POISON MALICE TWISTED

A DARK FAE ROMANCE

STEFFANIE HOLMES

Cover design: Seventhstar Designs

ISBN: 978-0-9951424-0-4

❀ Created with Vellum

POISON MALICE TWISTED

**She's sweet, forbidden poison – and she's the only one who
can save him**

Aisling is the last witch standing. She guards her family home
and the source of their power from the fae eager to devour it.
Grief and loneliness mark her days, twisting her up inside until
the night she opens her door to a dark stranger…

His malice threatens to undo them both

Even among the fae, Niall is considered broken. War has stoked
his lust for blood, for cruelty, for control. All he knows is death
and depravity until the day he steps inside Aisling's home and
finds everything he's ever wanted…

A forbidden attraction so strong, so twisted, they cannot resist

But Niall's vow requires that he sacrifice it all.

Every day that Niall and Aisling give in to their twisted desires, the house moves closer to ruin. Corrupted magic seeps from every crack, the walls draw closer, and the house is torn apart between the fae and human worlds.

If the house falls, both their worlds fall with it. But the only way to save it will force Aisling and Niall apart for all of eternity.

Poison Malice Twisted is a standalone dark paranormal romance novel of love, sacrifice, and weird architecture by *USA Today* bestselling author Steffanie Holmes. This story of a clever witch, a wicked fae prince, and a house with a mind of its own contains scenes that may disturb and delight.

Grab a free copy *Cabinet of Curiosities* – a Steffanie Holmes compendium of short stories and bonus scenes – when you sign up for updates with the Steffanie Holmes newsletter.

JOIN THE NEWSLETTER FOR UPDATES

Grab a free copy of *Cabinet of Curiosities* – a Steffanie Holmes compendium of short stories and bonus scenes – when you sign up for updates with the Steffanie Holmes newsletter.

www.steffanieholmes.com/newsletter

Every week in my newsletter I talk about the true-life hauntings, strange happenings, crumbling ruins, and creepy facts that inspire my stories. You'll also get newsletter-exclusive bonus scenes and updates. I love to talk to my readers, so come join us for some spooky fun :)

A NOTE ON DARK CONTENT

I'm writing this note because I want you a heads up about some of the content in *Poison Malice Twisted*. Reading should be fun, so I want to make sure you don't get any nasty surprises. If you're cool with anything and you don't want spoilers, then skip this note and dive in.

Keep reading if you like a bit of warning about what to expect in this dark fat book.

- Niall is NOT a nice guy. He's killed a lot of people, and he has no remorse about this.

- There's a bit of body horror in this book – eating hearts, pulling teeth, etc.

- Niall and Aisling have a messed-up Dom/Sub dynamic, and engage in knife/edge play. This is not true BDSM as it's not bounded by kink rules (hard to do, when Niall's fae and wouldn't know a safe kink relationship if it smacked him around the head). If the lack of discussion about boundaries/safe words is a trigger for you, this is not the book for you. All sex is consensual.

I promise there will be hot, dirty, sex, mystery, dark magic, and a house with a mind of its own. If that's not your jam, that's totally cool. I suggest you pick up my Nevermore Bookshop Mysteries series – all of the mystery and hot book boyfriends without the gore and trauma and violence.

Enjoy, you beautiful depraved human, you :) Steff

All houses wherein men have lived and died
Are haunted houses. Through the open doors
The harmless phantoms on their errands glide,
With feet that make no sound upon the floors.

We meet them at the doorway, on the stair,
Along the passages they come and go,
Impalpable impressions on the air,
A sense of something moving to and fro.

– Henry Wadsworth Longfellow, 85

1
______

AISLING

*I*t all started with the crack.

Aisling noticed it at breakfast; a jagged fissure snaking its way across the dining room wall, splitting apart the faded wallpaper. She walked over and peered inside the crack, searching the blackness within for some clue, some sense of what lay on the other side. She longed to thrust her fingers into those black depths and probe their secrets.

She *itched* to poke the bear. And by bear, she meant the unfathomable darkness that yearned to swallow her.

Aisling cupped her hands behind her back, fighting against the urge. She knew if she stuck her hand inside, all she'd be left with was a bloodless stub.

And what'll that do to my chances of becoming a world-famous juggler?

Even inside her head, Aisling was a mouthy bitch.

This particular crack was low on the wall, and it must've been growing for some time. It was quite long and wide, and had already begun pulling in the furniture. It had taken a corner of the armoire already. Around the fissure, the walls were blackened, rotting away as the void gnawed at the house.

Cracks in the walls of old houses weren't that uncommon. When Hollythorn House had been just a house, a lattice of cracks marred several of its once pristine walls, causing Aisling's father great concern over the house's structural integrity. Grandmother June had brushed off her son-in-law's protests. "These cracks are like the lines on my face." She had rubbed her withered cheeks. "They're part of the history of this house, the wisdom of its twilight years, the natural decay of its life. Let her grow old gracefully, just like me."

Of course, Hollythorn wasn't *just* a house anymore.

The crack's presence was a bitter end to a beautiful moment, one of the first they'd shared together in months. Bethany – the younger by six years – was barely talking to Aisling anymore. *Call it teenage hormones or post-apocalypse depression, I'm calling it 'my kid sister is a pain-in-my-ass.'* Before the war, they had always shared everything. Bethany would take the train into the city to stay with Aisling for the weekend, and Aisling would sneak her into clubs and fill her teenage head with strawberry daiquiris and big dreams for the future.

Now, Bethany spent hours sitting in the blue drawing room in the east wing, watching out the bay window as the house swayed over the edge of the precipice, eyes unblinking as lightning snaked from the swirling miasma below and crashed against the icy sky. Aisling knew she had to do something to bring her back from the edge. Bethany was the only family she had left.

That morning, Aisling found just the thing – a jar of strawberry jam hidden behind the beans in the pantry. She thought they'd used up the last of the jams two months ago, and it was supposed to be several months before another jar appeared. Grandmother June's pantry enchantment had been slowing down over the last year. Food now took months to replenish, and Bethany's gardening experiments in the frozen greenhouse attached to the kitchen garden had been a failure. You couldn't grow strawberries in sub-zero temperatures without sunlight, so their dreams of daiquiris in the drawing room remained only dreams.

Aisling clutched the jar to her chest, stroking the lid as though it were a precious jewel.

She set the dining table with the nice china and collected some fabric flowers from Grandmother June's sewing room – which today contained an ornate staircase that had never been there before – to place in a vase in the center. She even opened one of their few remaining bottles of grape juice and poured them each a glass. Widdershins – their grandmother's soot-black kitten with white socks who'd survived in the house as long as they had – crept inside and curled up on the rug under the table.

Everything looked perfect, like a scene from their childhood – one of Grandmother June's make-believe fairy picnics. Aisling fingered the jam jar and had to bite her lip to resist throwing it across the room.

I want cocktails and dancing. I want friends with mundane problems – cheating partners, bosses making lewd comments, secret drug addictions. I want a mortgage and a vacation to the beach and fucking student loan payments. I want to go back to the club and have my Dom spank me until I'm crying. I want little white pills to transport me somewhere else.

I want out of this house.

Instead, our world has shrunk so small that I'm excited about a jar of jam.

Bethany entered the dining room just as Aisling was folding the napkins. She tossed her brown ringlets over her shoulder. Bethany had their mother's unruly hair and petite build, her heart-shaped face and pixie features, whereas Aisling took more after Grandmother June – olive skin, narrow nose, huge brown eyes, long everything; long face, long legs, long fingers good for scratching down her Dom's back...

No. Don't start thinking about kink, or you'll be excusing yourself for the bathroom, and Bethany needs you.

"What's all this?" Bethany peered at the table. "Is that jam? I didn't think we had any jam."

"I found some at the back of the pantry. I thought we'd have a celebration."

"What are we celebrating?" Bethany pulled out her chair and started spreading a thick layer of jam across her cracker. Aisling wanted to tell her to use less, to ration the jam so it would stretch further, but she didn't have the heart. Not when Bethany was smiling her first real smile in months.

Instead, Aisling sat down opposite her sister, spread an even thicker layer on her own cracker, and took a big bite.

The jam was almost thick enough to disguise the stale taste of the cracker. Aisling took a swig of juice. Oh, it was heavenly, like swallowing a rainbow. Maybe she didn't need little white pills after all. Maybe she just needed to count her fucking blessings.

Jam, check. Sister, check. Cat, check. Two available hands to flick the bean as much as I like. Check and check.

Aisling glanced up at the calendar she had pinned to the wall. She'd made it from pages torn from a book on butterflies she found in the library. It was a pretty crude tally, just numbered boxes with crosses through them over pictures of red admirals and holly blues. She didn't even bother with the days of the week anymore. What was the point?

"We're celebrating survival." Aisling made a quick calculation in her head. "For thirteen hundred and twenty-two days, we've kept this house safe."

"What good is survival without *life*?" Bethany set down her cracker. She stared at a spot behind Aisling's head. "We have nothing inside these walls but a library full of books about things we'll never experience."

"The world in those books doesn't exist anymore," Aisling said.

"I don't care!" Bethany slammed down her glass so hard, grape juice splashed across the tablecloth. Widdershins sprung to his feet in alarm and darted from the room. "I want to swim in the ocean again, or feel grass between my toes, or fall in love. At least you got to leave home and get a job and a boyfriend. I never got those things, and now I never will."

"Be grateful for small mercies." Aisling squeezed her knees together as she thought of Guy leading her around on a chain at the club with his long black coat swishing, and his snakebite piercings bobbing as his mouth curled up in a wicked smirk. Guy, who refused to leave the city with her because he wanted one last party before the end of the world. "It's more to miss."

"I can't stand seeing the same walls day in and day out. We're prisoners here, Aisling, as surely as we would be if *they* got in and took us. We might as well be dead."

"Don't say that." Aisling's heart hammered. The jam on her tongue tasted too sugary, too sticky. She tried to swallow, but it wouldn't go down.

Bethany's thoughts were too similar to hers.

We have each other.

"Why not? It's true. Grandmother June has trapped us here, and for what? To save this house? She loved Hollythorn House more than she loved us—oh, no..." Bethany's gaze landed on the wall behind Aisling. Without turning around, Aisling knew from her sister's stricken expression what she would see: the dark fissure slowly opening across the wall.

The crack.

"Bethany, I'm sorry." Aisling squeezed her eyes shut, fighting back the urge to cry.

"I'll get some boards." Bethany rose from the table, pushing her half-eaten cracker away. Aisling reached for her, but Bethany ducked around her outstretched fingers. As she swung open the heavy door to the hallway, Aisling glimpsed her sister's eyes – they were empty. If Bethany didn't feel anything about the crack...

Her own eyes pricking with tears, Aisling cleared away the dishes and ate the rest of her sister's cracker. It tasted like cardboard. She pushed the dining table closer to the door, away from the crack. Bethany returned a few minutes later, carrying several pieces of a mahogany bookshelf they'd chopped up last month.

"This is the last of it." Bethany dropped the wood in front of the crack and pulled out her hammer, all business now. Her cheeks were dry of tears, her eyes dead. Her no-nonsense demeanor frightened Aisling more than her outburst of emotion. Bethany had been morose for weeks now, but this was different. This was as cold as the winter outside.

"Let me help." Aisling picked up one of the wooden boards. Bethany snatched it from her hands.

"I'll take care of this. You get the sealing stones." Bethany held the wood up to the wall and started nailing it in place, her strikes cool, efficient, the sound jolting through Aisling like thunder.

Not wanting to upset her sister again, Aisling ran from the room. She found the sealing stones in Grandmother June's desk in the blue drawing room, alongside other magical implements she didn't know how to use. The drawing room was toward the front of the house, overlooking what would have been the front yard but was now a barren, icy field between the house and the iron fence encircling the property. They'd chosen this room as their safe store, as it was furthest from the known locations of the void, and would be one of the last rooms to crack. Aisling grabbed the velvet bag of stones from the desk drawer and ran back to the dining room.

"Bethany, I've got them—"

Aisling's heart stopped beating. Bethany wasn't standing behind the table. Instead, she lay facedown on the floor in front of the wall. Her face was turned toward the doorway, frozen in a look of such intense horror that Aisling's stomach turned.

Her sister's left arm had been completely torn away.

Bethany wasn't bleeding. The burning darkness of the void had staunched the wound.

Her severed arm was nowhere to be seen.

Aisling turned from her sister and threw up on the rug.

"Bethany?" Her sister's name dragged against her raw throat. Aisling dropped to her knees and pressed her fingers to her sister's wrist. Bethany's skin felt clammy. She had no pulse. Aisling rolled Bethany over and tilted her head back, trying to remember everything she'd learned about mouth-to-mouth on that first-aid course she'd taken for work. But it was a lifetime ago now and she couldn't exactly get a refresher course.

Bethany's glassy eyes stared back at her, open but no longer seeing, and Aisling knew it was too late. Whether she was dead from the shock of losing her arm or from making contact with the void, Aisling would never be able to ask.

Behind Bethany, the fissure had opened even further along the wall – a gaping black tear all the way from the gilded portrait of their grandfather above the fireplace to the small cameo of a cat along the right edge of the wall. The gap at the midpoint was the breadth of Aisling's outstretched hands, and it tapered to a point at the ends – like a pair of black lips curling up in a mocking grin. The two boards Bethany had nailed up were its crooked teeth.

On the edges of the crack, inky black tendrils curled outward, giving off an acrid, smoky stench.

Bethany's hammer lay on the thick carpet in front of her, a single nail poking from the board above it, only half nailed in. One of her shoes had rolled off under the table. A thin trail of black smoke rose from the insole.

Did she accidentally touch the void, or did she throw herself into it?

Both answers sucked.

Aisling sank to her knees in front of the wall, her heart breaking inside her chest. The pain of her loss was physical – a searing heat burning through her body, as though she'd been set on fire. She pounded her fists against the floor, her cries of desperation echoing through the heavy, silent house.

Seconds, minutes or hours later, Aisling rolled over, her eyelids drooping, her nose stinging and her face sticky with tears. The grief ebbed, still sitting beneath her skin but no longer burning her alive. She rubbed her eyes, and her gaze fell on her sister's shoe, sitting empty and lonely where she'd left it under the dining table.

Now I'm the only one left.

2

AISLING

Aisling hadn't known war was coming for her until the bombs started dropping.

She had been your typical twenty-two-year-old. She had an architecture job she loved in the city, an apartment, a boyfriend, a sex club, a latex bodysuit, a penchant for loud music and an even louder laugh after a few drinks.

She was too busy drinking cocktails at trendy speakeasy pop-ups and trialing paleo recipes to pay much attention to news headlines. World Wars were things that happened in the distant past, something to feel sad about during history documentaries. Even when friends at the club talked about joining up, she didn't realize how up-close-and-personal this war had become.

If she *had* known, it would've meant sweet fuck-all. What could she have done? Joined the thousands of protesters clogging the streets? Written letters to politicians? Made spellcakes for peace and protection with Grandmother June to burn over a bonfire?

None of it had made any difference in the end.

In a twisted way, Aisling was grateful for those final months of her normal life lived in ignorance, writhing on a St. Andrew's Cross at her sex club like she alone knew the meaning of 'pain.'

Those were the memories she clung to now.

Her beloved city was burned. Her boyfriend was crushed in the rubble. The air itself became poison. The act of living was pain. Aisling fled to the only place she thought might be safe – Hollythorn House, where she spent her childhood summers with crazy Grandmother June and her witchy potions and stories of the fae. Grandmother June said she'd placed so many magical protections around the house it could literally withstand a nuclear holocaust. Aisling didn't believe in fairies and magic, but she definitely believed in Hollythorn's isolation and Grandmother June's fully-stocked root cellar.

I'll hide at Hollythorn until we win the war.

Until things can go back to normal.

Then, the fae came.

Fairies, fey-folk, pixies, darklings, the wild hunt, the Sidhe. Creatures Aisling knew only from her grandmother's storybooks swept over the Earth – not adorable little sprites, but vicious warriors with swords of bone and hearts carved in stone. They emerged from the irradiated forests and the charred meadows – a race lain hidden from human eyes until the poison of human war had seeped into their realm. They had left humans in peace for centuries, but now, they came for vengeance, for survival.

And nothing would ever go back to normal.

It turned out, Grandmother June's stories were true.

She was a witch, and all her crazy hippy friends were witches, and she passed down her powers to her daughter Alice, who supposedly passed them down to Bethany and Aisling – not that the sisters knew how to use them. *Thanks for nothing, Mom.* A whole family of witches hid under Hollythorn's roof from the end of the world – with all the power the fae needed to restore their realm, if only they could get inside.

The day the fae attacked Hollythorn House, Grandmother June hid Aisling and Bethany in the pantry while she and their mother and father and the other witches in June's coven fought against the fairy host that marched across the countryside to lay siege to their stronghold. Aisling held a trembling Bethany as the house shuddered around them from the force of spells being hurled back and forth. The air crackled and sizzled with restless energy, like a thunderstorm building up indoors. Cans and jars of preserves toppled from the shelves, their sharp edges raising bruises and cuts on their skin. Aisling's chest tightened with fear when she heard her father screaming.

The fae battled with Grandmother June and the coven for days. One by one, June's witches fell. The fae tore out their hearts to take back to their queen. Aisling's father took a sword to the abdomen and died of his injuries. The fae were breaking down the door.

With the assistance of Alice and June's two sisters – what remained of their coven – June bound herself to the house so the fae could not take her and her magic. She hid her magic in Hollythorn's walls and floors and moldings, but the spell killed her. It was supposed to stop the fae from seizing her power. They couldn't bleed magic from walls like they could from veins.

Instead, the fae dragged Hollythorn House – walls and doors and furniture and iron gates and witches and all – to the very edge of their realm, to the place where the frozen wasteland of the fae world met the boiling earth and the nothingness of space between them. This edge-place kept the house preserved while the fae figured out how they could get inside it, like a particularly recalcitrant nut they needed to crack.

But Hollythorn wouldn't crack. Instead, it fought back.

The house now teetered on the edge of a great cliff overlooking the void of space that divided the two realms. It defied logic – the entire east wing was suspended in midair hundreds of feet above the vast, bottomless chasm from which a great storm constantly churned. The frog-pond in the corner of the front yard glowed green from radiation, and the ground around it burned so hot they could lay down a frying pan to cook eggs. Winds wailed through the chimneys and dark clouds crashed against each other, battering the house from all sides and often completely obscuring the view of the fae mounds through the windows.

Over the years, the house had succumbed to the incredible forces exerted upon it. Rooms stretched and distorted. The ballroom was now larger on the inside than it was on the outside. Staircases descended into nowhere, and doorways into strange new rooms appeared randomly. The iron fence that surrounded the property grew in height – now it was taller than the gabled roof. The house kept adding and changing as it strived to protect its secrets from the fae.

Cracks formed in the walls as the house was pulled in both directions. Between those cracks, an unholy darkness lurked. If the void took you, you didn't come back. That was how Aisling had lost her mother three years ago, and her sister today.

Aisling was now twenty-five years old, and she was the last witch left alive. She would protect Hollythorn House from fae attacks and repair what she could. But she knew the cracks would grow bigger, the rooms would refuse to obey the laws of physics, and the house would one day swallow her up.

3

NIALL

Niall bent over the body of the witch and yanked his blade from her back. Blood spurted from the wound. A few drops sprinkled over Niall's boots, scenting the air with the sweetest smell in the world – the acrid tang of a dead witch's blood.

Niall wished he could take a bath in the stuff, but it was too precious for that. He settled for rolling her over, slicing the skin of her breast to swing her ribs open like the wings of an eagle unfurling before flight, and tearing out her heart.

Blood caked his forearms as he held up his prize. It quivered in his fingers as a crimson fountain spurted from a severed artery down the front of his tunic. Niall could barely make out the haze of blue light glowing faintly around the edges.

"There's barely anything left of her," he growled.

"Who cares? We need all of it." Odiana held out a sack made of woven grass, and Niall tossed the heart inside. Odiana threw the sack over her shoulder and grabbed the witch under the arms. She left a crimson trail across the linoleum as she dragged the body to the waiting wheelbarrow. The fae kept every witch carcass they could find. They gave the hearts to their Summer Queen and made their bones into talismans to ward against the encroaching ice and the evils that dwelt within it. "Are there any more?"

Niall glanced around the shop. The aura could sometimes be difficult to see, especially with all this human junk crowded together. The presence of so much iron made his head spin and clouded his vision.

Focus. Lay aside your hatred and bloodlust. Your brother needs you.

He squinted into a dark corner, where several carved walking sticks had been stacked alongside some old shovels and farm implements – the metal components now caked with rust. He ignored his body's urge to shy away from the metal and walked around the shovels, careful not to touch them as nausea clenched at his stomach. Decades of raiding expeditions into the human realm had hardened him against the effects of iron.

As he moved, Niall caught the blue glimmer of an aura near the back of the pile. He pulled out a beautifully polished stick – its handle inlaid with a shimmering moonstone. It thrummed in his fingers, giving off its own energy even through his thick gloves. In the light, the aura was much clearer – a blue shimmer extending down the length of the shaft.

"Here." Niall tossed the stick to Odiana. "This one."

Without any regard for the beauty of the craftsmanship, Odiana tossed the wooden stick into their wheelbarrow, on top of the witch's carcass and a pile of other blue-tinged human objects. Like Niall, she wore gloves pulled up to her elbows for handling the objects, made of the pelt of a selkie and stitched with rows of human teeth to protect their skin against iron. Even so, she didn't have Niall's tolerance for the objects, and she bent double over the wheelbarrow, clutching her stomach as her face twisted in agony.

Normally, only the warriors of the Slaugh had their queen's permission to cross into the human realm, but Niall had insisted on working with Odiana, and not even the queen herself would risk pissing Niall off. The fae didn't quite know what to do with Odiana – unlike other court-born fairies of her beauty – ice-white hair, porcelain skin, cheekbones that could carve up a man, eyes like faceted crystal – she had no care for dancing and song and possessing beautiful objects. To her, real beauty was in the orbit of a planet, the reaction of chemicals, the perfection of a mathematical equation. Her potions could create glamours and changelings and gift temporary invisibility, not because she was a skilled herbalist but because she understood how fae magic worked more than anyone. She might have been called a scientist, if that wasn't a human word the fae abhorred.

Niall had known her, and trusted her, long enough to know that if anyone could save the fae, it would be Odiana. He needed her by his side, to see, to know.

And he needed her *not* to see. She trusted him, and that meant he could exploit her.

"I'll stuff huffing this up the hill," Odiana said in her breathy voice. "You hunt for more imbued junk." Niall often teased Odiana that she pronounced every syllable as though she were whispering in a lover's ear. The fae were sexual beings, capable of fierce seductions when the mood so took them, but Odiana was a walking erotic manifestation who tempted him at every turn. But Niall would never give in to that particular impulse, not when he knew how much his brother loved her. Niall's profligate ways were reserved for the lesser fae.

A few minutes later Odiana returned, sans wheelbarrow, looking puffed and sickly. Niall handed her a battered toaster and a small carved wooden duck. Odiana held the bird up to the light. "This thing?" she asked, scorn dripping from her words.

"Oh yeah, it's humming with magic."

Odiana wrinkled her nose. "I'll never understand what would possess a witch to deposit their sacred magic into such grotesque objects."

"I think it's clever." Niall watched the edges of the blue aura pulse against the yellow aura of Odiana's fingers. "If you were a witch and fae broke into your house to take your magic, the last place they'd expect you to hide it is inside a hideous duck."

"Not so clever," Odiana grinned as she pocketed the duck. "We have you."

"The witches didn't exactly know about my abilities when they did this." His whole life, Niall hid the fact he could see the aura of an object or person who wields magic. To him, the whole world glowed with different shades of shimmering blue and yellow, but that was not a kind of magic known to the fae. Fae could cast glamour and heal wounds and influence luck and resist pain. Slaugh like Niall had heightened senses for stealth in battle. But seeing magic itself? It was the kind of power they reviled. The first blood Niall spilled had been to protect his secret. And now he was the future of his race. His queen's blessing chafed at him, making him restless, more thirsty for blood.

"All the better for us." Odiana grinned her enchanting smile. "Maybe one day soon I'll actually be able to extract the magic from all this junk, and your love for dusty human crap will be justified."

Niall punched her playfully in the arm. Their friendship was forged in their youth, built on a foundation of competitiveness and seasoned liberally with insults. They knew more secrets about each other than fae were usually willing to share, and that knowledge gave Niall a sense of calm when he was with Odiana. Calmness was a rare gift. The rage that burned inside him – the blaze of white-hot fury that could usually only be sated by human blood or fae depravity – quieted in Odiana's presence.

Back in the glory days, Niall relished every ride of the Slaugh upon the Earth, every chance to slash and maim and hurt. The Slaugh were the only fae allowed into the human realm – they had the queen's blessing to ride across the land, searching out witches for the queen's pleasure – sometimes replacing them with changelings and dragging them back to the fae realm for the queen to enslave or torture, sometimes cutting them to pieces and sucking their magic from the marrow of their bones.

When the humans aimed their nuclear weapons at each other and scarred the Earth with poison fire, the witches died along with the humans. Without their magic to sustain the Summer Queen, her grip over their realm faded and the Endless Winter crept in. The ice edged down from the mountains and never retreated. On the other side of the mountains, they knew the Winter Queen and her court grew stronger in their rule, but even she too would fade if the balance could not be restored.

Niall could no longer remember the feeling of grass rustling against his ankles or warm sun touching his skin. All he knew now was ice that matched his heart.

The fae hadn't known that witches had been protecting their magic for years, siphoning it off into objects so that if the fae took them, they would never give the queen enough power to dominate both realms. But Niall knew. He'd seen the objects in their homes glowing with the delicious blue aura. Now that only a few witches were left alive in the irradiated wasteland, those objects were the fae's only hope.

If Odiana could figure out how to extract magic from a wooden duck, she could extract it from Hollythorn House. And the Summer Queen would have what she needed to thaw the ice.

Niall had been watching this tiny village for weeks, observing nine humans and one witch sleeping in a protective huddle on the floor of the pub and attempting to grow potatoes in the poisoned fields. Niall had seen the witch enter this shop on numerous occasions to take tools, but yesterday he'd watched through the window as she picked up a small necklace from a cabinet and clasped it in her palm. Her eyes closed. The witch swayed gently, holding the necklace to her heart. The necklace glowed with bright blue light.

Niall rode on the village with five Slaugh warriors. They left no survivors.

He hadn't mentioned the necklace to Odiana.

While she struggled outside with the full wheelbarrow, Niall pawed through decades of carefully collected artifacts from the broken earth, searching for his own gold.

———

HE FOUND the necklace tucked behind a display of trinket boxes and spice jars. The metal burned his fingers even through his tooth-mail gloves. He placed the necklace inside a box lined with witch-bones and slid the box into his pocket just as Odiana came up behind him, a dusty book gripped in her hands.

"Find anything else?" Her voice was hoarse from the iron exposure.

Niall shook his head, brushing his hands on his green trousers. He kept his voice hard – the voice he used to command his men. "Let's go."

"You read my mind." Odiana sniffed, her perfect nose twitching. "This place reeks of humans."

Niall followed her to the top of the street, where she'd left the wheelbarrow. She dropped the book on top of the corpse, staining its cover with the witch's blood. Niall shoved the barrow through a doorway in a stone garden wall into a deserted street. His boots kicked fresh snow, its surface puckered only by their previous footprints and the rut from the wheelbarrow. Odiana elbowed him aside to pick up the handles of the wheelbarrow and shove it into the recalcitrant snow.

The box in Niall's pocket dragged like a lead weight.

Odiana followed the rut from their earlier journey back down the hill, but even so it was slow going in the unrelenting snow. Niall lifted his head as they rounded the crest. The skyline of the Summer City rose before his eyes – once beautiful spires of gnarled wood and clover-dusted mounds pierced the turbid sky, turned white and misshapen by the unceasing blizzards. Icicles lined dead tree branches and clung to the stems of once-living flowers – jagged teeth that bite by bite had devoured their green lands.

Behind the valley, Niall could see the outline of Hollythorn House high upon the hill. The gothic-style mansion towered over the blackened fields and charred forest that surrounded it. Twin turrets flanked the main wing, high round windows glaring at him like two beady eyes. A low porch shaded the front door, the broken arches like a row of sharpened fangs. The iron fence that had grown twenty-foot high surrounded it like a cage.

His throat closed.

The house glowed with a fierce blue light only Niall could see, a light so intense it warmed his skin even through the unrelenting cold.

A shiver ran through Niall's body as he stared at that strange house. Niall had been on the battlefield the day the witch fused her magic to the house. He'd seen his Slaugh brothers fall under an onslaught of magic as the walls glowed with blue light so bright he'd had to turn away. He'd nearly died himself as he carved into his own chest with his knife for one final fae-spell. But even ten-score Slaugh warriors spilling their blood for their queen was not enough, or was too much, and ever since,

Hollythorn stood sentinel on the hill, straddling the two worlds – a terrifying specter that loomed over the abandoned city, beguiling in its promise as a conduit of unlimited power.

Hollythorn was a place of mystery and superstition to the fae. No human could have survived inside for all these years, and yet lights went on and off in the manor's windows. Sometimes, smoke could be seen pouring from the chimney, and once or twice the front door even creaked open a crack. Niall and his brother Eamon used to dare each other to run up the scorched hill and peer through their iron bars for as long as their stomachs could stand it.

Once, Niall saw a dark-cloaked figure float slowly across the upstairs window. He couldn't make out a face or even the color of her hair, but he knew he was looking at the most powerful witch that ever lived. He pressed his face so close to the bars he burned two vertical scars over his cheeks.

The image of the shadow gliding with inhuman, impossible slowness haunted Niall's dreams ever since.

He'd been seeing it a lot since his father's death. Niall's language was blood and violence, not omens and portents, but even he knew the dreams were a message.

Although the skies were always cold and grey – the same broken sky since the Endless Winter began – above Hollythorn, black clouds swirled, raging and crashing against each other as the energy of the void collided with the two realms. As Niall watched, lightning arced down from the sky and struck the iron fence surrounding the house. The fence crackled loudly, but did not break.

Odiana shuddered, placing her hand over Niall's. "It's not natural," she said. "That much raw power. It's no wonder it's still standing after all this time."

"We should burn it down." Niall's words were harsher than

he intended. Hollythorn House held a special place of hatred within his black heart. If it wasn't for that house, he wouldn't be standing there with guilt clutching his chest and a magical necklace gnawing a hole in his pocket.

"Don't you dare. I'm so close to figuring out how to extract its magic, and then this whole shitshow will be over. We'll have our green fields back." Odiana kicked a snowdrift.

"You are?" Niall's fingers skimmed the edge of the box. His leg throbbed from being in such close contact with the metal necklace, but he welcomed the pain. Pain drowned out everything, even Odiana with her voice of velvet. Maybe it would drown out Niall's guilt.

Guilt. Who would have thought? Niall had never felt guilty before. Everything he'd ever done had been with complete malice of forethought. Niall had never experienced this constricting in his chest or the nauseous tumble of his stomach before, and he hoped he'd soon be rid of it. He fingered the box again.

Niall jerked his head up. Odiana was talking at him, and he wasn't even listening. Niall removed his hand from his pocket and focused on what she was saying.

"—we know witch magic is housed in their hearts, and it travels around their bodies in the bloodstream, right? Well, I think these objects have a heart, too. We find the heart, we get the magic. It's that simple."

Niall thought of the wooden duck. "I think you need to see a healer, because you've got a fruit bat loose in that skull of yours."

"Not a physical heart, *obviously*. Something that binds the witch to the object – something personal to her, like a song or a story or a particular piece. If the witch's lover gave her that duck, then the heart is in the memory of the giving, stored within the object. We get that, we get the magic." Odiana caressed the bloodstained grimoire. "It's a pity we can't keep a witch alive so we can extract these stories from her. I know you'd have fun with that. But the queen forbids it. I found this book that's part diary, part magical grimoire. I'm hoping it will contain the memories we need."

Niall looked to Hollythorn again. "What kind of heart do you think that house has?"

"One as black and twisted as yours. Let's get out of this cold." Odiana gave the wheelbarrow a defiant shove, heading toward the withered rowan bushes that led to the underground tunnels where the fae now lived. "Come meet me in the circle after I deliver these? I need a few glasses of nectar wine to put the color back in my cheeks."

Niall shook his head, resting his hand on his sword, the hilt stained wine-dark with dried human blood. "I need to sharpen this."

Odiana made a face. "Gross. Sometimes I don't know how we're friends."

"Because it's better to be friends with the sword-wielding maniac than get on his bad side?" Niall lifted an eyebrow.

"True." She stood on her toes to lightly brush her lips across his cheek. "Tomorrow, then."

"Tomorrow."

He watched her descend the carved steps into the gloom of the lower tunnels. He didn't know if there would be a tomorrow. The fae had once used these passages for storing food or as a hiding place when their kingdom was attacked by other creatures, the kinds of creatures who now roamed freely, emboldened by the ice.

Odiana didn't see Niall cast a final glance over his shoulder at the house.

She's right – you do *have a heart. I left mine behind when you took my only family from me. You sucked it up into your blackened depths and you fed on my malice until you became malice yourself. You and I are the perfect enemies.*

I promise you this, house – before I leave this broken earth, I will see your walls crumble to dust for what you've done.

4

———

AISLING

*A*isling wanted to bury Bethany in the family cemetery. Which was so much hard work it made her back ache just thinking about it. But what were sisters for if not to make your life miserable, even in death?

The eastern gardens bordered the void and were too dangerous to navigate now, but the cemetery was to the west, at the far end of a long, rectangular field bordered by fruit trees where Aisling and her cousins used to play soccer. It would be one of the last corners of the house to be devoured. The grass was no longer green, of course, but a brown mat frozen solid beneath a layer of dirty ice, cracked and pitted in places where lightning had struck it. The field had been stretched and warped so that it now took Aisling half the day just to trudge from the house to the cemetery, dragging her sister's body, her tools, and the homemade gravestone in a tarp behind her.

Snow pelted Aisling as she reached the cemetery. She dropped the tarp outside the gate and collapsed on the icy ground to catch her breath. Behind the low iron gate, four rows of neat graves lined the path leading up to the altar – a slab of stone the size of a coffin with channels carved in it for libations.

Grandmother June performed some of her rituals at this altar, calling on her ancestors to aid her magic. Here she'd forced Aisling's mother Alice to lie naked on the cold stone for hours as part of her initiation.

To be fair to Mom, if June made me lie out here in this weather, I'd probably want nothing to do with magic, too.

Aisling remembered visiting the cemetery when she stayed with Grandmother June. Her grandmother would grip her hand tightly while she recited stories about the ancestors who resided in those graves, and how the fence was made of iron to keep the spirits of the dead trapped inside.

Iron, it turned out, was good for barriers.

Bethany never much liked the cemetery. "Grandmother June lives in a world of the dead," she said sourly, kicking a stack of books in the upstairs bedroom they shared whenever they stayed over. At the time, Bethany was a moody twelve-year-old who would prefer to spend the summer with her friends. "She doesn't know anything about celebrities or fashionable clothes, but give her some dusty bones in a moldy cemetery and she's happy."

"I like Grandmother June's stories." Aisling felt defensive on their grandmother's behalf, not least because she liked to be the favorite. June had made a particularly good batch of hazelnut brownies earlier that afternoon, and Aisling was hoping for a second portion. And unlike their parents, who dumped them with June so they could go off on boozy vacations, June *listened* to Aisling. She was more like a friend than a grandmother – the good kind of friend, the friend with wisdom and hazelnut chocolate brownies. June treated Aisling's stories about school and boys and college applications with the gravitas they deserved.

"This whole house is like a mausoleum to our famous witchy family." Bethany used air quotes around the word 'witchy.' "It's ridiculous. All the furniture in this house belonged to someone who died. And those creepy portraits everywhere! You're sleeping in a dead person's bed. Just think about that."

You're in the world of the dead now, sis. Aisling dragged the stone through the gate, struggling in the deep snow. Her hands burned from the frigid air, and she nearly dropped the stone on her foot as she set it in place beside the one she made for her parents all those years ago.

The stones were dwarfed by the structure immediately behind them. Lady Aisling Greymouth – the first witch in their family, for whom Aisling was named – built her ornate mausoleum in the corner of the small plot. It was an above-ground structure, decorated in the gothic style Lady Greymouth had so favored, with flowing vines and winged cherubs dancing around the marble arches flanking the twin iron doors. Inside, she and the other twelve members of the original family coven were buried, watching over their descendants for eternity.

When Aisling was younger, their family would meet at the cemetery every year on Samhain. Grandmother June would throw open the doors to the mausoleum, and they would perform a short ritual at the altar and offer up flowers and wine as gifts to honor Lady Greymouth and the family. When they found June's lifeless body in the ballroom after the spell, also on Samhain, they carried her to the cemetery and gave her a coffin beside Lady Greymouth. It felt fitting.

Aisling and Bethany had continued the Samhain ritual for as long as they could after the house was brought into the fae realm, but now the door was frozen shut, and the mausoleum was half-buried under a pile of snow, and was a half-day's walk from the house. The final winter was closing in.

After some maneuvering and chipping away at the ice on the step, Aisling finally got the stone to stand straight. Shoving her hands deep into her pockets, she stood back and admired her work. Bethany's stone was simple – Aisling was not much of an artist with a chisel. She'd pulled up one of the paving slabs from the floor of the greenhouse, and managed to carve her sister's name. She wanted to add some Avenged Sevenfold lyrics – Bethany's favorite band – but she ran out of space and patience.

Aisling broke up the dirt with an ice pick, then dug it out with a shovel. By the time she had a shallow hole, the sky had darkened and the ribbon of irradiated fire that bordered the void provided her only light. Her back screamed and her hands were cut and broken – she felt like she'd just finished a particularly punishing BDSM scene, only without the pounding industrial music or the deep existential purr of sexual gratification. Luckily, the cold wind kept her sister's body well-preserved beneath the linen tablecloth Aisling was using as a shroud.

Aisling rolled Bethany's body into the grave and covered her with a thin layer of dirt and snow. She knew Bethany's corpse couldn't rot in this cold, and no insects or carrion animals would come to eat her.

There's only one kind of carrion beast who survives now. Aisling leaned back on her spade and stared through the gaps in the towering iron fence. The fae city was only visible from certain places on the property, and it too warped and changed so she sometimes saw it from a different angle, or upside down, or tangled with vines or cast in glittering ice or resplendent with fresh and verdant foliage.

Tonight, it was the usual scene – white spires cloaked with ice and snow pierced the empty sky. A few lanterns glinted between the buildings, their light casting a pale glow across the white city. A few trails of smoke from fires. Aisling never saw fae in the city – she figured they fled from the ice. But she sometimes saw their faces near the fence – the fearsome Slaugh warriors with their warpaint and bone blades weaving magic in the air as they tried to break through her iron barricades. They only ever appeared for a moment, but that was more than enough to fear them.

She wondered if those few remaining fae were just as afraid and lonely as she was. Was outside looking in any better than being inside looking out? But then she felt guilty for considering it while standing over the graves of her parents and sister, who died trying to protect their magic from the fae.

I'm not that desperate for company.

I'm not.

I miss her already.

Bethany — my sulky, petulant, artistic, bold, brittle, alluring, sarcastic, brilliant sister.

Goodbye.

I guess I'll be seeing you soon.

Aisling allowed herself one final tear. A single, solitary drop of water for the sister who had been taken from her.

Then it was time to get back to work.

5

———

NIALL

"That's good, Niall." Laneth used a pair of bone forks to pick up the necklace. "That's very good, indeed."

"It's worth two hundred teeth, at least." Niall's chest weighed heavy. As he stood across from Laneth, watching the enormous man paw at the tiny box with his tooth-mail gloves, he felt small, helpless.

Niall had never felt helpless in his life before he met Laneth.

He didn't like it. He wanted to knock the fae's head off for making him feel helpless, but that was exactly the point, wasn't it? Laneth could make Niall dance like a puppet because he held the key to Niall's guilt.

Laneth dropped the necklace on the table, next to the small pile of human teeth Niall had pried from the mouths of the villagers while Odiana wasn't looking. "I was thinking one hundred." he grinned.

Laneth rarely smiled, which made his grin all the more alarming. He wiped a sticky hand across his face, leaving a trail of grease. Laneth operated the poppy dens under the nose of the Summer Queen, and not even the finest herb soaps in the kingdom could rid his skin of the thin layer of tar from his clan-destine haunts.

One hundred teeth was ridiculously low. Niall knew he could get triple that if he took the box to one of the court fairies. Laneth knew it too, which was why he was grinning. He knew Niall would never risk selling a magical object to anyone else.

Niall gritted his teeth. "Fine. Take one hundred off, plus thirty-six human teeth. That means he still owes—"

"Eighty-eight thousand, nine hundred and sixty-four teeth." Laneth's nose twitched as he calculated the math in his head. He may have been large and greasy, but he wasn't stupid. Far from it, which was what made him so dangerous.

The number buzzed inside Niall's head, so huge and impos-sible even after all these years. Niall was used to being feared by humans and fae alike, but Laneth seemed to derive a wicked pleasure from having Niall under his thumb.

If Niall had a problem with someone, he snapped their neck. No more problem. But if he snapped Laneth's neck, the greasy bastard would probably just grow another.

If Laneth died, everything Niall worked for died with him.

"Can I see him?" Niall asked. His teeth stung from the humil-iation of asking. Niall asked permission with his blade, not his lips.

Laneth waved his hand. He was already engrossed in his new prize. He moved the necklace to his workbench and aimed one of his lanterns at it, inspecting it from all angles. Laneth had the same goal as Odiana and every other fae with a brain between their ears – to figure out how to extract magic from objects. Only if Laneth discovered a way to extract magic first, he wouldn't share it. He'd sell it to the highest bidder, or worse.

Niall left Laneth admiring his new acquisition and wandered down the stone steps into the tunnels beneath Laneth's residence. The hunched brownie Laneth kept as a servant waved him through without asking his business. Niall was such a frequent visitor that he was well-known in Laneth's labyrinthine lair. As he passed, the brownie gazed up at him with pleading eyes.

"Please..." she begged, holding out her arm so Niall could see the ugly scars that marked Laneth's experiments on her. Niall didn't even slow down.

One... two... three... Niall trudged past the empty cells, his boots shuffling against the stone cobbles. Down here, the air hung heavy with damp and the nauseating tang of iron. The odor of bodily fluids flared in his nostrils. A pitiful place for pitiable men.

Niall stopped in front of the final cell.

"Eamon."

"My brother." A hand reached through thin iron bars to clasp his. The fingers felt thin, brittle. Not at all like the fine hands of the fae Eamon had once been.

"I have paid another hundred and thirty-six teeth from your debt." Niall dropped Eamon's fingers and stepped away. Being close to the iron bars robbed him of his mind and dropped his stomach into his knees. He couldn't imagine the torture his brother endured trapped inside, let out only for Laneth's experiments.

"I've told you before, don't do this," Eamon's voice pleaded. "I made this mess. I was the one stupid enough to gamble away all my teeth."

"Not just your teeth." Niall touched the hilt of his sword. Even in this vile place, the purple aura surrounding Eamon glittered like gold. With the years of torture he endured at Laneth's hands, Eamon's aura had never diminished. He still held the dank, mysterious power inside him, which meant that Niall would never stop trying to free him. "You bet my teeth, our father's teeth, teeth you didn't possess, more teeth than I hope to pull from humans in my lifetime. So don't tell me what to do, little brother."

"You don't understand the danger." Eamon's words trailed off as he coughed and hacked. "You don't see what I see. The world isn't the same anymore."

An image of their ice-choked city filled Niall's head. "I'm not blind. Or stupid. I see enough."

"That's not what I meant." Eamon pressed his body against the bars. His flesh sizzled against the iron, but that wasn't what drew a cry from Niall's throat. Someone had made a series of long cuts across Eamon's chest, slashing across his heart. The wounds bled openly, unable to close because of the proximity to metal. "This isn't our old fae rivalries any longer. The queen thinks your blade will protect her in her weakness, but every time you give Laneth another magical item, he stockpiles that power. Have you seen his aura?"

Niall thought back to a moment ago, when he'd spoken with Laneth. "He looked like the same smug bastard I've come to know and loathe."

"He's not. Look at the fingers on his left hand."

"He wore gloves to handle the object."

"His fingers glow *blue*, Niall." Eamon grabbed the bar and shook it. A singeing smell tinged the air as the metal burned his skin. "He's close to figuring out how to extract the magic, and when he does... he's not in this to thaw the ice. He wants to wear the crown."

"Then he'll have to walk over my dead body to get to it," Niall growled.

They fired these same tired words back at each other every time Niall visited. The first time Eamon told him Laneth had a desire for the crown, Niall laughed so hard he spat up blood. But with every visit to the human wastelands, and every witch the queen carved up that didn't yield enough power to turn back the Endless Winter, Niall felt the air shifting. In the dark tunnels beneath the ice, the court fae no longer had their trooping and nectar-gathering and mischief to distract them. They were starting to ask, 'why can't the queen bring back the summer?' And there was Hollythorn on the hill, mocking them with its power – so close and yet another world away.

And in the middle of it all was Laneth, supplying them with the poppies that made them feel so good, dangling them all on strings, cackling as he made them dance.

Laneth who now had a blue aura – a *witch* aura – on his fingers.

Fuck.

Niall forced himself to look at his brother. Eamon had been a beauty once, inside and out, but their father didn't know what to do with a beautiful son, with power that didn't come from fists or blades or teeth. So their father cut that beauty out of him.

Being surrounded by iron for so long had given Eamon's skin a reddish hue. His teeth pulled away from his gums, giving him a monstrous scowl. His one remaining eye appeared sunken into his skull, and the raised ridges of the cross-shaped scar across the ruined socket were crusted black with filth.

Eamon dropped the bar and looked away. He was one of the few people who could bear Niall's stare for any length of time, but even he had his limits.

"How's Odiana?" Eamon asked the wall.

"Fine." *Bereft of you, even after all these years.*

Niall stared down at his sword. His brother's eye stared back up at him, encased in dried tree sap and set into the hilt.

A gift from Eamon, and a curse.

"She's had some success with the magic, too." Niall wanted to tell Eamon about the heart of objects, but he wouldn't put it past Laneth to have spies in the shadows.

"Laneth was telling me. That's why you have to be careful. Protect her, *please*. I think he knows more than he says—"

Eamon's words cut off as a sound echoed along the tunnel. Footsteps. Voices, low and urgent.

Niall's muscles tensed, his instincts honed for danger. He stepped into the tunnel entrance and drew his sword, admiring the way Eamon's purple aura danced along the blade.

He beheaded the first royal guard before the fae even saw him.

Niall's blade sang in the air as it drank the blood he spilled. In the close quarters of the tunnel, they could only come at him two at a time, and he cut them down as soon as they appeared. Blood splattered across his face, and he licked his lips to taste their folly. He felt the sting of an arrow in his shoulder, but he didn't lower his arm. *They won't take him from me. He's had his punishment a hundred times over—*

"Niall, *stop*."

Odiana. Her voice snapped him from his bloodthirsty trance. "Stand aside," he growled at her as she faced off with him over the pile of dead fae, using her body to block another cohort of the queen's guard from his wrath.

"You know I can't do that." Odiana tried to peer around him, but his bulk blocked most of her view. "What's going on here, Niall? I saw you take that necklace that should have gone to the queen, and then I followed you to Laneth, and I knew things were bad, but you can still salvage this. You—"

"Odiana?" Eamon croaked through the bars.

Odiana froze. Niall could see how pain of her name on his lips bit her like it had teeth. Her features twisted as she saw what she'd lost, and what she was about to lose again because of her own mistake.

The guards pushed past her and entered Eamon's cage. They had a key which they used with care through thick teeth-mail gloves. Three of them vomited before they were able to drag Niall's brother away from the iron. For the first time since Hollythorn's arrival Niall stared at his brother without iron bars between them, but Eamon still did not have his freedom or his good name as Niall had planned.

Eamon didn't have the strength to cry out as they dragged him away. The remaining guards looked to Niall with trepidation – they didn't want to have to subdue him.

"You have condemned him a second time," Niall hissed at Odiana as he sheathed his sword and stomped after the guards. As he rounded the corner of the tunnel, he thought he caught a glimpse of Laneth's face hidden in the shadows.

He was smiling.

***

THEIR GRIM PROCESSION passed through the vast courtly chambers, where bodies writhed over one another as the queen's fae sought warmth the only way they knew. They had not taken the back way – the queen wanted all the kingdom to see the enemy she had dragged up from the depths.

Niall's rage burned in his throat like a hot coal. His fingers drummed against the hilt of his sword as the blood crusted under his nails. It keened to be released again, to carve his rage into fae flesh. But that wouldn't help Eamon.

Laneth's smile taunted him from the shadows.

Accusing eyes studied Niall from around the smoking fires, and their whispers carried through the vaulted ceilings like a song. A brownie spat at his feet, bold in her disrespect. He recognized her. He'd had her in his bed last moon. He left her in tears, her skin raw and reddened from his proclivities.

His status had always kept his bed warm, despite his brutality. He needed to hurt, to maim. He needed to see his handiwork on their skin, to know for a moment that he was real and so were they.

The chamber guards parted to admit them, their swords pointing toward the ground as a sign of respect. They were Slaugh captains – they did not want to see their general fall, but they would not dare stand beside him. His crime was too great.

They did not allow Odiana or Laneth inside. Odiana called his name, her voice frantic, but Niall couldn't reply without uttering a curse he could not take back.

He did not blame her for following him, for calling the guards. He knew who had earned the full force of his rage. Niall sensed Laneth's eyes on him, *felt* his smile searing on his skin. *I'll cut that smile from Laneth's lips before this night is through.*

Niall raised his hand to his eyes to shield himself from the approaching light, and followed his brother's jailors down the steps into the throne room. Ahead, his brother cried out as the full force of the light hit him. It was enough to blind a fae used to the gloom of the tunnels. Niall gave himself a moment for his eyes to adjust before he stepped into the circle of flames.

Enchanted fires burned all day and night in the throne room – their orange flames simulating the light and warmth of the sun. Glass panels polished to a high sheen covered every inch of the walls, and faceted crystals hung from the ceiling to reflect the light back into the center.

Niall parted the strings of crystals and followed the guards into the inner sanctum. He threw himself to the ground, brushing his forehead against the dirt. Even with the fires burning day and night, the floor was ice cold.

"You may rise," a thin voice croaked.

Niall was first to his feet, first to lay eyes on the Summer Queen as she peered down at their party from atop her throne.

She'd been beautiful once – with hair of spun silk that glittered in the sunlight, skin as smooth and pale as the shell of a bird's egg, and eyes like sinking your bare feet into dewy grass on a summer's morning. But when the Endless Winter enclosed their world, it took the summer from her eyes. She wilted like the flowers she commanded, and her eyes became shards of amethyst – hard and cold.

She touched the vine that grew from her chest to wrap gnarled fingers around her limbs. The vine had once formed a beautiful pea-green dress that she adorned with flowers, but it too had shrunk and dried from the cold, leaving her withered body naked and cold. Only a single flower grew from her now, poking from her chest over her heart – the last spark of life in this lifeless place. When the last petal of this flower wilted and died, she would be no more. The last Queen of Faerie would become dust.

Niall was one of the few who knew how close she was to death. If the court fae knew how bad things had gotten, they would switch loyalties to Laneth in a heartbeat. The fact she allowed Eamon into her throne room didn't bode well for his survival.

Before the guards could speak, Niall rushed forward, tugging open his grass bag to uncover the witch's heart. "My Queen, I brought you a gift."

She took the heart in her hands and bit into the flesh. Blood trickled down her chin. The flower in her heart perked up.

"I executed this man once before," she said, a note of whimsy in her voice as she peered at Eamon with cruel interest. "Would you care to explain to me how he now stands before me, very much alive, with my most celebrated warrior as his protector?"

In the blinding light, Eamon's aura glowed a brilliant purple that glittered from every mirror. All that magic the fae wished to waste because of fear and retribution. Niall touched his brother's eye, drawing strength from their connection. He commanded the Slaugh; he had power over the fae, and the queen knew it. He could use that power to save Eamon.

He cleared his throat and spoke the truth, for that was all he could speak. "My Queen, Eamon owed Laneth money. The scoundrel decided he could not extract such sums from a corpse, and he coveted Eamon's power. Instead of taking Eamon to his death, Laneth hid him away in the deepest, darkest tunnel. He's been trying to extract Eamon's power, and he's been after me to pay Eamon's debts. I am guilty, but it is a guilt born of loyalty to you, to my brother, to our fae who have suffered—"

"You dare speak of loyalty?" The queen took another bite. Her aura briefly shimmered before dying away again. "You were on the battlefield the day your brother killed hundreds of our finest fae with his wicked magic. You were there when your own father was cut down. Where's your loyalty to them? You side with this criminal, the unnatural creature who is no more fae than a demonic goat."

"He is my blood."

"You're a warrior, Niall. You bathe in blood. You know it's nothing special." She sighed with disappointment.

"Please, My Queen, Eamon has lived in torment behind iron bars." Niall looked over to his brother's hunched form and swallowed a hard lump in his throat. "Whatever perverse magic he possessed has long ago been sapped away. He's no danger to the fae, and he might even be of use. He has been Laneth's prisoner and knows Laneth plans to overthrow—"

"*Silence.*"

Niall cut off his words with a snap of his jaw. Rarely had the queen raised her voice to him.

"Laneth has been a loyal servant to me. He has taken advantage of your deception to learn about Eamon's magic. I have read the bones." The queen swept her arm behind her, where a witch hung from branches of her throne, his hands pierced with thorns. His ribs had been swung back, his stomach opened. Two bogies snuffled, fighting over the remains of his entrails. "Eamon's presence has called the ice and held it close. He was the one who brought the bad magic to our realm. He was supposed to die to cleanse our land, and while he lives we will continue to suffer."

"That's not true. His magic cannot control the weather. He didn't do this. The humans did. The *witches* did—"

She spoke over him. "We will eject this poison magic from our midst and our summer will return. I have decided the sentence. Since Eamon brought Hollythorn to our realm, he shall return there. If he makes it inside, we will know the truth of his magic, and he may choose if he wishes to help his people by releasing its magic for us. If he does not, then justice has been served."

Niall *roared*. The flames leaped and flared as his anger took form – a beast torn from the depths of his soul who wanted only to spill blood to drown the injustice of it.

It's my fault the house is here. I sent Eamon into battle knowing he couldn't control his power. I wanted him to spite Father. He shouldn't die because of my malice.

A hand fell on Niall's shoulder. He grabbed it, twisting it against his thumb to break the bones. But then he caught the flash of purple light through the haze of his rage. He dropped the wrist and Eamon clutched his arm, his voice soft and pleading even though he'd been sentenced to death. "Please, brother. Let me do this. I want to atone."

You shouldn't have to atone for magic you didn't ask for, magic you can't control.

I was supposed to keep you safe.

"Spread my word through the kingdom – tomorrow, at twilight, Eamon will atone for his crimes by walking through the gates of Hollythorn." The queen licked witch blood from the tips of her fingers, her cracked lips smacking with satisfaction. "May this be the first day of a long and fruitful summer."

6

AISLING

*A*isling woke to warm fingers caressing her face, the tips lighting fire across her skin. The man lay beside her – his features calm, serene. He mouthed something to her, his tongue touching the front of his lips in a way that was utterly tantalizing.

The crash of the surf drowned out his words.

They lay on a beach, the sand warm beneath her naked skin. He draped his arm across her side. Their legs sandwiched together, limbs tangled off the end of the blanket in the white sand. With his fingers he traced the line of her chin, dancing along her throat, over her collarbone, darting along the edge of her naked breast before moving back to her throat and squeezing just tight enough to stutter her breath.

Aisling's body tingled with need. She kept her gaze locked on the man. His eyes were a blue so cold and vivid she couldn't believe they were real, that they gazed at her, at *her,* with such a violent craving it felt as though they melted away her skin.

A lock of his dark hair fell over his face, and she reached out to tuck it away. Really, it was just an excuse to get her hands on his body, to drag her nails across the hard muscles of his chest. The minuscule space between them seemed like an abyss. Aisling's body ached to be pressed against his, to be consumed utterly in the flame of his desire.

Her hand moved through the air in front of her in slow motion, as though she were pushing through molasses. Finally, her fingertips brushed his cheek. She sucked in her breath as she ran the tips over his coarse stubble.

His hand circled her wrist, holding her touch at bay. His fingers dug in, making her squirm with delicious pain.

He opened his mouth to speak again. Aisling caught the first breath of his word, then...

He disappeared.

The whole beach sucked into a black void.

Heart pounding, Aisling jerked herself upright. Her hands thrust out, searching for the warmth of his skin.

Then she remembered.

She wasn't lying on a beach at all, but splayed out in her bed, the covers in disarray around her. The man wasn't beside her. He was a figment of her imagination, invented to keep her sane all these years.

She'd never even been to a beach like that before. Summer beach trips with Grandmother June were to a sacred cove with sheer cliffs and waters too violent for swimming. She'd constructed the vision of an endless expanse of pearly white sand and crystal water from Treasure Island reality TV shows.

For the last six years, Aisling had seen the boy in her dreams. When she first met him in her final year of high school, he'd been a boy of her age, his strong shoulders and haunting face making her pulse quicken and an ache settle between her legs. They held hands and danced at the prom in her imagination, and she'd felt like every romance book ever written had been inspired by that night. Her real prom date was a bitter disappointment compared to the dream man.

Now he was no longer a boy at all, but a fully-fledged man with broad shoulders and a strong jaw and scars decorating his skin, barely recognizable from the gangly kid she'd once danced with. He had the hunger of a man, too – the way he held her and touched her and trapped her with his fierce possession awoke something dark and hidden inside her. The way he hurt her and made her wet had first kindled her interest in kink.

Those deep pools of intense blue that stared out at her from the veil of her subconscious had stayed the same all these years.

He's not here. He's not real.

Aisling allowed herself three deep breaths, three still moments where she could withdraw the image from her mind, to rub away the impression of the man's fingers digging into her throat. Then it was time to begin the day.

She threw off the covers and went into the hall, ignoring the door directly on the left of her bedroom. It hadn't been there yesterday, and she'd opened enough strange doors in this house to find its presence uninteresting.

When she and Bethany visited June growing up, they shared a honeysuckle-yellow room on the second floor at the end of the east wing, overlooking the rose gardens. But ever since that room had been swallowed by the void, Aisling had been sleeping in the old servants' quarters, housed along a dim, narrow hall behind the kitchens. The rooms weren't nearly as grand as the rest of the house. June decorated them with simple IKEA furniture and rented them out to backpackers. But Aisling preferred things simple – less opportunity for ghosts lurking in the corners or dark cracks to go unnoticed.

Widdershins skidded around the corner, purring with delight as he rubbed up against Aisling's bare legs. Even though he had to be at least five years old by now, he still acted like a kitten. A tiny speck of something stuck to his tail. Aisling pulled it off and held it up to her candle to inspect it. It was the flowering head of a stalk of wheat.

"How did that get here, boy? Come on, tell me. Where do you go?" Aisling picked up the cat and cradled him in her arms. Widdershins had been showing up with all sorts of weird smells and objects lately.

Widdershins' whole body vibrated with the intensity of his purr. He didn't reply. Cats never did.

"At least you're real." She snuggled against Widdershins' warm fur, wishing it was the man's long hair rubbing against her cheek.

IN THE LIBRARY, Aisling drew out the map she had made and spread it across the desk, holding the edges flat with other heavy volumes. She dipped her pen nib in the bottle of ink and scrawled a big, black mark through the dining room, digging the nib into the paper with such force she carved into the desk beneath.

Another room – and another witch – bites the dust.

During their first month in the house, Aisling found the original floor plans in a drawer in the attic, back when the attic was still a place they could freely go. She'd unrolled them with wide eyes, immediately understanding what they represented. *My architecture degree isn't as nerdy and useless as Bethany claims.*

She took the plans downstairs to show her sister.

"Why do we need dusty old drawings?" Bethany stuck out her lower lip.

"I'll show you." Aisling spread out the drawings across the library: The first floor on the desk, with the old red telephone weighing down one end and a glass paperweight on the other.

The second and third floors on the wide leather sofas that sat opposite each other in front of the fire, and the fourth sheet containing the floor plans for the attic and basement on the colorful Persian rug. She took up a pen and inkwell and started to make notations.

First, Aisling marked off the far end of the east wing, drawing crosses through the neat boxes on either side of the hallway. The bedrooms on the end of the hall had been completely enveloped by the void. Aisling had stood on the landing at the top of the staircase, watching the doorways buckling as they were crushed by the overwhelming power that pulled them between the two worlds. Cracks crisscrossed the wallpaper like spiderwebs, creeping like vines overtaking an abandoned building.

Only, Hollythorn House wasn't abandoned. It still housed a family that loved and hated it in equal measure.

Next, Aisling created a key of notations to mark the strange things they witnessed around the house. Red Xs marked walls where long cracks appeared. Blue circles were places where they heard knocking sounds coming from within the walls. Little musical notes were where they'd heard voices; the little girl singing nursery rhymes in the guest bathroom, the high-pitched shrieks from the back of the pantry. Blue droplets showed the cascade of water that fell from the ceiling in one of the servants' rooms.

As time passed, Aisling continued to mark parts of the house that became lost, and mapped the new additions as best she could. Some rooms crumbled into decay, others were dragged into the void. Some morphed into strange caricatures of themselves. As well as the room itself expanding in size, the floor in the middle of the ballroom bounced and buckled when you stepped on it, throwing you about like a giddy dancer. The hall hung with mirrors in the east wing stretched on into infinity.

The conservatory grew vines that twisted and burrowed their way through the surrounding rooms, and seemed always to be creeping closer.

The house had seen every event history could imagine. In the library there were books showing drawings of the Greymouth family at dinners, hosting balls and elaborate costume parties, or taking tea on the lawn back when Hollythorn was just an ordinary manor house with rooms that were the same size on the outside as they were on the inside. The house had withstood wars, rebellions, electrification, the installation of internet cabling. But then, *the* war had come. The great, deadly war that scorched the earth and left behind a barren, desolate wasteland.

In its own way, the house had survived that, too.

Aisling stared at the X she'd made on the map, and counted the safe rooms she had left. There were only ten in all, including her beloved library. The house had once had thirty-two rooms. Eventually, the void would win, and Hollythorn – Aisling's whole world and everything in it – would be consumed by the vastness of the void.

There's nothing left to do but dance.

Well, that or throw herself on the floor and howl that she wanted her sister back. That or give in to the gnawing, baying hounds of grief and loneliness that snarled and snapped in her chest, threatening at any moment to bite off a limb.

Aisling chose to dance.

Grandmother June didn't believe in computers or phones, but she did believe in dance parties at all times of day and night. Some of Aisling's favorite memories from Hollythorn were dancing around the ballroom with Bethany to Grandmother June's favorite records – Nina Simone, Chuck Berry, David Bowie. At university, Aisling had fallen in love with a rockstar – a skinny boy named Guy with a leather jacket and mascara-rimmed eyes.

The kind of boy who sang the stars and took her to BDSM clubs and fed her need for submission, for control, with his mouth and his fingers and his rope tricks. Through him, she'd brought the fantasies from her dreams to life. She went on tour with him over summer break and danced every night in smoky clubs, filling her veins with crunching guitars and cataclysmic poetry. When she fled the city, her record collection came with her.

Aisling shoved open the doors to the ballroom and stepped inside.

Marble and gold greeted her like old friends. The ballroom spread out before her like her grandmother's arms embracing her. This room was everything June was – bright and fun and luscious and exhilarating and queenly and ridiculous. It stole Aisling's breath.

But as beautiful as it was, the ballroom was also... wrong. The whole thing was now the size of a football field. One wall wobbled, like a jelly mold set out on the table. Bethany had thrown a teacup into it once, and it had never come out again. The floor sank slightly in the center, buckling like a Dali painting. A gilded staircase had appeared in the far corner two years ago – the steps leading in a spiral down into the darkness below. Aisling had never dared to follow it.

Sometimes, late at night, on the edges of her dreams, Aisling heard the fluttering notes of the piano playing the waltz. She wanted to tell the dream man about the music, but she couldn't. Not while he was standing right there, being all big and menacing and beautiful and *hers*.

Aisling put on one of Guy's band's records. Her hands slid down her body as her mind traveled far away from Hollythorn and loss and grief, to the pulsing post-punk and industrial music at the kink club where she used to hang out. She thought of the man in her dreams, his fingers tight on her throat or slapping her skin until it bloomed red. She closed her eyes and could almost imagine his fingers touching her.

She danced. She danced for the end of the world, for the sister that couldn't, and for the man who lived only inside her head.

7

NIALL

Niall dreamed about the woman again.

She danced across a marble ballroom – a human room – as a piano played a beautiful waltz, a flowing emerald gown spinning around her as she twirled in time to the music. She threw her head back, her bow-shaped lips parted in ecstasy and her long neck stretched out as the swelling violin caressed her curves. Brown waves spilled down her back like a chocolate waterfall.

Niall's fingers ached to curl around that neck, to squeeze her flawless skin *just* enough that she'd gasp, that those pretty lips would fall open in a desperate plea for air, that she'd know his power as he towered over her. That she'd *thirst* for his power. He could practically feel her body tremble as he pressed his lips to hers – not with fear like the others he'd lain with, but with a need that burned as deep as his own.

Instead, he remained glued to the wall, his body frozen by some invisible force even as his cock hardened to a stiff rod. He couldn't even move his hands to touch himself, to stroke away the fire that crawled beneath his skin. All he could do was stand and stare as she moved to the music.

She is not for you.

He wanted her, oh how he *craved* her as he'd craved nothing before in his life, more than sunlight and blood and the warmth of a fresh witch's heart pulsing between his fingers. He wanted her with an ache that reached from his heart to his cock to the soles of his feet. He wanted her as a lonely bear trying to make friends with a bee. As soon as he touched her, he'd crush her beneath his giant paws, and she would be only a memory.

At least in his dreams, she was safe from him.

The ballroom rose high above his head, ornate columns circling the checkered marble dance floor, their gilded blooms holding up a vaulted rococo ceiling painted with prancing deer. Candles burned in sconces along the walls, casting a warm, flickering light that reflected back in the polished stone, so it appeared as though hundreds of fireflies trailed around the girl.

She is for loving, for tenderness.

I can give her only pain, only blood.

She threw out a shapely leg and spun in a pirouette, her arms above her head. The music changed – the waltz growing darker, the music crunching and roaring as it sped up, humming in the air like a living swarm. Niall had never heard music like that outside of his dreams. It was music for slaying, for bloodshed, for nightmares worse than death, but the girl loved it. She danced harder as she laughed – a tinkling, musical laugh that made his heart soar and his cock pulse with angry urgency.

Her laugh turned into a scream.

The floor of the ballroom dropped away, bending toward a great churning black hole that opened up beneath the glittering chandelier. Her leg collapsed beneath her. She toppled over, crashing against the marble.

Niall's heart dropped to his knees. The ground tilted steeper, and she began to slide toward the swirling chasm. Her fingers clawed at the smooth stone, searching frantically for a hold. Her screams seared his soul.

He willed his limbs to move. He remained frozen in place, his feet glued to the floor. The music screeched, pounding in his ears as he stood mute, watching the floor tilt further, sending the girl sliding closer to her doom. He flicked his gaze around the room, searching for another way to rescue her. His eyes fell upon a dark figure – a hooded shadow – floating along the back of the room.

It was the same hooded figure he'd seen in the window at Hollythorn House.

"What are you doing here?" he managed to choke out. Helpless anger welled up within him. *How dare that witch just stand by, while the girl... while my girl... while she was...*

"Help me!" the girl wailed. The music swelled louder, pounding in his ears.

The figure turned toward him, a blackened shadow where a face should have been. Then, as quickly as it had appeared, it was gone. Niall's limbs regained movement. He tore himself away from the wall and leaped toward the girl, his arms outstretched, hands reaching for her, reaching...

It's not too late. It's not too late.

"Help me! Heeeeeeeeelp..."

"Ooof!" Niall landed on something hard. His head throbbed. His eyelids fluttered open, and slowly the world around him came into view.

He was on the floor in the small, drafty alcove off the Slaugh barracks that now passed for his home, his blankets in a tangle at his feet. In his throes, he'd managed to knock over his scabbard. His blade had slid out across the floor, and his brother's eye stared up at him accusingly.

He rubbed his eyes. He could still hear the music screaming in his head.

It's a dream. Only a dream.

But that was the problem.

Niall *shouldn't* dream. He should sleep soundly each night on a pillow made from the skulls of witches he'd slain. (Not really, but it was a joke Odiana liked to make.) Dreams were messages, visions of what had been or what would be. Slaugh like Niall didn't have the power to dream. Only courtly fae like Odiana had that power.

But Niall had always dreamed of the girl, as long as he could remember. He dreamed her even before Eamon's eye had given him powers no other fae had ever possessed. He never told anyone about the dream girl, not even his brother or Odiana. He wanted to keep her for himself, to possess her utterly, even if only in the dream world.

Always the dream was the same. Always she danced for him with those eyes that begged for his touch, those parted lips that spoke of secrets written for him alone, that if he was broken then she was broken also. And always he was powerless to stop the floor from swallowing her.

If he told Odiana, she'd make him visit a dream-nymph. The fae placed a great deal of importance on the meaning and symbolism in dreams. They would think something significant of a Slaugh dreaming. Throwing bones or carving out the guts of a deer might reveal why he dreamed of the girl.

But Niall didn't want to know why she came to him. He didn't want to ask the question in case it made her go away.

He ran a hand through his long curls and stared up at the picture on the wall behind his bed. It was painted on paper made from reeds that had been woven and hammered together and then dried in the sun. It was a drawing of Niall as a boy, his head bent in concentration as he sharpened his blade against a whetstone, every detail rendered to perfection, right down to the bead of sweat rolling off his forehead.

Eamon painted it.

Eamon who could have been the brightest, the most precious fae of all. Eamon who should have been the next Summer King if not for the uncontrollable magic that sizzled on his fingers, magic that no other fae had ever possessed.

Eamon who was being sent to his death at twilight, even after all his years of suffering in Laneth's hands.

Eamon who would die because the witches of Hollythorn refused to die with honor.

It should be me.

I won't let it happen.

Niall's throat closed as a plan formed in his mind. He pulled on his coat of teeth, fixed his scabbard around his waist, and shoved a bone dagger into the top of his boot.

I will set this right. I will give Eamon the life he was supposed to have.

He had a few hours until twilight, and all the malice and cunning in his heart he needed to pull off his plan. All he needed was something from Odiana's lab.

Odiana's laboratory was near the surface – a room too chilly for fae to live, which showed just how little the queen valued Odiana's work. She had a brownie guarding the door. It flitted in front of Niall as he approached.

"You can't go inside. There are sensitive spells—"

The brownie's words turned into a shriek as Niall drew his blade through its stomach. Blood splattered across Niall's eyes as the brownie collapsed on the ground, desperately trying to hold in its own entrails. Niall's dick swelled at the sight of that helpless creature peering up at him as if it might draw some sliver of kindness from Niall's bleak heart.

Niall drove the hilt of his sword down on the brownie's head, staving in its skull. His cock tugged at his pants, his balls tightening. Killing was the only thing that gave him pleasure.

Killing, and the girl in his dreams.

Niall stepped over the brownie's body and shoved open the door. He knew what to look for – Odiana had described it perfectly. On the long wooden shelves about her desk were rows of potions. He selected a lurid green vial and tucked it into his belt.

As he stepped back from the desk, he noticed what Odiana was working on – a strange device wreathed with thorn-covered vines, containing three glass vials filled with liquids, a set of bellows, and a small, blackish-red organ Niall thought might be a human heart.

He touched the vines gingerly, pricking his finger on a thorn. He remembered what Odiana had said about magical items having a heart. *Is this what this device is supposed to do? Will it find the heart of an object—*

"For a great military tactician, you're awfully predictable."

Niall whirled around, his sword raised. Odiana stood in the doorway, the light of a torch creating a halo around her golden hair. She narrowed her eyes at him, and he could see she'd been crying.

"The Slaugh don't respond to subtle tactics," he shot back. "You point them at your target and unleash their fury."

"You killed my brownie," she said.

"Plenty more where it came from." He knew she wasn't angry about the brownie.

Odiana's shoulders trembled, her hands curling into fists at her sides. "He's been alive all this time, and you *hid* him from me."

"I was trying to avoid exactly this happening," Niall growled. "You leading the queen's guard directly to him and sentencing him to death. Again. I had everything under control."

"He was rotting in an iron cage while Laneth did experiments on him. You were stealing magical objects from under the queen's nose. What part of that is under control, exactly?"

Niall wouldn't admit she was right, but she was right. "I'm going to fix it."

Odiana's gaze fell on the vial under his belt. "You're going to disguise yourself as him and walk into Hollythorn yourself. I'm not sure that's an accurate definition of 'fixing' anything."

"This is his time now, Odiana. His and yours. This is what you've always wanted. Be with him. He'll look like me, but it will be Eamon on the inside. Help him control his power. Help him fit in so that no one suspects."

"And what of you, Niall?" she whispered, reaching for his arm. "You'll be reduced to ashes and dust before you even reach Hollythorn's front door."

"If anyone has the strength to survive Hollythorn, it's me."

It was as close to a lie as Niall was capable of telling.

I was always supposed to die at Hollythorn. I'm returning things to the way they should be.

Odiana stepped up to him, her eye blazing with defiance. She pressed her lips to his. It was not a lovers' kiss, but the kiss of a priestess to her sacrificial victim. A kiss of honoring, of devotion.

"You call yourself a monster, but I feel the heart that beats in your chest," she whispered against his lips, her hand curling across his chest to rest over his heart.

Niall's body remained rigid. Her eyes fluttered shut. She stepped away, sniffing, and reached for the object on her desk.

"In case you're as strong as you say – I haven't tested it, but if you find the heart of the house, replace it with this and you will draw out Hollythorn's magic. You know how to use it?"

"I just wander about yelling, 'here, heart of the house! Come out, come out, wherever you are,' right?" Niall wiped a strand of her winter-white hair from her eye.

Odiana yanked the thorn heart from the desk. She removed a vial of blood from the shelf, emptied it into one of the glass jars, and then adjusted the thorns. She shoved the heart into his hands, along with a round quartz crystal. "*Now* you can wander around yelling nonsense. Use the crystal to activate it. It would work better if we had blood from one of the Hollythorn witches, but this will have to do. Don't fiddle with anything else."

"I've got it."

"If you run into any problems..." she swallowed hard a couple of times before continuing. "Or if you find something that might be of use to me, post a note through the fence. I'll come to the house every week and check for your word."

"You won't regret this," Niall squeezed her arm, giving her one of his widest grins.

Odiana's eyes met his, and he was shocked at the pain he saw there. Odiana was always so controlled, and now she was looking at him as though she was about to beg him to stay. She shook her head, focusing her gaze on something behind his head. "Get out of my sight, Niall."

He did that, shoving past her. He didn't want to watch the strongest, toughest fae he knew cry.

8

NIALL

Niall dragged his legs through the snow, his shoulders heavy from the weight of his teeth-mail, his bow, and the thorn-heart bumping in his grass bag. The guards who escorted him, of course, could see none of that. To him, he appeared as Eamon, dressed in rags and struggling under the weight of his crimes – Eamon the broken, the condemned, the bringer of poison magic.

Eamon had refused to take the glamour potion, as Niall knew he would. Luckily, his brother was weak from his captivity, and Niall was able to force it down his throat. Disguised as Niall, Eamon wandered free into Odiana's arms, his face a picture of misery, while Niall wearing the glamour of his condemned brother was marched toward his fate.

It took them hours to reach the edge of the city and ascend the scorched hill. A procession of fae braved the frozen lands to see the traitor punished. They sang and jeered and danced around him, belting out keening songs about the wrong he'd done at the Battle of Hollythorn. They brought along rotting food and excrement to throw at him. Their queen was not in attendance – she could not risk revealing her weakness. Neither was Odiana – Niall trusted she was somewhere with Eamon, making up for all their years apart.

Laneth marched at the front of the line, bearing the queen's standard with solemn pride even as he plotted to overthrow her.

Hollythorn loomed above them, a dark beacon of gloom, the symbol of everything that had gone wrong in Niall's life. Behind it, the black sky crackled. Jagged lightning splintered against the scorched earth. Even from out here, he could hear the creaks and groans of the structure fighting against the two forces that battled to possess it. The whole house glowed with a bright blue aura – the deepest, most vivid blue Niall had ever seen.

Niall knew no one else could see the aura, but you didn't have to see it to know the house brimmed with enough magic to bring back the summer and all future summers.

Through the iron bars, he could see the short path to the front door, choked with weeds and littered with the bones of the fae who'd fallen trying to enter the house. Some had lain there since the Battle of Hollythorn. Others were foolhardy youth or condemned criminals like him.

Do my father's bones lie there?

As the fae beat their drums and chanted for his death, Niall's hand closed around the latch of the wrought-iron gate. Even through his glove, the metal burned his skin. Niall gritted his teeth against the pain. Behind the pain was something else – a subtle heat thrummed through his fingers. Magic brimmed from the old gate, ripe for the taking.

As Niall steeled himself against the iron eating at his skin, dissolving his organs, rending his bones, his ears rang with a familiar sound. The waltz from his dreams playing over and over, calling him inside.

"This is for you, Eamon." Niall drew up every last scrap of strength inside himself. He swung open the gate and stepped onto the path.

9
———

AISLING

Aisling always secretly knew she'd end up alone.

She deliberately saved some of the books for this reason, choosing instead to play board games with Bethany and explore Grandmother June's treasures together. She hated herself for planning on Bethany's death, as though by considering it she somehow brought it about. But her plans had given her what she needed to survive in the house alone – a structure to her days, and memories with her sister she could play back like a favorite TV show.

Aisling lay on the floor of the ballroom, where she'd collapsed hours before, and replayed her memory reel. They dragged down trunks of Lady Greymouth's ballgowns from the attic before it became lost to them, and hung all the dresses in the wardrobes. They paraded around the house in the gowns, pretending to be celebrities on the red carpet or ladies in a Regency romance novel. When her mother was alive, Aisling made her sit and tell them stories from her imagination, enjoying these tales that starred her and her sister because they were always changing, always new.

Now that it was just her, she could make a start on the task she set herself. When you were alone, the way Aisling and their sister had been for three years – and the way Aisling was now in a way she couldn't quite comprehend fully – the only way to prevent yourself from going insane was to give yourself a task to complete.

Or you could drink all the alcohol, smoke all the weed (June was a recreational user, so fresh plants of her own spliced strain were included in the pantry enchantment), and descend into a grief-fueled rampage. Which was definitely still on the cards, but Aisling wanted to try the sensible option first.

Aisling's self-imposed task was to read every book in the library and to create a catalog of what she discovered.

Aisling liked catalogs, ordered lists, maps of hazards to avoid. She needed order, control. It was the only thing she had left.

She'd already made a list of the first books she wanted to read. Once the raw pain of her loss had dulled to a cold ache, she rose from the ballroom floor and reset the record player. Music could drown out the crushing loneliness, for a while.

Aisling propped the ballroom doors open so the music would swell through the house. She nodded her head along with the pounding drumbeat as she dug out the ledger book she had been saving for her purpose. For the first time in several months, her heart beat with excitement. It felt good to have a purpose.

A wave of grief laced with guilt rolled over her, knocking the wind from her lungs and nearly sending her to the floor again. *How can you feel excited about anything when your sister is gone?*

She battled against the grief. Before Aisling found kink, she'd struggled with her anger. Every part of her life seemed determined to destroy her carefully constructed order. She carried the burdens her flighty mother and timid father didn't care for. She didn't dare show a hair out of place or the scent of emotion, or her teachers, her peers, her boyfriends would see her for who she truly was.

She kept it all inside. All the emotions that felt wrong, imperfect, messy, selfish. All the broken pieces of herself that didn't fit with the image of Aisling the valedictorian, Aisling the perfect daughter, Aisling the girl everyone wanted to be friends with. She pushed them down down down like they were clothes bulging from a too-full suitcase, until eventually, the zippers burst.

The double line of scars along the insides of her legs gave her control back.

She cut to release the pressure.

She cut to *feel* when her feelings were wrong.

She cut right through her first year of college. She cut so she could sustain her 4.0 GPA. She cut so she could earn her prestigious architecture internship. She cut so she could keep smiling even when she wanted to scream. She cut harder and deeper, right up until the first time she'd gone with Guy to the kink club.

And then she didn't need to cut anymore.

Overnight she stopped scarring her body – she didn't need to bleed to release herself when there was a whole room of kind, brutal, willing Doms who'd happily tie her up and spank away the wrong feelings. On the St. Andrew's cross or locked in a spreader bar, Aisling had found her home.

But then came her imprisonment in Hollythorn. She had no one to play with when she most needed the release. She'd tried a few things on her own, but nothing takes the fun out of surrendering yourself in a scene like having to be in charge of your own domination. She masturbated a few times a day because there was fuck else to do, but it wasn't the kind of release she craved.

But maybe, maybe, she'd find that release in books.

Down in the library, Aisling stacked her chosen volumes

under her arms. Plumes of dust rose up around her as she hunted out books she hadn't seen in months or years. She was about to sit down on the lumpy chintz chairs under the window when the thought occurred to her that she could read in the blue drawing room instead. Hollythorn was *her* house now, and there was no rule that said she couldn't read there if she wanted to.

The library was in the west wing, and it was the first room along the wide hallway that opened off the large foyer that served as a through point for the house. Aisling stepped out onto the marble floor, and her gaze instantly swept upward. The entrance hall was open to all three upper floors of the house. Twin staircases swept up from the ground floor, their carved mahogany balustrades depicting fat cherubs and swirling clouds. Between the staircases, large double doors led into the ballroom beyond. The history books Aisling had read about the house often talked about the lavish parties Lady Greymouth held – with enough guests to fill both the entrance hall and the ballroom and spill out into the gardens beyond.

Lady Greymouth had a natural eye for architecture. Even with all my schooling, I don't know if I could design something this exquisite.

The west wing, where the library was located, swept off from a wide archway located near the foot of the staircase. The drawing room was the first room along the east wing, accessed through an identical archway on the opposite wall. It had once been a grand receiving room, hung with elaborate tapestries and delicate French drapes, its large bay windows looking out over the front yard. The tapestries had long since been obscured by a thick layer of dust, and the dark gloom of the overgrown garden, the towering iron wall, and the abyss beyond pressed against the windows, obscuring most of the view, save the bay window that looked out over the porch. Bethany liked to sit at their grand-mother's desk under the window, scribbling drawings and scrawling angry messages in one of her many notebooks. But Aisling rarely went into the drawing room – it had been their grandmother's favorite room, and her mother's as well. Her mother's distinct sandalwood perfume lingered on the moldy furniture. From the window above the desk, one could glimpse the frozen fae city between the clouds. Seeing smoke billowing from their underground chimneys and the occasional fae child playing in the snow made Aisling's blood boil.

But not today. Today, she ached to smell that perfume again, to be in the room where the three women she most loved in the world had passed their days. As Aisling moved across the large entrance hall, a heavy stack of books and her ledger cradled against her chest, there came a knock on the door.

10

AISLING

*K*NOCK *KNOCK.*

Aisling froze, the books teetering in her arms. *I must be hearing things. It's the knocking in the walls again. We haven't heard it in months, but it must be back again. It's trying to fool me into trying to open the front door—*

KNOCK KNOCK.

"Never open the door," her mother had warned her more times than she could count in her final months. "Even if the house allows you to."

KNOCK KNOCK.

Hollythorn House was protected by Grandmother June's powerful spells, but opening the door created a chink in the armor, a portal through which fae could pass into the house. It was like inviting a vampire over the threshold. The house knew this, and so it kept the door tightly sealed, except for a couple of rare occasions where it had creaked open a crack before slamming shut again. In their first months inside the house, many fae had braved the burn of the iron and the threshold spells to fling open the gate, run along the path, and try to gain entrance through magical spells or brute force. The moment they passed the rust-covered iron statue of a serpent that sat in the front yard, their bodies collapsed into the weeds.

Fae hadn't tried the gate in many years, and Aisling only rarely saw their faces peering through the iron bars, their features wracked with pain as they endured the proximity of iron to catch a glimpse of their prize.

Bethany had tried to open the front door once, during one of her screaming fits where she declared that death by the fae was better than being stuck inside for all eternity. She'd pulled and pulled at the handle, but the door wouldn't budge. The house knew how to protect itself and its inhabitants.

KNOCK KNOCK.

The sound was definitely coming from *outside* the house. Her heart pounding, Aisling stood bone still, listening hard. Through the frosted glass on the side of the door, she could see a shadow moving on the porch.

A fae has reached the porch. That's never happened before.

Her heart in her chest, Aisling raced into the drawing room. She dropped the books on the writing desk and leaned across, wiping her sweaty palms on her skirt as she peered through the bay window out over the porch. The shadow moved in front of the door. Snowy footprints led from the cracked steps toward the door.

KNOCK KNOCK.

The music pounded in her head, and the knocking fell in tune with the drums until Aisling wasn't sure whether the knocks came from the shadow outside or from inside her own head.

KNOCK KNOCK.

Nope, those are definitely outside.

She tore her gaze away from the shadowy figure and looked to the wrought iron gate at the end of the overgrown path. She gasped as she saw the gate was open, creaking as it swung on rusty hinges. Who could it be? That gate was a hundred times larger than it was the last time a fae came through. What fae could have the strength to endure touching so much iron to walk right up to Hollythorn House, past the serpent statue, and knock on the door?

Who is so bold or so desperate that they would accept that pain?

Maybe... maybe they're not a fae at all?

Aisling leaned further, her knee digging into the hard wooden chair. She could just make out the outline of the figure's face as it beat at the door with both hands.

It *was* a fae.

Aisling could tell by the slightly upturned edges on his ears and the weird green clothes he wore. Unlike the proud and regal fae who attacked the house all those years ago, this one was hunched and filthy, his body jerking with unnatural speed, as though every moment caused great pain. He raised his fist to knock again. Lightning cracked behind him, illuminating the dark stains and sores on his skin and his swollen, sunken gums.

She leaned so far forward her nose smushed against the glass. Her knee slipped out from beneath her and she toppled forward, hitting the window with a dull thud.

The fae spun around, giving her a glimpse of the X-shaped scar slashed across his face where an eye socket should have been. His remaining eye found hers.

Aisling's breath stuttered.

A jolt ricocheted through her body as though she'd caught her hand in an electrical socket. She lost her grip on the windowsill and toppled backward, stumbling over the chair and crashing to the floor.

That eye.

It looks just like the eyes of the man from my dreams.

But that was impossible. This man's face was completely different – he had that horrible scar, for a start. His body was strange and twisted, hunched from pain. His movements were jerky and rapid, not controlled and arrogant.

And he was *fae.*

Surely I wouldn't dream myself a perfect boyfriend and make him fae. I'm not that much of a masochist.

Heat shuddered through Aisling's body. She didn't know if it was from fear or desire. She lifted her eyes to the bottom of the desk. *Whoever he is, he's right out there, just on the other end of the porch—*

RAP RAP.

The sound was right above her. Aisling yanked her head up and smacked her forehead against the underside of the desk. Cursing as pain surged through her skull, she crawled backward, using the chair to hoist herself into a kneeling position. Her knees scraped the wooden floor, and she flashed back to the times she'd knelt for the man in her dreams, causing heat to pool between her legs.

From here, concealed by the heavy desk, she could gaze up at him without him being able to see her. He definitely wasn't her dream man, but there was something about him that called her dreams to mind, that made her long to fling open the door and fall at his feet, or into his arms.

This is ridiculous. He's fae. He's here to attempt to take the power from the house, as they've all done before. Nothing else.

But still...

How can he have the same eye? That same orb of brilliant ice. That can't be a coincidence. Grandmother June said nothing was ever a coincidence.

Aisling's eyes followed the fae as he leaned forward and rapped on the window again. She pulled herself up, her eyes peering over the edge of the desk. He jabbed his finger toward the door – a short, assertive motion that seemed so out of place on his ramshackle form. It made her heart flip. He was not the one in charge here, but it didn't stop him from seizing control.

His lips – cracked and coated in dried blood – moved in a blur. He was speaking to her, but all she could hear through the glass was a muffled moan.

"Speak louder!" Her words came out a whisper. Aisling cleared her throat and tried again. "I can't hear you!"

His lips moved again, impossibly fast and with fresh blood seeping from his wounds. Still, she couldn't discern his words. *It must be the protection spells messing with the sound.*

Aisling's heart raced as she hoisted herself from the floor. The fae jumped back with a start, his single eye rolling down her body in a way that made her heart pound faster. His features were a mix of rage and need and raw fear.

She jabbed her finger in the direction of the front door. "Go back there!" she shouted. "I'll come meet you."

He didn't move. His eye bore into hers.

Aisling tore her gaze away and forced her limbs to move. She rushed into the foyer and flipped up the mail slot on the door. A gust of frigid air hit her face.

"Who are you?" she whispered into the slot, her stomach churning in anticipation of his answer. "Why are you here?"

A shadow passed over the slot as he knelt down, and she found herself only inches from a ruined socket and an icy iris boring into her with a stare so intense she felt as though he saw right through her skin. Aisling swallowed, her head thudding against her chest.

"I need to talk to you," he said. "Open the door."

Open the door.

The way the words fell from his lips, dripping with menace... This was a man who was used to being obeyed.

He even sounds like the man from my dreams.

"We can talk fine how we are." Aisling's guard instantly

raised. She was horny, not stupid. He might have an eye and a voice from in her dreams, but he was also fae, which meant he couldn't be here for any good reason.

Perhaps he's using glamour. He's tried to dress himself in the skin of my dream man to get me to open the door, but the spell is breaking down because of June's protection spells.

But how does he know what the dream man looks like? Sounds like?

"You're the one who called me here," he rasped into the slot. "You're the one invading my dreams. Open the door."

What?

Okay, this wasn't normal. His having her dream man's eye was one thing, but for him to also have a dream that involved her was something else entirely.

That means something. I just have no idea what.

Is it prophetic? Do we share some kind of magical connection?

Did he eat my dream man and steal his eye? He is fae, so I wouldn't put it past him.

Aisling hadn't had much cause to pour through the old family grimoire (she'd given up after it had become apparent there were no answers that could free her from the house. It was all a bunch of magical gobbledygook). She would have to carefully study the section on dreams. Later. When she'd stuffed her bleeding heart back into her chest.

"If your dreams are keeping you awake, I don't see how that's my problem." Aisling settled for bravado to cover her own sweaty palms and wild thoughts. "The guy in my dreams is way hotter than you, and human. So... bye fae-licia."

"You have a ballroom with a gilded ceiling. You play your music and you dance and you wish for someone to dance with you. There's a hole in the floor. You'd better be careful or you'll dance right into it." The words sound like a threat, a promise.

"So you've come to gloat at my imminent demise?"

He snorted. "Your 'imminent demise'? Who talks like that?"

"*I* talk like that." Aisling's fear made anger rise quickly in her stomach. How dare he come to *her* house, terrify her, and then mock her? Dream man would have never done that. "I've lived in this house a while. There are lots of books. I read them because I've got nothing better to do. Thanks for the creepy but useless warning. I promise I won't dance into a giant wormhole. You can go away now."

Aisling tried to slam down the mail slot, but he jammed his fingers through it. The tip of his finger grazed her cheek.

His touch... it was *everything*.

An electric jolt raced through her body, lighting up long-dormant parts of her. He could have jerked his hand away, but he kept his finger pressed against her skin – a promise, a threat, an invitation. The burned tips brushed her cheek, but they didn't feel burned and cracked – they felt soft and warm and familiar. *She* could jerk away, but she was frozen by a touch that hummed with the power of her dreams.

From the other side of the door, the fae let out a strangled snarl, as if he too had felt the connection between them.

Aisling jumped back. Her skin burned where his finger had touched her.

The house let out a long-suffering groan.

"You..." the fae snarled, his voice like a bass riff reverberating through her body, right to her toes. "I've come for you. You need to let me inside."

I've come for you. Oh, how many nights had she wished for this very thing to happen, for the dream man to show up and rescue her from her prison. But now she didn't know what to do, what to believe. And worse still, she was all alone, with none of the more experienced witches in the family to guide her.

Again, she reverted to bravado. "You're fae. I can't trust you."

"You will." A fork of lightning reflected in the verglas of his eye.

"That's rather presumptive of you. This house has protected me from the spells and blades and other weapons your kind have thrown at me. These walls keep me safe, so I don't see why letting you behind them is a good idea. You haven't given me a good reason to open the door."

He roared, slamming his fists against the door. "I'll die out here. I can't go back through the gate. The iron is eating away at me. Is that what you want?"

Is that what you want?

Yes.

No.

Fuck no.

I don't know.

She wanted her dream man, but not like this. Not a broken, one-eyed fae who carried his voice.

"What happens in your dreams?" she finally managed to ask, her voice a whisper. "What happens to me?"

"You're in trouble, and I try to save you, but every time I fail." His eye blazed with fury. "Not this time."

Aisling stared into that eye. What she saw there terrified her. She saw her own turmoil reflected back at her. He looked desperate, and terrified. That was not the way of the fae.

Her fingers itched to reach out and touch him, to feel the shimmer of their connection again. She knew this was so so stupid, but knowing, and being alone and doomed, were two different things. She longed to brush her lips against his ruined face, to kiss the pain away, to feel her body react the way it did in her dreams.

He may not be the dream man, but he could be enough.

Aisling's hand poised over the door handle. She couldn't trust him, but she trusted the house. If it let him inside, she'd know he was safe. *Maybe Hollythorn knows that he's here to help me...*

The door didn't budge.

Disappointment flooded through her along with a sense of relief. Aisling slumped against the door and jammed her fist in her eye to hold back the tears. All around her, the house groaned with protest.

I'm alone.

I'm safer alone.

I'll die alone.

She'd never know what it was like to stand beside him, to gaze into his eyes without a door in the way.

But then, he'd never have the chance to betray her.

He banged on the door. "What are you doing?"

"I can't let you in, even if I wanted to." Her voice came out as a sob. "The house won't let me."

As if responding to her sobs, the front door clicked. The handle spun of its own accord. Aisling leaped away in shock.

The hinges creaked as the door fell open.

11
____

AISLING

For the first time in almost four years, Aisling saw the front porch.

Her eyes drank in the details; dark stone – darker than she remembered – dotted with still darker bloodstains from the battle, the posts cracked and buckling, leafless vines weaving between the lattice balustrade. Broken ribcages and skulls grinning up at her, covered in a thick layer of ice.

And she saw *him.*

As the door crashed against the wall, the fae stood on the threshold, towering over her. Like a blanket falling from a ghost costume on Halloween, his broken skin slid away, revealing a second skin beneath.

He is *my dream man.*

The man with the mesmerizing eyes. The man who held her, whose touch lit up her body. The man who touched her exactly the way she longed to be touched, his pain swallowing hers so that she was light and free. The man who seemed to watch over her shoulder when she had to venture into the parts of the house that were not safe. It was him. He was *real.*

And he was a fae.

Dreams are your mind's conception of the world, Grandmother June had once told her. *You see what you want to see.*

She'd wanted a man. A friend. A lover. A Dom. Someone to talk to, the way lovers talked in books. So she'd created him.

But how is he here, standing on my threshold?

How did I never guess he was fae?

He had the same features common in the fae; that proud, arrogant nose, the strong chin held high, the slightly pointed tips of the ears, the piercing eyes that seemed to stare into her soul. Long dark hair hung in ringlets around his face, and two discolored scars ran vertically down his sharp cheekbones – burn marks from where he'd pressed his face too close to the iron fence. His mouth quirked into a haughty smile that made her knees weak.

The clothes he wore beneath his disguise marked him as a warrior. The rows of human teeth stitched on his coat clattered together as he moved. He'd probably been on the battlefield four years ago. The sword that hung at his side might have killed her father. His biceps tugged at the leather of his teeth-studded coat. Tattoos of fae symbols and arcane languages trailed along his neck. The tips of his ears swooped back into pixieish points. But he was no pixie. He exuded danger.

And she wanted it.

"It looks as though I've been invited." He flashed her a wicked grin that transformed his face into something utterly, terrifyingly, enchanting.

"I... I..." Aisling's grandmother screamed warnings inside her head. *He's fae. Run away. Slam the door in his face. Punch him right in his perfect fae nose.* But Aisling's body called to him, longing to know more about him, and to do many other things besides. The house welcomed him, and she didn't know what that meant.

She didn't move, and her mind turned to mush. She couldn't articulate what she wanted to say.

Her mother's voice drummed in her ears. *Never let the fae inside the house. You're safe in the house as long as the fae can't get in.*

She should be running for her life, but something in his eyes kept her glued in place. Behind that arrogance, that bloodthirsty cruelty, lurked something else, something she could only see because she knew him from her dreams.

Fear.

He was afraid.

Aisling wanted nothing more than to run to him and fall into his arms. Her whole body ached with need for him, for the release he represented. She knew his fear because she shared it. She knew what it meant to crave control in a world that had fallen apart around her.

Sucking in her breath, Aisling stepped back and gestured into the hall behind her. "If you come inside, you won't be able to leave again," she said. "Not unless the house wants you to. There's some pretty powerful magic in these walls, and I don't know what it will do once it senses a fae inside."

"I have nothing to go back to."

He hitched up the grass bag he had slung over his shoulder, next to a quiver of arrows and a curved wooden bow.

He raised a heavy boot and lurched forward.

Aisling sucked in her breath. It seemed he held his breath too as he moved his foot over the threshold. The house paused its creaking and groaning. Even the storm raging outside quieted for a moment. The world teetered on edge, waiting to see what would happen next.

His heavy boot thudded against the marble floor of the entrance hall, the sound ricocheting through the empty, cavernous gallery like a gunshot. His other boot followed.

He was inside.

Aisling barely had time to gasp before he seized her under the arms and hauled her to her feet. She gripped his shoulders, the teeth biting into her skin. This close, she was struck mute by the obscene beauty of his features. He pressed her back against the wall, trapping her beneath his weight.

"What are you?" he hissed. "How have you survived inside this house? Why are you in my dreams?"

"If your reason for coming here is to get those answers, you're going to be bitterly disappointed." Aisling used the self-defense moves she'd perfected after too many nights out at grubby heavy metal clubs to squirm out of his grip. She hated her body for how much it didn't want him to stop touching her, but she needed to see for herself. She needed to *know*.

The door is open. Is it open for me?

Aisling skidded across the marble and shoved her arm out, trying to pass over the threshold to the outside.

Her hand slammed against an invisible barrier. *So much for that idea.*

The fae came up beside her. He tried to pass his hand back through the door alongside hers. His hand came up against the same hard, invisible surface. He tried to push against it, his muscles bulging with the effort. Aisling would've been salivating if she wasn't so terrified.

But no matter how much he pushed, his hands remained stuck in midair, the barrier before him unyielding.

"You weren't kidding," he breathed, a shadow of fear passing over his face once again.

Aisling nodded. The door handle flew from her hand, torn away by some secret wind. The door slammed shut. The frame rattled. The outside world disappeared, swallowed in the gaping silence of the house.

Aisling faced her dream man.

She looked up at her guest, her heart pounding. He was *real.* He was *here.* "I told you. You're stuck here now. Do you want a tour?"

12

NIALL

A tour?

I've just forced my way into her house and she's offering me a tour?

He glared at the witch. *Is she on drugs? Humans had the strangest drugs.*

He swept his eyes over her body, taking in the strange and sublime sight of her. Everything about her was exactly as it was in his dreams. No – it was better. That long tangle of hair begging to be fisted. Long legs he wanted wrapped around his torso. Those huge, dark eyes that bore into his soul. Her cheeks reddened under his gaze, but instead of looking away, she did the same back to him – devouring him with her eyes. Her aura pulsed with brilliant blue light.

Nothing about this makes sense.

Niall hadn't expected to live this long. He hadn't expected to hear the music from his dreams as he walked the path to Hollythorn's front door. He certainly never believed he'd be inside the house, staring up at the majestic room with its enormous iron chandelier that didn't seem to affect him.

And *her*. He never dreamed to find her here.

Or that she'd be a witch.

Something moved in the shadows at the end of the hallway. A jet-black cat wandered into the hall. When he saw Niall standing there, he arched his back and hissed.

"Widdershins! What's—"

Her words cut off into a scream. Niall darted across the hall and grabbed the creature by the scruff of its neck, his other hand jerking the dagger from his boot. His sinuses itched. The cat swiped at his face.

So iron doesn't affect me inside, but cats still do.

Niall pressed the blade to the foul creature's fur.

"No!" The witch threw her body underneath his arm, covering the cat's body with her own. "You can't hurt him."

"He's a cat." The creature wriggled in Niall's arms, swiping angry claws in the air.

"He's my only friend." She yanked on Niall's arm, which had absolutely no impact on him, but he admired her trying. The mail-teeth of his armor dug into her skin, leaving little marks that set his blood boiling with lust. "Drop him, please."

The softness of her voice spiraled Niall into his dreams, to the very edge of a gaping hole and this beguiling woman he couldn't save. She begged him then and he'd remained frozen. She begged him and he failed her. As he failed his father, his brother, Odiana.

I don't have to fail her again.

Niall dropped the cat to the floor. It landed on all fours like the diabolical creature it was.

The witch dropped down beside the cat and tried to pick him up, but he jerked away with a hiss and bounded into the shadows. A few moments later Niall heard him meowing piti-fully from somewhere in the depths of the house.

"What do you have against cats?" The witch folded her arms and glared at him.

"Cats and fae are lifelong enemies."

"Let me guess – they're the only creature who can see fae as they truly are." She looked him up and down again. "Cats are excellent judges of character. He would've seen through that glamour of yours even when I didn't. If you lay a finger on him, this mail coat won't save you from me."

As she said it, her fingers closed over his arm, her eyes fluttering shut. They were pressed together, her chest heaving against his with each shuddering breath. Every place where she touched him burned with forbidden hunger.

A fae and a witch.

Talk about mortal enemies.

It took all of Niall's self-control to tear himself from her. Her back slammed into the wall as he darted back across the room. Her eyes fluttered closed again, and the way she bit her lip suggested that she liked the pain.

No. This is dangerous.

He needed distance to think, to plan. The thorn heart snagged on his coat.

I'm stuck inside Hollythorn House. With a witch.

With my witch.

And the spell that might save my realm.

"Can I ask how you are keeping a cat in here?" Niall said through gritted teeth. His hand flew to his sword, touching his brother's eye as he turned sideways, knowing his witch could probably see his cock straining against his breeches. "I haven't seen a cat since the Battle of Hollythorn."

Anger flared in the witch's eyes. It was a good fucking look on her. "That's because you ate them all."

Niall shrugged. "Not me. I'm a vegetarian."

"Is that true?"

"I answered your question. Now answer mine."

She bit her lip again. She was afraid of him, but she *liked* that fear. "Widdershins was my grandmother's cat. He came through to this realm with the house, with what remained of my family. He doesn't seem to age, and he knows this house better than I do. He disappears for days sometimes. I don't know where he goes, but he always seems well-fed, and sometimes he brings back objects that don't belong in the house. Once he came back covered in duck feathers, and I'm going to bet there are no ducks in the Summer City, either."

Now he had some distance from her, Niall gazed around the entrance hall, taking in the marble, the baroque tables stuffed with hideous knickknacks, the enormous chandelier creaking above their heads. Bright blue light clung to every wall, every object. Despite himself, he stretched his hand up toward the chandelier, running his fingers over the metal. *How is it that I'm standing directly beneath it but it doesn't make me sick?*

In fact, he'd been feeling much better since he stepped over the threshold.

What is this place?

His eyes darted over the enormous portrait hanging above the twin staircases that rose up toward the first floor. The woman in the portrait wore old-fashioned human clothing, and her eyes seemed to follow Niall as he crossed the floor. She looked like the witch who now glared at him from across the grand room.

"This is a big house."

"You get used to it," she sighed. "My name is Aisling, and the cat is Widdershins. How about we agree that we won't kill each other or hog all the hot water, and I'll give you that tour?"

"I'm Niall." He stared down at his hand clasping the hilt of his sword like it might give him answers. "I won't kill you. Or the cat. And I'm fae, so you know I cannot lie."

Aisling looked like she had a million questions for him, but instead of asking them, she pushed off the wall. "This way." She led him into the west wing, holding open the doors as he could peer inside. "Here's the library, and the smoking room. Across the hall we have—"

"Why is that door blocked off?" Niall ran his fingers along the boards nailed over the first door, feeling a coldness creep over his fingers that was somehow darker and colder than the Endless Winter.

"Don't touch that." She shoved him aside. As her palms slammed into his chest, a jolt of fire raced through his veins, sending a wave of warmth crashing through his whole body.

Niall slammed into the wall, knocking a gilded frame askance. Instinctively, his hands rose up, one cupping her around the neck, the other grabbing her hip to hold her in place and stop her attack. Aisling yelped, the sound stifled by his hand on her throat.

"Let me go," she whispered.

But that wasn't what her body said. Her fingers clamped against him and her eyes had this wild and aroused anxiety. Her lips parted, and although she didn't say the word, Niall felt her *please* in his bones.

Fuck.

Niall had always known Hollythorn had the power to save the fae, but if he'd had any idea of the treasure inside...

He leaned forward, his lips an inch from hers, so close that heat burned between them.

"As you wish." He dropped his hands. She crumpled at his feet, hitting her knee against the wall. She peered up at him, her skirt riding up her legs, her head level with his crotch. There was no way she couldn't see the effect she'd had on him on her knees down there.

Her ruby-lips parted, and it was so easy to imagine sliding his cock between them, fisting her hair in his hand as he made her take him in. She bit her lip, and he wondered if she imagined it, too.

Fuck, this witch will undo me.

"There are things you need to know about Hollythorn House." Aisling breathed hard as she crawled away from him, away from the boarded-up door. Niall balled his hands into fists. The palms still stung with warmth from their connection with her skin. He needed to get control of himself, and he couldn't do it around her. "The house sits part in the fae realm, part in the human world."

"I know *that.*"

Aisling ignored him, continuing her explanation as she moved down the hallway. "The two realms butt up against each other, forcing the house apart. And between the gaps, the void creeps in. It's capturing the house, room by room, altering it into something completely other. If you're not careful, it will capture you, too."

"That's impossible."

"I agree. It *is* impossible. Hollythorn House is a paradox. It shouldn't even exist. But it does, and that's why it's more than just a house. You'll see for yourself. Some rooms change shape. Some rooms change position. I only just found the upstairs bathroom again yesterday. That's the first I've seen of it in months."

"And this room?" Niall nodded to the boards.

"Some rooms, like this one, will eat you alive. It ate my sister." Her voice snagged on the last word.

"Your sister?" Niall's eyes narrowed. "There are more of you in here?"

Aisling shook her head. Her eyes closed again, and her back straightened. She looked to be steeling herself against some internal battle. She lost. A tear forced itself out the corner of her eye and rolled down her cheek.

Tears did things to Niall. His brother's tears made him want to burn the world. Wet streaks of their father's rejection on Eamon's cheeks had driven Niall to make the decision that had led him to this moment. The tears of fae he took to his bed made his blood boil and his cock rock-hard. But that tiny drop of weakness made him want to scoop her into his arms. And that was more terrifying than the prospect of being trapped in this house forever.

Aisling turned her head away. "No, there's no one else. I'm alone."

"You're not alone anymore." He stepped toward her.

She darted away again, swinging her body the way his dream girl did when she danced. His breath closed in his throat. At this rate, he wouldn't survive this tour without either imploding from need or throwing her against a wall and rutting out this madness.

"Shall we continue the tour?" Aisling moved down the hallway, not waiting for his reply. She showed Niall through the few rooms on the west wing that were still accessible before bringing him back into the main entrance. They walked past many metal objects that had no effect on him. As they crossed the marble toward the ballroom, a knocking sound came from the hallway they'd just occupied.

"What's that?" Niall whirled around. His hand darted instinctively toward his sword, but he didn't yet draw it.

"I don't know," Aisling said honestly. "I've heard the knocking ever since I could remember. Every year it grows more frequent. Here's the ballroom with the gilded ceiling. It's one of my favorite rooms in the house, which is saying something. I love this house. At least, I did before it started trying to eat me. I trained to be an architect, you know. When I drew plans for my classes, I always based my designs off Hollythorn. The proportions are *perfection*, and don't get me started on the complexities of this ceiling—"

She kept up a stream of chatter as she threw open the doors. Niall's breath caught in his throat. He forgot the knocking.

This is the room from my dreams.

The room where she danced.

The room where I lose her.

And what a room. Niall had never seen the like of it in all his trips to the human realm. It was larger than the queen's palace in the Summer City, stretching on into infinity. Gilded deer leaped across the vaulted ceiling, and pillars of wooden vines twisted around the outside of the room. The dance floor – made from cream and black marble tiles arranged in a checkerboard pattern – gleamed as though it had been used only yesterday. A dusty grand piano stood silent in the far corner. On top was a wooden box that emitted Aisling's music.

"It's grown several times its original size," the witch said. "It doesn't seem to want to stop."

She looked like she wanted to say something else, but instead, she pointed to the wooden box in the corner. "That's the record player. That's how I play the music you heard. You can see where the floor has—what's wrong?" Aisling looked at him again, those big eyes wide.

Niall turned away, shocked by her question. What was he giving away in his eyes?

"It's exactly as it was in my dreams," he said.

"That's nuts. You can't have seen this room in your dreams. No fae has ever seen it." She flipped through cardboard sleeves painted with images of men and women holding strange instruments, and selected a round, black disc from one. "Maybe you just saw a room that looked like it. Lady Greymouth – she's my ancestor who designed this house – modeled this room off the ballroom at Manderley. A lot of ballrooms of the era follow this style—"

Niall shook his head furiously. "It was this very room, only it was smaller, and that staircase wasn't there. You were here, dancing to a beautiful waltz. Then I saw a shadowy figure behind you, and the floor opened up and sucked you in. I tried to save you, but I was frozen in place. Is that what you saw in your dreams about me?"

Her face flickered with fear again.

"Let's go to the west wing now," she said. "You can tell me more about why you're here."

13

AISLING

*A*s quickly as she could, Aisling led him through the rest of the accessible rooms downstairs, explaining as many of the house's quirks as she could remember with him standing there, being all imposing and gorgeous and distracting. She talked so much she hoped he'd forget she hadn't answered his question.

As she led Niall along the second-floor corridor, where the manor's main bedrooms were, Aisling noticed the bathroom had disappeared again. When she opened the hallway door where it had been only this morning, all that greeted her was a red-brick wall. A lone spider clung to the mortar.

Aisling slammed the door shut. Niall laughed. His laugh was like glass shattering, like ice cracking against the edge of a lake. It was cruel and intoxicating, like a force of nature. Against her better judgment, Aisling found herself smiling, too.

"Those are all the rooms. The rest of the house belongs to the void. Let's have tea."

Careful rationing of her grandmother's tea stash meant that even with the enchantment malfunctioning, Aisling had two whole boxes of English Breakfast to offer. She didn't even know if fae drank tea, but Niall followed her and watched as she fixed the tea with shaking hands. He walked around the kitchen and touched all the appliances. He didn't seem affected by the iron and metal in the house the way he'd been outside.

He accepted a cup and allowed Aisling to lead him to the blue drawing room. He slumped into her mother's old chair as though he owned it, and brought the dainty china cup to his lips, pausing there while he waited for her to settle.

"Why did you come to Hollythorn House?" she said. "Why, after all these years, did a fae make it to the porch?"

"Hang on, let me taste this first." Niall took a tentative sip, smacking his lips. "Seems to be free of poison."

'I'm not kidding around here, fae. Tell me or I'll give you a bedroom with an attitude problem to match your own."

He grinned at that – a wild, dangerous grin that made her stomach purr – but set down his cup, shifting his enormous frame uncomfortably in the dainty chair. "Fine. Here's the story. I didn't come here of my own will. I was sentenced to death. Or rather, my brother was sentenced, and I used glamour to take his place."

"You're telling me the fae who've come through the gate before were condemned criminals? Hollythorn House is a giant electric chair?"

"Some of them. Some were just young warriors trying to prove themselves."

Aisling swallowed. "What was your brother's crime?"

She wasn't sure if she wanted to know.

"Eamon is... different. He has a magic that's never been seen before in the Summer City. My father feared and hated him for this power he couldn't control. He hid Eamon's magic from the other fae and maimed him so he couldn't become a Slaugh warrior. But all my brother ever wanted to do was fight, and I thought he should have his chance. When we marched on

Hollythorn, I took him onto the battlefield alongside me. When the battle turned against us, you witches cut down my father. I waded into the fray to rescue his body, but I became trapped in the spell you were casting on the house. I would have been pulled into the void. Eamon did it to save me."

"Did what?"

"He sent Hollythorn House into our realm." Niall's gaze lifted to the ceiling. "So you see, *I'm* responsible for all this. I deserve to be here."

He stared at the teacup, his eyes wide. He looked surprised at his words, as if he wanted to stuff them back inside himself. His hand flew to the hilt of his sword, and Aisling noticed him caressing an object buried in the hilt. It looked a little like a jewel, and touching it seemed to ease the dark in his eyes.

Here was this fairy, his body built for dominance and war, but his eyes betrayed the turmoil within his own mind.

Of course, fae can't lie.

I bet that's annoying.

At least I have an advantage over this guy.

"So you haven't been sent here to cut out my heart?" Aisling said.

Niall laughed, a grating, barking sound that made her start. "Your heart wouldn't help her grow a single flower. The Summer Queen is dying. She would need more magic than all the witches of the world once possessed."

"She needs Hollythorn." Aisling knew it. Of course she did. But she didn't want to have to look over her shoulder, wondering if her dream man had come to stick his blade through her heart as she slept to take the house's power for himself.

Fae can't lie. If he says he was condemned to death, then it's the truth.

Besides, I'd like to see him try to wrest June's heart from the place.

"I'm not here for Hollythorn," Niall growled, his fingers gripping the chair arms so hard he cut the fabric to tatters. "I wouldn't be here at all if it weren't for you. I'd be dust scattered on the path outside."

Aisling set her cup down and moved to the window. She peered out at the fence, and could just make out the shadows of figures darting through the mist. "Your executioners are still out there. If they saw you enter the house, will they send others to try it?"

"They might, but those warriors will fail. I'm the strongest of the fae, and even I barely made it. Besides, they still have no way of extracting the magic from the house – until they have some spell or device that works, they probably won't send another. The queen won't want to waste a loyal soldier. She needs every one. And you have a new protection now – me."

"No offense, but I trust this house more than I trust you."

"Wise, but unnecessary. My friend, Odiana, is the fae who will figure out the puzzle of Hollythorn's magic. She's also the only one apart from my brother who knows it's me inside. She won't do anything to Hollythorn while she believes I live."

Aisling drummed her fingers against the windowsill. "What I want to know is, why haven't you stuck that sword of yours through my heart yet? I know the fae well enough to know you don't do anything out of the goodness of your heart."

Niall gulped a huge mouthful of tea and swallowed before he said, "I told you. I see you in my dreams."

And I see you. The words were on the tip of Aisling's tongue, but she bit them back. She needed to be reticent, to retain some semblance of control over this situation. And she didn't want to admit what they got up to in her dreams. Right now, Niall was scared and amenable, but if he got over that, he'd just be an ordinary fae, cruel and capricious. She didn't want him to have anything on her.

She narrowed her eyes at him, not sure if she was ready to

believe it was that simple to him. She was a witch, he was fae. They should never be dreaming of each other. *None of this makes sense.* "Anything else you're not telling me?"

Niall inclined his head. "I'm being honest, Aisling. I cannot be anything but honest. But if you want another truth, a truth that exists alongside the truth of our dreams, it is this. The witch inside these walls killed my father." He kicked off his heavy boots and stretched out his legs. Aisling couldn't help dragging her eyes over the tattoos peeking out from the hem of his breeches, along the curve of his strong calves, up to his muscled thighs and what waited between his legs... "Perhaps I also wanted to see if he still left something of himself behind. I wanted to understand."

It seemed he did. As they drank the rest of their tea, Niall asked question after question about the house, and as the minutes turned into an hour, and then two hours, Aisling found herself increasingly opening up to him. As the hours wound by and Aisling talked more to Niall, she felt her unease melting away. It felt so good to talk, so good to toss her hair and be something other than a sister again. Dare she hope that her dream boy was truly real, truly made for her?

Dare she hope that Niall's presence in Hollythorn House was a good thing?

14

NIALL

It was difficult to tell time was passing in Hollythorn House. Aisling said the grandfather clock in the hall and the small clock above the fireplace in the drawing room had both stopped a couple of years ago. There was a sundial in the overgrown backyard, but no sun to read it. The sun and moon were mostly hidden through the black clouds. While exploring the room, Niall found a wind-up pocket watch in a desk drawer, but it seemed to be acting up; the minute hand swung madly around as though it were a compass trying to locate north in a room filled with magnets.

Not that he minded. He was alive, which was more than he expected. And he was with *her*. He wanted to learn as much about Aisling as possible. In real life, she was so much more beautiful than his dreams – her eyes like giant brown saucers, her curves delicious, her lips crying out to be kissed. Niall knew he was staring at her, but he wanted to commit every feature of her face to memory in case he woke up and this was just a dream and he truly had died on the steps of Hollythorn House.

As Aisling talked about her parents and grandmother, spinning some story about an imaginary world she invented as a child, her brown eyes seemed to grow wider. They gave her face a wide-eyed innocence that was utterly intoxicating. It was the kind of face Niall longed to corrupt. He crossed his legs, hiding his stiffened cock in the folds of his pants. His whole body shimmered with energy. He had never felt this attracted to someone before.

She's a witch.

And? The idea of bedding an enemy made Niall's dick jerk with anticipation. Her conquest and domination would be all the sweeter.

And he would conquer her, he decided. He needed something to do if he was trapped in Hollythorn until he found the heart of the house.

You can't think about that now, he admonished himself. *Focus, in case she asks you something about what's in your bag.* He'd already told her more than he'd ever intended, more than he'd ever told another soul who wasn't his brother.

'I'm not here for Hollythorn,' he'd said to Aisling. It had to be the truth – he wouldn't have been able to say it otherwise. But then, the house had stripped him of his aversion to iron, so perhaps it had given him the gift of lies as well. Or perhaps Niall was acknowledging that he was here for Eamon, he was here to settle the debt he owed, and any magic he could extract to save his people would simply be a nice cherry on top.

But the more Niall talked, the fewer shadows he left behind to hide his secrets. And now that he was here, and she was sitting there looking equal parts innocent and wanton, he wasn't going to ruin things by telling her the truth. He was stuck in this house now, indefinitely – he was damn well going to make the most of it.

Besides, I'm not the only one trying to deceive. Aisling must need her delusions to survive living in this house her whole life.

He remarked that the changes in the house almost seemed

designed to test a person's resolve. Aisling laughed, the sound like a trickling stream. "This house casts its own spell on you." She sipped her second cup of tea. "After a while, you can't help but feel enchanted by it, to want to protect it at any cost, even if it's just you standing alone against the fae and the void."

"You don't have to do it all yourself any longer," he growled. A fierce wave of resolve flared in his chest. This was his dream girl, and he would protect her at any cost.

You have to be careful, he warned himself. *Don't get too carried away with Aisling. You have to betray her in the end.*

Aisling yawned. Her long eyelashes tangled together as she struggled to keep her eyes open. She rose from her chair to draw the drapes, shrouding the room. "Follow me," she said. "We'll find you a bedroom."

Aisling led him past the kitchen, where a small suite of servants' quarters led off a narrow hallway. She showed him a bedchamber, much roomier and nicer than the underground alcove in the barracks, and only a few doors down from hers. A small window high above the bed looked out across the frozen lawn. The bed was made up with sheets and a floral duvet, and there was a wooden chair and cupboard on the opposite wall. A painting over the bed showed a woman relaxing in an armchair, a black cat curled in her arms. Niall scanned the walls for cracks but could see none. "It will suffice," he said.

"If I were you, I'd move the bed over to this corner." Aisling pointed into the easternmost corner of the room.

"Why?"

"You'll find out. I can help you if you like."

Niall peered even closer at the wall above the bed. "It's safe where it is?"

"As safe as anything is in this house."

He laughed at that. "This isn't a trick, witch? I'm not going to get sucked into the void in my sleep?"

"I'm not deliberately trying to kill you off. At least, not yet. But there's—"

"Then I think I'll leave it where it is," Niall grinned at her. "I'm going to be here a while. I need to get used to this house's quirks."

"Suit yourself." Aisling's brown eyes swept over him, an unreadable expression on her face. Niall stepped toward her, drawn to her. All evening he'd sat across from her, holding himself back from grabbing her and doing what he wanted to her, what her body begged him for. Now, in the gloom of this cozy room with an inviting bed right there beside them, his fae desires pulsed through his veins. His self-control ebbed away, the voice of reason in his head fading to a dim murmur.

"Niall?" Aisling looked up at him. Damn, she was hot. The air between them sizzled with energy, the pull of their bodies undeniable. Niall reached out a hand and tucked a strand of hair behind her ear.

As his fingers brushed her cheek, a spark shot down his arm, opening a quivering warmth in his chest and jolting his cock to life once more. A faint moan escaped his lips. He bent his head toward her, ready to devour her—

Aisling's breath hitched. Her eyelids fluttered, and her lips pursed in a way Niall found irresistible. He cupped her cheek with his hand and pulled her toward him—

Her eyes grew so wide they practically bugged out of her head. She ducked under his arm and darted toward the door. Niall's hand remained frozen in the air, his cock aching in protest.

"Come back—"

"Don't do that," she choked out, gripping the doorframe like it was the only thing holding her upright. Niall realized she was shaking.

"You want this," he growled. He wanted to touch her so badly, to know that she was real.

"Niall..." She sucked in her breath, her hands straight at her sides. She didn't look at him. "It would never work. You're fae, I'm a witch. Your people are trying to kill me and take my house. I hate you for that. Let's not complicate things."

"But don't you want this?" He balled his hands into fists. He felt angry, cheated. How could she deny the connection between them? She was *his* dream girl.

"It doesn't matter. Just... forget it, please. Rest well, Niall." She backed into the hall, kicking the door shut with her foot. It slammed against the frame, the sound echoing through the large room.

Your people are trying to kill me and take my house. I hate you for that.

Niall's body knotted with tension. He stared at his fist, then smashed it against the portrait hanging beside the bed. The frame splintered and cracked, and the canvas tore away as his fist slammed into the wall behind.

He yanked his hand back, his knuckles stinging. He felt a little better, but the tension still hadn't left his body. There was no way he could hope to get any sleep now, and he had a long time to wait before it was safe to explore the house on his own.

If she didn't want him, if she rejected him, then he had no reason to feel guilty about what he needed to do next.

He gazed at the torn portrait, really seeing the image for the first time. It was a woman sitting by the window in the drawing room. He recognized the window frame and the writing desk beside her, although the neat garden visible through the window had very much changed. She wore an elaborate gown of silk and brocade, and the painter had taken great pains to detail the embroidery around the hem and the folds of fabric swirling around her feet. In her hand sat a closed volume, and a black cat stood regally beside her chair.

What struck him most about the portrait was the woman's remarkable resemblance to Aisling. She was older, in her late thirties in human years, he guessed, but she had the same wide brown eyes, luscious lips, and delicate bone structure. Her breasts practically spilled out of her corset, which cinched in at her waist and accentuated her already ample curves.

It must be one of Aisling's ancestors, he realized. Most likely, it was the same woman in the portrait above the staircase. She and Aisling could practically be sisters. The resemblance really was remarkable. He could just imagine Aisling bustling around the house in a corset, her pert breasts spilling out over the top, always wet and willing to bend over his knee—

Stop thinking about her. Aisling had made it clear she wasn't interested. She'd embarrassed him, made him feel small. He would have to give it time before he considered more forceful action, as much as his cock still rigidly refused to obey. Knowing she was sleeping only two doors down the hall made it even worse.

This will be a long night.

Niall slipped off his tunic and went into the small bathroom across the hall to wash. Luckily for him, the servants' bathroom was still exactly where it was supposed to be. A thin bar of soap, a tub of baking soda, and a bottle of vinegar sat on the edge of the claw-foot bath – Aisling had explained these were substitutes for shampoo, since she'd run out. Niall didn't know what shampoo was, so he settled for splashing some water and soap on his face.

As he stared at his reflection in the mirror, he wondered how his brother was doing. Eamon would have to wear Niall's face from now on and perform his duties with as much malice as Niall himself employed, or the fae would become suspicious.

Odiana would keep him supplied with the potion to create his glamour, and they could finally be together after all these years.

Being trapped in Hollythorn was a small price to pay, especially if Niall could emerge with the heart of the house.

The edges of the mirror rippled with eerie blue light. Every surface of the bathroom gleamed with the aura of its stored magic. No wonder the rooms had a mind of their own.

Niall dared a smile. Aisling may not yet be succumbing to his charms, but he *had* done what he'd set out to do. He was inside Hollythorn, the house that terrified even the toughest fae. He was still alive, and he had unveiled the mysteries that engaged even the wildest fae imaginings. If Odiana's thorn heart worked, he would thaw the Endless Winter. And the girl in his dreams had turned out to be very real and very, very enticing. Even if she didn't want him right now, a few days or weeks together in the house and she would change her mind.

He would give her no choice.

Niall returned to his bedroom, checked the door had firmly closed behind him, and lifted his bag from where he'd dropped it beside the bed. He unfolded the cloak he tied around the thorn heart. He'd doused it in the glamour potion to disguise it as a pile of ordinary clothes, but the spell had lifted as soon as he stepped inside the house, so he needed to keep it hidden.

He ran his fingers over the blackened heart at its center, careful not to snag his skin on the vicious thorns. He reminded himself of Odiana's directions. He glanced at his watch before remembering it was broken. It was too early yet, anyway. Aisling would have only just gone to bed. He'd have to wait, and patience wasn't exactly a Slaugh personality trait.

Niall lay down on the bed and stared at the ceiling, trying not to think of Aisling. It was impossible. His thoughts kept returning to her beautiful lips, her curves, her bouncing curls. He began to compile a list of things he could do to her body once she submitted to him, how he would touch her, torturing her until he tore each orgasm from her lips...

Stop thinking about it. He got up and paced across the floor. The movement only seemed to make him more agitated and aroused.

He had no idea how much time had passed. He had to stand on the bed to gaze out the high window, only to discover it looked toward the back of the property, where the tempest of clashing worlds raged. For a time, he watched dark clouds smash against one another, giant forks of lightning illuminating barren flowerbeds and, toward the rear of the lawn far in the distance, what looked like a small family cemetery. A fork slammed into the side of the house. Niall jumped back as the wall shuddered. Hollythorn groaned.

Something wet fell on his shoulder. Another droplet splashed against his cheek. Suddenly, he was standing beneath a shower, his wet clothes clinging to his skin as more and more water poured on top of him. Niall glanced up into the black void of the roof. Was there a leak somewhere? That seemed unlikely – he would have noticed a draft. Besides, it wasn't raining outside.

This is what Aisling meant about moving the bed. Niall laughed as he wiped slick strands of hair from his sopping forehead. He rolled off the bed and watched the ceiling rain down a giant puddle on top of the sheets.

She did this on purpose, to see how I'd react.

This is nuts. I'll have to sleep on the floor.

The thought made him laugh even harder.

He squeezed out what water he could from his breeches and used the curtain to dry his face and hair. *How much time has passed now? Will it be safe to sneak away to search for the heart yet?*

Niall pulled open his door and crept down the hall. He pressed his ear to Aisling's door, straining to discern any sound.

He heard a faint snuffle, followed by a gasp. *She's still awake.* Niall listened for a few more moments, then pulled away as he realized the sound was sobbing.

Aisling was crying.

The sound made his chest ache. He longed to shove open the door, wrap her in his arms, and kiss the tears away.

What is happening to me? One look at that girl and I've turned into a foppish court fae. I don't comfort sobbing witches. I whip them until they have something to really cry about.

Annoyed at his own sentimentality, Niall returned to his room to wait a bit longer.

The ceiling rain had stopped, and the puddle on his bed had completely disappeared.

15

AISLING

isling did not sleep.

The tears of grief that fell every night dried up some time ago, and her mind turned again and again to the fae in the room down the hall. Was he struggling to sleep, too? A warrior like him, hardened for battle, she imagined he slept like a baby with no care for the disturbance his presence caused.

Three times she yanked off the covers, swung her legs out of bed, and took the first steps toward the door, her body humming with desire for him. Each time, the part of her mind that still saw sense yanked her back.

Your hormones are in overdrive because he's the first man you've seen since the fae killed your father. He's gorgeous, he's in your dreams, but he's fae. Just because he's now trapped here with you doesn't mean you have to have anything to do with him.

Her cunt ached with protest.

Remember, it's the fae who brought Hollythorn House to this realm in the first place, who doomed you to this isolated life. Niall and his people view this house as a source of energy, a powerhouse they want to be able to tap into whenever they choose. He might be condemned, but he won't go quietly into the void. He has a plan, and although he can't lie, he's not revealing all of it. Want to bet a million dollars his plan involves running you through with that bone blade of his?

But how come he dreams of me? Aisling argued with herself, round and round in endless circles. *If he wanted to kill me, he could have done it already. He wanted me in his bed tonight. Surely that means something?*

It means he knows how to play a witch. Your sister is dead, and all you can think about is a fae. What kind of a person are you?

At the thought of her sister, fresh tears welled in Aisling's eyes. Bethany would have known what to do about Niall. She'd probably have scratched his eyes out the minute he stepped inside.

But Bethany wasn't here when Aisling needed her more than ever. The only person here was Niall. And she couldn't very well ask him. She knew from what her grandmother had told her that fae were sexually charged – they often used their magnetism to lure unsuspecting humans into traps. In fae society, lovemaking was part of a magical binding. Sex made them stronger. A guy like Niall, with his muscles and malice-laced smile... he would have fucked his way across the fae realm. He knew how to make himself into something she desired, but that was just the point, wasn't it? She wanted him, and she almost didn't care if it was a game. She hadn't played a game with a real cock in so long.

If he's after my magic, he's going to be bitterly disappointed.

June's magic was locked in the walls of the house, and nothing Aisling tried could remove it. She doubted the fae had any other bright ideas. And her own magical abilities were limited to an uncanny memory for song lyrics and a pasta sauce recipe friends described as 'worthy of the gods.' Alice rebelled against her kooky upbringing and wanted her girls to grow up 'normal,' so by the time she started dumping Aisling and

Bethany with June every holiday, they were too cynical to believe in any of June's spells or potions. Aisling had been initiated into her grandmother's coven, but she'd never actually performed a spell or twitched her nose and made something happen.

But she didn't need magical abilities to know she should beware of Niall. Yet she couldn't deny how Niall pulled her in with that sinful smile, those cold eyes that seemed to see right into her, and the pain that crept into his voice when he spoke of his brother—

Stop it. Stop thinking about him. Go to sleep.

Niall... fuck... Niall...

She growled with frustration. *This won't do. I'm never going to get to sleep unless I...*

Aisling slid her sheets back. Her panties were already wet from thinking of him, from replaying that moment when he bowed his head to hers, so certain as he took what he wanted from her. So certain she would let him.

I wish I let him.

She closed her eyes and drew herself into one of her dreams. She imagined lying on that perfect dream beach, the waves lapping at her toes, her body naked and laid out on silken blankets so the sand wouldn't get everywhere. Her wrists tied behind her head by something. Her legs tied as well, so she couldn't move even if she wanted to.

She didn't have to decide. She didn't have to make a move or second-guess herself or deny what she truly wanted. She didn't have to be the good girl, the perfect girl, the girl who never made waves.

She could surrender.

She could simply *be.*

Aisling's breath hitched as she pictured Niall above her, his mouth curling up into a wicked grin. His weight shifted the sands beneath her as he knelt over her. He bared his teeth and took one of her nipples in his mouth, tugging it and teasing it, biting down hard enough to draw blood.

Aisling pinched her nipple between her fingers until it stiffened to a hard nub.

His grin grew wider as he slid that vicious bone blade from its scabbard and drew it across her chest. He didn't break the skin, but he threatened it, using the knife like a feather to tease paths of fire across her breasts, over her navel. Aisling gasped. She could almost feel the weight of his thighs weighing down her legs, his breath hot on her skin as he chased the blade with ghostly kisses.

She pushed her fingers inside herself. She was wet, so wet. She imagined his body bending over her, his mouth hitting her cunt, attacking her clit with hard, relentless fury as he drew that knife slowly across her skin.

Her blood burns in her veins. "Yes." Aisling hissed the word between her teeth. She did not want Niall across the hall to hear, did not want him to know what he was doing to her in her imagination.

A lie. She wanted him to know. She wanted to replace his ghost fingers, his ghost lips, with real ones. She wanted to truly feel the chafe of a rope around her wrists. She wanted to truly relinquish her control and be herself again.

But she would settle for this... this piece of him she took right now. She tore her own pleasure from her lips as her fingers swirled faster, as she bucked her hips to meet her own punishing pace. His name was on her tongue as the pleasure sliced through her – like his knife splitting her open from nose to navel.

Aisling sagged against the bed, her fingers cramping, her legs jelly. She pictured Niall lifting his fingers, coated with her juices, to his mouth and licking them. Licking them clean like he needed her taste to live. It was the last piece of the fantasy she needed to be able to fall asleep.

She rolled over and tucked her head in her hands, enjoying the wetness between her legs and the satisfied hollow of her stomach. *That's the best orgasm I've had in months.*

But it didn't satisfy that craving that tugged inside her, that dark and secret part of her that needed more than a vision to survive. She felt like a shipwrecked sailor, washed up on a desert island and forced to survive on coconuts and tiny fish. She could fill her belly, but she could never satisfy the hunger that gnawed inside her.

She was starving, and a fairy feast had just walked in her front door.

16

NIALL

*H*ours passed. He sat outside Aisling's room long after she stopped crying. Just when he thought she must have been asleep, she spoke his name with a tight, strained sob, and he'd nearly shoved open the door and crawled into her bed to tear his name from her lips once more.

Back in his room, Niall pulled all the drawers out of his dresser and examined the scanty contents. Behind one drawer he found a dark crack in the wood – a gateway into the void. Aisling must not have known about it – otherwise he was certain she'd never have given him the room.

She wasn't trying to kill him.

At least, not yet.

And that made what he was about to do even worse.

He held his hand in front of the crack to feel the bitter cold blow across his palm. The wind made a whistling noise as it was thrust from the crack. Niall moved his head closer. It almost sounded as though—

Niall. Come to me, Niall.

The wind was calling to him through the void.

Hurriedly, Niall replaced all the drawers and backed away.

He stood still, straining to hear. Was that his name hanging in the air, the black void calling him through the dresser? Or was he just imagining it?

What kind of sorcery is this?

How has Aisling survived in this house for so many years? I've only been here one day and already it's fucking with my head so much I doubt I'll ever sleep again.

Speaking of Aisling... surely she's asleep by now?

Niall grabbed the thorn heart from where he'd set it down on the floor. He didn't dare put it on the bed in case that water – if it even *was* water that had been falling like rain – drowned it and rendered it useless. Without Odiana's knowledge at hand, he wouldn't be able to fix the heart if it broke.

With the heart tucked under his arm, Niall crept into the hallway. He listened at Aisling's door again, straining to hear the faint sound of regular breathing. She was finally asleep.

Niall crept along the servants' corridor behind the kitchen, careful to tread near the edges where the wood was less likely to creak. At the top of the short flight of steps, he headed toward the sealed-off dining room.

If the void was open behind those doors, the magic would be stronger there – a chink in the house's armor. Also, Aisling had lost her sister there. If the heart of the house was a story, like Odiana said, then the dining room held Aisling's sad tale.

It had to be the heart of the house.

The dining room door glowed with blue light, like the entrance to some post-apocalyptic dance club. Niall ran his fingers along the edge of the top board, feeling a faint cold breeze against his skin, similar to the one coming through the crack in his bedroom. Noise whispered through the gaps in the boards. At first, Niall thought it was just wind, but as he fiddled with the glass vials on the instrument, he realized they were words.

Come inside, Niall. Come inside. I want you.

It was the same chorus of voices that had called to him from behind the dresser. What was going on? How did anything inside the void know his name?

Niall knew how to swing a sword and fire a bow. He knew all the best places to cut a witch for maximum pain. But creepy voices calling to him from the void turned his blood cold.

His heart pounding, Niall set down the thorn heart and backed away, until he was pressed up against the same wall where he'd held Aisling earlier. The corner of a portrait nudged his ribcage.

He held the small crystal between his fingers, rubbing it the way Odiana had shown him. He stared at the thorn heart.

The crystal's green aura pulsed wildly. It grew warm in his hands, tugging his fingers in the direction of the heart. The three vials inside the thorny wreath always glowed faintly with bright blue magic, then they flickered out.

Nothing happened.

The crystal went cold in Niall's fingers.

What happened? Why won't it work?

Niall picked up the thorn heart and checked all the vials. But they were positioned exactly as Odiana had shown him. Nothing seemed to be moved or broken. He re-activated the crystal, but this time he couldn't even get the thin blue aura to appear.

Anger surged through him. He'd come all this way, managed to get himself trapped inside the house, ready to do something truly selfless by sacrificing his own life for the fae who condemned his brother, and Odiana's precious heart didn't even *work.*

The rage coiled inside him. Before he knew what he was doing, Niall swung the instrument at the wall. It collided with a photograph of Aisling and her sister as children and knocked it from its hook.

The frame fell, the glass smashing across the rug. The photograph slid out, the edge creased and ruined. Niall bent to pick it up and noticed a second photograph shoved behind it.

He pulled out the image. His eyes widened. His chest twisted and his cock hardened between his legs.

Well, well.

Aisling stared back at him from the image, her long hair pulled up in a severe ponytail. She lay face up on a sculpted couch, her hands tied above her head and a rounded gag trapped between her teeth. Her legs had been tied together with rows of intricate knots, the rope biting into her flesh and causing her skin to blush with pink welts and—

"Reeeeeeow!"

Niall's foot collided with something furry. Sharp pain arced up his leg. The photograph slipped from his fingers.

"Widdershins? You shouldn't sneak around in the shadows like that." In the gloom, Niall could just make out a pair of yellow eyes as the black blight darted down the stairs. He gave Widdershins a twenty-second head start, then picked up the photograph and the thorn heart and started down after him.

I'll have to keep looking.

Back in his room, he found Widdershins curled up in the center of the bed, her yellow eyes staring daggers at him. Happy to concede the strange bed to the cat, Niall pulled the pillows off and made a nest for himself in the center of the room, as far from both the ceiling rain and the crack as he could get. He lay down, weariness creeping along his limbs now that he could see the full horror of his situation.

He slid the photograph underneath his pillow.

Niall fell asleep staring out the window at the swirling maelstrom, his mind on the life outside these walls he'd thrown away and on the girl sleeping only a few doors away whose skin made such pretty welts.

The girl he wanted with a want that burrowed under his skin.

The girl who was completely out of reach.

17

AISLING

She woke with a start, sensing a foreign presence in her room. She opened her eyes, scanning around her for the source of the uneasy feeling clenching her gut. But the grey light from her window had only just begun to creep across the bed, and all she could make out were the blurry edges of her furniture.

"Rise and shine," a deep voice whispered, close to her ear.

Aisling shrieked and scrambled away. She whirled around. As her eyes adjusted to the dim light, she could just make out Niall leaning over the bed, his handsome face inches from hers, in an eerily similar position to the one he'd been in during her fantasy.

He held something long and dark in his hands. A weapon?

He lied. The fae fucker really is here to kill me!

Aisling dived across the bed, trying to kick her legs free of the duvet. She kept one of her great grandfather's rapiers in the corner of the room. If she could just reach it...

Her leg broke free. She grabbed the rapier hilt and whirled around, directing the tip at Niall's throat. "Get away from me," she growled. *I knew you couldn't trust him,* her brain screamed.

"Hey now, is that any way to greet the bearer of breakfast?"

"What?" Aisling breathed hard. Niall lifted his hands, holding the object in the square of grey light streaming from the window. He was holding a tray. On it sat two bowls heaped with porridge, topped with huge dollops of jam.

A lump formed in Aisling's throat. He'd brought her breakfast in bed. The last time she'd had breakfast in bed, she'd lived three months in Hollythorn and was recovering from a fever. Her mother brought her dry crackers and the last of the orange juice. She'd got gritty crumbs all through the sheets. It wasn't a very pleasant memory.

Now, this handsome boy leaned across the bed, the tray poised on his long fingers, a mysterious smile playing out across his lips. He wasn't wearing a shirt, and the hard muscles of his chest called her, begging for her to run her nails across the intricate tattoos winding their way across his pecs. He tweaked the tip of her sword with his finger, causing the blade to shudder.

He grinned wider.

"Do you even know how to use that thing?" he asked, a sneer in his voice.

Aisling's whole face burned as she realized she was wearing nothing but a threadbare lace summer nightgown that had once belonged to her grandmother. The faded white material probably showed *everything*. She tossed the rapier aside and crossed her arms over her chest, hoping Niall wouldn't see her nipples standing erect.

Her mouth watered, and not just for the warmth of the porridge. Beneath her folded arms, her nipples rose like hard stones.

He used the last of your jam, her sensible self scolded. *And that's at least six days of porridge in those bowls. You should be scolding him.*

Instead, Aisling managed a small smile. "Thanks," she said, her stomach flipping.

"I figured it's the least I could do after barging into your house yesterday." Niall set the tray down on the bed in front of her like a peace offering. He climbed across the covers and settled himself against the headboard, leaning on his side with one strong arm behind his neck. He patted the bed beside him, as if it was *his* bed and he was indulging her by allowing her to sleep in it. "Shall we?"

Aisling's body hummed with electricity. *Ignore it,* her brain screamed. *It's his fae magic. He makes everyone feel like that.* But somehow, she didn't quite believe it. Without even realizing she was doing it, Aisling slid down beside Niall on the bed, laying on her side so she faced him, propped up on her elbow. The tray sat between them, a barrier of precious food.

Niall's eyes blazed a trail across her body. Aisling positioned her arm across her chest and reached for the bowl closest to her. Niall snapped out his wrist and brushed his fingers across her knuckle. Sparks of electricity shot along her arm, surging through her chest, lighting up her dark and secret fantasies.

She jerked her hand back. "Why do you keep touching me like that?"

"You feel it too." Cold blue eyes burned into hers.

"I don't know what you're talking about." Her fingers fumbled with the spoon.

"The energy... whatever it is... that flows between us," Niall lowered his voice. "Whenever we touch, it's as though I'm caught in a lightning storm. It hurts, but I don't want to be anywhere else."

Ain't that the truth.

Aisling stared down at her bowl, trying not to notice how close his leg was to hers. If that tray wasn't between them, she could reach out and trail her fingers along his thigh—

No. Don't be ridiculous. He's fae.

"And when you combine it with the dreams I've been having," Niall continued, his fingers creeping across the sheets toward Aisling's. She gulped, but couldn't find the words to turn him back again. "It all points to something connecting us. Something I don't think has anything to do with this house. Don't you agree?"

Aisling squeezed her eyes shut. *Don't tell him,* she warned herself. *Don't give him that power.*

"I had the dreams before I came to the house."

Great. Way to listen to yourself, Aisling.

Niall's body shuddered. His lip curled back in a shit-eating grin, like a spider watching a fly struggle in its web. "Before... Hollythorn?"

"Yes. You've been in my head for years before the battle, okay? I don't know if I trust you. But you're right – there's something very odd about you and me. We should both have all the information if we're going to figure it out, especially if any of your friends decide to come after you. That's only fair. How long have you had the dreams?"

"My whole life." Niall's long eyelashes blinked across his eyes. "What do we do in your dreams? Is there a shadowy figure? Do you fall into the ballroom floor?"

Aisling's entire body stung with heat. "No shadow. We... lie like this," she whispered, gesturing to the space between their prone bodies that cackled with untaken vows. "Usually we're on a beach, but sometimes we're other places. Wild places, like a forest or beside a river. Never inside the house."

"What do we do?"

"We talk, and... other stuff." *Oh, would that the floor open up and swallow me now.*

In this house, that was at least a reasonable request.

Niall grinned. "We fuck?"

The way he said the word, so crass, so oddly human and yet so confident, a flicker of interest darting across his tongue, his arrogant features fixed on her, begging her submissive soul for worship. A shiver ran through Aisling's body that had nothing to do with the cool air.

Niall placed his hand on her thigh, the thin material the only thing separating their skin. Energy surged through his fingers, snapping against Aisling's skin like the promise of more contact, a bit of pain to take away the edge of her needing. Everything in the world ceased to exist save for that hand, those fingers, so close to her... to where she ached...

He's fae he's fae he's fae he's fae...

Aisling grabbed the bowl and gulped down a spoonful of porridge, barely tasting it. She had to change the subject, quick. "You don't seem too upset about being trapped here. You might not see your family again."

"I don't have much of a family anymore." A shadow passed over Niall's face.

"You said your father died in the battle. But what about your mother?"

"He killed her," Niall said. "After my younger brother was born. He thought she was the source of his poison magic, so he cut the poison out of her. He made me hold her down while he slit her throat."

Fuck. That's brutal. Remind me never to ask a fae about their family life again.

Niall's hand crept to the hilt of his sword, which rested in the scabbard at his side. She wondered if he slept with it, and assumed he did. He stroked over that same inlaid object, his fingers deft, reverent.

"This magic your brother has, what is it exactly? What makes it so different from ordinary fae magic?"

He gave a dark chuckle. "He can shift houses across realms, for a start."

"Besides that. Go on, fae. Indulge me. Explain fae magic as if I'm a sheltered witch who has no idea what the fuck you can actually do with those fingers."

Oh, how that arrogant smile did things to her insides. "Ordinary fae magic is... just that. Ordinary. Straight out of your human storybooks. Court fairies have their glamour potions, their changelings, their unbreakable contracts, and their siren songs that lure humans to their deaths. Us Slaugh have our heightened senses and our resistance to human weapons. We have our bloodlust and our ability to hunt as one across the earth. But Eamon could do things no fairy should be able to do. He could see the future – he would get these terrible visions of blood and death and ice that sent him into screaming fits for days. He could move objects with his mind, bring things to him just by thinking about them. He could *see* magic and identify different types by its color, which meant he could recognize a witch standing among humans simply by the glow of her skin. And he could shadow-shift – become a shadow that prowled in the darkness."

As Niall moved his fingers from his sword to pick up his spoon, Aisling peered at the gem with curiosity. *It's not a crystal. That's a—*

An eye.

Fae are fucking gross.

"No fae has had such power before," Niall continued. "And what was worse was that Eamon couldn't control it. My father couldn't abide that. He needed to have complete dominance over everything, including our family. He needed Eamon to fall into line, and he needed me to help put him there."

From the darkness in his voice, Aisling knew he'd been

asked to do things that were etched onto his soul. Niall scraped another spoonful into his mouth. "But that's okay."

"It is?"

"Yes." he shrugged. "Father is dead. Eamon is free. I am here with you. Now, what do you do all day?"

"I slap mouthy fae who don't give me straight answers to my questions."

Niall rubbed a hand along his jaw. "I doubt I'd feel so much as a sting, little witch. Go on, entertain me."

"What do you mean?"

"I mean, you don't just lounge around in diaphanous lace negligees, waiting for fae servants to bring you your every desire?" He grinned that wicked grin again. "Not that that's a bad way to spend the day or anything..."

"You like lounging around in lace negligees yourself, do you?" she shot back, relieved she could use sarcasm to cover for the fact her body flushed at the idea of a shirtless Niall granting her 'every desire.'

"Ah, she's a quick one." Niall set the tray on the small table beside the bed and leaned toward her. The gap between them narrowed to a sliver of no man's land, a barrier that kept her safe and trapped her at the same time. She breathed in the scent of him, heady and masculine and somehow woody, like the smell of the hardwood furniture that filled the house. "Go on, what's fun in this house?"

I know what would be really fun...

"I don't know," she managed to choke out, shrugging her shoulders. "I read. I play with Widdershins. I walk around and make sure the house hasn't lost another room. My sister and I would play games sometimes. We have chess and backgammon and—"

Niall's eyes bore into hers. "That's it? That's what you've been doing your whole life?"

"Not my whole life. I used to have a life, a job, a boyfriend—"

"Mmmm. I believe you." His arrogant mouth tugged as he slid something onto her bowl.

Aisling's cheeks reddened as she held up a corner of the photograph.

"I bumped into a photograph in the hallway." Niall flexed his broad shoulders. "The frame smashed and I found this image tucked away behind it. Why were you hiding this?"

"It's... like I said, it's my old life." Aisling tried to shove the image under the blankets, but Niall grabbed her wrist.

"Let go of me," she whispered.

"Tell me what this photograph means."

That voice – commanding but thick with desperation – hummed against her bones.

"It's kink." She wriggled beneath him, but that only made him lean closer, his crotch resting over hers so she could *feel* his hardness digging into him. Invisible lightning flashed between their bodies. "It's something humans do, *consensually,* when they need their sexual release tinged with something else. For me, it's pain. I like pain. I *need* pain."

"These ropes around your legs." Niall traced the edge of the photograph, his hips grinding against hers.

"It's kink. My friend ties me up like this. The rope feels amazing against my skin, especially when it bites. Sometimes I would hang upside down."

"And those stripes on your skin?" His finger jabbed. The growl in his voice pooled heat in her stomach.

She couldn't bear the intensity of his gaze. She turned away, but she knew from the sharp intake of his breath that her red cheeks only made him more aroused. "Marks from a whip."

"Is that what you want?" His breath teased her ear.

No. Not from you. Not from my enemy.

Yes.

More than anything, yes.

Her body responded to the weight of him pressing her into the bed, to that haughty command in his voice, to the hard cock digging into her thigh.

Please, yes.

No, no.

"If this is who you are," he growled the words against her skin, reaching his tongue out to lick them away. "Why hide it away behind another photograph? Why not display it in this sepulchre to your ancestors?"

"Because my younger sister lived here, too. She didn't need to see me like this." Aisling squirmed, but there was no escaping his weight, even if she wanted to. The heat pooling between her legs suggested she very much did not. "I hid it there because... because I liked knowing I still kept part of myself. This house hadn't taken everything."

"Your sister." Niall leaned back on his elbows, his cold eyes delving into hers. She caught a tremble in his voice, something he wasn't telling her. "Your sister who is in the void."

She nodded. "I answered your questions. Now let me free."

"That's not what you want." His fingers tightened around her wrists. "Turn over."

Any witch in her situation would use this opportunity to shove the bread knife between Niall's ribs, but Aisling didn't have the strength. Not when he used *that* voice, the one that demanded obedience, the one that promised pain.

Slowly, slowly, aware of his eyes on her skin, aware that her nightdress had ridden up over her thighs, Aisling turned over.

The bedsheets shimmered against her skin. Every movement felt like a caress. Her nightshirt twisted around her middle, riding up so that her panties rubbed against Niall's breeches. Aisling's cheeks burned deeper as she felt how wet she was.

A low growl escaped Niall's throat. "Is this how you want it?" Niall's voice rasped. His body hovered over hers, not quite touching, letting the electrical storm between them do all the work. "Is this how I make you wet?"

The scabbard of his sword rubbed against her thigh.

Aisling whimpered. Niall's fingers circled her wrists. He held her down with one strong hand while he nipped and bit a trail along her spine. "Like this?" he growled in her ear. "Answer me."

"Yes."

Aisling needed to tell him so many things, about boundaries and safe words and edging and aftercare, but she couldn't form sentences, not when he was everything she'd needed for so long, not when the proximity of her body pushed out her grief and replaced it with the most dangerous bliss. "Yes."

"And you want this?" His voice was ragged. He fisted the fabric of her nightgown, dragging it up to expose her ass.

Her skin prickled with nervous anticipation. If she were at the club with Guy, she'd know exactly what was coming next, and she'd relish the knowing – the squeak of Guy's boots against the polished wood, the creak of leather as he selected his implements, the intake of breath from a bystander watching the scene. But here there was no knowing. Here, Niall's breath grazed her neck and his knife touched her skin and she had no idea if he would fuck her or kill her.

And maybe he would kill her. Maybe he would tear her ribs open and pull her heart out through her chest, the way she'd seen the fae attack her grandmother's coven. Aisling didn't care anymore, as long as he kept holding her hands and breathing those sweet, forbidden words against her ear.

"Y-y-yes."

She didn't know what he would do if she said no. He was her sworn enemy, and he could snap her neck without breaking a sweat. She'd let him take away her power, her ability to fight back. And yet, she'd never felt more powerful.

She gasped as he tore away her nightdress, as he slid his knife over her thigh to cut away her panties. He growled low in his throat as he drank in her naked body, her bare ass pointing up. The sound of him pooled liquid between her legs. Niall grabbed a handful of her hair, tugging so that her neck arched back toward him. His fingers were rough as they trailed along her spine. The scabbard grazed her again, and it was like another hand, another cock, doing things to her.

He grunted as he fiddled with something. Then a moment later, something bit across her ass. Aisling yelped as the pain bloomed, burrowing its way inside her to where it was needed most.

The sting of a whip. No, not a whip. The leather belt of his breeches.

Her body hummed with energy, lit up like a Christmas tree taken down from the attic after a year in the dark. He tugged her hair, and her scalp burned with color and heat and *need*.

Fingers reached down to touch her between her legs. "You're wet." He sounded surprised.

"More," she begged.

He withdrew his fingers. Aisling angled her hips, chasing the ghost of his rough touch, only to be met with another sting of the whip. She cried out as the pain bit deeper, as it reached into her most lonely and vulnerable places and laid it all bare before him.

Niall laid blow after blow across her ass, never hitting the same spot twice. He wasn't like Guy and the other Doms she'd played with at the club. He had no control, no rhythm. He abandoned himself completely to the role of tormenter, but he seemed to understand exactly what she needed. He dropped her wrists and thrust his fingers between her legs, stroking her clit as he latticed strokes across her skin.

Fat tears rolled down her cheeks as the pain undid the laces holding her loneliness inside her. All that was Aisling – all her need for control and order and maps and plans – fell upon on the bedsheets, until she was just a quivering mess of nerve endings and fucked-upness.

She came with a scream that tore through the empty rooms of Hollythorn. She unraveled from the outside in, not caring, not thinking, only feeling, only *being*.

Fuck, it was *magic*.

When she could move again, Aisling looked over her shoulder as Niall slid off the end of the bed. He stared down at her with a need that had etched itself into his skin. The belt dropped from his fingers.

The tip of his cock peeked from beneath his tunic, a beat of pre-cum rolling off the tip. Aisling licked her lips, and Niall's shoulders shuddered.

What would he make her do now?

What would she do?

Anything.

She'd forgotten what it felt like to be vulnerable, to be beautiful in her abandon. To be alive.

She needed more. She needed him.

Niall blinked. With a great effort, he drew himself back from the knife-edge he walked on. He grabbed the tray and turned away from the bed. His scabbard hit the doorframe as he fled the room.

His rejection crushed her. She rolled over, savoring the rawness of her skin against the sheets.

The tears fell thick and fast now. Tears she cried for Bethany, for her life before, and for losing the only man who might have made this miserable existence worth living before she'd even tasted his cock.

Why did he leave? Did I frighten the fearsome fae warrior?

Am I that sick? That twisted?

She heard him call back to her from the hallway. "Throw on some clothes and show me this library."

18
___

NIALL

I need pain.

Her cherry-lips parting, begging him for more...

Niall had never before experienced a sexual act like what he'd done with Aisling. Sure, he'd whipped pixies until they bled, but it had always been about him, about pouring the rage inside him into another vessel so the snarling voices in his head would quiet for a moment. This time, he wanted to hurt Aisling, but not for himself. For *her*. Because she needed it. Because she *begged* for it. And then she surrendered to the pain with such complete trust and serenity that he couldn't help but wish he could give her everything she needed a hundred times over.

In her bedroom, his mind had spun with all the depraved things he could do for her, anything to elicit more of those sweet mewling noises from her.

He'd never considered pain could be a service, that in his depravity he would find some dark and secret place of his heart where he *wanted* to serve.

That was the problem.

That was why he ran.

She was a witch. His need to hurt her was tied up with his

duty – he *should* hurt her, harm her, tear out her heart for his queen to devour.

He couldn't pretend what he just did had anything to do with duty.

Niall fled through the house, down to the kitchen with the dishes in his hands. He felt like a coward. His balls ached. He'd pushed his fingers inside her and felt the silky warmth of her folds, and now he couldn't think of anything else, even as he swore to himself that he wouldn't give in.

He would possess her utterly. He would make her body quiver like that over and over again. He would make her scream his name and beg for his cock, but he would never submit.

He would give her the pain, yes, but he wouldn't give her any piece of himself.

He had so little left.

Aisling wandered down to the kitchen as Niall washed up the dishes. Her nose was red from crying, and a strange feeling that might've been regret if fae felt such a thing twisted in his gut. She peered around the kitchen with amused disgust. "You made porridge with jam. How did you manage to use every dish in the house?"

"It's a skill."

"It's not your only skill, fae." She looked at him then, and the rawness in her eyes made her more naked than when he fucked her with his fingers.

Aisling elbowed him out of the way of the sink and ordered him to clean up the globs of porridge stuck to the stovetop, the floor, even the ceiling. Niall had never been ordered to clean before – that was what brownies and boggarts were for. But he found himself using his knife to chip away at the dried porridge while Aisling finished the mountain of dishes.

Aisling sang as she worked, swaying her hips with a beat that existed only in her head. Niall watched her out of the corner of his eye as he wiped down the counter and returned the jam to the pantry.

"How come you still have so much food left?" He gestured to the shelves of boxed and canned supplies. A cold twisted in his gut. She'd been feasting in this house while the fae starved through the Endless Winter. "I've never even heard of Frosted Flakes and KitKats. This is all food from the human realm. It should have run out years ago, like your shampoo."

"We're witches, remember?" Aisling slammed the pantry door and placed her body in front of it, her eyes flashing. He'd put her on edge, and he wasn't sure why. "The pantry has a replicating enchantment on it – any item that's removed and eaten will magically be replaced by a new box. It's a very powerful piece of magic worked by my grandmother and mother when Hollythorn was being pulled through to the fae realm. But they're both dead now and it's wearing down and I have no idea how to fix it. It used to take minutes for a new box or can to appear. Now, it takes months. If I don't ration carefully, we will run out of food."

Her unsaid words hung in the air, unspoken but understood. *And now you're here, this food will have to feed two.*

"And the water? Where's that come from? The house can't be hooked up to a city supply."

"It wasn't on the water main back on Earth, either. The house collects its own rainwater. My grandmother enchanted it to collect and melt ice and snow from outside, and to filter out the radiation." Aisling ran the tap to wash her hands. "Thankfully, that system still works perfectly. If it broke down, I'd be dead before I knew it. You, I'm not so sure about. You fae seem to have a radiation tolerance."

When the kitchen was spick and span, everything back in its exact place, they went to the library. Aisling swung the heavy door, holding it half-open as she shifted her weight from foot to foot, caught on the threshold by some internal dilemma.

Niall shoved his way past her.

His gaze swept around the room, taking in the shelves piled with books, the drafting table where drawings of the house were pinned in place, the chintz chairs by the heavily-draped bay window – the stuffing tumbling from long gashes made by Widdershins' claws, the dusty scientific instruments lined up above the fireplace, the old-fashioned bright-red dial phone still sitting on the corner of the desk. The corners of his lips turned up in delight.

He may not have found the heart of the house yet, but he stood inside its brain. Somewhere in this room would be the map, the formula, the answers he needed. And the sooner he found the heart, the sooner he could rid himself of this witch who made him feel things he didn't understand.

"I usually sit here." Aisling dropped into the less-battered of the chairs. She stared up at Niall with those wide, dark eyes, as if daring him to make the next move.

"Go about your business. Don't let me stop you." Niall moved along the shelves, his finger rubbing along the spines of the books. His lips moved as he read the titles to himself, his eyes widening as he gorged on the knowledge to be found within. He thanked his mother silently for insisting he learned to read, but that only brought up the memory of her blood flowing between his fingers, and he had to hide that away again.

Niall jabbed his finger at the gilded frame that hung on the wall beside the library door. The woman wore a pink gown and held a matching feathered mask on a stick. Her face was rendered in soft brushstrokes, her hair cascading down her back in luscious curls, and she stared over her shoulder at someone outside the portrait, a half-smile playing across her lips. She looked so like Aisling, they could be sisters. "This woman is everywhere. She's the woman in the entrance hall, and there's a portrait of her in my chambers, as well."

"She was my great great great great great great grandmother, the Lady Greymouth."

"That's a lot of greats."

"Well, she deserved them. She was an amazing woman. She designed and built Hollythorn House, including the carvings in the ballroom and stormwater system and the secret sex dungeon we've never been able to find. When you build a place like this, you get to stick your portrait everywhere."

Aisling dropped into a wingback chair, folding her legs to give Niall the shapely line of her calves. Her ankles were so thin he thought he might be able to wrap his fingers around them and touch the tips together. He imagined what she'd look like with those ankles tied together, perhaps hanging from the chandelier, those pouting lips open to accept him...

His cock grew hard again. He turned back to the portrait, needing a moment. "You look a lot like her. She's older, and I can't imagine you wearing that frilly dress. But her eyes, her facial features, the fact she had a secret sex dungeon..."

Aisling shifted in the chair behind him. Tension touched the edges of the room. He didn't know how to navigate this *pull* between them. Sharing this house with his sworn enemy should be easy – he either killed her or imprisoned her while he searched for the heart of the house, his ticket back to fae society. Instead, he was tripping over his tongue trying to make conversation with her, to draw out her stories as if they might be a light in the darkness.

Instead, he spent every moment thinking about the wet heat between her legs.

"Lady Greymouth was quite remarkable," Aisling said. "We don't know a lot about her, but there's this story of how she came upon the land for the house. She was on her horse, riding across the country to meet with her solicitor or something, when she decided to take a shortcut through the Wilcox estate. Unfortunately, the horse threw her and she fell and hit her head. In the middle of the day, in the hot sun, she could have died! Luckily, one of Wilcox's workers – a man named George – stumbled upon her and brought her around. She was so smitten with the view that greeted her when she opened her eyes—"

"I bet she was." Niall winked over his shoulder.

"Don't be ridiculous." Her face flushed. "I was talking about the view of the landscape, not George. *Anyway,* Lady Greymouth immediately demanded George take her to his employer. She presented Lord Wilcox with a proposal – he would sell her the field where she had fallen, as well as the eight fields surrounding it, and George's contract as well, into the bargain."

"See, she *did* fancy him. Bet he spent a lot of contractually obligated time in the sex-dungeon—"

"Will you let me finish?"

Niall inclined his head, and she continued. "Wilcox hadn't even intended to sell the land, but there was no arguing with Lady Greymouth. She gave him some gold she had on her person, got her land, built this house, and gave George his own cottage and plot as thanks for saving her life."

Niall said. "I think I would have liked her."

"Even the whole giving-George-a-free-house part?" Aisling quirked.

Niall thought of the sprites and boggarts who served the court fae or rode sometimes with the Slaugh to serve them on the battlefield. "Sure. Slaves are annoying. You have to feed them or they fall over. Food is expensive. I'm anti-slavery, pro-sensible investing."

"George wasn't a slave, but it figures a fae would be anti-slavery because of the benefit it would give to *him.*" Aisling picked up a book from a stack on the desk. "Lady Greymouth also fought to keep the fae out of the chest cavities of her fellow witches. Many of your kind who came to the human world for witches' hearts died by her hand."

"A brutal woman. I like her even more." Despite himself, the corners of Niall's mouth pulled up into a grin. "I've never seen so many books in one place before. I don't even know where to begin."

"You can read, can't you?" Aisling sounded unsure of herself.

"My friend taught me." His mother began his lessons, and Odiana instructed him in secret after her death. He remembered Odiana's perfect features furrowed in concentration as she ran her finger over the page, forcing him to follow the letters. "Fae live far longer than humans. There is time even for warriors to learn useless skills like reading."

"It's hardly useless."

"To a witch, maybe. But the only book my father had was a manual on weaponry."

"You had no books in your home? No stories?"

"Fae do not tell stories, we *are* the stories."

Niall felt Aisling's eyes on him as he circled the room. There were books on every subject – books on cookery and herbal medicine and gardening and human mythologies and ancient and modern architecture and many many many with cats on the covers. Niall itched to take one – not a cat one – and curl up in the chair next to Aisling. He allowed himself a moment to imagine the peace of reading alongside this witch as if there were nothing between them but air and time.

Niall toyed with the corner of a gardening book. *Aisling is wary. She's afraid she told me too much about the pantry enchantment. I should wait a few days before trying to get more information—*

His father's voice battered against his skull. *The Slaugh don't wait. They don't play games like court faeries and pander to the sensi-*

bilities of pretty young witches with welts on their asses. The Slaugh have one purpose – to ride across the human realm on a cloud of bloodshed.

To hunt.

To kill.

"Where are the magic books?" Niall barked.

Aisling dropped the book in her lap. "Why?"

"A family of witches must have an interesting collection of spell books. I want to read them."

"Again, why?" The wariness crept back into her voice.

"Because I'm trapped in this house and I have nothing better to do and you won't let me eat the cat. Because I'm interested in your family. Because I may find some answer that will free us both."

Because I want to sit beside you and breathe in your scent all day—

She shrugged. "You hoping for a handy 'suck out Hollythorn's magic' spell, right? Not happening, fae. I've pored over all those books, and so did my mother and grandmother. There's nothing that will help us, and even if there was, what would be the point in freedom? My world is an uninhabitable wasteland, and yours is rapidly heading for a new ice age. Why would I leave Hollythorn House just to hand my heart to your queen on a platter?"

Because maybe we can thaw the Endless Winter. Because maybe if I save the fae I can find a way to keep you for myself. "I'd like to read them anyway."

With an exaggerated sigh, Aisling flounced to her feet and led him to a shelf in the corner. She indicated the two rows of leatherbound books on the bottom shelves. "By all means, knock yourself out. Here they all are."

Niall selected an old grimoire that had belonged to Aisling's great grandmother Ama. When he sank into the chair, the fabric molded itself around him, cushioning his weary muscles in a way no fae furniture ever had. His brother, ever the poet, might've said it was like being embraced by a lover, which made Niall uncomfortable because he'd never been embraced before.

The pages crackled under his fingers, the paper old and brittle. Ama had been an experienced herbalist, and she filled her grimoire with complex diagrams of plants and flowers, along with recipes scrawled in loopy, unreadable script. Niall's eyes darted hungrily over the pages, surprised to feel the thrill of the hunt seeping into his veins. In this room was the answer, he knew it. He would find his way to the heart of the house.

Beside him, Aisling shifted in her chair. As he read, Niall's senses took in every creak and shuffle and tap. He knew without looking up when she stopped turning the pages and was studying him over the top of her book.

Such insolence. His father's voice pounded against Niall's skull. *She should be punished.*

An image of Aisling bent over the library desk, his hand on her throat, holding her down as he spread her legs and reddened her backside.

Yes, she should be punished.

Niall set the book on his thighs, hiding his engorging erection.

He knew that punishment could feel good, that pain could be a penance. It was why he'd swapped places with his brother, after all.

But Aisling wouldn't be a punishment for him. She could be his salvation if he allowed himself to surrender...

No.

Niall didn't want to look at her, didn't want to give into his twisted cravings again. He forced himself to focus on the book, on the drawing of a lily, its petals delicately rendered with loving care.

He looked up.

Aisling snapped her chin down toward her own book, her shoulders tensing as she fingered the corner of the page. *I'm just reading, nothing else,* her body language said, but her pulse quickening in the vein in her neck betrayed her. And just like that, Niall's balls were screaming at him for release.

How am I going to be able to live in the same house as this witch? How will I resist her?

19

AISLING

"I have a problem," Niall said.

They were eating breakfast together in the window of the drawing room, in the new 'breakfast nook' Niall made for them. He had pulled a small table and two chairs from one of the opulent guest suites upstairs and set it up where the writing desk had been. The desk had been banished to the dark corner of the room, boxes of her grandmother's magical tools stacked on top of it – a fact that made Aisling instantly love the drawing room again. Niall made the table look festive with a lace tablecloth and the finest silver. On the wall behind the table was the mural they'd painted of Widdershins wandering down a sandy beach – Aisling had tried to make it look like the beach in her dreams, but she wasn't that great at art. Niall was even worse, but the sloppy mural with the stick figure cat made her feel giddy.

Having Niall here makes this so much more bearable.

She had counted the days on a new calendar – eighteen in all since Niall had stepped over the threshold. They'd flown past like no other days in the house ever had – days laced with luxurious breakfasts and reading in the library and violent chess games and sexual tension that sizzled between every glance, every touch. Niall walked around shirtless a lot, making it hard for her to breathe. And if she couldn't breathe, she could give no space to her grief. He hadn't tried to kill her yet, so it was good news all around.

Aisling set down her spoon and met Niall's ice eyes. "What's your problem?"

"When I came here, I didn't expect to survive. And so I didn't pack any spare clothes," Niall held out the front of his shirt and wrinkled his face in disgust. "I've been airing these out overnight, but they're starting to reek."

"What about that bag you brought with you?" Aisling said. "I thought that had clothes in it."

Niall's jaw tightened. "It had a few things. Mostly spare weapons. But... I lost it, to the void at the rear of the master bedroom upstairs."

"You didn't tell me."

"I didn't want to bother you. Besides, you seem to prefer me naked."

Aisling snorted into her porridge, even as her body flared with heat.

Niall lifted one arm above his head, sniffed his armpit, and wrinkled his nose. "Seriously. Smell me. I smell worse than a boggart in a thorn-apple bush."

"Then get away from me." Aisling shoved him away, her body shivering with delight as their skin connected again. She'd gotten more used to the sensation when they touched, but that didn't mean it had stopped. If anything, the sparks between them grew stronger, more urgent. Like an itch that couldn't be scratched.

After they'd cleared up the breakfast dishes, Aisling showed Niall the small doorway at the back of the kitchen. "Here's the laundry." She gestured to the large enamel tubs and old-fashioned wringer.

"What is this sorcery?" Niall touched the handle of the wringer, wrinkling his nose. "It looks like a torture device."

Aisling brushed aside the lust that fizzled in her veins at the word *torture* on his tongue. "That wringer has been here for over two hundred years. Grandmother June liked to do things the old-fashioned way. A good thing, too. Because if there'd been an electrical washing machine, I'd be screwed."

"Can't you just enchant some little birds to do your chores for you?" Niall asked. "I saw that in an old human storybook once."

"There aren't any little birds around here," Aisling said. "And Widdershins is afraid of water. You're going to have to use good old-fashioned elbow grease."

"Help me. Show me what to do. I usually had a—" he stopped talking abruptly. A good thing, as Aisling had a feeling the words 'slave do it for me' were about to come out of his mouth.

"Crank handle. Push clothes through. It's pretty easy," she grinned. "Besides, you're so strong, and you've only got one outfit, not including your tooth-mail which, honestly, you never have to wear again. You'll be done in a flash."

"You're cruel, witch."

"Get used to it, fae." They started calling each other witch and fae in that teasing, cruel way that had over time become not so teasing and cruel, and more affectionate and sweet. If anything about Niall could ever be called sweet. Aisling worried that by doing it, they were removing the power from the words, bringing themselves closer than they should be as the differences between them broke down. But she couldn't help it. She was close to Niall, whether she wanted to be or not.

And she couldn't deny that even as she tried to resist the pull of their bodies, she longed for them to be closer still.

"Don't watch," Niall turned away from her and tore off his shirt. His back muscles rippled as he bent down to unbutton his pants. Aisling stood in the doorway, transfixed by the way he moved, each action purposeful, controlled, but hiding an untamed fury just below the surface. Complex tattoos wound their way down his spine and across his shoulders. They depicted battles against fierce monsters, souls burning in bright orange fires, their tortured faces contorting as they were consigned to ash. Why would someone immortalize such sights in their flesh?

Niall would, because his whole world is death and fury.

"I know you're watching." Niall didn't turn around as he turned the tap to fill the tub with hot water. The muscles of his ass pulled taut as he stepped out of his pants. Beneath, he wore a pair of shorts made of some kind of linen tied with a drawstring around his waist. The muscles of his thighs pulled at the shorts, which did little to disguise the curve of his tight ass. Aisling gulped, her face stinging with embarrassment.

She didn't turn away.

"How do you know?" She wet her dry tongue.

"I can feel your eyes on me." He glanced over his shoulder and flashed her a wicked grin.

Those icy eyes saw straight through her. Aisling's cheeks burned with heat. The room suddenly seemed very small, the walls bending inwards to swallow her. "I don't exactly have a television in here." She tried to keep her voice light. "This is the best show I've seen in years."

"I read about televisions, but I've never seen one. The fae have no use for such things." Niall tossed his pants into the steaming water and stepped out of his boxers. *Oh god.* Aisling's stomach churned. Every nerve ending in her body was on fire, and he wasn't even touching her. He wasn't even *looking* at her. All he needed to do was stand in a room and she wanted to fall to her knees for him.

I'm sick.

The air around her sizzled with energy. Turn around, turn around. But she knew he wouldn't. He liked being in control like this, making her suffer until he could tear her needs from unwilling lips. She tried to avert her eyes away from Niall, but they remained transfixed on his thighs. Several long scars crisscrossed his back – like whip marks but crueler – Niall hadn't been whipped for pleasure.

"What are those marks?" Aisling asked. She couldn't keep the need from her voice.

"Lashes," Niall scrubbed the armpits of his shirt like he didn't have a care in the world. He still hadn't turned around or given her any indication he knew what he was doing to her. *Is he hard? Is he getting off on denying me?* "The fae are harsh on those they feel are less than perfect."

"How were you less than perfect?" Aisling asked, unsure how someone with a body like that could be anything but worshipped.

Niall continued scrubbing, still not turning around. "I disobeyed my father. He was the commander of the Slaugh, and he used to take me on his hunts in the human realm. One day we found a witch hiding in a forest. He ordered me to drain her. She was old and I could see that her au—I sensed she had little magic left inside her. I said the exercise was pointless. We would dull our blades for no reason. She was more valuable to us alive, where she could be questioned, made to give up other witches. Father thrashed me for disobeying orders."

Aisling swallowed. "What happened to the witch?"

"He drained her himself, then tossed her body to the wolves."

Tears stung her eyes, though she wasn't sure where they came from. "I'm sorry."

"Why?"

"That you were thrashed. That you couldn't save her."

That you didn't have parents who loved you.

That you won't let me anywhere near your fae dick.

"Save your apologies, witch." Niall's voice had a ragged edge. "Don't make the mistake of thinking I was trying to save her. If she'd been kept for questioning, she would have been tortured. Father might even have done her a mercy."

The brutality in his words stung her. She forgot, sometimes, that Niall was a warrior bred for killing. As nicely as he treated her, that wild, bloodthirsty part of him bubbled beneath the surface, that part of him he'd let her see when he thrashed her with his belt.

He's fae. Her grandmother's voice echoed in her ears. *He eats the hearts of witches and wears human teeth for magical protection. What did you expect?*

Aisling's gaze swept over his body again, and her grandmother's voice died away, drowned out by his smooth skin, the taut muscles of his thighs, his warrior's body...

Turn around... turn around...

Niall rinsed off his shorts in the warm, soapy water, then emptied the tub to rinse them. She watched him in silence, in awe of his graceful, light movements, the way his muscles shifted, the way he utterly refused to turn even though he knew she was watching.

He's fae he's fae he's fae he's fae...

That's it. I can't take it another second.

"Niall?" She took a step toward him. "How many... how many have you killed?"

"Don't ask that question." He placed his shirt between the rollers and started to crank the handle. The machine was heavy as fuck, yet he made it look effortless. "You won't like the answer."

He's fae he's fae he's fae he's fae...

Aisling tore herself from the room, slamming the kitchen door as she ran from his villainy, from his indifference. She didn't stop running until she reached the ballroom. She threw open the door and ducked inside, sliding the gilded bolt into the lock to seal herself in. She flung herself down at the piano, her fingers shaking as she set a Blood Lust record in the player, her body aching to dance away the rejection that burned under her skin even as tears streamed down her cheeks.

20

NIALL

*A**isling.*

Niall flung the blanket off. His body was drenched. At first, he thought the rain had moved across the room and was now soaking his new bed, but as he wiped a hand across his forehead, he realized he was, in fact, bathed in sweat.

He'd fallen asleep, even though this sleep cost him precious time. He'd been dreaming, but he couldn't remember what about. That disturbed him. Fae who dreamed always remembered their dreams. *Always.* That was why there was a whole sect dedicated to deciphering them. That was why whole wars had been waged for the prizes promised in dreams.

All he knew was that the dream unsettled him. It wasn't the same vision he usually had of Aisling falling into the hole in the ballroom floor. He'd woken with a fresh and terrible fear that Aisling was in danger – not in the dream, but right here, in Hollythorn House.

In her room.

Niall hadn't seen her since he chased her out of the laundry. He'd finished wringing out his clothes and jerked off in angry strokes into Widdershins' cat blanket. His balls stopped hurting, but he didn't stop thinking about her. About what her eyes raking over his naked body had done to him, about the twisted things he planned to do to her. About the sleeping herbs he'd placed in her morning cup of tea to knock her out by lunchtime.

But then she got too close.

All those questions. About his scars. About his father. He told her the truth because it was either that or silence, and if he let the silence stretch on she'd ask more questions and he'd have to stop her with his cock. But another truth scorched his tongue, begging to be unleashed – that Niall's father lashed him within an inch of his life that day because Niall had unwittingly revealed he could see the witch's aura, and his father couldn't abide another son with Eamon's curse.

And that truth was dangerous.

Just like Aisling.

So he reminded her what he was, and she fled. Of course she fled. He *hated* that she fled. He raged that his dream girl couldn't love his malice the way she loved his pain. He loathed that he wanted her to.

As quick as the anger came, it was replaced by another sensation – worry.

He was worried about her. The fact that she would fall into slumber with tears in her eyes because of what he'd said made him feel all... odd. Like he'd misplaced something important. He'd paced around the house all afternoon, moving listlessly between the rooms as he waited for a sign that the drugs had taken effect, unable to sit still or focus on a task. He should've been using this time to prepare for tonight, but all he could think of was *her*.

Aisling didn't come down for lunch. When he went to his room to get his things for the journey, he'd heard her breathing heavily in her room. At least he knew she was alive, although she didn't strike him as the type to hurl herself out a window.

And now he'd gone and fallen asleep himself, and his body crawled with the sensation that something was wrong, that somehow Aisling was in danger. All his attempts to remind himself that it was only a dream, and dreams didn't mean the same things to humans, didn't assuage him – not in this house, especially not with the rasping voices whispering his name from the other side of the crack.

Niall threw himself out of bed. He still wore his scabbard, but he didn't know what he'd face out there so he pulled on his tooth-mail, grabbed his bow, and tossed his quiver over his shoulder. He yanked out an arrow and loaded the bow, then darted into the hallway, his senses on high alert. He scanned the corridor, searching for something that shouldn't be there.

Something brushed against his ankle. Niall leaped back, swinging his bow around to meet his foe. A pair of yellow eyes glared at him from the darkness.

"Meeerrrrwww."

Niall slackened his grip. "I nearly killed you, you daft cat."

Widdershins fixed Niall with a withering stare, then trotted past him into his bedroom. Niall didn't have to glance over his shoulder to know there was now a black lump sleeping in the middle of the bed, luxuriating in the dent left by his warm body.

Niall focused his attention on the corridor again. He stepped out of his doorway, nudging the door to the bathroom open with his toe. He swept inside. Nothing. Next was Aisling's room.

Niall pressed his back against the wall and pushed the door open a crack with his foot. He swung himself around so his back was against the door. He lifted his bow, nocked an arrow, and pulled the string back against his shoulder.

Aisling lay in her bed, the sheets twisted around her body like the ornate drapery of the portraits downstairs. Her head rested on her hands, her bow-shaped lips parted slightly, and her long lashes tangled together like the limbs of lovers. She wouldn't be waking any time soon.

Niall nudged the door open further and stepped into the room, swinging the bow around as he searched every corner for the creeping danger of his dream.

There's nothing here.

The raw panic in his chest subsided to a dull ache. It *was* just a dream, as all human dreams were. Echoes of thoughts and emotions being sorted at the end of the day. But what did that mean? Did it mean he was human now? But then how could he still see auras? How could he still not lie?

I sound just like Aisling with all these damn questions.

Aisling. She murmured in her sleep, her plump lips moving softly around a word he couldn't discern. Her chest rose and fell with a steady rhythm, so perfect, so vulnerable. She was just so fucking *vulnerable* like this. She had no idea he was here with her. He could do anything to her. *Anything.* His finger twitched on his bowstring. He put the arrow away and rested the bow on the end of her bed.

He inhaled her scent. Apples and figs and vanilla edged with scarlet musk. The scent of the bright summers that had never felt like home to him, of long days and languid nights that he now missed with a fervor that cracked open his heart. A scent that lingered at the back of his nose all day and all night. A scent that said, *this is not for you.*

She'd kicked her leg out from beneath the covers, and the welts from his belt stripe across her thigh were just visible in the murky gloom. His chest squeezed.

She wears me on her flesh.

He swallowed and tasted vanilla. He wanted to taste her. He wanted her to come apart under his tongue and then roll over and dream about how much she liked it. He wanted her to wake up wet and aching and not understand why but know that he was responsible, that he possessed her even in her dreams.

He wanted to wear her orgasm on his tongue.

Niall summoned all the self-control he'd never had to command. He grabbed his bow and backed out of the room, pulling the door closed behind him. He returned to his own room and set down the bow and quiver. Widdershins opened one sleepy eye and yawned at him.

Niall's foot brushed the bag containing the thorn heart.

I've wasted too much time already.

He grabbed the heart and headed back into the corridor, uncovering the strange and ghastly thing. The vials pulsed blue as he walked past Aisling's door. He noticed he'd left her door open a crack.

He stepped toward it, thinking to close it so that when Aisling woke from her drug-induced slumber she didn't notice it was open. She'd lived in this house too long to not notice a little difference like that. As he grabbed the handle and pulled the door closed, he thought he saw a glint of light – a flicker of lightning from the window behind blazing on the surface of an open eye, staring at him.

Niall blinked, and the flicker had gone.

Is it Aisling? Has she woken up?

She can't have woken up. I gave her enough of that herb to knock out a horse.

"Aisling?" he whispered into the night. He received no reply.

I imagined it. Or it was the light catching a piece of jewelry or one of those hideous dog statues that seem to be everywhere.

The door clicked shut and Niall continued on down the hall, tracking the same path he'd followed many nights before this on his hunt for the heart of the house.

No matter how many times he visited the library, it never failed to fill him with wonder. He hated himself for being here, in Aisling's favorite place, without her. Keeping the secret didn't bother him – lies rolled off his back like raindrops in a storm – but being in the library alone felt somehow sacrilegious, as though he were trespassing in some sacred temple. But tonight, it would be a quick visit. Niall had another mission in mind, and he needed to get going if he hoped to return before she woke up.

He wanted to see if the heart of the house was a literal heart.

Niall tore a page from Aisling's ledger book and scribbled a note to Odiana outlining his lack of progress. Next, he went into the foyer and pushed open the mail slot. He peered through but couldn't see anything beyond the iron gate. No fae guarded the house. No fae waited for a sign.

No one expected him to return.

He pierced the note on the tip of an arrow, inserted the tip through the slot, and drew back his arm. He braced his body for the bite as the arrow ricocheted off the invisible barrier and bounced back at him, but to his surprise when he released the string the arrow flew true, straight out the mail slot and through the bars of the gate to land somewhere on the other side.

Hopefully, Odiana will be the one to find it.

That done, Niall crossed through the kitchen and headed out the back door, through the ruined greenhouse where ice staved in the glass panels and vines snaked across the frozen ground, and out through the walled garden into the field beyond.

The freezing wind bit at his cheeks as he peered down the length of the frozen lawn to the cemetery miles in the distance. Niall could only just make out the line of the fence and the tip of the mausoleum Aisling described peeking through a mound of snow.

Lightning cracked overhead as he moved to the edge of the garden, stepping into the shadow of the leafless bushes and the towering iron fence. Niall closed his eyes and touched his hand to his brother's eye. He whispered the word his brother taught him.

Cold swept over his body – not on top of his skin but *inside* it. Cold in his bones, cold wrapped around his organs. A kind of cold that lived and breathed, that had form and desire all of its own. A cold where shadow things lived.

Niall opened his eyes.

He was a shadow-thing now.

Like his ability to see auras, this power – this shadow-shifting – had only come to him after he started carrying his brother's eye. Somehow, Eamon had given Niall these two gifts even as Niall stole his sight and his beauty. Odiana was the only one who knew about the auras – although his father suspected something – but no one knew about Niall's ability to move through shadows like he was part of them, silent and stealthy and as fast as a light being snuffed into darkness.

There were nights like this, when the cold burrowed into his heart and marrow as he saw through eyes made of night, as he moved with silent speed to overtake an enemy or reach a creepy cemetery before his pet witch woke up, that Niall truly believed his brother might be a god born to fae. And the fae don't have gods.

And then, there were days – like the day when Niall's father beat him – that he realized Eamon's gifts might actually be a curse.

In his shadow state, the world remade itself in facets of light and dark. In the dark, he could be everywhere at once, see everything without seeing at all. It was addictive to lurk, to hunt, to creep. But if he stayed too long in the shadow shift, he found himself forgetting. The cold squeezed and squeezed until he wasn't sure what bits of Niall were left.

Even moving in the shadows, it took Niall hours to reach the cemetery. It had moved even further from the house than

Aisling had described when she told him about it. He didn't tell her that every detail of it had been etched into his memory. That there was where her grandmother had slain his father across a stone altar.

Niall fell from his shadow-shift just outside the cemetery gate. He sagged in the snow, sucking in air, holding his hands to his mouth to puff his warm breath on them. Even when his eyes adjusted to the normal world again, he couldn't shake the creeping cold that still clung to his insides.

Maybe that's what I am now. I'm a creature of cold malice.

Niall shoved the gate open and stepped inside. The first thing he noticed was the stone Aisling made for her sister Bethany propped up near the base of the mausoleum. He kicked away drifts of fresh snow and saw the corpse peeking out from beneath the ice, buried so shallow he could still make out her features. A faint aura of blue light bloomed across her chest.

Niall's fingers danced on the hilt of his sword as he debated cutting out her heart. He wondered what it would taste like, if it would give him power like it did the Summer Queen. But he thought of Aisling's tears and stepped away, kicking the snow back over the shallow grave so that he wouldn't be tempted.

You're here for another heart.

Niall wiped a drop of snow from Eamon's eye. *Is this what you're reduced to? You, who've torn the hearts from the chests of a hundred witches, can't bear to see one of them upset?*

He didn't know if it was his father's voice or his own.

Niall shoved his blade into the mausoleum's lock and broke it free. He shoved the heavy door open, revealing a circular chamber containing a central plinth where the body of Lady Aisling Greymouth lay inside her stone coffin. The lid was carved with her likeness, and even in stone Niall marveled at the beauty of her features, so like her descendant sleeping back at the house.

He moved around the circle, reading the names on the coffins resting in niches around the walls until he located the one he was after.

June Greymouth.

It took little effort to slide the heavy lid away. And there she was, her wizened face just visible beneath a thick layer of ice, remarkably preserved for someone who died so long ago. June Greymouth – the witch who started it all. The one who'd killed his father and given her magic to the house rather than see it in the hands of the fae.

In every story Aisling told, June was the central figure. She was the keeper of the family's magic, the coven leader, the source of all knowledge and direction.

June was the heart of the house. She *must* be.

And Niall might desire Aisling with a fire that burned in his veins, but that would not stop him taking pleasure in what he was about to do.

He dropped to one knee and brought the tip of his dagger down on the ice, again and again and again. Ice chips flew in all directions as he drilled his way down to the witch who condemned his brother, who started the Endless Winter by refusing to give up her powers. He smashed and chipped his way through her frozen skin to reach her ribcage. He broke a rib free, holding it up to the light to see the blue aura. There was none, but she'd been under ice for so long, he didn't know what that did to the magic.

Niall snapped off ribs and punched through tissue until he cracked through to an empty cavity. He swept the ice chips aside. Rage mounted in his chest and a red mist closed over his eyes as he realized what had happened.

Someone else had already removed the witch's heart.

LETTER SHOT THROUGH MAIL SLOT OF HOLLYTHORN HOUSE

Dear Odiana,

I'm alive. So that's interesting.

Don't worry about me. I'm fine. A witch lives here, Aisling. Can you believe it? We're getting along as much as can be expected. She has yet to succumb to my infinite charms, and I haven't eaten her heart yet.

There's a whole library of magic books, including many written by the witch who bound herself to the house. She's buried in a mausoleum at the bottom of the garden, and I'm going to dig her up and place her organ inside the thorn heart and this will all be over, I'm certain of it.

Don't do anything rash. Keep my brother safe. Break his dick with your lust — you deserve it.

Niall

21

AISLING

"I'm bored," Niall announced, throwing down his book.

"How can you be bored?" Aisling looked up from the page she'd read twenty times already. She'd decided to forgive him for the laundry thing. She didn't want to waste her days holding a grudge or judging him for who he'd been outside Hollythorn's walls. Inside, he'd been... not a gentleman exactly, but a strange comfort. "We've only been reading for half an hour."

Aisling stifled a yawn. She slept long into the morning, unusual for her, and her mind flitted with the edges of weird, Niall-filled dreams. She'd woken with a fierce hunger and a desire to do exactly what they did now – if he wouldn't give her his dominance, then he could at least give her another day sitting across from each other in the library, sneaking glances as they pretended to read their respective tomes.

Niall made a face at the stack of family magic books on the desk beside him.

Why does he want to read our grimoires? Is he just curious about my family?

Is there something he's not telling me?

Then she felt bad for doubting him. The doubts came from her dreams, from the weird taste in her mouth when she finally woke up. The dreams made her uneasy. They weren't her usual dreams where she and Niall did filthy, depraved things on the beach. She could remember only flashes, sensations – a looming presence, a frozen heart, a lone glowing eye tinged with purple glaring at her from the shadows.

He's trapped in this house, same as you. And he has nothing to go back to if he wants his brother to live. He can't lie, unlike you, and if he was planning something devious, he wouldn't be so quick to down books for some crazy adventure.

Unless he's trying to trick you, her mother's voice drummed against her skull. *Maybe everything about him is a trick.*

It can't be. He dreams about me. He didn't make that up. I'm not going to justify my choice in companion to a voice in my head. I miss you and June and Dad and Bethany, and he's the only one who's come knocking.

"Half an hour? Really? It feels like longer." Niall swung his muscular body out of the chair. "Let's do something fun."

"I didn't know Slaugh knew the meaning of the word." Aisling felt her yawn transform into a smile. "What's fun to a fae? And don't say eating my cat."

Niall's gaze swept over her body. "I can think of a few things."

She pressed her legs together, trying in vain to calm the heat pooling there under the intensity of his gaze. "We agreed the other morning was a mistake."

"We did?" Niall tapped his chin, his head tilted as he thought. "Pity. Because I've been thinking how good you'll look with your wrists and ankles shackled to that desk."

Aisling's heart skipped a beat.

"You weren't thinking about that in the laundry room," she shot back.

"Wasn't I?" Niall touched his tongue to his lip. "Or have I

been thinking about nothing else since? Have I been cursing myself for reminding you what I am?"

She didn't have a reply to that.

Niall's fingers touched the hilt of his sword, and a darkness passed in his eyes that squeezed thorns into her heart. "I can give you what you need, what we *both* need, but I didn't think you'd want it from a fae. My hands are stained with the blood of witches, blood I savored taking, blood I would lick clean from their bones. Do you want truly want them on your skin, wrapped around your throat, inside you?"

"I know what you are. I know what you've done. But you're here and I'm here and..." she nods to the pile of books stacked between them, their half-empty teacups and cookie crumbs. "I don't hate you. I know I should, but I don't. And I don't think you hate me for being what I am. And I'm curious what your idea of 'fun' might be."

"Slaugh love two things. We fuck, and we fight. Come on." Niall grabbed her hand and yanked her into the hall.

"What are you doing? Let go of me!" Aisling yelped. Niall laughed his dark, cruel laugh as he dragged her down the hall. The house spun around her, the flocked wallpaper making crazy patterns across her eyes. Electric energy spread up her arm and through her body, making her feel giddy.

They stopped in front of Niall's room. Aisling's heart pounded against her chest. *We're doing this now...* she squeezed her legs together, relishing the anticipation of—

Wait, what's he doing? To her surprise, Niall dropped her hand. He ducked inside and returned with his bow and quiver.

"What's that for?"

That evil grin again. "Target practice."

"Am I the target?"

"Do you want to be?" Niall's eyes raked over her body. "I do so love the thrill of a hunt."

Even though she was certain he was talking about a hunt that ended in him tearing her apart, Aisling couldn't help the flush of heat rocketing through her body. She studied the weapon with interest. "How many people have those arrows killed?"

"Not as many as my blade," Niall said, that glint of bloodlust never leaving his eyes. "The bow is for long-distance, and I like to kill up-close and personal."

He's talking about witches. He's talking about tearing out the hearts of witches and stomping on their heads and bathing in our blood. But still her body betrayed her, her clit humming and begging for attention.

I'm completely screwed up.

Yup. Living in a horror-funhouse with your entire family dead tends to do that to a person.

"You'll enjoy this. It's a useful skill to have. One day, something may come through the front door from your nightmares instead of your dreams."

"I think that's you," she shot back. Niall grabbed her wrist and pried open her fingers, wrapping her hand around the bow. Aisling lifted the weapon, and there was something about holding it that made her clit hum all the louder.

Power.

She was drawn to the bow in the same way Niall drew her – she needed to feel powerful, like she was in charge of her life again. She'd been a prisoner for nearly four years. She'd watched, helpless, as everyone she loved was killed by war or fae or taken by the void, she'd read and she mapped and she planned, but she'd never had agency to take action.

That was what being a submissive was all about. People who didn't understand kink thought the Dominant was in charge, but the opposite was true. The Dom was in service to the Submissive. The chains around her wrists or the bite of a paddle on her ass didn't take away her power. She awakened it. She *commanded* it.

This bow gave her something to fight with.

Niall gave her someone to fight *for*.

"We'll have to go outside to shoot, and it's freezing." She pouted, but it was a teasing pout – the kind she'd use on Guy when she wanted to be punished. "The arrows won't even penetrate the garden wall—"

"We're not shooting at the garden wall, and we're not going outside." Niall gestured to a shelf of dog figurines on the side table in the hall. "You're telling me that none of these creepy statues deserves to die a horrible death?"

Aisling stared down at the ugly dogs, with their huge eyes and dopey faces and comically large paws. Aisling's great-great aunt Celeste, who lived in Hollythorn before June, loved dogs. She'd owned seven fox-terriers who had left their own mark on the house in the form of several small dog-flaps between rooms, and a wall of canine portraits in the east bedroom wing. June also added to the ceramics collection with tables and shelves filled with gilded otters and garishly painted teddy bears scattered all over the house. The dog ornaments were some of Aisling's least favorite.

She couldn't believe she was considering it. These statues had been in her family for generations, and many of them were cast in gold and inlaid with precious stones. They could be worth a fortune. Never mind that when she was small, Aisling once spent the whole day hiding in the closet to escape their creepy faces. On her bad days, she'd run past the table so she didn't have to look at them.

Why do I still keep them out? This is my house now. When June inherited the house from Celeste, she installed a popcorn machine in the portrait gallery and added a foot spa to her bathroom. If I hate the dogs, then why are they still here?

Holding on to June's things wouldn't bring back the life she'd lost. How odd that it had taken Niall's appearance to make her see that. Aisling grabbed the tallest, ugliest dog and thrust him at Niall. "Go on then. Turn me into Robin Hood."

———

AISLING DARTED THROUGH THE HOUSE, picking out her least favorite knickknacks – a leering monkey holding a banana in a suggestive way, a fat fairy with garish pink wings, and several of the worst dog figurines. Niall rustled around in the greenhouse and came back inside with a small potting bench, which he set up at the end of the hallway, in front of the boarded-up dining room door. They lined up the figurines along the bench and backed up until they stood in the entrance to the grand hall.

"Have you ever used one of these before?" Niall handed the bow to Aisling. She'd done archery at college as part of her dorm's social club, but the bows were heavy and an arrow fletch sliced through the skin on her arm, so she'd quit after one try and drank wine in the sun with her girlfriends instead.

Despite being larger than the college ones, Niall's bow was as light as a feather. *This is what fae do with their magic instead of figuring out how to stop the impending ice age. They make impossibly light bows to help them more effectively hunt witches.* She ran her fingers along the sinews (not wanting to know what creature he pulled them from), over the smooth limbs inlaid with precious woods. *Such a beautiful piece of killing art.*

"Nothing like this. It looks complicated."

"It's not. I'll show you." Niall stepped behind her. He placed his arms around her waist. Her back rested against his hard stomach. Energy sizzled around them, wrapping Aisling in a shimmering cocoon. Niall's breath brushed her ear as his body caged her in place.

Don't think about it, she told herself. Concentrate on the bow.

Niall laced his fingers between hers, placing her fingers against the string. "Do you feel this little bump in the string? This is the nock point. You hold the string between these fingers." He adjusted her hand. Aisling's body sang with energy. She held her breath as he fussed over her, too afraid to move and spoil the moment.

Has he ever done this before? Taken this care to show someone else how to use his weapon?

Does he know he's arming me against himself?

"You notice the V-shape carved into the arrow? To nock an arrow, you rest the arrow against this wooden peg, then shove the string into the V, just above the nock point."

She did this. He patted her arm, and the act of him approving of her gave her such a jolt of pleasure she nearly dropped the arrow. "Draw the arrow back. If you find it difficult, it can help to push the bow forward while you pull."

Aisling drew the string back toward her ear. The bow creaked as it tightened. The weapon wasn't so light anymore. Her arms ached from the pull of the string as the bow fought against the force she exerted.

"That's good," Niall said. "Is the weight okay?"

"It's okay if I can let it go really soon," Aisling said through gritted teeth. Her arm wobbled. *How did the bow get so heavy so fast?*

"Line the arrow and the sight up with your target, and let her sing."

Aisling let the string go. The arrow flew from the bow, zipping down the hall before embedding itself deep into the wooden panel of the door, an inch above a grinning dog's head.

"Not bad." Niall handed her another arrow.

"Not bad? I missed completely."

"At least you got in the general vicinity of the targets." Niall grinned. "The first time I tried to shoot, I ended up with six arrows in the ground about ten feet in front of the targets. It took me ages to get the hang of it. Eamon, of course, got his arrows all in the center of the target, a perfect score. My father was so frustrated with me, he threatened to post me to the Dullahan if I didn't improve."

"The what?"

"The Slaugh's headless division," Niall said. "Fae like me with giant black steeds and no heads who feed on human souls. They have a high mortality rate. Lots of accidentally flying into buildings and impaling themselves on fenceposts. Go on, try again."

Aisling nocked her second arrow, pulled back the string, and let it fly. It smashed into the dog statue, shattering it and scattering broken porcelain across the hall.

"I got it!" Aisling jumped with excitement.

"That's my witch." Niall grabbed her arm, causing another wave of heat to course through her.

His words echoed in her chest, drumming against her pounding heart. His smell swirled around her, an earthy scent of fire and freedom, another world from the mustiness of the house. Aisling looked up, captured by that icy stare. His chest was so close, all she had to do was tip forward and she'd be right up against him.

Touch me, her body begged. *Please, kiss me.*

Possess me.

Niall's body shuddered. His hand flew to her neck. Rough fingers squeezed the sides, not hard enough to cut air but commanding enough that she was at his mercy, just where she wanted to be. He tipped her head back, exposing her throat, tumbling her hair over her shoulders. He opened his lips, as though he were about to speak. But no words came out.

Aisling fixated on those pouty lips – perfect bows, like the weapon that hung from his back. She wondered what it would be like to run her tongue along them, to feel them slide over hers, to have them nip and nibble at her skin.

She swallowed. His fingers tightened their grip, pooling heat low in her belly.

This is insane.

She tore herself away, staggering backward until she slammed into the dining room door. Shrieking, she leaped back, her heart pounding against her chest. She shook her head, her hand touching her throat where the ghost of his touch still threatened to undo her.

Whatever magic had been pulling her toward him, the spell had most definitely been broken.

"Pick up your bow." Niall's words were taut with malice.

She didn't want to find out what he'd do if she disobeyed, so she scrambled to raise the bow once more and fire the next four arrows. Three went wide, but her fourth shattered the fat lady statue. Her enormous head rolled across the floor, and Aisling kicked it against the dining room door with glee. It bounced against the wood and came to rest against the foot of the bench.

"How do we get the arrows back?" she asked, staring at the shafts sticking from the wood like porcupine quills, the red fletchings gleaming in the low light like droplets of blood.

"Just grab them at the base of the shaft and pull. They'll come out eventually."

She tweaked the nearest shaft. It seemed pretty stuck in there. "But... have they penetrated the door? What if the tips are inside the void?"

"It's fine." Niall drew up beside her, and with a flick of his wrist dropped all the arrows onto the floor.

She couldn't believe the way he just flicked those arrows out of the wood like it was nothing. He'd scattered wood chips over the thick carpet from where the wood had splintered. She couldn't describe what staring at those wood chips made her feel, kind of giddy and lightheaded.

He had his hands around my neck. How easily he could break me in two.

How much do I want him to break me?

"These arrows are fae arrows," Niall said, his icy eyes meeting hers. "They're enchanted to return to me. But yes, I am strong. Maybe that will come in handy in this house."

"Oh yeah? You going to move furniture for me?"

"Witch, I can move *worlds* for you."

Aisling snorted. Niall frowned. "What's so funny?"

"You are." She thrust the bow into his hands. "Your turn, Super-fae."

"Watch and learn from the master." Niall's fingers moved lightning fast. In seconds he nocked an arrow and drew back the bow. Just as he let the arrow fly, Widdershins careened around the corner of the entrance and scampered across the hall, the arrow heading straight for his head.

22

AISLING

"No," Aisling screamed.

Widdershins darted into the bathroom just as the arrow flicked past his tail, missing him by a few hairs and embedding itself in the wall behind with a thunderous *CRACK*.

Aisling darted into the bathroom and scooped up Widdershins, but he was too freaked out to accept a hug. He drew a deep scratch across her arm and jumped down, disappearing into the bathroom again. Aisling sank to her knees, clutching her chest as her heart rate returned to normal. From on top of the bathroom vanity, Widdershins yowled with rage, his tail puffed up in agitation.

Niall sank against the doorframe. "Stupid animal. He shouldn't have run out in front of me."

"No, not stupid." Her hands balled into fists. "You aimed for him."

I never should have trusted you.

"I did not."

"You can't seriously expect me to believe the great fae warrior didn't hear a little cat approaching?" Her body trembled. "You tried to hurt him *on purpose*. You—"

Niall's face twisted with rage. Aisling had no time to react as he flung himself at her. Her legs slammed against the clawfoot bath and she toppled backward, saved from slamming her head against the brass taps by Niall's fingers closing around her throat again.

This time, he squeezed. He squeezed as his eyes clouded with rage and *need*. Aisling gasped for air, but he gave her nothing. Red welts appeared at the edges of her vision. He jerked her head up, dragging her so that she was pressed against the pipes, the taps digging into her ass.

"Know this, witch," he whispered. "I am fae, and fae do not lie. If I hurt you or your cat, I will do it staring you in the face, not stabbing you in the back."

Aisling's feet swung in the air, tangling around the plastic shower curtain. Her fingers scrambled for purchase. She knocked the shower mixer, and a rush of hot water poured down on both of them.

Niall peered up at the water cascading from the rain shower above. His grip on Aisling's throat loosened. He tilted his head to the side, a sadistic smile playing across his lips. Aisling followed his gaze to her chest, where the water soaked through her shirt, turning the fabric see-through and plastering it to her skin. Her nipples hardened into round peaks.

"Don't you dare," she glared at him.

"Don't I dare what?" Niall reached up with his free hand and unhooked the shower head. He turned it over in his hands, watching with academic interest as it sprayed water all over the bathroom. A stream hit Widdershins, who howled with outrage and darted from the room.

"What's his problem?"

"Cats don't like water," she gasped out. "They, um, find it..."

Aisling lost the words as Niall trained the nozzle on her

breast, right against her nipple so the warm stream assaulted the sensitive bud. She threw her head back as the water pounded against her, unrelenting in its pressure. She gasped and fought against the harshness of it – it felt like her nipple was being waterblasted off her body.

Niall's fingers circled her other nipple, rolling it between his fingers and then pinching it until the pain bloomed across her chest, sending a trail of fire straight between her legs.

"But you're not a cat, are you, my witch?" Niall murmured as he angled the shower head for maximum pain. "You like water very, very much."

His strong arms held her upright, pinning her so she couldn't escape. Aisling thought she might come just from the wrongness of it, from the thrill of submitting herself to this torture devised by a fae. Her eyes swept over his body, drinking her fill of his hard muscles, the shape of his long, hard cock straining against his soaking breeches, his icy, fathomless eyes, and that quirk of his mouth as he watched her writhe away from his assault.

Just as she felt her orgasm dancing on the edges, Niall dropped the shower head. She moaned with frustration, but he wasn't done with her yet. Niall tore down the shower curtain and ripped off a strip of material. With the hose clamped between his teeth, he wrapped the plastic strip around her hands, binding her wrists tightly to the overhead pipe. Aisling opened her mouth to ask him what he thought he was doing, but she didn't have a chance to get words out as his lips clamped around her nipple.

Aisling thought she'd seen the magnitude of his dominance the other morning. She was ecstatic to discover how wrong she was. While Niall's teeth nipped at her sensitive bud, he aimed the head between her legs, chasing her ache with its pounding hot pressure. She arched her back toward him, desperate for more until the pressure became too much, too hard. But when she tried to pull away, he refused to allow it.

"I want you to come undone for me," he demanded.

And she did, she did. The laces that held everything inside her sprung free, and Aisling tumbled to pieces. Her heart broke open, and for a moment she had no more grief, and it was the most wonderful feeling in the world. That water hurt and hurt but it was the best kind of hurt, the kind that burrowed into her bones and obliterated everything else, until she was freefalling into Niall's arms, until she was slick and spent and wet and *free*.

Niall looked up at her, meeting her eyes with his ice-cold orbs. "When you're like this, I want to devour you. I think, this time, I will."

He caught her legs, pulling her off the ground so she swung outward. Aisling gasped as her arms took part of her weight. A delicious ache tugged at her shoulders. The pain woke her body once more.

Niall held one giant hand down her back, his fingers splayed wide, taking some of her weight so her shoulders didn't do all the work. It was something a human Dom would do, caring for his Sub in the middle of a scene, knowing she wasn't in a headspace to ask for it herself. She didn't expect such care from Niall – who wore his malice like a badge of honor – and noticing it made her heart squeeze so tight she struggled for her next breath.

With his hands holding her firm, he nibbled on her stomach, tugging at her skin to create a line of red welts from her breast right the way down down down to...

"Oh," she gasped as his lips kissed her clit. This wasn't a chaste kiss, but the devouring he promised. He drank her like he'd been in the desert for years and she was the first drop of water on a parched tongue. His lips and tongue and teeth were everywhere at once, and his brutal grip didn't allow her a moment's respite.

Her hips twisted as the first wave of heat shuddered through her. He pushed two fingers inside her and she felt herself pulse around them, around *him*. And that was it. That was what she needed. The heat spread across her belly and flared along her restrained arms and rushed to her cheeks and burst around her broken, aching heart.

She'd never come so hard or so long, swinging there in the shower with a fae's lips against her cunt. She'd never needed it so bad. She arched and rolled and cried out as she rode each delicious lash of pleasure until it crested and broke, until she broke over him, until her eyes came to rest on his ice-cold orbs, anchoring her with a window into something dark and cruel breaking inside him.

What she saw was him touching his lip with his tongue, and the taste of her unbinding his own laces, letting free something he'd never allowed himself to feel. He was feeling it now, and his face twisted through the intensity of it until he didn't look like Niall any more but a broken, wild thing trapped in a hell he couldn't escape.

Niall backed away. His hands jerked from beneath her, dropping her into the bath. She fought for purchase against the slippery surface as panic cooled the heat in her blood.

"Niall, what is it? What's wrong?"

His eyes... fuck. He looks like he's seen a ghost. Or like a little kid afraid of the monsters under his bed.

Niall grabbed the towel rail and hoisted himself from the bath, sending baking soda containers and loofahs flying in all directions. His hard cock tented between his legs, and he moaned as he gripped it as if being hard for her caused him pain, as if his body had betrayed him.

She twisted against the restraints, her panic becoming full-blown fear. "Niall, let me *down*."

Something's gone horribly wrong with Niall, and I'm tied up naked, completely at his mercy.

23

NIALL

iall's cock throbbed. He felt like he was about to split open from the pain of holding on to his release. When Aisling came, her pink lips parted and he imagined sliding his cock between them, tangling his hands in her hair to make her do it just the way he liked it. He imagined her body responding not with disgust, but tightening and purring beneath him as he fucked her mouth, taking everything he had to give and begging for more.

No. No no no no.

I have to stay in control.

I can't do it if... if she likes it.

"Niall?"

Aisling's foot slid on the surface of the bathtub. Before he knew what he was doing, Niall reached out and caught her before she fell and took too much weight on her arms. He held her there, struggling for breath, for air, for command of himself. The head of his cock jerked as it brushed across the hair on her pussy, and he nearly burst right there. Her chest heaved against his, and those doe eyes begged him.

"Niall," she whispered.

His name on her lips was more than he could bear.

He wanted to hurt her.

He *needed* to hurt her.

He wanted this thing that was more than hurt and pain, this clenching of his chest when he looked at her that felt both horrible and wonderful. But he was wrong and evil and he would betray her, and he could not take this from her too, not after all he planned to take.

She'd bewitched him. He didn't know what he was around her. And he had to be strong or... or...

With a roar, Niall shoved her away. He scrambled out of the tub, his feet sliding on the wet floor. The shower nozzle sprayed across the tiles. He gripped the wall for balance as he fled like the coward he was, running from the witch who seemed made to drive him wild.

Her cries followed him down the hall. "Niall, you bastard. Let me down."

I can't, Aisling. I can't. If I go back in that bathroom, I'll have to be inside you. And you'll see everything about me. You'll know my truth, and it will break you.

You're my poison. If I drink from you, I'll die and you'll be alone again. And I will never give you pain like that, I promise you.

I won't fail you again.

You may hate me now, but at least you'll never mourn me.

24

AISLING

*N*iall *can run all he likes, but he can't hide from me in Hollythorn House.*

Aisling rubbed the welts on her wrists as she padded down the hallway, following the wet footprints. Once she'd calmed herself down and regained the use of her legs, it had only taken her a few minutes to undo Niall's knot. *He can't have gone far.*

He hadn't. Niall stood in the kitchen doorway, his back rigid. He didn't know she was in the hallway, watching him. His eyes were focused on a black shadow that glared at him from the windowsill.

Widdershins jumped down and padded toward Niall. He didn't arch his back. Aisling looked from cat to fae, wondering what was going to happen.

Niall knelt down, his hand hovering over his heart. "Look, cat. I didn't intend to hit you with that arrow or spray you with water."

I know, Aisling thought as she looked over his face. *I believe him, and not just because I know he can't lie. I believe him, but I don't understand. Malice is in his blood. He is the fae who hurts. But this is... it's* almost *an apology.*

Widdershins regarded Niall as if he were a bug not worthy of squashing. He turned his back, raised a white-socked paw, and washed himself.

"If you truly want to win over a cat, you need to feed them." Aisling stepped toward the cupboards where she kept his food. "I'll get him a treat."

She felt Niall's eyes on her as she set down Widdershins' bowl. A million questions flooded through her. In the shower, he'd cradled her as he ate her out, he made her feel *safe*. But when it came to his own pleasure, he couldn't do it, even though his dick looked painful with how hot and swollen it was for her. For all his malice, he didn't want to take from her. Why?

Niall is fae. His race takes great pride in their cruelty, their remoteness. Any other fae would have deliberately aimed the arrow at Widdershins, and then skinned him and made him into a delicious stew. But Niall jerked the arrow away. And he looks genuinely upset right now.

He's here with me because he sacrificed himself. He gave his life to his brother because he thinks this is all his fault. He's not as cruel as he believes himself to be.

Is this another sacrifice? Is denying himself some kind of penance?

What for? What else has he done?

And why does he believe it's so terrible that I won't ever accept him because of it?

LETTER SHOT THROUGH MAIL SLOT OF HOLLYTHORN HOUSE

Dear Odiana,

Still no heart. Someone cut it out of the witch's chest. If I had Eamon's love of betting, I'd wager a hundred teeth that her coven cut it out of her to bind her magic to the house. Which means it's somewhere inside Hollythorn, right?

Somewhere inside a house that grows extra rooms and eats hallways and rains indoors. Should be a breeze to find.

And yes, I could torture the witch until she told me where it was, but I'm saving that in case I have no other choice. There's so much I want to tell you, but it's hard. I don't have the words for what this house is doing to me. It's fucking me up.

I need to know what's going on out there. Has Eamon kept his disguise? What of Laneth? Eamon was concerned about him making a move for the crown. What about your experiments? Have you discovered anything more about removing magic from objects?

Write back to me. You were always a lousy shot, but if you can get an arrow into the mail slot, it should reach me.

Niall

25

———

NIALL

Niall's days in Hollythorn House bled one into the next.

Every morning he woke Aisling with some kind of culinary masterpiece (although he learned from her scoldings to ration a bit better), and they explored the house together, finding their own fun in the strange and altered rooms. They bounced Ping-Pong balls off the wobbly wall in the billiards room and made a fort out of blankets and cushions in the upstairs lounge. They shot arrows at the strange and hideous statuettes and tossed the pieces into the dining room void. Aisling sat him in a nest of pillows in the ballroom and gave him a music education, explaining the history of punk and metal music and blasting his eardrums with songs that sounded like war. He particularly liked a band called Iron Maiden.

Sometimes Widdershins trailed around their heels, sometimes he had already vanished into the depths of the house, hiding in the places only a cat knew.

Sometimes Niall's cock hurt so much from wanting her that he couldn't breathe. Sometimes he vowed he'd stop denying himself, but then she'd smile at him and he'd feel lightheaded and he knew he couldn't touch her or he'd pull her into an abyss even darker than the void.

Sometimes it wasn't his cock that hurt, but his chest.

His heart.

After their explorations, they read in the library or played games together in the drawing room. Niall with all his military training grew quite good at chess, although never good enough to beat Aisling.

And they talked.

Niall never tired of talking to Aisling, even though nothing about her made sense to him. She told him about a life on Earth that she couldn't possibly have lived, a life that had to exist only in her imagination, built of other people's stories she read in this library. He ached for her because this life was so real for her, but it could never be real and he could do nothing to change that.

She told him about Bethany, about being the older sister and the responsibility she felt to keep her safe. She railed about the grief and guilt that crushed her chest and hardened her heart, because Bethany had died and she lived. That part made sense to Niall. He knew it all too well.

Sadness, grief, fear... the words rolled off Aisling's tongue as she described her own life. She wore them with pride – badges of honor, for humans found honor in their ability to be broken. Words like this were poison to Niall, denied by his fae upbringing and his life of soldiering. And yet, as days passed in the house, he felt himself beginning to succumb to them. He dared to speak them aloud, to give voice to feelings he'd never understood.

When he looked at Aisling, he did not see the weakness his kind expected to see – he saw instead a woman of great courage, a warrior in her own right.

His equal.

His undoing.

She asked Niall questions he couldn't answer, questions with answers that would sear his soul in the telling. She asked about the eye set into his sword, and about his family, and about why he became a warrior. She asked if fae and humans could ever be friends. She asked him what he would give to thaw the Endless Winter and make the world whole again.

Niall's lips remained sealed. He could not lie to her, and the truth would break her. So he stayed silent.

I won't fail her again.

But he already had, hadn't he?

While Aisling spoke to him, her eyes would often drift away, the irises circling the room, checking the walls, the ceiling, searching for the cracks that would signal the approach of the creeping void. Her body tensed up, shriveling into herself. When her gaze eventually settled on him again, her body would unravel, relax. Occasionally, he even caught the glint of a smile, a rare diamond that filled him with a terrible sadness.

For years she's been trapped inside this prison, watching the walls collapse around her, knowing it will eventually take her with it.

Niall balled his hands into fists, rage flooding his body. She shouldn't have to live like this.

You're not supposed to care, his father's voice burned in his mind. *You cannot be weak.*

Aisling kept up her practice on the bow, and she begged him to teach her to use the sword. Niall refused. He didn't know what would happen if she touched his blade. Would Eamon's magic be transferred to her? Would it allow her to see him for what he truly was?

He hated saying no to her. Aisling was a practical, measured person. She would make a fine fighter. It would give her another skill to use against the fae when they finally came for her.

When he located the heart of the house.

Perhaps he didn't like the idea of giving her the means to kill him, should she discover his secrets.

Perhaps he didn't want her soft hands to touch an object so tainted by his malice.

Every night while Aisling slept the sleep of the dead, Niall moved about the house, using the thorn heart and activating crystal to try and locate the hiding place of June's heart. When that failed, he retreated to the library to squint at the pages of the family grimoires – his only light the flashing lightning of the void beyond the window.

There has to be something in these books, something that would tell me how that infernal witch did it.

As he pored over Aisling's family history, his stomach churned with guilt. He never lied to Aisling; fae couldn't lie, but they were experts at hiding the truth. And the truth was that Niall still had one foot back in the fae realm with Eamon and Odiana. He still wanted to thaw the ice and stop Laneth from taking the crown. And that left him all twisted up inside because achieving those things meant betraying Aisling.

If he didn't find the heart of the house, his brother, his queen, Odiana, and all the fae would die or worse if Laneth took the crown. But... *if* he was the one to find it, then he could use that to bargain for Aisling's life. He could save her. But she would never trust him again.

26

AISLING

"Why are you smiling about?" Niall asked Aisling as he slid into the chair across from her in the library. From the smug look on his face, she knew he thought she was smiling because he'd woken her up by tying her legs to the bed and whipping her until she came. She rubbed her smarting legs against the edge of the chair. That had been pretty amazing, even if he still refused to let her touch him, but that wasn't what had her so happy.

"I'm smiling because it's Twinkie Day," Aisling grinned.

That wasn't strictly true. Aisling was smiling because she was thinking about Niall. She was replaying her favorite moments of the last two months – painting a mural of Widdershins on the wall of the drawing room, shooting arrows at the ugly dog statuettes, cleaning the kitchen together after another of Niall's culinary disasters.

The whip marks he laid along her skin.

The delicious, throbbing tightness between her legs from his fingers fucking her senseless.

The dark, depraved things he whispered in her ear.

And that haunted, broken look in his eyes when he thought she wasn't looking.

He was her perfect nightmare. Niall made Hollythorn House more than a prison – with him it became a source of joy and wonder. Aisling hadn't felt either of those things in such a long time.

And she felt something else too, a tugging in her chest whenever he caught her eye, a quickening of breath whenever he smiled, a sudden bereavement after he left the room.

She ached constantly to have his cock inside her, but she ached for something else too, something she couldn't quite describe. It had something to do with the electric energy that surged between them, drawing them closer whenever they were together, urging them to touch.

But all this happiness bore an edge of guilt. Every moment she shared with Niall was a betrayal of what June and her parents and Bethany died for. But Aisling didn't fucking care anymore. They'd left her all alone to face the fae, and she *needed* this. She needed the marks on her body to feel alive.

She needed him.

"Twinkie Day? Is that some kind of witch holiday?" Niall picked up June's gardening diary. "I thought they all had weird German names that sounded like sexually transmitted diseases."

Aisling swatted his arm. "You're ridiculous. How do you even know what sexually transmitted diseases are?"

"The queen made my friend Odiana research them so she could make strict rules about fae/human interactions," Niall said with a cruel quirk of his lip. "Odiana's experiments were great fun."

"I don't even want to know. Twinkies are a kind of snack, back in the human realm. They're little spongy loaves of happiness. My grandmother had two packets in the cupboard when she set up the food regeneration spell, and today is the day when they come back."

Aisling opened her diary to show Niall where she'd marked it carefully on the calendar. The food regeneration spell worked to a pretty reliable timetable, even if it was gradually wearing down. She mapped the food deliveries as her ancestors before her mapped the phases of the moon and the stars in the heavens.

"Intriguing. I eagerly await your strange human delicacies."

"What gave you the idea I'd be sharing?"

"Because I gave you three orgasms this morning," Niall said. "And because if you do, I'll teach you how to fight with a sword."

Aisling sat up straighter. Ever since she'd seen Niall twirling around the entrance hall, sparring invisible enemies with his curved bone blade, she'd been bugging him to teach her. So far, he'd steadfastly refused. She didn't know what had changed his mind, but she'd happily give him a Twinkie in exchange for sword fighting lessons.

She would give him a Twinkie anyway, because... she wanted to.

"Follow me." Aisling bounded to the kitchen, relishing the movement of air against her welts as she moved. Niall trailed behind her, and she felt his gaze caressing her thighs, admiring his handiwork, his claim on her body.

He still hadn't fucked her. He still wouldn't let her touch him, and they hadn't got any closer to a kiss than that moment when they were shooting arrows... and it meant she spent every moment thinking about his lips, imagining what he'd taste like, how he would tangle his fingers in her hair and—

Get a grip. You can't survive thirteen hundred and ninety-eight days in this house to fall apart over a fae.

Aisling threw open the pantry door, eager to tear open her sugary treat. She scanned the second shelf on the left, where the

Twinkies appeared. There were two granola bars and a single, banged-up apple. But no Twinkie boxes.

"Where are they?"

"Maybe that infernal feline knocked them down?" Niall offered. Aisling ducked down below the shelves, running her hand between the sacks of flour and baskets of onions and potatoes. She found a lot of dust and crumbs, but no Twinkies.

Maybe I got the day mixed up. She scanned the calendar hanging on the back of the door, which she used in case she ever lost the library. *Nope, they should definitely be here, along with a fresh box of tomato soup and some canned green beans...*

Aisling scanned the next shelf. The beans and soup hadn't arrived, either.

Panic rising now, Aisling shifted all the boxes on the shelves. Maybe they'd been moved to another shelf... but no, there were no Twinkies in sight.

Come to think of it, the entire pantry looked a little bare. Yes, Niall ate more than Bethany ever did, but that didn't explain the barren shelves. Aisling checked the calendar again, panic rising in her chest. There should've been more potatoes arriving last week, and a whole bunch of canned food that was missing. She'd been too wrapped up in Niall to notice.

Shit.

"Aisling," Niall growled.

"There should be two bags of potatoes," she said, pointing at the corner where there was only dust. "They were supposed to regenerate last week. And another jar of milk. June's neighbor used to give her fresh milk every week in exchange for June's sleeping draught, and even though the neighbor's dead we should have had a new bottle four days ago. I've been so preoccupied with... with..." Her cheeks flushed as she thought of Niall's tongue tracing the welts of his belt against her ass. "I didn't notice the food supply has been depleting."

"It's fine. We'll just ration strictly and eat less to allow the regeneration to catch up—"

"That's not it." Aisling ran a finger down the chart. She hadn't been ticking items off the way she usually did, ever since her and Niall... became a fucked-up package of poison and malice and pleasure. But she could see that she had missed at least four key regeneration days, with nothing to show for them.

"Fuck." She pounded her fist against the door. It figures, just when the universe sought to give her something to make her stay in Hollythorn House actually fun, it took that away by allowing them both to starve to death. "We're running out of food. The pantry enchantment must be broken."

"Can I help?" Niall asked.

"Unlikely, unless you're an expert at fixing witch enchantments?"

"I'm not, but you are."

"Excuse me?"

Niall indicated the empty shelves with a sweep of his hand. "You're a witch, Aisling. All this runs in your veins. I know you say you don't have the skill to do this kind of enchantment, but we both know that's bullshit."

"It's not. I don't have a magical bone in my body. If it weren't for Hollythorn and the fae, I'd still believe magic and fairies were for storybooks. My mom resented June's unusual parenting style and her hippie, magical upbringing. She never wanted us to learn the craft, but she still shipped us off to June every year so she could have her fun."

She couldn't help the resentment creeping into her voice. How was it possible to hold so many opposite feelings inside her? Aisling loved her summers at Hollythorn, but she resented her parents for forcing them on her.

It's Niall – he brings all this up because he's a walking contradiction. Aisling knew her feelings for Niall were tied up with her grief and loneliness, and the bond of guilt they shared as older siblings who'd failed. But she also knew that as much as she hated what he was, she felt something for him that was deeper than the pain he gave her.

"You don't have to be taught. You're clever enough to figure it out on your own." Niall grabbed her hand. Energy leaped from his fingers and rocketed along her arm. He dragged her to the other side of the pantry, where the regeneration spell was set up.

It consisted of a small wooden box containing several crystals glued into place on a white cloth scrawled with sigils. As Aisling picked it up, it hummed in her fingers. Aisling stared down at it, completely lost. It was like staring at the papyrus of hieroglyphic script hanging in Grandmother June's bedroom – completely alien to her.

"Do you sense anything?" Niall asked.

Aisling shook her head. *What does he expect me to do?* She touched her finger to a green stone. It gave her a jolt so painful she yelped and leaped back, clasping her finger.

"It stung me," she cried out.

"Is it supposed to do that?"

"I don't know!" She sucked on her finger. "This is hopeless."

"It's not hopeless. You're being awfully defeatist for the girl who's lived in this house for her whole life. Where will you find the answers you need?"

"In Grandmother June's spell books." Aisling ignored the weird thing Niall said, because he said a lot of similarly weird things and she put it down to him being a fae and not used to listening to witches before he killed them. "But she doesn't have a diagram of this spell. Bethany and I looked for it when the deliveries started to slow down. She wouldn't have had time to draw one before the fae showed up at the house... but I guess there may be some other information I can use, a similar spell or some information on crystals."

Niall patted her arm. "It figures your solution to a problem is to read a bunch of books. Come on, let's go to the library."

He placed his hand possessively on her lower back, his fingers splayed wide, as he directed her out of the kitchen. Aisling's heart flipped as they navigated the hall together, the energy of his touch coursing through her body. *Who are you really, Niall? Why do you make me feel this way? And why, when you are the enemy who has kept me trapped here, am I so desperate to trust you?*

27

NIALL

"I've got it!" Aisling cried out.

Of course she did. He knew she'd figure it out. She reminded him of Odiana, the way she threw her whole self at a task.

And it didn't hurt that he'd pointed her in the right direction with some of the spells he'd read in her family grimoires. He wanted to see what she could do, what her family's power was truly capable of. Her aura shimmered with power – more than he'd seen in a living witch in his entire life – and he wanted to see her use it.

Niall put down the spell book he'd been poring over and leaned across to where Aisling jabbed her finger at a page.

"This says crystals need to be charged by the light of the moon, or their power will diminish over time." Aisling read the page in excitement. "We never did this. We never even knew you *could* charge a crystal as if it's a goddamn battery. No wonder the unit is malfunctioning. But at least this means the solution might be relatively simple. I just need to move the crystals under a window, where they'll have some exposure to the moon. Hopefully, the recharging will still work through the storm."

"How will you touch them without getting hurt again?" Niall looked at the red welt on the tip of her index finger, and his stomach twisted with anger. He wanted the bruises on her body to come only from him, to be marks of his possession. Thinking of the crystals hurting her made him want to throw the contraption across the room.

"I figured that out, too. I don't move the crystals individually. I cast a charm around the whole unit and move it as one." Aisling made a face, like she couldn't believe she could do such a thing. "Once the crystals are charged, I should be able to touch them without a problem, and we'll be back in business."

Niall leaned over and planted a kiss on her forehead. Her warm skin sizzled under his lips. He placed a finger under her chin, tilting her face up, her lips just an inch from his—

I could do it.

I could kiss her and touch her and glide inside her and make her scream my name until the windows crack.

He wanted her so bad that every waking moment she crawled under his skin, and every night she haunted his dreams. Niall had lived with an empty stomach and thirst drying his throat, but he'd never known hunger like this – hunger that gnawed on his insides, that made him wish he'd been born a stone so he couldn't feel the pain of being beside her but without her.

And now he'd done it, he'd kissed her hair, felt the softness of the strands whisper against his lips. He'd drowned himself in her fig and apple scent, and her eyes gouged holes in his skin.

Aisling's eyes widened. "Niall..."

"I know, I know. I'm fae, you're a witch." But he couldn't tear his finger from her chin. He couldn't stop the hunger that boiled and bubbled and wished for what was forbidden.

"That's not what I meant." She planted her hands on his chest, as if she was about to shove him away. Niall willed her to do it, to be the one to break the spell she held him under, because he was gone, gone, gone. Aisling glared at him with a look of stubborn determination. Her fingers curled in the fabric of his tunic, her nails scraping over his skin. "You like to play these games with me. You touch me but you refuse to let me touch you. I want to know why."

Her hand drew up his thigh, her fingers grazing the edge of his cock through his breeches. Niall grabbed her hand and twisted, trapping her wrist against her breast.

"That's enough," he ordered.

"That's not what your erection says," she shot back.

"We're not doing this."

"Why the fuck not? What difference does it make? If this about your stupid fae pride – not wanting to be with a witch, to admit that you feel something for me, that you feel something at all – then you're an idiot. It's the end of the fucking world, Niall. We're going to die in this house, so why not chase what little happiness is left?" She stamped her foot. "Answer me, dammit."

He wanted to flog that insolence right out of her, but he suspected that was exactly what she wanted. That was why she pushed him like this, because she wanted to kneel, she wanted his palm across her ass and his cock in her mouth.

Being close to her now, when she was this feisty, his resolve crumbled.

No. I won't fail her again.

This was why fae never kept secrets. Because truth didn't eat you up inside the way this did.

Niall stood up, intending to leave the room and master himself. But Aisling grabbed his hips, yanking him toward her so that her face pressed against his hardness. Her hot breath burned him through the thick material, tearing a groan from his lips as he danced on the edge of losing his shit. Aisling's shoulders heaved, her breath fast, excited. She didn't expect to be allowed this audacity, but Niall couldn't move, couldn't touch her, or he'd spill his seed and his truths, and it would all be over.

Her teeth gripped the string of his breeches.

Niall's chest constricted. Aisling peered up at him with those wide, lovely eyes, the string dangling from the side of her mouth. The air sizzled with anticipation. They both stood frozen, waiting for the other to make the next move.

Slowly, with an impertinent smile, Aisling drew her head back, tugging at the string. The waistline loosened, the fabric shifted over his cock, drawing his ragged breaths as he fought for command of himself, as he willed himself to stop her.

One hand still held her wrist, but the other fisted at his side. Niall's fingers brushed his sword, touching the glassy surface of his brother's eye. Before he knew it, the blade was in his hand, pressed against Aisling's throat as he held her down against the chintz chair.

"Niall..." Those eyes were as big and wide as the moon.

He held the blade steady, the familiar weight of it bringing him back to himself. He needed a moment to breathe, to think, to remember. But it was hard when he straddled her like this, his swollen cock pressed up against her thigh as she stared up at him.

He didn't know what he was going to do.

My sword is an extension of my body. It cuts what I need it to cut, and I need her to save my people.

I need her to save me.

"I can't do this," he growled, but he couldn't move. He couldn't step away or drop his weapon. Instead, he turned the blade, drawing it down the front of her shirt, slicing through the fabric like it was made of air.

The ruined fabric fell to the sides, revealing her breasts, naked and round and impossibly perfect, the nipples hard as pebbles.

Aisling's chest heaved. She bit her lip in that way that drove Niall insane, and an un-fae-like sound tore from his lips as he battled for dominance.

Niall's eyes fell to the vein in her neck, bulging as she swallowed, as her blood pumped with fire. The edges of her were ringed in shimmering blue magic.

"Do you see what you do to me?" he roared. "You make me wild. And that's *dangerous*."

He drew the flat edge of his blade across her skin, teasing that vein in her neck, warning her what he was capable of. How many witches had he knelt over with this same sword in his hand? How many times had he plunged the tip into warm flesh? And now...

and now...

"Don't you understand?" Aisling cried back at him, her eyes shimmering. "I want *you*, Niall. Not some castrated version of you. I want all of you, *especially* the dangerous parts."

Niall swallowed. He couldn't breathe. He felt like he was drowning and flying at the same time. He had his dream girl beneath him, staring up at him like he was a god, and he held his knife against her skin and it was so hot and so fucked up he was going to come any second.

Aisling shivered beneath him as Niall moved his blade across her chest. The tiny hairs on her skin stood on end as he caressed her with the cool bone, leaving pretty pink trails he longed to kiss. He couldn't help himself. He shoved a hand under her skirt.

She was soaking wet.

Niall's breath hitched. His hands locked tight. He couldn't move, couldn't breathe. His sword poised on her skin, the tip pointed directly at her throat, jabbing into her skin just enough to draw a droplet of blood. Her warm juices soaked his fingers.

Aisling's eyes fluttered, her eyelashes tangling together as she reached up to touch his hand. She slid her fingers over his, stroking his brother's eye and sending a shudder of electric current through his body.

"Don't stop," she whispered.

Fuck.

"As you wish." Niall gritted his teeth as he dragged the blade over her breast again. He flipped it over so that the edge touched her skin this time. As he drew it lightly across her once more, he pushed a finger inside her.

She was so slick and wet and tight and hot and *perfect*. He pumped his fingers into her, watching her pretty lips fall open, her hair tumble over her shoulders, the wild need in her eyes cloud as she passed over into pleasure.

The orgasm rippled through her, drawing a long, happy sigh that echoed inside his skull. She clenched around her fingers, and it was like a fist clamping around his lungs. He gasped for air. His balls screamed. His cock was fucking *done* with the torture.

Niall drew back his sword arm, not wanting her to cut herself as she writhed beneath him. Instead, he slid the blade across his own chest. It bit into his flesh, drawing a long, shallow cut that stung and bled and sang with power. The cut and the final clench of her around him did him in. He bellowed as his balls emptied and his cock pulsed a release so intense he lost his vision. His seed spilled down his leg, pumping in great bursts. He tossed the blade across the room and fell against her, smearing his and her blood across her chest as his body bucked and shuddered.

When it was over, when he stilled, he found himself lying across her, covering her body with his, feeling her warmth seep into his skin and the cut across his chest sting and her impossibly soft lips pressed into his collarbone.

"Niall?" Aisling murmured.

He tore himself away from her, struggling for breath as he felt his release trickle down his leg. He wiped a smear of blood from his pec as he hurriedly retied the drawstring.

She came from my sword against her skin.

I came from just the feeling of her orgasm on my finger and the blade in my flesh.

She is for me.

She was everything he never knew he wanted, and she didn't know that he'd already destroyed their future. That his dreams could mean only one thing – a premonition.

A warning.

A threat.

Hollythorn House would take Aisling from him, and he couldn't save her.

He'd tried to hold back. He'd tried to give her what she needed without causing her more pain. But denying her had led to *this*... Niall touched the cut he made in his chest, over his heart, feeling his own blood pulse with need of her.

We can't go back from this.

She belongs to me, and I belong to her, and even if our days are numbered, I will spend every spare moment making her smile, making her scream, making her lips fall open to whimper my name.

"Niall?" Aisling touched her hand to his cheek – so soft, so searing. "Are you okay? Did you hurt—"

"How can I hurt when I have you?" Niall wrapped his hands around hers and pulled her to her feet, steadying her against him until she was strong enough to stand. She tried to say something, but he held his finger to her lips. They had time still for the things they needed to say. "Come on, let's get these crystals charged."

Aisling didn't say anything as Niall helped her to the kitchen. She had a blissed-out smile on her face as he settled her at the table. He wanted to feed her something sugary, but all they had left was apple juice, so he poured her the rest of the carton, stroking her hair while she drank.

How is she mine? What does she see in my savage, lonely soul?

She finished her juice and had perked up a little. "I forgot the spell book in the library."

Niall rushed back to collect it, presenting it to her with a flourish. Her cheeks flushed as she tore her eyes from the cut across his chest to bend over the book.

As Niall watched Aisling work the charm on the pantry to remove the unit, he saw something she could not. Tendrils of shimmering magic unwound themselves from the moldings and ceiling beams, their blue tips curling along Aisling's arms and into her hands, which glowed with a brighter aura than the rest of her body.

The house fed Aisling's power with its own. The more she practiced her magic, the more it fed into her, until her body shimmered with the blue aura, making her even more beautiful and even more dangerous.

Interesting.

"Got it!" Aisling cried in triumph as she slid the white cloth onto a large serving platter, crystals and box and all. She pushed past Niall and dashed into the library, where she placed the unit on the table in front of the window. Luck was on their side, for according to the chart Aisling had made (yet another chart), it would be a full moon that night. A couple of days at the window, directly in the path of the moon's light, should have the unit fully operational again.

In theory.

Niall hoped like hell Aisling was right. He'd been hungry for her for so long, he refused to lose her to actual starvation. If it came to it, he'd allow her to eat his flesh. It would be the greatest honor to know that in death he became part of her, that he'd sacrificed himself so she would live.

28

NIALL

*L*uckily, Niall didn't need to offer up his body as sustenance.

Two days later, he was reading in the drawing room when he heard Aisling's cry of triumph.

He didn't look up immediately, too engrossed in the book. He'd taken one of the thick magical volumes from the library and was thumbing through the pages. This time, he wasn't searching for the heart of the house, but anything to explain how Aisling's body had somehow suddenly become alight with magic from the walls. If he could figure that out, he wouldn't even need to locate the heart of the house. All he'd need...

...was Aisling.

The possibility plagued him these past two days. The answer should have been simple. He'd entered Hollythorn to find a way to extract its power for his queen, to free his brother and all their people. This right here was his answer. He would let Aisling take in the power of the house and then he would cut out her heart and take it to his queen.

Simple.

Not simple.

He wouldn't do it.

She was his. He wouldn't hurt her unless she begged for it with those doe-eyes of hers. The idea that anyone might hurt Aisling made his blood boil, the same way the rage inside him burned at his brother's wrongful treatment.

Even if it meant the fae would die, he would not cut her heart from her chest.

But there could be a way to have both – to use the magic and spare Aisling's life. He couldn't talk with Aisling about it, not without revealing the deception he'd been trying to uphold. He would continue his investigations with casual indifference, looking for an answer that would give him everything he wanted, even as he knew he had no right to want at all.

The magic books were a shambles of notations and doodles and scattered, half-finished thoughts. It was impossible to find what you wanted to know.

Where is the heart of the house?

How can magic be taken from walls and stone and given to a human?

Why was the house giving Aisling magic now?

Niall stared over the top of the book out the window into the grim storm. Beyond the iron fence, the lanterns of the Summer City should have been visible. He saw only towering plumes of smoke. His stomach twisted. *What's going on out there? Is Eamon okay? Why won't Odiana write back to me?*

His fingers itched to write to her again, to tell her that he'd seen the house push magic into Aisling. That maybe she'd be able to use that to find a solution, as long as Aisling survived it.

But a voice in his head that didn't belong to his father told him to hold off, that he needed more before he could convince cool, headstrong Odiana to spare a witch.

Aisling's face appeared at the doorway. "I did it!" She waved a packet in the air. "I got it working again!"

"I knew it." Niall crossed the room, thinking that this might be it – the moment he kissed her, the moment his walls came crashing down. But she was too busy shoving a spongy cake into her mouth.

"Mmmmmmfgg mmmmmphh." Aisling's whole face was alight with joy. Niall had never seen her like this before. It almost made him feel jealous of the... what were they called? Twingles?

"What was that you said?" He leaned forward, holding his hand behind his ear. "Was it, 'Niall is one handsome fae and I'd like him to suck my nipples'—"

Aisling swallowed, then thrust out a packet toward Niall. "Shove one of these in your mouth so I can have a moment of peace."

Niall took one of the packets in his hands. The treat was coated in plastic, one of the habits of humans he was all too glad the fae hadn't adopted. He peeled back the wrapping and pushed out the treat. The buttery cake sprung beneath his touch. Gingerly, he bit off a corner.

Whoa. The saccharine-sweet taste danced across his tongue. Flavor exploded in his mouth. Sickly sweet cream flowed over his tongue. He chewed slowly, not wanting any part of the delicious treat to be wasted.

It tasted nothing like nectar cakes the fae made – it tasted fake and cloying and incredible.

"Good, huh?" Aisling grabbed another.

Niall swallowed the last bite. "Can I have another one?"

"Sure." She passed him a second packet. Niall tore it open and stuffed the treat into his mouth. "You need to fuel up for my sword-fighting lesson."

At the mention of a sword, Niall's cock swelled to life. After the other day, when he held his sword against her skin and came so hard he momentarily lost his sight, he would oblige any whim of hers.

Especially when he got to see her just the way he liked her – surrendered and trusting and powerful.

He didn't know what he would do to her this time. He didn't know what seeing her with a sword in her hands would do to *him*. All he knew was that he would teach her to fight, to win, to revel in bloodshed, and she would love every moment of it.

She will truly be mine.

Aisling looked at him expectantly, her face frozen in a half-smile.

"Fine." He gulped down the last of his Twinkie, which tasted like cardboard now that all he could think about was her fig- and vanilla-scented skin shuddering beneath his blade. "I'll teach you a few simple moves."

Aisling set the box down on the table and dragged him out into the hall. "Come on, then."

"Right now?"

"Yes, of course now." She took down two swords from their hooks on either side of the front door and handed one to him. "Let's use these. I don't want to learn with your sword, no offense."

He understood. She'd seen fae weapons take out her family. To have his blade against her skin was one thing, but to train to kill with it...

"Right." Niall stared down at the blade in his hand, feeling oddly disconnected from it. He'd fought with swords his entire life and had trained hundreds of Slaugh warriors. A blade like this in his hands became an extension of his malice. Yet, when he thought about teaching Aisling, all his knowledge flew from his head, replaced by a vision of her spread out before him, her pearlescent skin painted by trails of blood.

As her teacher, you'll need to correct her stances, help her with her holds, grapple with her in the cross... all excuses to get close and personal, to show her that you're here to protect her, that you'll die for her.

All excuses to press a blade to her skin again, to feel that excitement bubble inside her as she dances with death.

To know that you can slide the tip between her ribs and end your people's suffering, if only you had the courage.

Niall shook his head, trying to shake off the last thought, the voice that belonged to his father. *You were the coward, not me. You were too afraid of what the fae would think of Eamon's powers to accept him as your son. I don't listen to you any longer.*

He drew up to his full height and held the sword in a low guard. "First, you need to learn the proper stance. Your legs are too far apart. Useful for other things, not so much in battle."

Niall explained some of the concepts behind fighting with the two-handed sword she'd chosen, then ran Aisling through the different guards, brushing his fingers against her skin as often as he dared. He showed her how to stay light on her feet, how to move her weight as she stepped or swung to give herself more power or a quicker reaction. He rested his hands on her thighs as she swung from her hips, and his whole body surged with desire. Sweat poured down her face, glistening on her skin, reminding Niall of what else they might do that would make them sweat like that.

Next, he showed her a couple of basic defensive blocks that would work with her steel against his bone. Any fae she fought would have bone blades, so Aisling needed to play any advantage she had. They drilled the blocks over and over. Trying to dissuade her from continuing, Niall flung himself at her with all the speed and force he could muster. Again and again, he beat her back against the wall of the ballroom, disarming her or ending with his blade pressed against her throat. He expected her to balk, to beg him to take it easy on her, but every time she met his eyes with her damnable fire. She swung her sword to clash against his, her lips pursed with determination as she tried to match his strength with her own.

Every time they ended up in the same deadly dance – Aisling pinned in his arms with his blade dragging across her skin. The slightest shift of his weight and he could drive it through her, yet she gazed up at him with perfect trust.

With perfect lust.

Her neck arched and her lips parted. He knew from her heavy-lidded eyes what he'd feel if he reached between her legs – her wetness, her desire.

Niall's cock was in agony. His limbs shook from the effort of holding himself back. He needed her. He craved her, and she was right there for him, on the point of his knife, begging him to unleash himself on her yet again.

Aisling was the only person who stared down the truth of Niall's cruelty and refused to shy away. She saw him for who he was and wanted him. She *welcomed* him.

No, that wasn't the truth.

Because he hadn't given her the truth, had he? Enough truth to satisfy the fae court, but not the truth that mattered. Aisling bared herself for him and he couldn't do her the same courtesy even as he vowed to protect her.

"Again," he roared, throwing himself away from her. She'd noticed his raging hard-on because her eyes flicked to his crotch as they parried, but she kept fighting, kept trying to beat him.

They danced around the entrance hall, their breath coming out in short gasps. Her hair clung to her back in wet ringlets. Their swords clanged together, echoing through the massive house. He'd never seen anything so arousing in his life. His cock throbbed angrily against his leg.

"You're getting tired," Aisling huffed as she raised her sword again. She licked her lips.

"Never." Steel met steel. This time, Aisling caught his blade in exactly the right place, at exactly the right angle. She applied pressure, leveraging him into a compromising position. *WHAM.* She slammed the pommel of her sword into his cheek.

"Argh!" Niall dropped his sword and cupped his hand over his stinging cheek. Rage bubbled inside him. *He* was the master here, not her.

"I'm sorry!" She rushed at him. "I didn't mean to hit you so hard."

"It wasn't hard," he said, rubbing his cheek. The cut stung, but the pain was nothing. His chest swelled with pride, with admiration. She beat him. "Nice job," he added gruffly, the rage ebbing.

"You're getting slow," she teased. "We should take a break. My poor, broken soldier. I can think of just the thing to ease your pain..."

She dropped her sword on the tiles and pressed her body against him, letting the blue magic that curled around her mingle with Niall's own aura – a swirl of color and light more beautiful for how forbidden it was. He drew in a deep breath, savoring the scent of her after battle, sweaty and heady with bloodlust of her own.

Aisling's smile turned his insides out. He was past the point of denying her. He tossed down his own weapon and resisted the urge to fall to his knees before her.

"I'm yours to do with as you wish," he said. The words came out hoarse, tight with need.

"I know." Aisling slid her hands into the waistband of his breeches. Niall's breath stuttered as she pushed the fabric over his thighs, dragging it down to reveal his swollen cock, the head crowned with moisture.

Aisling knelt before him. For a fae, kneeling meant accepting the dominance of another, but as Aisling's eyes blazed up at him, he knew she was the one with the power here. That she wanted this as much as him, that what they shared as their skin sizzled with energy was more than lust, more than 'kink.'

She leaned forward, her eyes closed, her lips wet with anticipation. It was the way she looked a few hours ago when she held that first Twinkie in her hands. She reached out with her tongue and tasted him, licking down his shaft and circling the head.

Niall drew in a ragged breath. A fresh bead of pre-cum rolled down his shaft.

When her hand closed around his cock, he knew he couldn't fight her. *Weak,* his father's voice boomed through his head.

Her lips circled the head, drawing him into the warmth of her mouth. Niall couldn't hear his father any longer.

All he could hear was the deep, satisfying moan as she took him into her mouth, all of him.

If this was weakness, then he'd be weak for Aisling any fucking time she wanted.

He belonged to her. He was hers to worship, to use, to command as she chose.

Her eyelids flickered open, and those huge dark eyes watched his face as she held the base of his shaft and took him right in until his head pushed against her throat and her lips kissed the hairs of his stomach.

"You're so beautiful like this," he moaned.

In response, she rolled back on her heels, drawing him out before slamming her mouth down onto him. Niall tossed his head back, his fingers tangled in her hair, guiding her, revering her.

For the first time since he'd taken his oath to serve the Summer Queen, his sword fell from his hand. The pommel clattered on the marble tiles.

He did not care.

How could he care with Aisling's lips wrapped around him? With the plum of her mouth slicking down his shaft?

Aisling dug her nails into his thigh as she took him deep. She tilted her head back, tumbling her dark ringlets over her shoulders, and he felt his length squeezed by her throat. She moaned with the joy of serving him, as if it was all she'd wanted to do these long months they'd been dancing around their feelings.

Her moans undid him. Her plump lips stretched around his shaft sent him careening over the edge. Niall came with a roar that shook the windows, with the knowledge that Aisling knelt for him and him alone, not because he forced her, not because he deceived her, but because *she* wanted to.

She wanted him.

All of him.

Even the bloodshed. Even the malice. Even the twisted heart that took pleasure in the chaos and pain he wrought.

Niall's balls tightened, and he clamped his hand around her head as he held himself inside her, chasing the warmth of her mouth through his pleasure. Aisling took it all, swallowing him down like she couldn't get enough of him.

When he was spent, Aisling rocked back on her knees, staring up at him with a wild, dangerous smile on her lips. "See, that wasn't so bad."

Behind her head, Eamon's eye swirled to face him.

It blinked.

Niall turned away so it couldn't watch him, judge him. He could still feel it staring at him.

He turned from the woman on her knees for him, the woman with a waterfall of dark hair tumbling over her shoulders and swollen lips and wide, caring eyes.

He turned and he ran.

29

AISLING

*H*e ran again.
Bastard.

Aisling rocked back on her heels, forcing her fists into her eyes. She could still taste his saltiness on her tongue. She promised herself she wouldn't cry. She'd already spilled too many tears over Niall.

No. No tears. Her tears belonged to Bethany. To her parents and her grandmother. Tears weren't for fae warriors who said things like 'how can I hurt if I have you?' and then ran the fuck away rather than risk being the slightest bit vulnerable.

No tears.

Only wrath.

Aisling pulled herself to her feet. Her knees burned from the hard marble, but it was the right kind of pain. The kind only Niall could give her.

He's not getting away from me this time.

For all his fire and fury and 'I've killed hundreds of witches, you can't handle my depravity,' Niall couldn't even face his own emotions. She'd seen it flash in his eyes as she swallowed – that darkness inside him breaking open – the lid of a puzzle box that could never be put back together again.

Luckily, Aisling knew a little about handling stroppy Doms. She dusted off her knees and looked around, trying to think where he might've gone. Widdershins sauntered over from the ballroom door and rubbed against an object on the ground a few feet away.

Niall's sword.

She picked it up and studied it, running her fingers along that vicious curved blade. The edges were chipped from where her metal weapon had connected with it. She let out a long breath as she remembered the last time she'd seen a blade like this – when she and Bethany had been shoved in the pantry, she'd glanced over her shoulder out the kitchen window to see the fae host outside, hundreds of bone swords glinting in the air as they bore down on Hollythorn House.

Niall had been out there. This blade might have slain her father or one of June's coven.

Aisling turned it over. The eye glared up at her, unblinking, unmoving. Aisling ran her fingers over it again, wondering who it belonged to, why Niall had it in his sword. He'd dodged the question every time she asked, which meant he thought she wouldn't like the answer. And that made her all the more desperate to know.

Aisling tucked the blade into her belt. Something else caught the corner of her eye, something that wasn't as it should be. She stepped toward the window and peered across the front yard, beyond the iron fence, beyond the thrashing storm.

Weirdly, there were no lights visible in the Summer City, just scattered plumes of smoke. *Odd.* She didn't know what that meant, but she suspected Niall knew, or guessed.

"Come on, Widdershins." She lifted her cat onto her shoulder, where he kneaded her sleeve with gusto. "Let's go find my emotionally-stunted fae and kick his ass."

30

NIALL

One of the benefits of being trapped in a labyrinthine house was that if you wanted to hide, Hollythorn would make you a hiding place. Niall took the stairs three at a time, his thoughts a wild tangle, his balls empty, his cock still warm from the ghost of Aisling's mouth.

He rounded the corner and came across a hallway he'd never seen before. He didn't stop to check if the familiar cracks of the black void crisscrossed the walls. He didn't care if he tumbled into oblivion. He turned down the hallway and tried the first door. It flung open and he ducked inside.

He gasped as golden light bathed his body. Warmth caressed his skin – a warmth so foreign to him that it felt uncomfortable, as though it dissolved his insides. But as his eyes adjusted to the gleaming light and the warmth braised his skin, Niall let the warmth melt the ice that clung to his chest. It claimed him, making him anew, lighter and warmer and dazzling.

His feet scuffed golden sand. Water lapped in gentle waves, tugging, even though there was nowhere for it to go but break in salty sprays upon the walls.

A beach.

The house has given me a beach.

Niall slumped down in the sand, trying to force his body to stop shaking. He knew exactly where he was, which meant it was only a matter of time before—

"Niall."

She found him. He was her dream man, after all.

Aisling slid onto her knees beside him. She had her metal sword shoved through her belt, which he adored. She held up a handful of sand and let it trickle through her fingers. "I've never seen this room before," she said. "But I know this beach. I love the beach. June would take us for walks sometimes in a sacred cove near Hollythorn. There were cliffs—" she pointed over her shoulder, to the door cut out of a limestone cliff-face that had grown over the wall "—where we'd hunt for fossils. For my thirteenth birthday, June's coven held a ceremony in the cove. We had a bonfire and danced naked under the full moon. That's the first time I dared to believe that magic could be real, because there was something magic in the air that night."

Niall nodded. He couldn't speak.

"But that wasn't this beach. I've only visited this beach with one other person," she said. "With you. In my dreams."

Something slid across his lap – his sword. He'd fled without it. Eamon's eye glared up at him, still and secretive. Niall knew he hadn't imagined it blinking. His brother was trying to tell him something about the Summer City. Something he didn't want to hear.

I failed him. And I'm failing her.

Aisling prodded at the eye.

"Start talking, fae. Or I start stabbing your favorite body parts."

"I..." he wrung his hands. "I can't—"

"You can. It's easy. Open mouth, speak true things. Come on,

Niall. You're afraid of something. I need to know what it is so we can fight it together."

He sighed. "I'm the one who's supposed to protect you."

"Get over it. Haven't you fae ever heard of feminism?"

"In my dreams, I can never protect you. The figure in the shadows always gets you in the end. You want to know what a Slaugh could possibly be afraid of? Watching someone I love die and not being able to do anything to stop it. I've only loved three people in my life, and..." he swallowed. He didn't have the words.

"Your brother?" Aisling pushed.

"I thought I was protecting him by taking his place." Niall glared at the window on the other side of the narrow strip of lapping ocean. The skyline of the Summer City stretched beyond, shrouded in darkness, with those ominous pillars of smoke rising into the black clouds. "But instead I've left him alone out there, and Odiana. And I can help them, but it means—"

He stopped himself. He couldn't tell her. He couldn't bear to see her turn on him, or worse, to know he did this but to care for him anyway.

"How can you help them? You're trapped in here." She knitted her fingers in his, squeezing hard. "That's not your fault."

Niall stared at the sword in his lap, at her delicate wrists with their prominent veins now wreathed in luminous blue light. She had taken in more magic. Her body *hummed* with it. Something had activated in her, and the house was siphoning off magic into her. Magic that could save his people. "I didn't want to teach you to fight. If I did that, I admit that I believe there's a time when you won't have me."

If I teach you to fight, I admit I will betray you.

"You know that's ridiculous, right?"

"Carrying a sword like this means carrying the ghosts of

your victims. I'm never going to let you be in a situation where you're alone and defenseless, where you may have to live with the knowledge of the lives you take. I'm fae – guilt is foreign to me. But you have no such protection."

"Am I the third person you've loved?" Aisling asked, her voice soft, her fingers dancing in his.

Niall looked away, ashamed of his weakness, terrified to think she might not feel the same. "That's what I said."

"It's actually not, but I'm learning how to translate fae." Aisling gave a short laugh. "And is this macho toxic masculinity bullshit why you won't let me touch you? Why you keep running away every time you get too close to your emotions?"

"More or less," he muttered.

"Hear me, because I'm not saying this again. You don't come into my house and make that decision for me. I didn't ask for you to come, and I didn't ask for... for *us*. For this fucked-up thing that we have. By teaching me how to defend myself, you *are* protecting me. You're giving me another tool to keep myself alive, as I've done all these years. I won't be bound to you in the same way I'm bound to this house. I will be my own person, and I will make my own decisions. And I choose you, Niall. Do you hear me? I choose you. Because I love you too, you idiot."

Niall blinked.

I choose you.

I love you, too.

Nothing Aisling could have said would've rocked him more than those words. All his life, Niall had been chosen. He'd been carried along with the will of others. His father had chosen him as the son born into bloodshed. The Summer Queen chose him as the enforcer of her order. Even Odiana had chosen him as a shield to enable her to continue her work unmolested.

But Aisling... she was choosing *him*. Not Niall the warrior. Not Niall the executioner or Niall the twisted sadist. She chose

Niall. Just Niall. He didn't know who he was without his sword, but as she clutched it in her tiny hands, he realized that he wanted to know.

More than anything, he wanted to be worthy of her choosing.

He pointed to the eye. "When I was seven years old, my father made me cut that eye from my brother's head."

Aisling started, dropping the sword into the sand like it burned her. "That—that's horrible."

"He bled so much." Niall shook his head. "I've killed many, witch and human and fae, in bloody and brutal ways. But his screams are still the ones I hear in my dreams."

"Why would he make you do that?"

"Father feared Eamon's powers. He said that Eamon could destroy the kingdom he helped build, but I think he was more afraid that if Eamon used the full force of his powers, the fae wouldn't need Slaugh anymore. So much of fae magic comes from the eyes – from manipulating the world you see and altering the vision of others, so Father had me take one of Eamon's eyes to diminish his power. To protect the fae from Eamon. It was my initiation into the Slaugh. It was to test my loyalty." Niall's hand trembled. "I passed."

"That's horrible. Your brother must have hated you."

"Eamon doesn't know how to hate. If I hadn't done as Father asked, we both would have suffered worse punishments. He had this sword made for me, to remind me I think that I should nurture my own gifts – loyalty, brutality, protectiveness. But like my love, his gift is also a curse. When I carry it, I have some of his powers. I can see the auras of magic in people and objects. Fae glow with a golden yellow, like the sunlight we miss so dearly. Witches are blue. Eamon is the only aura I've ever seen as a deep, rich purple. I'm the reason the fae have collected so many objects imbued with witch powers. I can see them. I can see this house glowing with lurid blue light. And you. I can see you."

"Right. Wonderful. It would have been great to know this before, fae," Aisling said. "Any other magical powers I should know about?"

"Yes. I can do this thing called shadow-shifting. I can become a shadow, and move wherever shadows lurk. It's handy when tracking—" he'd been about to say *witches*, but stopped himself "—prey. And for eavesdropping. But I can't hold the shadow form for very long or it starts to consume me. Maybe it already has."

Aisling laid her hand across his. "In this house, we are not the sum of our powers and our mistakes. Maybe that's what Hollythorn gives us – this chance to exist between ourselves."

"I shouldn't have kept this from you."

"No, you shouldn't have. Why did you?"

"Because I thought if you knew, you'd see me as an enemy coming to take your power. That wouldn't be a false impression. It's what I did back in... in the world."

Aisling sighed. "I've never been worried about that. Hollythorn can look after herself. And after that first night when you didn't kill me in my sleep, I figured you're all right for a fae. So can you maybe stop being so sulky and just let *us* happen? I'd like to have sex at least one more time before the void takes me."

"Very well." Niall gestured to her weapon. "Pick up your sword. I'll show you how to stab a man through the throat."

Aisling grinned as her hands closed over the hilt. "That's more like it."

LETTER SHOT THROUGH MAIL SLOT OF HOLLYTHORN HOUSE

Dear Odiana,

I'm still here, and still safe. Something strange and wonderful has happened.

I am in love.

There, I said it. Yes, this is Niall speaking. Yes, my mind and sword are still sharp, but for the first time in my life, my heart is light. I know how you've felt, loving my brother for all those years. I hope the two of you have had a chance at happiness.

The other day, I saw Aisling draw down magic from the walls to help her perform a spell. She didn't even realize she was doing it. There's something in that, but I'll report back once I know more. There has to be a way for us to use Hollythorn's magic without hurting Aisling. Please, help me figure it out. As Aisling says, I was born for kink, not to think.

Have you heard of kink? It's this thing depraved humans do. It's delightful.

What's with the smoke? Where are the lights?

Niall

31

AISLING

"**W**ake up," a deep voice whispered in her ear. "I have a surprise for you."

Aisling opened one lazy eye, the voice not quite calling her from her dreams. How could it, when the boy in her dreams and the man leaning over her bed were one and the same?

"Get out of here," she murmured, catching the gleam in Niall's eyes. She'd learned that it meant only trouble. "I was on the beach with this hot guy..."

"Not until you agree to come with me." Niall yanked the covers, trying to expose her. Aisling thrust out her arms to stop him, aware that her nightdress had hitched up around her waist and she wasn't wearing anything underneath.

Especially aware as Niall's gaze swept over her, as she felt the power of him bear down on her. Even just having him stand over her with his fae bearing and knowing what he was capable of with his blade against her skin sent her into wild, dark places.

"Give that back!"

Niall yanked all the covers – including her – onto the floor. Aisling shrieked in delight as he climbed on top of her, pinning her arms to her sides with his knees. She gasped in the scent of him, all dark forest depths and smoky firelight. The tiny hairs on her skin stood on end.

I was going to ask him something... it was important... she searched her mind for the niggling feeling that she had something vital to discuss with Niall, something that had kept her tossing and turning after waking from a dream last night. But his eyes held her in their thrall, and her thoughts turned to soup as her body surged with the strange energy that forever zapped between them.

"Whatever shall I do with you?" Niall's lips hovered dangerously close to hers. She could just move her head slightly and press her lips to his. *Our first kiss.*

But she wanted to draw it out, to savor the thrill of being in his power.

She wanted Niall to be the one to cross that line. For Niall, a kiss was more intimate than anything they'd done before.

Then she remembered what disturbed her last night. She woke up to go to the bathroom. As she staggered back to bed, something caught her eye in the shadows. Lightning cracked outside, and the bolt of light had been reflected off a shiny object in the shadows.

It looked suspiciously like the glassy surface of Eamon's eye.

There had been something else, too – a heaviness to the shadows in the hallway, a solidity that felt... off. Aisling might've put it down to Hollythorn had she not known about Niall's shadow-shifting power.

He was there last night, lurking in the shadows. And he didn't want me to know it.

The memory sent a shiver down her spine that had nothing to do with her desire. Niall hadn't mentioned any nocturnal walks around the house, and since he told her pretty much everything these days, that didn't bode well for the bond of trust between them.

Fae couldn't lie. All June's books confirmed that. But they had their ways of obscuring what they didn't want you to know.

He's hiding something else, but what?

I told you never to trust a fae, her mother screamed inside her head.

Aisling hated the idea of Niall wandering around Hollythorn alone, touching things that had been part of her family for centuries, exploring the house unaccompanied. Last night, she'd been too shaken by his shadowed presence to confront him about it. It wasn't until she got into bed that she realized what it might mean.

You don't want to admit to yourself that he could be lying to you. Her grandmother's voice thundered in her ears.

Aisling suspected that was true, and now, watching that wicked grin spread over his face, feeling her skin tingle at his touch, she was more confused than ever.

Niall didn't kiss her. He slid off the end of the bed, grabbed her hands, and tried to yank her upright. "Come on, witch. I can't wait for you to see this."

"Yeah, sure." Aisling's body sang with energy from where their skin met. She rose, rubbing the bare skin of her arms. She yanked on a pair of jeans and pulled on a bra. *I'm the last human alive and I've been trapped in this house for four years and I'm putting on a bra? For him? I'm fucked.* On her dresser, the long, thin kitchen knife Niall had shown her how to use to gut a fae just yesterday glinted from beside her jewelry box. Aisling tucked it into her back pocket as she pulled on a shirt, her heart pounding, then followed Niall down the hall. He had a lantern in his hand, which he swung in circles.

"You're not gonna believe it." Niall's voice rose with excitement.

He led her up the stairs to the second story of the eastern wing, where the guest and master suites were located. Aisling didn't go up there much, evidenced by a thick layer of dirt clinging to the hall furniture. The rooms were too large for the lights to permeate, and she couldn't know what might be hiding in the corners she couldn't see. The attic had already succumbed to the void, and long black cracks crisscrossed the ceilings on this floor, spreading out like a poisoned web ensnaring everything in its path.

"We have to be careful up here," she said, her stomach flipping. *Is this a trap? Is this what Niall was doing late last night – plotting to get rid of me so he can steal my power?*

No. She refused to think it. Not after everything that passed between them. Niall kept his powers secret from her, but everyone had secrets. Hell, this house was a pile of secrets on top of secrets. She remembered Niall's voice cracking when he told her it was his job to protect her. *No, Niall loves me. Niall is safe.*

Her hand dug into the back pocket of her jeans, closing around the narrow blade. *But I'm going to keep this here, just in case.*

Niall led her past open bedroom doors. The lantern in his hand cast a small circle of light around them, illuminating corners of enormous armoires and ornate four-poster beds in the depths of rooms that had warped beyond recognition. He paused at a door near the end of the hall, a door that Aisling couldn't remember being there before.

"Oh," she beamed, the tension in her stomach relaxing slightly. "You found the upstairs bathroom again."

Niall shook his head. "Even better."

He swung open the door.

They stood in a room Aisling had never entered before. It was enormous – three times at least the size of the ballroom downstairs – and seemed to stretch on and up into infinity. Tall trees sprouted from the floor, pushing up the rotting floorboards as they twisted around each other, creating an indoor forest. At the foot of one of the trees, she noticed a small, enamel basin. Above the basin, a black-stained mirrored cabinet protruded from the wood. Behind those, a clawfoot bath hung from a tangle of vines.

This is the bathroom. But now it's so much more.

"Wow," she breathed, turning in a slow circle to take it all in. The foliage from the tall trees spread so thick she couldn't see a ceiling above it. Vines tangled between the trunks, creating a storybook jungle. Along the vines, Niall had strung strings of fairy lights he must've found in the Christmas decorations. They glowed with warm light, creating dappled shadows across the uneven floor. She had no idea how they were glowing, since the house had no electricity. In the distance, she heard the chirps of birds and the rustle of leaves blowing in the breeze. She rubbed her arms. *How is there even a breeze?* "How... how did you find this place?"

"Sometimes, I have trouble sleeping," Niall said. "You might have heard me wandering around at night."

Aisling nodded. *I wasn't mistaken. I did see him in the shadows. He's admitting it.* The tension in her body relaxed completely. She felt awful about the knife in her pocket. Of course, Niall wasn't lying to her. After all this time, she should know him better than that. She should stop judging him just because of the shape of his ears and the things he'd done.

"Recently, I've been exploring this wing," he grinned sheepishly. "At first, I wanted to see if I could find out where the water in my room was coming from, but then I got interested in what the rooms up here were doing, how they were changing. Last night I came up and found this door. I had to show it to you. Come on."

He grabbed her hand and led her down a short path into a small clearing. Leaves and twigs crunched under her feet. Aisling breathed deep, tasting the crisp air, a flood of memories from her childhood rushing back to her. Pushing Bethany on a tree-swing at the end of Hollythorn's garden, foraging for wild herbs with June, reading under the large oak outside her college dorm. How long had it been since she'd seen a tree that wasn't choked to death by ice or radiation?

Niall was saying something, gesturing frantically. Aisling looked where he was pointing. Her heart soared.

On the floor in front of them, underneath the globes, Niall had spread out a picnic blanket and several cushions. Aisling recognized them from the couch in the master bedroom sitting area. A bottle of wine sat in a bucket of ice, along with two crystal glasses. On her grandmother's best china sat delicate scones with jam and real whipped cream (where on earth had he got *that?*), and small finger sandwiches stuffed with delicious things. Much more sensible portions. Niall was learning.

"It's beautiful," she breathed.

"I thought we could eat breakfast without getting crumbs in your bed." Niall dropped to his knees. He reached up a hand and pulled her down beside him. Aisling picked up one of the scones, holding the treat in her hand. She couldn't believe he'd made this, all of this.

He did this for me.

"How did you make these scones? Where did you get the cream?"

"Your grandmother has recipe books. They explain how to skim the cream off the top of the milk and whip it." Niall raised his fist to flex his biceps. "I figured it out. By the way, don't go into the kitchen. It looks like a cow exploded in there."

She laughed, her body feeling light. The blade in her pocket dug against her thigh. She wished she could remove it, but she didn't want to explain to Niall that she had mistrusted him. Not when he'd done all this for her.

No one has ever done something like this for me, ever.

Aisling bit into her scone. Oh, it was amazing. The light, fluffy cake was cooked to perfection, and the sweet jam and cream sang on her tastebuds.

I can't believe he did this for me. I can't believe he cares so much.

"You have some cream on your lip." Niall set down his sandwich and leaned toward her to wipe it away. "Here."

The world stood still. Aisling's lips parted, ever so slightly. The energy around them rose in a crescendo, pulsing against her bare skin. Her eyes locked on Niall as he leaned closer. His finger brushed the corner of her lip. Time skipped a beat.

His lips seared against hers, hot and fierce.

Yes.

Finally.

This kiss wasn't tender and sweet. It was a kiss of hunger, of desires long held in check and now pouring forth without restraint. Aisling returned the kiss in kind, sinking into the heat of him, aware of her skin burning as the energy sizzled up from inside her. Niall's hands wrapped around her, mashing her body against his, as if the air between them was offensive to him.

Niall pushed her back, resting her against the trunk of a tree. His hands explored her body, his touch laying trails of fire over her skin. This wasn't like the touches they explored before – this wasn't about dominance or kink or pain. This was them, together.

Aisling's tongue explored his mouth, seeking to discern every corner. *Is this what it's like to kiss someone you love?* Her fuzzy mind managed to express the thought as her stomach dropped into her toes and she felt like she was floating and falling at the same time. *The romance books don't lie. This is incredible.*

Niall grabbed the edges of her shirt, tugging it upward. Despite the thrumming of the energy against her skin, the motion cut through her haze, and she trembled against him.

"Niall," she spoke against his lips, "I'm scared of this."

"It's okay. I'm scared, too."

"Really?"

He laughed a little, deep in his throat. "Mostly, I want to be as close to your gorgeous body as I can. But yes, I'm scared. I'm scared that I'll mess this up and I'll lose you."

"That won't happen."

"If you say so," he murmured against her, his hands skimming her hips, caressing her curves in a way that made her heart leap against her chest. "I've never been with a witch before. We don't even know if our bodies fit together. Do you want me to stop?"

"Don't stop."

Her body screamed. *Don't stop. Don't ever stop.*

Niall sat back a little, his icy eyes regarding her. "You trust me?"

The knife scraped against her thigh. "I shouldn't trust you. You're fae."

"I didn't ask if you *should* trust me. I asked if you do. In this house, we're no longer fae and witch. We're Aisling and Niall, and right now," he grinned wickedly, "Niall wants to tear off Aisling's clothes and lick her all over until she begs for mercy."

Aisling's body shuddered. "If you insist," she said, her voice trembling as much from excitement as from nerves.

"All I get is an 'if you insist'?" Niall's lips brushed against hers again. "Where's the enthusiasm?"

"What are you waiting for, a written invitation?" Aisling thought for a moment, but only one line – a ridiculous one, from a trashy romance Bethany loved – came to mind. "Fine, fae, take me in a manly fashion?"

"If you insist." Niall pressed his lips against hers, and the fire lit her up within. She rose up to meet him, cupping his face in her hands. She pulled his shirt over his head and ran her fingers over his body, satisfying her urge to explore the curve of his shoulders, the tension in his muscles, the tautness of his chest and abs. Her hand skimmed the waistband of his trousers, and his whole body shuddered with need.

"You're mine, Aisling," Niall murmured against her lips. His hands found the hem of her shirt again. He lifted it over her head and flung it aside. He reached behind her and unclasped her bra.

Aisling sucked in a breath as Niall's hands explored her breasts. He held each one in his hands, weighing them possessively as if deciding which to lavish with attention first. He ran his tongue along the cuts and welts he'd made – the marks of his possession on her body.

"You're so beautiful," he murmured. He bent his head and took a nipple in his mouth. Aisling gasped as his tongue slid over her sensitive skin. Instead of his usual violent tongue, he gave her only the lightest touch, like a feather, like a warm summer breeze. His fingers burned as they stroked her body, and a fountain of need welled up inside her.

"Niall..." she whimpered, tangling her fingers in his hair, watching him as he teased her nipple with his tongue, swirling around the sensitive bud before running his teeth along the edges, nipping and biting at her skin. The sharp pain delighted her, and the need inside her swelled.

But Niall wasn't going to give her what she wanted so easily. He moved his mouth to the other nipple and gave that one the same light treatment. Aisling moaned as her nipple hardened, arching her back to seek the wicked heat of his mouth.

Niall's hands slid down her body, fiddling with the button on her jeans. The well inside her turned into a groaning, desperate *ache*. She tried to help him with the buttons, but he slapped her hand away.

"Naughty witch." He kissed her again with all that graceful fae arrogance that made her knees weak and her toes curl.

Niall unbuttoned her jeans and slid his hands along her hips. Aisling lifted herself off the ground so he could push her jeans over her hips and yank them from her legs. As he did, the knife clattered from her pocket.

"What's that?" Niall reached over to pick it up.

"No, don't!" Aisling tried to grab his hand, but it was too late. He picked up the blade, turning it over in his hands. Her face flushed. "I saw you in the shadows last night when I was in the bathroom. Well, not saw exactly, but I *felt* you. I thought... I don't know what I thought, exactly, but you wouldn't tell me where you were taking me and I had to be sure—"

"Good." Niall tossed the knife aside. "I wouldn't trust me, either." She started to apologize, but he covered her mouth in ravenous kisses.

"Lie back," he ordered her in that easy, commanding voice he knew drove her wild. His fingers tugged at her panties. Aisling obeyed, breathing in as he slid her underwear down over her hips. She was completely naked in front of him.

Her stomach tightened with nerves, which made no sense because she'd been naked with him before. But never like this, never her heart on display alongside her skin. According to June's stories, fae found witches repulsive. That was why there weren't hybrid children wandering around.

Aisling gazed at Niall's face, searching for the revulsion. All she saw there were his stony features softened by the lantern light, and his blue eyes dancing as they took in her body.

"Niall..." Her stomach twisted. Her body hummed with life, with promise, with *magic.*

"You're perfect like this, witch. All undone for me."

Niall leaned over her and ran his fingers down the insides of her thighs until she bit her lip with frustration. He pushed her legs apart, spreading her before him. Aisling felt so exposed, so *worshipped*. She was a goddess of the forest, and he would give her sacrifices even though he didn't believe in goddesses. He would give her anything she asked.

As Niall continued to caress her thighs in languid circles, he lowered his face between her legs. Before Aisling could move, he flicked his tongue over her cunt, drawing along her whole length before circling around that one spot from which her unrelenting ache originated.

Aisling moaned, digging her fingers into his shoulders as his touch shuddered through her. Niall licked her again, slowly, arrogantly, building upon the ache inside her until her body sang under his touch.

"You taste amazing," he breathed against her.

"I—" Aisling tried to speak, but Niall's tongue worked its magic on her, rendering her speechless. He licked her again, slowly, and then sucked her clit into his mouth, swirling his tongue around it until Aisling thought she might pass out from sheer ecstasy.

She stopped worrying about what was going to happen after they came undone for each other. She stopped thinking about his presence in the shadows. She stopped thinking, full stop.

Niall worked his tongue faster, flicking it again and again. Aisling's veins thrummed with energy, her blood heated to the boiling point. All rational thought passed from her mind, all of her doubts about Niall and her nervousness and her fear. All that remained was the growing ache inside her, the ache that spread through her limbs and pounded at her skull. The ache that thrummed along with the beat of her heart.

As he continued to lick her with that furious rhythm, Niall pushed a finger inside her, then a second. Aisling tossed her head back and screamed as the ache in her belly burned through her veins. A wave of pleasure erupted, thundering through her body, jerking her limbs and snapping her thighs against Niall's face. Stars danced across her vision. The forest around her went supernova – the birth of a new world all happening inside her veins.

The pleasure coursed through her, dulling into a pleasing ache. She regained the ability to move of her own accord. Smiling his self-satisfied fae smile, Niall crawled up alongside her, wrapping her in his arms. Aisling rested her back against his chest, enjoying the warmth coursing through her and the way the energy swirled around them both, wrapping them in an invisible cocoon. She'd never felt so good, or so safe, in her whole life.

"There will be plenty more of that today," he whispered in her ear. "If you're good."

"I'm always good."

"That's up for debate, witch." He nipped her ear. "I told you being stuck in this house with me would bring residual benefits."

Aisling smiled up at him. She couldn't think of a witty reply; her brain had turned to mush.

"Hey, don't go to sleep now." Niall prodded her thigh with his rigid member and dared another of his wicked grins. "I have plans."

She rolled over and pulled him on top of her, wanting to feel his weight driving her into the forest floor. Niall knelt over her, steadying himself against the tree roots. His eyes locked with hers. Aisling saw herself reflected in those icy depths – all the trust, all the desperation for someone to care, to understand. Niall grinned, and she grinned back.

He lowered himself over her, his shoulders shuddering as the tip of him brushed against her. He was trying to go slow, to make this romantic or some shit, but that wasn't Niall. She wanted him, not an act he put on to please her. Aisling tipped her head up to him and caught his lower lip between her teeth.

"Give me yourself," she said.

Niall obliged, driving into her with a single stroke. Aisling let out her breath as the fullness consumed her. A warm, delicious stretch spread through her whole body, the kind of stretch that was just this side of pain, the good side, the side where she liked to dance.

He kissed her, his hand behind her head, holding her right where he wanted her. He nipped and sucked as he moved inside her, drawing out with his hips before slamming back into her, filling her completely.

She lifted her knees, angling her body so he could drive himself deeper. The ache in her stomach returned, fiercer than before. She gripped Niall's shoulders, enjoying the way his muscles moved beneath his skin as he held himself above her. He thrust deeper, every stroke a delight.

His lips sought hers, his kisses frenzied, wild. That thin veneer of control he wore like a shield slipped away, and there was Niall, just Niall, beastly and feral and beautiful in his depravity. He took her like a god of wild places, rutting with his goddess under a blanket of stars. He took her with fierce possession, with savage kisses, with nails scratching and teeth bared and all his beautiful malice open for her.

And Aisling swallowed it all, all of him. She rose to her wild fae with her own fire and fury. Around them, the energy swirled, burning through their skin, wrapping them in the threads of their destiny.

I can't believe this is real. I can't believe Niall is real. He's perfect.

The ache spread through her again, growing out from her stomach, shuddering through her limbs. Aisling's mind exploded with color, and the entire universe – stars and galaxies and nebulae – danced across her vision, twinkling between the foliage above her head. The whole world a beautiful, luminous light that emanated from her body.

Niall's mouth closed over her collarbone, and his teeth dug into her skin, drawing blood which he lapped up hungrily. He came with a shudder, pumping inside her as his body rode her until the end. After two final, violent thrusts, he collapsed on top of her, soaked in sweat and completely spent.

They remained like that for several moments. The galaxy on Aisling's eyelids faded from her vision, and she could once again make out the towering forest around her, the sparkling fairy lights, the forgotten food spread across the picnic blanket, and the fae boy who lay on top of her, his hard face slack and content.

Niall rolled off her and gathered her into his arms. "Let's stay like this for a while," he whispered. She nodded, afraid that if she spoke, she would wake up, and this room, this fae, this moment would be another of her dreams.

He's my dream man, and he's perfect. He's mine.

Aisling stared up at the twisting vines entwining the ceiling of this mysterious room. In her prison, she had discovered the last thing she'd ever expected. She'd found love.

Fae and witch – forbidden, but unbreakable. Nothing would come between her and Niall now. Not even Hollythorn House.

32

NIALL

Niall carried Aisling back to her own bed, leaving her clothes abandoned on the forest floor. He laid her out on the sheets, running his hands over her soft skin. He couldn't get enough of her body – whether he was kissing her or whipping her, she was his.

When he'd first entered Hollythorn House – even though he'd been intrigued by her, and her appearance in his dreams – he'd seen Aisling the way any fae saw another they were attracted to; a conquest to be won by seduction or guile or coercion or force. But now, he saw her as something else entirely – as a bond, an unbreakable promise, a shining beacon that made him want to be better for her.

She was his, and he was totally and utterly hers.

All we have in this house is each other.

Niall lay down beside her, stroking her face. She smiled up at him, her skin glowing. The aura of her magic danced around her cheekbone, the blue fire radiating out from her like a supernova about to burst. She'd taken in even more than he'd realized. Her body *surged* with untapped power, and she seemed completely oblivious to it.

"I never thought I'd be happy in this house," she said. "Until you came along."

Niall's heart thundered against his chest.

"I've wanted you ever since I saw you through the mail slot," he told her. "Since I realized the girl in my dreams was real. But you're not her – she's just a dream figure. You're even more amazing."

"You came here to save your brother," she whispered. "And now you've saved me."

Just like that, with those simple words, all Niall's happiness drained away. All this – everything they'd done together – was based on lies. Hers and his. Hers, because she still told her stories that made no sense, because she was hiding the depths of her loneliness behind false tales of the world before. But his deception most of all, because he was pulled in two directions – as much as he loved her and would die for her, he still believed he could use her family's magic to break the Endless Winter.

He still believed he could be worthy of Eamon's love.

Niall had wrapped his lie in a heroic story of the brother he wished he could be, and that lie had become such a truth to him that fae magic couldn't touch it. *If Aisling knew about my desecration of June's grave, and the thorn heart, and the real purpose of my nocturnal wanderings, and the letters I sent to Odiana...*

The words were on the tip of Niall's tongue. He could tell her, rid himself of the guilt that stabbed at his heart, the guilt a fae should never have to carry.

As he opened his mouth to speak, Aisling leaned forward and kissed him, and all the words tumbled away.

NIALL AND AISLING didn't leave her bed for a day, save for when he took a trip down to the kitchens to collect food for dinner.

Between bouts of furious, kinky sex and tender lovemaking, they lay with their bodies entwined and talked about everything and anything. Aisling asked him about his powers.

"So I look blue to you?" Aisling's smile lit up her whole face. "Like a weird blue alien?"

"All witches are alien to me," Niall grinned back at her. "I think you look beautiful."

He didn't tell her that she'd grown more luminous ever since she fixed the regeneration spell, and then again after their time in the forest. He hoped Odiana had sent him a reply, that she might find a way to use Aisling's magic without hurting her. And then everything would be fine.

As the grey sky faded into darkness, Aisling's eyelids started to droop. Her head nodded against Niall's shoulder, and she began to breathe rhythmically.

As soon as he was certain she was asleep, Niall gently eased his arm out from beneath her, placing a pillow beside her to simulate the bulk of his body. Feeling like a complete bastard, he collected the thorn heart from his room and went to check the mail slot.

Nothing.

What the fuck was Odiana playing at?

Niall peered out the window, but the storm clouds had gathered close to the house and it was impossible to see anything beyond the gate. *What's going on out there? Are Eamon and Odiana okay?*

He crept upstairs to the hallway where he found the beach room, set the thorn heart down on the golden sands, and activated the crystal. Nothing happened.

So not the beach, then. But where? Where is this damn witch's heart?

As Niall hurried to the forest room to try there, he passed

alongside a long fissure in the wall. Dark tendrils of inky smoke curled on the surface.

Niall. Come to me, Niall.

The voice from the cracks called to him louder than ever. It was no longer a whisper, but a melodious singsong pulsing inside his brain. It was a woman with an enchanting voice, backed by a chorus of echoes that made it seem as though there were a hundred of her. She spoke to him every time he passed the living room doorway, or under the cracked ceilings of the first floor, and she called to him from the crack behind the dresser in his bedroom.

Niall knelt, holding the thorn heart as close to the crack as he dared. "What do you want?" he murmured, trying not to make a noise Aisling could hear.

The voice didn't answer. She never did. She just kept calling his name, over and over. The thorn heart flared with a hint of blue before falling quiet again. Whatever the voice was, it wasn't the heart of the house.

Ignoring the voice, Niall moved to the library. He tossed the thorn heart onto the desk and pulled out the thin volume he'd found the previous night. It had been tucked behind one of the larger books of domestic spellcasting. It wasn't a grimoire, but a diary. From the dates written above each entry, he could see it had been begun only a few months before the end of the world. It was written in Aisling's grandmother's slanted hand. Niall turned to the first entry.

The news reports are bleak. Alice phoned this evening. The cities are being evacuated as more bombs drop. Alice says they're been directed to go to a nearby camp, but she doesn't think it's as the government is making out. So she's bringing Dan and Bethany here, which might be the most sensible idea my daughter's ever had.

She can't get ahold of Aisling. I've been burning sage and calling her, hoping to give her the message to come here. If anyone can sense my magic without training, it's Aisling.

I'll go to the store tomorrow and buy as much food as I can. I have a feeling we'll be hiding here for a while.

Niall raged as he read. *None of this makes sense. Is this old bat deceiving herself, or did she write it to deceive any fae who might come across it?*

But it holds true to Aisling's stories. Is she in this with her grandmother? Did Aisling write this diary herself? What is she hiding with this delusion?

Niall turned the page to another entry, dated the following day:

I went to the store, but there was no food to be had. Old Mabel wasn't even working the register. The shelves were empty and people inside shoved what little was left into huge trash bags. A man at the door waved a tire iron at me and told me to move on. I gave him a lecture about speaking with proper respect to his elders, which he took in good stride, but he still wouldn't let me inside.

Fine. I have other ways of feeding my coven. It's taken me all morning, but I've figured out a replenishing enchantment for the food stores I already have. I'll need to wait until Alice and Dan get here to activate it, as it will take our combined power to make it work. It's one of the most draining spells I've ever concocted. My strength is gone. But if it keeps us alive, it will be worth it.

The news reports are looking worse and worse, and they don't see what I see – the hooves churning on the horizon, the flash of bone blades in the storm. Ours is not the only realm to be poisoned by the bombs. The Summer Fae are descending in droves, coming for the witches whose magic might save their world.

They won't take mine. I'll die first.

We'll make our last stand here at Hollythorn House. I feel it in my veins. These walls have always protected our family – they've been our fortress against whatever life throws at us.

I can't stop the Slaugh from riding, but I do have an idea on how to keep my coven safe.

And another.

I tried to phone my coven sisters. We need as many witches as we can to make this spell work. The phones are down, so I've had to resort to enchanting their Netflix. Much less accurate, but still effective. They must've seen my flashing message by now and will be on their way.

I hope.

Every word, every memory, was *wrong*. But it was written with such an earnest voice, the deception was remarkable. Niall turned the page, his eyes darting across the neatly-formed lines of text.

The fae have arrived.

We barricaded the house as best we can, but I fear they will break through in a matter of hours, if the radiation doesn't kill us all first.

All we have left is my final spell – dedicated at the altar of my family, my loves.

For them, I enter the flames with happiness, with a heart light as a feather.

For them, I bleed on this altar.

I will keep the walls strong and protect those inside. Alice and Dan and the girls will be safe as long as Hollythorn stands – as long as the altar has its sacrifice – and the power that the fae so desperately seek will be lost to them.

Niall remembered a stone altar at the cemetery. His father had fallen near there. But the witches had not been at that altar when they created the spell. They'd been inside the house. He remembered it distinctly, because—

Hollythorn is *the altar.*

As soon as the thought entered Niall's head, he knew he'd cracked it. Altars had no place in fae magic – for fae, magic was nothing more than a resource; something to be harvested, bartered, and spent when they saw fit. But humans with their poetry and their hungry gods saw magic as a gift from a power beyond their knowing. An altar was a doorway to the divine – and a witch or priest or acolyte had to approach that altar with purity of heart, knowing that to accept a divine gift meant to sever yourself from everything earthly.

To step through the doorway, an altar demanded *sacrifice.*

That was what June did. She sacrificed herself upon the altar of her family – Hollythorn, the seat of her family's power for generations. She stepped through the doorway and severed herself so that they would live. In doing so, she became the heart of the house. And now, the doorway yearned once more. June's magic was selecting another sacrifice.

Aisling.

The magic flowing into her... it was *purification.* It was fattening the lamb before slaughter. She'd been growing in power since Niall stepped through Hollythorn's doors. The house let him in. It knew about their dreams. It thrust them together because it knew she loved him enough to sacrifice herself for him. Perhaps it had planned this with Bethany instead of Niall, but then Bethany died and Aisling was alone, and leaping into the flames to escape loneliness was not a true sacrifice...

The altar demands a sacrifice.

No no no.

You won't take Aisling from me. Never.

Niall roared and kicked the bookshelf. Volumes tumbled down on top of him. Hard corners slammed into him, raising mounds of dust as they thumped on the floor. He grabbed the chair he'd been sitting in and smashed it against the shelves. Chunks of wood flew in all directions, and the house groaned in protest.

"I'll tear you apart with my own hands before I let you take her," he yelled, bringing the chair down again and again until it fell apart into splinters. He was just about to pick up Aisling's chair when something caught his eye.

The shelf behind the grimoires didn't reach quite back to the wall. The recess was shallower. Niall bent down to inspect it. He couldn't believe he'd never noticed it before, but with shelves jammed with books it was impossible to see.

He pressed his fingers against the wood. It didn't take long to locate a spring that pushed back. Niall released the spring and the wooden compartment slid open, revealing a dusty hole containing nothing but a small wooden box.

Niall's blood rushed in his ears as he removed the box and opened the lid. Inside, nestled on a cushion of velvet, was a shriveled black object.

A witch's heart.

June's heart.

The heart of the house.

33

NIALL

The altar demands a sacrifice.

Niall peered down at the leathery heart. He expected to feel something – elation, triumph. But he felt only the bleak cloak of despair.

He'd found the heart of the house, but it was useless. The heart's magic had been spent long ago. The heart had no aura, not a spark of magic remaining. Odiana was wrong – the heart of the house didn't contain the magic, it was the other way around – the heart *gave* magic. The heart *was* the sacrifice.

And the house wanted Aisling to be next.

Just to be certain, Niall removed the heart from the wreath of thorns and placed June's heart inside. He tried every variation he could think of with the crystals and vials, but nothing would make the heart beat again.

Hollythorn needed a new heart.

Above his head, the house groaned again. Niall got down on his hands and knees and picked up the books, stacking them up as best as he could remember. He tossed the pieces of the chair through the dining room door into the void, and replaced it with one of the billiard room chairs, hoping Aisling wouldn't notice.

He picked out the wood splinters from the rug with his fingers, accepting each one that stabbed through his skin as a punishment.

I doomed her. When I walked through that door, I anointed her the sacrificial lamb.

There has to be a way to reverse this. To make the house accept a different sacrifice.

More than anything, Niall wished Odiana was here. Within a minute she would have the whole thing straightened out.

That was it. They needed Odiana. She knew more about witch magic than any other fae, certainly more than Aisling. Odiana would be able to stop the house from taking Aisling, and then they'd be able to use its power to end the suffering of his people. Who cared if Hollythorn perished if Aisling was alive and the fae had all the magic they needed to flourish, and there would no longer be a need to hunt and harvest witches.

The eternal, damnable winter would, at last, be over.

Excitement hummed through his veins. Niall tore out another blank page from Aisling's ledger book and scribbled a note.

Odiana,

I've figured it out. The house is an altar, and to create the heart, it needs a sacrifice. The house must have a sacrifice. It wants to take Aisling; it's feeding her power now to prepare her, but we can't let it. If it takes her, then our chance to use the magic is gone.

If it takes her, I lose her forever.

I need you to come to Hollythorn. I can't figure this out without you. We'll save them together, you and me and Eamon. But you can't kill the witch. She is mine and I protect her. Know that you can take the magic of Hollythorn, but if any fae tries to harm her, I will kill them.

Satisfied, he went out into the hall, crossed the wide

entrance, and tapped the mail slot in the front door. It opened easily, as it had every other time he'd sent Odiana a note.

He tried the handle, but once again, it wouldn't budge. There was no way for him to walk to the gate to see if his previous notes had been removed. Tonight was clear enough to see the plumes of smoke rising from the Summer City once more, but again, no light, no signs of life. He'd never seen anyone close to the house, but then, he didn't watch all the time.

Niall settled for a silent prayer to Hollythorn House as he sent his arrow flying into the gloom.

Please let Odiana find my note. Please let it work so we can end it all, forever.

As soon as the arrow released from his hands, a rush of sickening guilt overwhelmed him. What was he thinking? He'd just handed Odiana – and whoever else she might be working with, including Laneth – all the knowledge they needed to take the house's power. In the right hands, what Niall knew could end the fae reign of terror over the remaining witches. But that wasn't how fae thought. Niall only thought like that because Aisling had got under his skin.

Fae thought only of obtaining more power, more magic for themselves.

Even Odiana would kill Aisling first, ask questions never – she'd do it gladly. Even Eamon would argue that Aisling's life – a witch's life – was forfeit if it brought back the Summer.

No one outside had chosen him. None of them would fight for him.

Only Aisling had chosen him, and he betrayed her.

Panic surged through him. *I've got to get that letter back.* He grabbed the door handle again, twisting it with all his might. It wouldn't budge. Niall planted his feet on both sides of the doorframe, braced himself, and leaned all his weight back.

The door didn't give.

Breathing hard, Niall backed up to the other side of the entrance hall, in front of the ballroom doors. He ran at the door, getting up as much speed as possible. He angled his shoulder at the center of the door and slammed into it, throwing his whole body behind it.

The door didn't even creak.

The house did, though. It moaned and groaned like it was mocking him.

Niall staggered back, pain ricocheting through down his arm. His heart hammered. *I have to fix this. I have to—*

Niall tried to shove his hand through the mail slot. Perhaps he could twist his arm down and grab the door handle from the other side and—

His fingers slammed against an invisible barrier. The house wouldn't let him even attempt it.

Anger bubbled up inside him. *Listen to me, you stupid house. I made a mistake, but I want to fix it. I have to protect her. I'm protecting you, too. If the fae take your sacrifice then there will be nothing left for you. Just let me outside and Aisling will be safe.*

As if in response, a great fork of lightning crackled across the sky, lighting up the windows like an air raid. The house groaned, but the door didn't budge.

Niall slammed his fist into the frosted glass beside the door. Pain arced up his other arm, but the glass didn't even crack. It was as if he'd just punched a brick wall.

Niall sank to his knees, clutching his aching fist. For the first time since his father made him take Eamon's eye, tears pricked the corners of his eyes, as he thought of what he'd done.

Aisling was his dream girl, and he'd handed her over to the fae.

34

AISLING

*A*isling woke up the next morning to grey light pouring in her window. Lightning crackled against the side of the house, shaking the wall. Aisling yawned, and stretched. She couldn't keep the smile off her face.

She threw her arm across the bed, expecting to feel Niall's warm skin and hard muscles. But all she grabbed were cold sheets.

"Niall?" She sat up, casting her eyes around the room.

He wasn't there.

Did I dream yesterday?

All the memories of what they had done together flooded back to her. The picnic, the room with the forest, the mind-blowing sex that didn't even need kink to be real and aching and beautiful, the hours of talking and laughing and entangling themselves between the sheets. She couldn't have dreamed it all, could she?

But where's Niall?

Aisling glanced around the room, more carefully this time. On the table next to the bed, she noticed a small tray containing her breakfast – a cup of tea and a small bowl of porridge. She dipped her finger into the porridge. It was ice cold. So was the tea.

Niall usually woke her up for breakfast. Sometimes he woke her with his head between her legs, or by nudging her lips open with a silver spoon. Today he dumped the tray and left.

What's going on?

Aisling pulled on jeans and a t-shirt and padded along the corridor. "Niall?" She poked her head into the kitchen. "Are you here?"

There was no answer from among the filthy pots and pans.

He wasn't in the greenhouse, either, or the billiard room.

She found him in the library, curled up in the second chintz chair, his head buried in a thick volume on magic. For some unknown reason, he'd replaced his usual chair with one of the uncomfortable leather ones from the billiard room. He didn't look up when she entered.

"There you are," she exclaimed, shaking his shoulder. "I was wondering where you got to. I thought I'd come down and put the forest on the map—"

Niall's head snapped back and his face tightened with rage. Aisling's heart pounded. *Is something wrong with him? Why is he looking at me like that?*

"I came here to read," he growled. "If that's okay with you?"

"Of course it is. This is your house as much as it is mine. You don't need my permission to read in here."

"That's right, I don't."

Aisling's body stiffened. What happened to the Niall from yesterday? The man who had made her feel like a goddess? His whole body dripped with hostility, his icy eyes glaring at her with hatred. It brought her back to the first night, the way he'd stared down at her with such unrivaled disgust that the woman from his dreams could be a *witch*.

"Is this a fae thing? You get all moody and temperamental

after sex?" She jiggled nervously in the doorframe, feeling like a stranger in her own home. "If so, let's stick with your head between my thighs from now on. Just as much fun, none of the drama."

"Last night was a mistake," Niall said without looking up from his book. "Witch and fae shouldn't co-mingle. It won't happen again."

Tears stung at the corners of Aisling's eyes, but she forced them back. She wouldn't give him the satisfaction of knowing he'd got to her.

"Fine," she backed toward the doorway. "I won't disturb you any longer. Thank you for breakfast."

Niall leaned forward. Aisling froze, thinking he was going to embrace her. Instead, Niall snatched the phone receiver from the desk.

"Why do you still have this?" he snapped, waving the mouth-piece in her face.

Why was he asking about the phone *now*? That phone had sat on the desk every day since she could remember. He must've seen it a hundred times, but now he was acting as though she'd deliberately placed it there to antagonize him.

He didn't deserve an answer, but Aisling responded automatically to that dark, commanding tone of his. "Grandmother June had all sorts of friends and social engagements, and mobile phones sometimes didn't work at Hollythorn, so she used the landline instead. I used to sit in the corner here and listen to her cackling away with her friends as she spread neighborhood gossip or exchanged recipes. I keep it here because it reminds me of her. You got a problem with that?"

Niall's eyes narrowed. He gripped the receiver against his chest. "You're talking about back in the human world, before the war, before the fae opened the void."

"Of course."

"Stop lying to me."

"I'm not lying."

"You are. Nothing you say makes any sense." Niall said, his tone accusatory.

"Why not?" Anger bubbled through Aisling's veins, replacing the despair she'd felt when finding him in this foul mood. How dare he talk to her like this, in *her* library?

"Because the nuclear war wiped out life in the human realm fifty-one years ago."

35

AISLING

hat? What is he talking about?

"No, it didn't. It was only four years ago. I have the precise date in my calendar if you want to look it up. I remember it distinctly, because I came to Hollythorn to escape the city—"

Niall shook his head. "That can't be. You can't *remember* it. That would mean you'd have to have been inside this house for more than fifty-one years." He jabbed at the book. "I'm reading here that humans live for maybe eighty years. If your stories were true, you'd be a grey-haired woman by now. You weren't alive when the war began."

"All this time, you thought I've been lying to you?"

"I'm saying that what you've told me can't possibly be true."

"Then that makes two of us." She glared back. "I've been in this house for fourteen hundred and twenty-one days. *That's* the truth. Now, you want to talk about lies? You're a fae, so you're not supposed to lie, but you've been keeping something from me. Why have you really been sneaking around the house at night?"

Niall slammed his book shut and threw it at the wall. Aisling flinched as it bounced off the shelves and clattered to the floor, the pages splaying open. "How come you've never tried to get out of this house?" he demanded, his hands balled in fists as he approached her. "How come you've never looked at ways to harness the magic buried in these walls to make your own escape?"

"I don't know how. It takes a whole coven – at least three witches working magic together – to pull off a spell like Grandmother June's. I never saw what they did that night – Bethany and I hid in the pantry. All the words in all these books can't make me into that kind of witch. I haven't had the practical experience." Aisling narrowed her eyes. "You can blame yourself for that. You and your queen took my family from me."

Niall jabbed a finger at the book. "It's all right here, Aisling. All of it. You could have used the magic from the house. The power in these walls could cast any kind of spell you want. You could have blown up the entire fae realm, got rid of the lot of us. You could have raised your family from the dead. So why didn't you? Why didn't you use the power you had, while you had the chance?"

"What do you mean, while I had the chance? I'm still here —" Her heart stuttered as she caught the agony behind his eyes. "What have you done, fae?"

Niall's hand flew to the hilt of his sword, his fingers wrapping around his brother's eye. He didn't answer.

He sneered, and the cruel cock of his mouth told her everything she needed to know.

"I don't believe you. You're not this cruel," she screamed at him, her heart shattering into a million pieces.

"I am fae," he said simply.

"No." Aisling's breath trembled. She stepped forward and grabbed his shoulders. "You're not. You're *mine.*"

She pressed her lips to his.

She *tasted* his cruelty – a tangy bite of tartness on his tongue, tinged with the ghost of the blood he'd spilled. She melted into him, drinking her fill, taking his darkest secrets into herself until she swelled with them – sucking out the poison that came between them.

Niall's wrong if he thinks he can push me away with words.

Guy taught her never to go into a kink scene with anger or hurt in her heart, that those feelings would send her over the edge into an abyss from which he could not save her. But Aisling had fallen into Niall's abyss a long time ago.

She knew exactly what he was doing – this was the stunt he tried to pull in the laundry. He was trying to make her hate him. She didn't know why.

"You need to run away," Niall choked out as his lips devoured hers. "I'll hurt you. I've already hurt you."

"So hurt me."

His fingers dug into her skin.

"Hurt me, Niall. Make me cry. That's what you want, isn't it?"

He roared as he flung out an arm, shoving everything off the desk – books and paperweights and pens and that damn red telephone crashed to the floor. Before Aisling could draw another breath, Niall threw her down on the wood surface, planting his hands on either side of her, trapping her within the cage of his body.

"Don't push me, witch," he hissed.

She kissed him again, bruising her lips on his teeth. He returned her kiss with a wicked tongue and hate spilling from his eyes. He was not gentle or kind, but his possession had her so needy that she moaned against his ferocious lips. He kissed her like he would bring down war upon her body. It was the opposite of the forest, and Aisling loved it. She *loved* him like this, wretched and undone for her.

Niall used his knees to shove open her thighs, grinding against her with urgent, warlike lust. She scratched her nails down his back, digging into his skin deep enough to draw blood, and she loved the way his body shuddered as his blood slid through her fingers.

I can hurt you right back.

Niall tore her clothes away with one hand. He growled low in his throat at the sight of her, naked for him, tilting her hips for him, bruised lips parted and desperate for him. She knew he wanted her to believe he was doing this because he hated her, because he wanted to hurt her, but she saw the raw need in his eyes.

He needs to hurt because he's hurting.

So she fought him. She fought against his restraint even though she knew it was pointless, even though she didn't want to be anywhere else in the world. She struggled and she wriggled and she cried because he needed to be a monster. He needed to feel wrong and guilty and twisted, and she would give him whatever he needed.

Niall slammed her wrists over her head with such force the wooden desk splintered. With the roar of a wild beast, he impaled her with his cock. It hurt oh so good. This was so different from last night in the forest. That was Niall and this was Niall too, and she loved both of them.

He bit down on her earlobe as he thrust into her. So big, so hard, so angry. Each slam of his hips shuddered the desk and sent her closer to the edge.

He slid his fingers into her hair, balling it up in his hand and yanking until tears sprung in her eyes. The pain rushed her body, giving her the sharp edge she needed to fall into oblivion.

Her orgasm tore through her, not an undoing this time but a *stampede*, a fucking herd of animals running through her veins to escape a predator, their blood boiling with adrenaline, their hearts thudding with fear. That was what it was to have pleasure ripped from your body by Niall – it was beyond control, beyond pain. It was pure animal instinct.

"Thank you," she whispered, her nails digging into his arms. "Thank you for your hurt."

Niall stared down at her, his face twisted as he realized what she'd done. But he was too far gone. The stampede sent him over the edge of the cliff. He threw his head back and roared with anguish as he slammed into her, filling her completely.

His cry bounced across the high-ceilinged room. Before Aisling could say anything more, he tore himself from her body, turned on his heel, and stormed from the room, slamming the library door with such force the house groaned in protest.

36

NIALL

There was nowhere in the house Niall could go to escape the guilt that gnawed inside him for the horrible things he'd said to Aisling and the even worse things he'd done.

He ran anyway, up the stairs, past the doors that led to the opulent bedroom suites and the ladies' drawing room. Past the gilded portraits of Aisling's ancestors, who frowned at him from their lofty heights.

You're an intruder on our altar, they seemed to say to him. *You shouldn't be here.*

You're right. I shouldn't be here.

Niall headed for the forest room. *I'll escape into the woods. Perhaps if I travel deep enough, I'll lose myself.* But when he yanked open the door, all he found was an ordinary bathroom – a marble sink and pale pink towels hanging over the bath.

Hollythorn House had a sick sense of humor.

Niall flung open a random door at the end of the hall and ducked inside, slamming it shut behind him. He found himself in the largest bedroom he'd seen in the house, containing not just an enormous four-poster bed, but a sitting room decorated in plush velvet.

He'd been in this room yesterday, only it had been on the opposite side of the hall. He'd taken the pillows from the bed to use in Aisling's picnic. Was that only yesterday? It felt like a century ago, when he believed it was possible to be happy.

As Niall stepped into the room, the floor stretched beneath him, pulling the wall with the window away from him, as if it didn't want him to see. A long crack ran along the wall behind the velvet chaise lounge. Niall stood in front of it and stared into the blackness. Inky tendrils of smoke curled out from the edges, and he stepped back before one of them could graze his skin. The familiar, singsong voice called to him through the crack.

Niall, come to me, Niall.

Niall yanked the dagger from his boot and sliced at the tendrils, hacking and slashing at the wall. As he drew back his blade, he saw the void had eaten it – all that remained was an inch of bone above the hilt and a curl of smoke.

Niall threw himself down on the bed, his eyes finding more black cracks on the ceiling – a spiderweb of darkness ensnaring the entire room. Aisling had been right when she said that these second-story rooms would be the next to go. No wonder they slept in the servant's quarters, ceiling rain and all.

He didn't understand this feeling that clenched his stomach. By all rights, he should have been ecstatic. The note he'd sent Odiana would save his brother, not to mention the whole of his race. They would keep Laneth from taking the crown.

All Niall wanted to do was take the letter back, to find a way to make it right with Aisling, and stop the fae from getting inside Hollythorn and destroying everything she'd given her life to protect. But there was no way for him to fix it, and so he was trapped here, trapped with his guilt.

Trapped on the altar as his dream girl became a sacrifice.

When Aisling'd found him in the library, all that guilt had coalesced inside him, and he longed to tell her everything, to spill his awful secrets and be rid of them. But he couldn't. The words wouldn't come. What had come was his rage – the same rage that burned in his veins on the battlefield, that made him crave torn flesh and warm blood.

Rage at his helplessness.

Rage because the only way to stop her from becoming the sacrifice was to take away her ability to give her life out of love.

If she didn't love him – and how could she love someone so twisted and cruel? – she couldn't lay down her life on the altar for him.

Niall watched the tears pool in the edges of Aisling's eyes and hated himself, but not enough to admit what he'd done.

He betrayed her without a thought.

He thought she made him a better person.

He was wrong.

And then there was what Aisling said, about coming to the house as a child. Despite what he'd yelled at her in the library, he didn't think she was lying anymore. So what did that mean? How could Aisling have spent four years in the house when the house had been on the edge of the void for over fifty?

"Meerrrw?" Two black paws landed on his chest. A wet nose butted his chin. Niall's hands reached for the cat, expecting it to rend his skin with claws and teeth. Instead, Widdershins yielded under his touch. He settled down on Niall's chest, his body vibrating with the force of his purr.

Niall stroked Widdershins' fur with the ferocity the cat loved. Widdershins dug his claws into Niall's shoulder and started kneading, his rumbling purr shuddering through his tiny cat body.

As Niall scratched Widdershins under his chin, a thought

occurred to him. Something Aisling had said to him the first day he was here, "*...he doesn't seem to age...*"

Widdershins was still a kitten, with kittenish habits. In Niall's timeline, the cat should be dust. In Aisling's, he should have been loping around like a grand middle-aged cat and sleeping on all the good furniture, not chasing strings of yarn across the ballroom.

Widdershins disappeared for days at a time. Sometimes he came back with objects that couldn't possibly be in the house. Often, his fur was covered in wheat stalks. And he was far too healthy and boisterous to be older, especially since he hadn't had something called 'a vet visit' in years...

Niall sat up, staring into the crack again. The void was devouring the house, piece by piece. It was altering the spaces, creating rooms where there had never been rooms before, moving the bathroom around, making storage closets the size of football fields and forests and beaches. If it could alter all that, could it not also alter *time?*

Niall pulled June's old pocket watch from the fold of his tunic and tapped the face, watching the second hand swing wildly back and forth.

Was time passing differently inside the house? It sounded impossible. They had day and night, just as the outside world did. And yet... it could explain their different timelines. It could be another weapon in Hollythorn's arsenal against the fae – the house would keep Aisling alive for longer to be its guardian. Its priestess.

That had to be the answer. It was the only explanation he could think of that made sense. Odiana would be proud of his deduction.

Niall threw himself out of bed. *Wait until I tell Aisling. She won't believe—*

He was halfway to the door before he remembered. He

couldn't tell Aisling, because currently, she wasn't talking to him. And he couldn't blame her. He'd been cruel. He'd never been cruel to her before. When he was around her, that side of his personality – the side that was pure fae – twisted into something that couldn't fathom cruelty. He blossomed under her love.

Until he'd messed it all up. Because as much as he loved her, *really* loved her, he couldn't tell her the truth. He couldn't bear to find out what she'd think of him if she learned what he'd done.

"There's nothing else for it," Niall scooped up Widdershins and headed for the hall. "You and I are going to figure this out on our own."

37

AISLING

Niall didn't come for dinner that night.

Aisling could hear his footsteps pacing back and forth across the upper story. Sometimes he ran, other times he slowed his pace or stood still for long periods. Occasionally, she heard a door slam or Widdershins' excited *meerrrw*. Her cat hadn't joined her for dinner, either. Were they playing together up there?

Was Niall hurting Widdershins?

Aisling peered out into the entrance hall just as Widdershins streaked past on the landing above, his tail kinked like a periscope as he gave little chirps of delight. He wasn't in pain. He was playing a game.

Who the fuck is this Niall who accuses me of lying, fucks me hard, and then plays games with a cat?

If I didn't know it was impossible, I'd say he wasn't Niall at all but some other fae disguised with glamour.

If Aisling were a braver person, she would go upstairs and yell at him, try to force to truth out of him. But after all the things he said in the library, after that darkness in his eyes when he fucked her, Aisling couldn't face him. She knew he was trying to drive her away because of his own guilt, but it still *hurt*. She couldn't bear to see his face twisted with rage like that; rage directed at her.

Aisling ate alone, hunched over a book in the corner of the library. She left Niall's plate of roasted vegetables on the first landing of the grand staircase, secretly hoping Widdershins would find it first and gobble it all up. It would serve Niall right.

She turned the page in her book, the words barely registering. Anger bubbled through her veins. Her stomach rumbled. *This is pointless. I need snacks.*

The thought of going to the kitchen and possibly seeing Niall there made her feel ill. *Maybe I'll wait here until he gets tired and goes to bed...*

Resolve hardened her. *Screw him. It's my house. He invaded it. I can go to the kitchen and eat whatever I want.*

Pretending she was braver than she felt, Aisling swung her body out of bed, flung on a dirty sweatshirt, and trudged down to the kitchen. She kept her eyes trained on the floor in front of her and her ears focused on listening out for Niall.

She reached the kitchen door with no sighting. Aisling pushed the door open with her foot, stood in the threshold, and listened. The only sound in the room was the steady *drip drip drip* of the sink faucet.

"Thank the gods for small miracles," she said, and went to the pantry. She grabbed the last two Twinkies, tore open the wrappers, and shoved both sugary treats into her mouth. She found an empty bowl and filled it up with an entire bag of M&Ms, and then a package of mini Mars bars. Taking her food to the table, she reached for a bottle of Scotch above the sink. She remembered a time Bethany visited her in the city, sobbing after her first high school boyfriend dumped her. Aisling had set the same junk food in front of her and handed her a glass of Scotch.

I told her there's nothing like whisky to wash down a heartbreak-induced sugar binge.

I'm wiser than my years.

Outside, lightning crackled against the side of the house, causing the walls to shake briefly, and the candle beside her to flicker. Aisling set down her glass and peered out the window, into the tempest that raged in what had once been the back yard.

The storm grew worse over the course of the day, the lightning strikes larger and more frequent. The waves crashing from the edge of the void sent showers beating against the side of the house. Darkness raged in the heart of the storm, a great black eye that had grown larger and closer and more menacing. And what was really odd was that she realized she could no longer see the wooden spires of the Summer City glowing on the skyline. It was as if all the lights had been put out.

Aisling squinted into the storm. There was something else out there, too. At the edge of the garden wall, she noticed a shadow moving. She squinted harder into the gloom.

It was a fae warrior with his bow drawn, the arrow aimed through the fence at the front door. Aisling gasped as he loosed the arrow. It bit the air, soaring through the gap in the fence, but as it neared the house the wood burned to ash.

The fae turned away, consulting someone in the shadows with angry gestures. Aisling felt relieved, but then she heard a creak, almost as though the gate had swung open.

But that's impossible. Niall said only he'd have the strength to—

KNOCK KNOCK KNOCK.

Aisling dropped the bowl. It smashed on the tiles, scattering candy across the kitchen floor. *That sounded like...*

KNOCK KNOCK KNOCK.

...like someone knocking on the front door.

38

AISLING

That was how it had started with Niall. The knocking on the door. Why had the door opened that day? If the house had never let Niall inside, then she wouldn't be feeling this pain.

Aisling stared at the kitchen wall, her mind reeling. *Has the house been trying to tell me all along that I'm better off without him?* Niall said the voice talking to him was telling him to throw himself into the void.

The house knew it fucked up.

It knew it let something inside that shouldn't be here.

Hollythorn House was trying to correct its error.

So what was this new knocking? Was it the house, finally figuring out how to correct its mistake? Or was it the fae, here to strip every last shred of magic from Hollythorn before enslaving her?

Only one way to find out. Aisling swung off the chair and raced into the hall.

As her feet pounded across the marble, Niall emerged from the top of the staircase. Aisling dared a glance up at him. He looked terrible, his face blotchy, his eyes ringed with dark circles. He walked hunched over, not standing tall and proud the way he usually did. He looked in every way the defeated man as he padded downstairs.

I don't care, she told herself, turning back to the door. *He deserves to suffer.*

KNOCK KNOCK KNOCK.

Niall reached the bottom of the staircase and came to stand beside her, his eyes glued to the door, which rattled on its hinges from the force of the knocking. The space in between them felt like a chasm – the energy that usually bound them acting more like charged magnets, forcing them apart. Niall's fingers brushed hers, but she yanked her hand away, shuffling a few extra inches away from him.

"The knocking?" he whispered to her. Aisling flashed him a filthy look. This wasn't about him. It was between her and Hollythorn House. She was about to tell him to piss off when through the frosted glass, she noticed a shadow pass the window. *Someone's out there.*

Fear closed her throat. More than anything, she longed for the comfort of Niall's embrace, the way being in his arms made her feel safe. But he'd wrecked it all, and she could never feel safe again.

Niall stepped forward, his arm outstretched for the door handle.

"Don't do that," she snapped. "We don't know who it is, and I don't trust the house to know best anymore."

Before Niall could reply, Aisling turned on her heel and ran for the drawing room. She heard Niall's footsteps on the marble behind her. She longed to turn around and run toward him, to feel his warmth easing her pounding heart. Again, she reminded herself that it wasn't possible. She would never again feel comfort from Niall.

In the drawing room, Aisling lit the lantern and yanked aside the curtain. She squinted out into the grey gloom. There on the porch was a fae woman, old and bent and gnarled, banging on the door like she was desperate to break it down.

The woman slammed her hands against the glass, yelling something into the dark room. Her white hair streamed over her shoulders in matted waves, and her ice-blue eyes were ringed with lines and dark circles. She was the most beautiful woman Aisling had ever seen, and as she tossed her head back and her perfect lips opened to yell something at the house, Aisling realized tears streamed down her cheeks.

Aisling strained to listen to the fae's words, but of course she could not hear through the deep magic of the house. Whatever she was yelling, the fae woman looked frantic, as though it were a matter of life and death.

Aisling grabbed a paper from the desk and scribbled a message. She pressed the paper up to the glass and banged on the window. But the fae was so occupied with the door, she didn't even notice. Aisling glanced back at Niall, who'd wandered in behind her. She didn't want to defer to him, but she felt helpless, unsure of what she should do. To her surprise, she saw that Niall's face had gone bone white.

"Niall?" she whispered. He didn't reply. Aisling waved her hand in front of his eyes, but he didn't even blink. He just kept staring wide-eyed at the woman, his face stricken with some deep-rooted pain.

"Odiana?" he whispered.

That one single word drove all the air from Aisling's lungs. She looked back at the woman, her tiny fists pounding against the front door, her face twisted with fear and desperation.

Niall had spoken often of his friend Odiana, a scholar who had stood by him even when his family had fallen in status. But how could it be her? Niall had lied about everything, so surely he'd made up this girl as well.

Besides, the girl Niall described had been a year older than he. This woman was *ancient*, the oldest fae she'd ever seen. Lines crinkled at the corners of her eyes, and her white hair was streaked with grey above her ears.

"Niall," Aisling shook his shoulder, her skin crawling from the contact. "That can't be Odiana. She's too old. Niall, can you even hear me?"

"It's her," Niall shook his head. He grabbed Aisling's hand from his shoulder and squeezed it, so hard that he cracked her knuckles. "I don't know what has happened, but I'm telling you, that's my friend out there. Aisling, we have to talk to her."

"It could be a trap." She yanked her hand away. *How dare he touch her, here, now?*

"It's not. It's not a trap. It's Odiana!" Before she could stop him, Niall ran from the drawing room. Aisling took off after him. *He's going to do something stupid.*

"Niall, wait, we have to think about this!"

She skidded around the corner, her feet sliding on the smooth marble. Niall was already at the door, his hand grabbing the door handle.

Aisling sucked in her breath, her fear rooting her in place. *The house will stop him. The house wants to keep me safe.*

The door handle twisted in Niall's hand. It clicked. Niall flung it open.

Aisling held her breath. She expected the woman to whip out some kind of weapon and blast them both away. She inched toward the wall where her sword hung, ready to defend herself. But the woman took a painfully slow step forward, her foot landing on the marble with a resounding *CLAP*.

She stood frozen, her eyes fixed on Niall with a haunted expression.

Aisling expected Niall to fling his arms around the woman,

but he didn't. Of course he wouldn't show emotion. Once a fae, always a fae.

"Odiana, is that really you? What happened?"

"Niall?" she gasped, holding her hand to her mouth. "What's happened to you? You're still... you don't look a day older than when you left."

"I don't understand. Obviously, I look the same. I've only been gone a few months."

Odiana shook her head. Tears sprang in the corners of her eyes. "No, Niall. You've been gone ninety-nine years."

39

NIALL

Niall sprung back from the door, yanking his hand from the door handle as though the metal stung him. Behind him, he heard Aisling gasp.

Ninety-nine years. He rolled the number around in his head, unable to comprehend it.

Odiana couldn't lie outright like that. This wasn't a fae deception. And he could believe the evidence of his eyes. It was Odiana standing in front of him, but not the same young woman he'd left behind. Now her beautiful face was pinched and stretched. Fae were blessed with long life and youthful looks, but if ninety-nine years had passed...

That meant the house slowed time down inside its walls, even more than it had for Aisling. The few precious months he'd had with her had cost him ninety-nine years from his life.

This is my punishment for my deception, my malice. This is what the house was trying to tell me. Maybe it wasn't trying to get me to kill myself, but to step back into time and have my life again. But it would've been a life without Aisling...

Niall's stomach churned as the full weight of the revelation crushed down upon him. His brother... the lights in the Summer

City burning out again, those plumes of smoke... what had happened in all those years while he was gone? While he'd been inside the house doing... what he'd been doing with Aisling, his whole life had been flashing forward around him.

He missed it all. He missed *everything.*

Niall leaped forward and grabbed Odiana's hand, trying to pull her further inside. Her skin felt different from how he remembered, not as smooth or supple. "Odiana, please. You must tell me – what became of my brother?"

Odiana yanked her hand away. "I'm not coming inside there," she declared, wrinkling her nose in a way that was pure Odiana.

"Just tell me, please. What about Eamon?"

She screwed her eyes up, as though it was painful to speak of. "He's dead."

Niall's whole world stopped.

"What happened?" he growled.

"You weren't here, is what happened," she yelled. "You should have let him die that day, Niall. That was right and fair and just. The guilt of it ate him alive, you know. In the end, he volunteered to go first."

"To go first? For what? Tell me." Niall shook her arm so hard she cried out.

"The Eternal Winter grew darker, colder. All the underground crops we were growing – the fungi and the moss and the grasses – they withered and died. We had no food. We were so cold. I couldn't make the potions to maintain Eamon's glamour. So very cold..." Odiana hugged her arms around herself. "In the end, no one had the strength to stop Laneth. If you were there, you would have stopped him. You would have made us fight. But you weren't there and Laneth was and we were so *hungry.* He convinced Slaugh and court fae to follow him. He said the Summer Queen had failed us, and it wasn't a lie. He slaughtered the queen and her loyal fae and threw them on the fires until they were nicely roasted. We cut their flesh away and we feasted. We feasted and we danced as we hadn't in years. But Laneth kept Eamon all for himself. He wouldn't give me even a rib, even a tooth. He ate Eamon and the queen, bones and heart and all."

My brother. Niall gripped the door handle as Odiana's words became real, became a truth that made him hate the truth, that made him long for a lie that wouldn't hurt as much as this. For once, all the rage in him stilled. All that was Niall stripped away from his bones, pulled out to sea on a wave of grief. His lungs filled with dark water. He couldn't breathe and it felt right, it felt right that he shouldn't breathe because Eamon didn't get to breathe.

A world without Eamon in it seemed inconceivable. Niall didn't know what to do with his hands, which trembled, or his eyes, which leaked salty tears. He did not know how to say the things that twisted in his mind or how to plug the hole that gaped in his chest.

Everything I did to save him has been for this – so Laneth could feast on his flesh.

Now Laneth has his power.

"He ate Niall's brother? Classic fae move," Aisling said. But she moved toward him and placed her hand on his arm. The warmth of her fingers sent a fresh wave washing over him, dragging him under grief's wretched spell.

Aisling knows this pain four times over, and she survived it. She is so much stronger than me.

Odiana ignored Niall's pain and Aisling's comment. "Laneth is king now. It's done. It can't be changed. But he can't control Eamon's magic, especially not now that he's consuming all those magical objects you sold him. He doesn't want anyone else to have magic but him. Now all he has to do is touch someone and he can pull their magic into himself. We're all walking ghosts now, just one magical spell away from death."

"That's not possible."

But even as he spoke the words, Niall remembered. His brother gave Niall some of his power when Niall took his eye. And if Eamon could share his magic with Niall, could he have also *taken* magic?

Odiana held up her hands, turning her palms toward Niall for him to see. His eyes widened as he saw. Or rather, didn't see. The yellow aura that glowed around the fae should be immutable, unchanging. But Odiana had only enough of the Summer Queen's magic for a single, tiny spell. And then she would be dead.

"I'm lucky," she said. "I still have a little left, enough to keep me alive. So many have died. That's why the fires still burn—"

"He can't do this to you." *If you'd been there, instead of inside Hollythorn House, you could have stopped this.* Guilt crashed against Niall's grief, swirling into a maelstrom that sucked him down into sunless depths. Sucked him back out the other side, where he could rage once more. Rage at himself. He'd been so selfish when he thrust that note through the door. He should have been more careful. In the wrong hands, that information...

"I'm going to find a way to stop this," he insisted.

Tears sprung in Odiana's eyes. "It's too late. He has your note and he's coming for Hollythorn House, Niall. He's assembled the Slaugh host for their most deadly ride of all. Desperate fae who he tempts with the promise of unlimited power, of a fae kingdom that will remake the Earth. Laneth will use his magic to break through Hollythorn's defenses, and they'll take your witch before the sacrifice."

"What sacrifice?" Aisling's eyes narrowed at Niall. "What note? What's she talking about?"

Odiana ignored her. "Laneth will have all the power he

needs to take not just Hollythorn's magic, but the magic of the void itself."

"That's insane."

"I know, but he's insane, so it makes sense." Odiana glanced over her shoulder. "I don't have much time. He has guards all around the house so none of us can get to you to warn you. I managed to take out one, but I don't have long before they discover his body."

"Odiana, you have to listen to me. Go get all the fae who are loyal to the Summer Queen, as many as you can. Talk to the warriors in my old regiment." Niall pulled out the hilt of his broken dagger and handed it to her. "Show them this and they'll know I'm still alive. We need anyone willing to stand up to Laneth. Bring them here and I'll find a way to let you inside. Hollythorn will be safe for you, I promise. Once you're inside, we'll use Aisling's magic to stop him. Our only chance is to use up the last of the magic before Laneth gets his hands on it."

"Niall, I don't think I'll find anyone. I have to—" Odiana's mouth hung open. Her whole body stiffened. She stared down in surprise.

Niall's eyes followed her gaze. An arrow pierced Odiana's chest, the bright-red tip poking through the front of her robes, the shaft ringed with blood. She made a gagging sound as she gripped the shaft with both hands, her eyes wide. Pain flooded her face.

"No!" Niall reached for her, meaning to sweep her into the house. Odiana toppled over, hitting the porch with a horrible CRACK. She didn't move as she rolled on her side, her piercing eyes staring up at the grey sky.

Now the rage boiled inside Niall. *This is senseless.* Odiana was probably the greatest mind the fae had produced in centuries, and now she was dead because she'd tried to warn him.

I'm a curse, a poison to anyone who cares about me.

From the gate at the front of the path, Niall caught sight of a figure. Wearing the tooth-mail of a Slaugh, the fae's long fingers gripped an empty bow, his eyes burning with triumph as he regarded the crumpled body of Odiana. He nodded at Niall and nocked another arrow. He raised the bow and drew the string back to his ear, a sadistic smile spreading across his face as he faced Aisling.

Niall slammed the door shut just as the fae loosed the arrow. The door shuddered as the arrow buried itself in the wood, splintering the door directly in front of Aisling's face. Aisling cried out, leaping back.

Niall grabbed her, wrapped his arms around her, and knocked her to the ground. He heard the glass shatter, shards skidding across the marble floor.

Aisling lifted her head, her eyes resting on the arrow quivering from the foot of the balustrade, where she had been standing only a moment ago. She blinked, her eyes widening as she stared at him with love he didn't deserve and could no longer accept.

"You saved my life," she whispered.

"Yours is the only life worth saving." Niall felt the warmth of her, the solidity of her. She was all he had left that was real and good and true, and he would lay down his life for her. "You're everything to me."

Aisling's aura swelled with blue light, and the magic swirled around him as the words left his mouth. He'd never meant anything as much as he meant those words. And even if she never forgave him for his lies, even if she refused to talk to him or touch him ever again, it was okay. For he had stripped himself of all the bullshit and avarice, and right here, right now, he was just Niall. She had given him this truth, and that could never be undone.

His arms around her grew heavy, weighed down by the hope

that surged through his body as she stared up at him with those huge brown eyes. He could see her weighing up his sins – even the sins she didn't yet know about – against what she felt for him.

Would it be enough? He wanted it to be, so so bad.

Aisling pursed her lips. She leaned forward. Niall was certain she would spit in his face. *It's the least I deserve.*

But she pressed her lips to his, her tongue seeking out his own. Niall deepened the kiss, pouring all his emotion into it, giving her back all the good that she had given to him. The magic surged around them, wrapping them in heat.

Aisling broke the kiss. "I love you, Niall," she whispered against Niall's skin.

"You shouldn't love me. I've done a horrible thing, Aisling. I may not have lied to you, but I deceived you about so many things." The words poured out of him, all the things he'd been holding back and dancing around, all the truths that had burrowed like rats into his soul. He told her about the thorn heart Odiana gave him, and how he'd been sneaking around the house at night trying to find its heart. He told her about sending Odiana the notes, and how confused and angry he was about the things she'd said and the things he read that didn't make sense. His words hitched as he spoke of how he'd figured out what the house was and what it wanted from her.

"I don't understand. The house isn't an altar. The altar is in the cemetery—"

"These walls are the altar of your family. They demand purification. They demand sacrifice. That's why the house let me in," Niall wiped a silken curl from her cheek. "You needed to fall in love, or you would have nothing to sacrifice."

Aisling shuddered, burying her face in Niall's shoulder. "This fucking *sucks.*"

"It does. It does suck. And I've made it a hundred times

worse. Laneth is coming for you, and all because I forgot what a fae would do for power. I should have realized what would happen if I sent that note, but you've made me a different person. Laneth will come and destroy the Hollythorn and take all your magic for himself."

"You were trying to save your brother," she sniffed. "I understand that now. And you were trying to save me."

"Was I? Or was I trying to save myself?"

"I think the fact that I don't currently have an arrow through my heart because of you answers your question." Aisling grinned. "I love you, Niall. I don't like being deceived, but I forgive you for it. Just don't ever do it again."

"Yes, ma'am." Despite the gravity of their situation, his heart had never felt lighter. There had to be a way to undo the damage he'd done.

"As much as I'd love to lie here with you all day..." Niall gestured to the arrow sticking out of the staircase. Aisling nodded. Niall sat back and helped her to her feet.

"How did that arrow break the glass?" Aisling reached for the arrow. It looked different from Niall's arrows. The surface shimmered with tendrils of green smoke. Niall had never seen green magic before. "Nothing should be able to get in here."

Niall slapped her hand away. "Don't touch that. It's been charged with Laneth's magic. It's powerful enough to penetrate the shield that protects the house, especially now that it's weakened."

"How is it weakened?"

"The house has been giving you the power, so it doesn't have as much as it once did. I've noticed your aura growing ever since you worked on the replenishment spell. I think the house has been siphoning power into you, and now that it knows the fae are coming, it's giving you the power you need to fight them off. But that weakens its own defenses. Even if it had its full power, I don't know how long it could stop these arrows or anything else Laneth wants to throw at us."

"Shit." Aisling stared at her hands, trying to see for herself what Niall saw.

"Shit is right." Niall slumped to the floor, burying his face in his hands. "I did this. I doomed us both."

"I've been doomed for years," Aisling said. "It's nothing new. I've been living like a ghost between these walls. It wasn't until you came along and showed me joy that I even saw I had a life worth fighting for. So, stop with the self-deprecating bullshit and give me a bit of that fae bossiness. We've got an army of magically-charged fae bearing down on us. What are we going to do?"

"I know exactly what we're going to do." Niall balled his hands into fists and glared at the hole in the glass. "We're going to fight."

40

NIALL

That night, curled up beneath the sheets of Aisling's grandmother's bed with his witch in his arms, Niall dreamed of Aisling.

In his dream, he stood at the window of the library, gazing out into the ruined garden beyond. Aisling stood on the lawn, ten feet from the window, her face downcast as she collected dried, rotten branches from what had once been a rosebush. The thorns pricked at her hands and fingers so that thin rivers of blood streaked across her pale skin.

Right behind her, standing near the garden wall, was the hooded shadow.

Niall banged on the window, calling her name over and over. But as loud as he called her and as much as he tried to get her attention, he could not make Aisling lift her head to see him.

Panic rose in his chest. If she was outside, then how would she get back in? Did this mean she'd found a way out without him? Was he destined to live out his days in Hollythorn House alone? That didn't even bother him. At least with the walls separating them, he couldn't hurt her.

What bothered him was the shadow creeping closer. If the shadow attacked her, he couldn't stop it.

Niall spun around, searching the library for something he could use to reach her. He grabbed the old red telephone on the desk and hurled it against the window. The glass broke. Cracks cascaded across the surface like spiderwebs. But instead of being clear, these cracks were black – a dark, threatening black. A black with form, with substance.

The void.

There was no time to think. The shadow inched closer to Aisling. It was standing right behind her, black hands raised to remove its hood. Niall flung himself at the window, desperate to reach Aisling before the shadow got her. His skin collided with the void, and he was burning, his body tearing into a hundred tiny pieces. The pain exploded inside him, and—

Niall opened his eyes, blinking until his vision focused on the lattice of cracks across the ceiling of the master bedroom. Aisling snuggled into his armpit, but even her warmth couldn't penetrate the chill creeping through his body.

Was it his imagination, or had more cracks appeared since yesterday?

Niall sat up, rubbing his eyes. He had to squint to focus on the tiny window, now fifty feet away from the foot of the bed on the other end of the stretched room. Outside, he saw the spires of the Summer City piercing the soot-soaked sky.

No longer shrouded in ice, the city gleamed with brilliant light.

The light of a thousand fires burning it all to the ground.

Niall's nostrils burned. An unmistakable scent permeated the room. He recognized it from his days in the army. It hung thick in the air as the Slaugh lined up for their ride. It clung to their skin as they raised their swords and bore down on their foe.

The scent of blood.

The fae were coming.

41

AISLING

That night, Niall locked himself in the kitchen, forbidding her to enter as he concocted some kind of fae delicacy that Aisling bet would taste like grass and mushrooms. All Niall's fae food tasted like grass and mushrooms. They weren't exactly known for their great culinary traditions, unless you counted raw witch hearts, which she did not.

While her stomach growled with trepidation, Aisling sat in the library and watched the fae army surround Hollythorn's fence. They were dressed in the same tooth-mail and trousers Niall wore. They walked with curved bone swords drawn and a quiver of arrows each across their backs.

They walked with faces tight with determination.

Behind them, the horizon glowed with brilliant fire.

The clouds swirled and shifted, converging in a way that felt almost deliberate. Aisling leaned back in the chair, peering deep into the grey cloud. *What is that?* She touched the glass window, tracing the design with her finger.

That cloud looks like a woman's face...

The phone on the desk started to ring.

42

AISLING

*B*riiiiing, Briiiiing.

Aisling whirled around, the fae outside instantly forgotten. She stared at the red phone, her heart pounding against her chest.

It will stop in a second.

Briiiiing, Briiiiing.

It kept on ringing and ringing, the shrill sound reverberating through the lofty room. Aisling crept toward the desk, her throat closing with fear. She reached out and grabbed the cord from the phone and traced it back until a small plug fell into her fingers.

Shit.

The phone's not even plugged in.

Nevertheless, it kept ringing, the red receiver jingling on its perch.

Aisling's heart raced.

She squeezed her eyes shut as she wrapped her hands around the receiver. It thrummed between her fingers, warm to the touch.

Slowly, sucking in her breath, Aisling raised the receiver to her ear.

"H-h-hello?"

"Aisling—" a voice rasped in her ear. Aisling screamed and threw the phone on the floor.

"Aisling... Aisling..." The voice called up at her from the receiver, muffled by the thick carpet.

This isn't possible.

It can't be.

With a shaking hand, Aisling lifted the receiver from the rug and held it well away from her face. "Who is this? How do you know my name?"

"The fire is coming," the voice said. "Hollythorn will burn."

"How do you know this?"

"Hollythorn will burn, but don't be afraid. The altar must be purified. The sacrifice must be made. I will protect you, Aisling. The heart will protect you until the last."

"Tell me who this is!" Aisling screamed into the receiver.

The phone made a clicking noise, then went silent.

Aisling slammed down the receiver and fell back in her chair. She couldn't stop shaking. Her fear rose in her chest and bubbled out of her as great, heaving sobs.

43

NIALL

*N*iall came running when he heard Aisling scream. The visions of his dreams burned in his retinas as he shoved open the library door, expecting to see her falling through the floor or torn in two by the shadow. Instead, Aisling sat on the floor, her back against the desk as she stared at the pieces of the red telephone scattered across the rug.

"What happened?" He dropped to his knees beside her. Two big brown eyes peered up at him, wide with fright but *alive*.

Aisling took a shuddering breath. "Something *insane* just happened. Someone called me on the telephone."

"What?"

In jagged words she told him about the phone call, about the rasping voice that said it would keep her safe at any cost. Niall helped her to her feet and set the phone back on the desk, returning the broken receiver to its cradle. Aisling inched away from the phone, as if it might explode at any moment. Something told him that if this rasping voice called again, they would want to get the message.

"We're going to need to think about defending the house,"

he said, coming to stand beside Aisling at the window, looking out over the assembling forces.

"Do you think they can see us?" Aisling asked.

Niall shook his head. "I think because of the time difference, we've never been able to see much through the windows of Hollythorn. Sometimes shadows move, but nothing we could identify as a witch. We should ready ourselves. How do you feel about brushing up on your magic skills?"

"Only if you give me more sword fighting lessons. I've been drilling the defenses—"

Widdershins darted between their feet and careened from the room.

"What's that in his paws?" Niall asked.

"One of those wheat stalks, I think."

"After him!" Niall dived from the room, chasing Widdershins down the hallway and into the grand foyer. If he could find out where Widdershins got that stalk—

"Niall, what are you doing?" he could hear Aisling clattering after him. "Niall, wait for me!"

Widdershins skidded across the marble floor, his back paws sliding out as he made a dramatic ninety-degree turn. He hurtled at the ballroom doors, throwing his weight against them. The door swung open and the cat disappeared inside. A moment later, Niall reached the door and shoved it all the way open. Widdershins was over by the wobbling wall, batting at the piece of wheat like it was the best toy in the universe.

"Come here, boy." Aisling took a step toward the cat, her arms outstretched. "Show me what you've got there."

Widdershins looked up at Aisling, then his gaze switched to Niall. That cheeky cat's lips curled up into a smile to match his yellow-eyed glare. Niall lunged for Widdershins, but the cat made a particularly acrobatic leap to trap the stalk, and both stalk and cat tumbled backward through the wobbling wall, disappearing into the gilded carvings.

"No!" Aisling shouted. Niall grabbed her as she rushed at the wall, holding her back while she kicked and screamed and clawed at his arms.

"You can't go after him!" he cried. "We don't know what's on the other side of that wall. It could be the void."

I won't lose you to the void. I'll die first.

Aisling didn't seem to hear him. In front of them, the wall wobbled, the carvings rearranging themselves before their eyes.

Aisling's body went limp. "He's gone," she whispered, sinking to her knees in front of the wall. "He was my friend, and he's gone."

Tears cascaded down her cheeks. Her body heaved with sobs. Niall had never been this close to human misery before, and the weight of it dragged open the Eamon-shaped hole in his chest until it was a giant, bleeding chasm. He pulled Aisling to him and kissed her tears as they toppled down her cheeks. "I don't think he's gone."

"He's in the void," she sobbed. "Like my sister, and my mother. There's no way anyone can escape."

"Don't write off that furball so fast." Niall held her shoulders so she could look into his eyes. "I believe time is passing differently in the house."

"How is that possible?"

"I don't know, but it would explain why you've only lived here four years while I've stared at the house on the hill for fifty-one."

Aisling's eyes widened. "And the dreams. It explains the dreams."

"It does?"

"It doesn't explain why we've dreamed of each other, but it does explain why you've dreamed of me for your whole life, but

I've only dreamed of you for six years. Because I've been dreaming of you for *your* whole life."

Clever. Niall never would have put that together, but Aisling had.

"You're right. And think about Widdershins. He's too old to still be a kitten. And what about all those weird things he brings back after he disappears? I think Widdershins has been going somewhere in the house where he stays young." Niall nodded at the wall. "I tried to follow him yesterday, but he's too fast for me."

"So *that's* what you were doing yesterday? I heard all this banging and crashing. I thought you were breaking down the walls to let your fae friends in."

His fingers squeezed her skin. "No fae inside apart from me. I'll die before I let them touch you. But as for that cat of yours, I think he'll turn up again—"

As if on cue, a faint *meerrwww* came from deep within the house.

Aisling's head snapped up. "Widdershins?" She tore herself from Niall's grasp and yanked open the door of the ballroom. "Widdershins!"

"Meeerrwww!" came the distinctive reply.

Now it was Niall who raced after Aisling. He followed her as she hurtled up the stairs. She ran left along the upper landing, yelling for Widdershins at the top of her lungs. By the time Niall reached the top of the staircase, the damn cat must have doubled back on itself, because a black smudge whizzed past him, diving into the master bedroom.

He thinks this is some kind of wonderful game. Niall ran into the bedroom, his ears pricked for the cat. He needn't have worried. There, lying demurely on the center of the bed, looking as though he were a king about to pass judgment upon his subjects, was Widdershins. He looked up and gave a dignified *"merrrw?"*

Aisling skidded around the corner and came to stand beside Niall. When she saw Widdershins, she burst out laughing.

"Oh, you ridiculous cat!" She bent over to sweep him up in her arms. But Widdershins was too fast for her. He dived off the bed, streaked the room, and squeezed through a hole in one of the large doors at the end of the room.

"Do you know what's in there?" Niall pointed to the large door at the end of the room. He'd tried to explore the door last night, but the room was locked.

"That's my grandmother's closet." Aisling withdrew a small keyring from the loop on her belt and inserted a key in the lock. "Grandmother June loved dressing up. She kept all these dresses, some of them belonging to my ancestors. She used to have these elaborate balls where everyone dressed up... nothing as fancy as Lady Greymouth's soirees, of course. But they were pretty cool. I keep it locked so Widdershins doesn't tear up the dresses, but I guess he found another way in."

Aisling turned the key and shoved open the door. Cascades of colors assaulted Niall's eyes. Clothes spilled from racks lining two walls of the enormous room, nearly the same size again as the master bedroom itself. Full-length mirrors were mounted on the end wall and behind the door, reflecting back on themselves like an endless hallway of clones. There were racks for blouses, belts, and coats. Rows of black boots and strappy red heels lined a shoe rack beside the mirrors. Makeup and glittering jewels spilled from tall cases. One full rack in the far corner was entirely dedicated to ball gowns – a sea of shimmering satin, lace, and beading.

Niall took it all in, unable to focus on just one detail, so assailed were his senses by all that human glitz and finery. Aisling beamed as she watched him. She didn't realize how the fae were attracted to riches, to all beautiful things they longed to possess but could not touch.

"This isn't a closet," Niall breathed. "It's a treasure chest."

"I know." Aisling grinned. "It's nuts. Women in my family love clothes."

As Niall spun around the room, taking everything in, his eye fell upon something hanging in front of one of the mirrors. Something that never should have existed.

The green dress.

Niall's mind swirled with the memory of the dream, as real to him as any memory. Aisling in that green dress, twirling and swirling around the ballroom in a graceful waltz, her hair swept back, revealing her graceful neck, and those hips, those glorious hips swaying and shifting in time to the music. He stood mesmerized by the door, trapped under her spell.

"Niall?" Aisling prompted. "Your eyes have gone all glazed. Is something wrong?"

"Of course not." He forced himself to laugh, trying to make his voice sound normal. He couldn't bring up the dream now, not with everything he'd broken between them. "I was just looking for that damn cat of yours."

"He's over there under the shoes. The wall behind there wobbles as well. Are you sure you're okay? You've gone all white, like you've seen a ghost."

"I'm fine, really. Can you get that thing out of his mouth? I need to see what it is."

Aisling bent down and dragged Widdershins out. He glared up at Niall with narrowed eyes as Aisling cradled him in her arms. Both his mouth and his paws were empty.

"He must've dropped it," Aisling said. "But how did he get up here after he disappeared into the ballroom wall downstairs?"

"I don't think either of these walls goes into the void," Niall stared down at the hands on his watch as they spun crazily. "At least, not exactly. I think there might be pockets of the house that exist in another time, or serve as portals to other times. That's why Widdershins never seems to age. His clock keeps getting reset."

"You mean, we could walk through the wall in the ballroom and end up in another time?"

"I don't know. It's just a theory, and one that's far too dangerous to test." He stared pointedly at her.

"Don't look at me. I'm staying as far away from anything to do with time travel as possible," Aisling shuddered. "Knowing my luck, I'd end up fast-forwarding to the time when the only safe room left in the whole house is the broom closet."

Niall grinned. He gestured to the dress. "Have you ever tried this one on?"

Aisling looked at the dress, and a deep blush came across her face. "It belonged to Lady Greymouth. I love that June kept her dresses in such good condition. Bethany always said that dress wouldn't suit me. The color would wash me out, and it's way too clingy."

"I think she's wrong. Why don't you try it on for me?"

Aisling looked ready to argue, but then her face broke out into a brilliant smile that made Niall's chest tighten. "Why not?" She grabbed the hanger and disappeared behind an ornate Chinese screen at the back of the room.

"You can do that out here," Niall called to her, grinning. "I promise I won't peek."

"A promise from a fae? We both know that's not worth the paper it's written on." There was a hint of a smile in her voice as she said it, but she stepped behind the screen.

He watched her clothes drape over the top of the screen, and something fluttered around inside the hole in his chest. A naked arm rose up, throwing over a scrap of fabric that must have been her bra. He groaned under his breath.

Aisling poked her head around the side of the screen, her naked shoulders smooth and white as milk. "Did you say something?"

Niall shook his head, momentarily lost for words. His hardness pulsed against his thigh.

She knows exactly what she's doing to me.

A few moments later, Aisling shimmied out from behind the screen, the dress hugging every luscious curve of her body. Niall's tongue froze on the roof of his mouth, and his chest constricted, so his breath came out in a short, sharp gasp.

She had never looked more beautiful. Not even in his dreams. The green of the dress enhanced her pale skin and made her large brown eyes appear even larger. She swept her hair back off her face so her cheekbones stood high and regal. The dress' straps highlighted the swoop of her collarbone, and the neckline plunged in the center, giving Niall a tantalizing glimpse at her cleavage.

Her hands and arms glimmered with a blue aura, more intense than he'd ever seen it. It lit her skin with an ethereal glow, making her appear otherworldly. How much magic shimmered inside her now? More than he'd ever seen in a witch or object before, except for Hollythorn, which still had so much more to give. As she moved, more magic flowed into her, dripping from the walls to crawl over her skin.

"What do you think?" A note of anxiety crept into Aisling's voice.

"I think your sister must have been insanely jealous to tell you that dress looked terrible."

Aisling beamed. Niall held out his hand. Aisling stared at his palm for a few long moments, and his heart sank as he realized she was debating whether or not to touch him. She didn't yet trust him. He guessed he couldn't blame her.

But then she reached out and clasped her hand in his.

Niall's breath caught. Her skin, warm and impossibly soft, sizzled against his.

Her touch sent a wave of fire through his whole body, his veins burning beneath his skin. Niall angled his body away so she couldn't see what she'd done to him.

Niall lifted his arm above his head, spinning Aisling around. She laughed as she twirled, the dress fanning out around her shapely legs and clinging to her hips. As she spun back toward him, he tugged on her arm so that her back fell against his chest, his arms across hers.

Her scent invaded his nostrils – sweet and rich, vanilla and fig and the musk of old books, treasures of the past he longed to explore. The sizzling energy passed between their bodies, pulling them together like magnets. But it wasn't close enough. Niall wanted to be closer, wanted to fall right into her skin, to bury himself in her warmth.

"Let's go," he whispered in her ear, relishing the way her body shuddered against his. "We don't want to be late for the ball."

Niall tore his body from hers, but maintained his commanding grip on her hand. His fingers seared with heat as he led her out of the bedroom and down the stairs, her dress flowing out behind her. In the entrance hall, Niall threw open the ballroom doors and escorted her inside.

"What are we doing?"

"Humor me, witch."

She narrowed her eyes. "You're not going to try something dangerous with the wall, are you?"

Niall lifted his gaze to the ballroom ceiling, taking in the gilded animals frolicking across the carved rococo arches, the towering crystal chandeliers covered with dust and cobwebs, the few faint black cracks creeping down the edges of the wall. He remembered the joy of the dream, and how it had turned into his worst nightmare.

Maybe this is a mistake.

Niall pointed to the center of the floor, where the marble had sunk into a dimple. "In my dream, you were dancing right here. You were wearing this dress. This *exact* dress. And it was so beautiful, I couldn't even speak."

"Why do you look so sad, then?"

"You died, remember? You fell through the floor. I couldn't save you."

She wrapped her arms around his neck. "If I die in this moment, wearing this beautiful dress, here in your arms, then I die happy. I never thought I'd be granted that kindness."

Behind them, the piano struck a note.

They leaped apart, both their eyes darting to the dusty instrument. The piano stood sentinel in the corner of the room, the bench pulled out as though someone invisible sat waiting for their cue. As Niall watched, frozen in place, a key compressed itself, and the note rang out through the room, perfectly clear. And then another, and another, the music forming a beautiful, slow tune.

"What is this?" Aisling's lip trembled. "It's never done that before."

Summoning his courage, Niall slunk across the room, until he was standing behind the piano bench. The tune continued to play, the exact same tune from his dream – a haunting waltz that echoed through every corner of the room.

He swiped his hand over the bench, but there was nothing there. The piano continued to play.

"Who's there?" he whispered at the bench.

Niall... the rasping voice called to him from nowhere and everywhere.

"Can you hear that?" he called to Aisling, his gaze fixed on the moving keys.

"Niall?" Aisling's voice choked with fear. "Help me."

He whirled around. Aisling held her hands up in front of her, staring at them in horror. "What's happening to me?"

Her hands no longer glimmered with the blue aura. Now they positively *pulsed*. The blue was so thick and deep he could barely see her skin beneath. That amount of magic could save the Summer City, if there was still a city to be saved.

That kind of magic could resurrect the broken, barren Earth.

"My hands..." Aisling gasped. "They're getting warmer. There's this weird tingling going up my arms."

"It's Hollythorn's magic." Niall reached out through the blue and grabbed her hand, gripping her hard. He could *feel* the magic pulsing through her – he'd never felt that before. "You've just been given a huge influx of power."

"But how... where did it come from?"

From behind Niall, the piano struck a deep, ominous chord. Niall raised his eyes to the ceiling, watching thin, almost invisible tendrils of blue light descend toward them. The tendrils curled and swirled as they became one with the blue cloud encircling Aisling's hands.

"I think the house is ramping up for war," he said. "You can feel the magic now, can't you?"

"Yes." Aisling stared at her hands with wide, fascinated eyes. "But the music?"

"I could be wrong, but I think Hollythorn is trying to give us a moment, the same way it let us find the forest and the beach. I thought the house was preparing you for sacrifice. But what if it actually *cares* about you? What if this is a gift?"

"You think the *house* is doing all this? That's crazy."

"Is it? Think about everything that's happened, all the times the house has kept you safe. Your grandmother sacrificed herself pouring her magic into these walls. She did that out of love for you – a pure, selfless act. Perhaps she poured some part of herself inside as well, and that part of her doesn't want you to make the same sacrifice, even though that's what the spell demands."

Aisling swiped her hand through the air, sucking in a breath as she felt the magic trailing after her. "So the house wants a sacrifice, but it *also* wants to protect me?"

"That's the best theory I have right now," Niall said. "And it ties in with that voice I've been hearing."

"How's that?"

"The voice wants me to step into the void. I think... I think it knows it needs a sacrifice, but it doesn't want that sacrifice to be you. So it's trying to make me destroy myself to save you," he swallowed. "The house knows I'm responsible for bringing the fae here. It knows they're coming. It's trying to change the future."

"Does sacrifice have to be death, though? If the house thought you were a danger to me, why couldn't it just let you leave the way it let you in? We'd be apart forever. Wouldn't that be sacrifice enough?"

Niall shrugged. That was a puzzle he had no answer for. "Maybe it thought you could use the company?"

On cue, the music started again, the notes of the waltz filling the air. Aisling smiled. She nodded to the playerless piano.

"Perhaps you're right." She held out her hand. "Come on, then."

"Come on where?"

"If war is coming, then let us take our perfect moment while we can."

Niall took her hand in his. He placed his other hand on the small of her back and twirled her under his arm until she laughed that musical laugh of hers. "As you wish."

44

AISLING

The music swelled, and so did Aisling's chest. The magic in her blood flared with heat as Niall clasped her hand in his.

She thought this feeling inside her was love, this weightlessness in her chest, the sizzling in her veins. And maybe it was love. Maybe it wasn't the replenishment spell that triggered this, but her feelings for Niall. She wanted to protect him as much as he wanted to protect her, and the house gave her the magic so she could do it.

Niall spun Aisling in a circle, holding his arm up so she could twirl beneath it. As she came back towards him, he spun her back into himself, so her back rested against his strong chest.

He kissed a trail of fire along her neck. Aisling tilted her head back, giving him access to her bare skin. Her whole body flushed with heat, not just from her desire, but from the magic that pulsed through her veins.

She felt so *different*. So *alive*. Her skin tingled. Her veins felt like they ran with liquid sunshine.

Niall's lips trailed up her neck. He gripped her chin in his fingers and turned her head, his lips commanding hers to relent. Aisling sank into the kiss. *This might be the last time I ever touch him like this.*

Please, she begged the house. *Please don't destroy Niall. He's the only thing I have left.*

He's all I have worth fighting for.

Niall's hands caressed her body through the silken dress, cupping her breasts, holding her against him so she couldn't escape even if she wanted to. His fingers sought her nipples. He pinched one through the fabric, causing it to harden into a pebble.

Aisling reached up and unhooked the clasps that held the dress, sliding the straps over her shoulders.

"Was this how your dream went?" she grinned as she stepped out of the dress, leaving a puddle of fabric on the floor.

"This is already much better." Niall swept her into his arms, his lips meeting hers in a ferocious kiss. Aisling's fingers dug under his shirt, running over the taut muscles of his back, over the raised scars that marked his skin. She lifted his shirt over his head, relishing the sensation of her charged skin against his.

His lips still locked on hers, Niall dragged her across the room until the backs of her legs banged against the piano bench. He shoved her shoulders down so that she sat on the edge of the bench, facing out into the room. The keys continued to pound out the eerie waltz. Niall's fingers twined through her hair, his body tense. Aisling ran her hands over his thighs, toying with the drawstring of his trousers.

"Don't tease me, witch," Niall growled.

He started to climb on top of her, his eyes cold with determination, but Aisling pushed him back. He'd given her so much, and this might be his last time as well.

She reached a hand beneath his drawstring and drew his length out. His breath stuttered as she admired him from all sides – the tautness of his skin, the veins standing out around the dark head, the way he jerked between her fingers whenever she breathed against him.

Aisling leaned over and took him in her mouth. Niall moaned as her tongue slid over his length. She gripped him with her right hand, her other running over his balls, holding them and teasing them, exploring everything about him.

She drew him back into her throat, as far as she could, sliding her hand along his shaft. He let out a low moan. She slid him out again, then took him in deeper, trying to fit as much of his length as possible while keeping the pressure strong. Niall's hands gripped her hair, tugging at the strands. She loved the way his muscles tightened when she drew him in, as though he was holding himself back, desperately trying to maintain control.

He tasted warm and slightly salty, just the way she remembered. She wanted to sear his taste onto her tongue forever. Aisling moved her hand faster, building a rhythm while her fingers danced across the skin on his thighs. Niall's breath came out in shallow gasps, and his fingers tightened around her hair.

She sucked him right to the back of her throat, loving the sensation of being completely full of him.

"Aisling, stop. No more." His fingers gripped her hair. His face twisted, poised on the brink between agony and ecstasy. "I won't be able to... I can't—"

Aisling grinned and dropped him. "Make me stop, fae."

"You bratty witch." Niall grabbed her roughly, tipping her back so she leaned against the bench. He yanked up her legs, placing one each on either side of him. He slid up between her legs, burying his face into her cunt. His tongue worked her furiously, forcing the ache through her body, bringing her right to the brink.

He sucked her clit into his mouth and she toppled over the

edge, into the galaxy of pleasure, the world within her where nothing existed but her and Niall and his tongue on her body and oh... her mouth was open and she was crying out, but she didn't register the sound. All that existed was the pleasure.

Niall didn't wait for her cries to die down. He flipped her body over so her legs hung off the end of the bench. He grabbed her around the thighs and dragged her back, driving into her with one smooth movement. Aisling drove her hips back, forcing him deeper. She gripped the end of the bench, her head tossed back as his length slid inside her.

From this angle, he lit up new places within her as he thrust hard and deep and furious. His fingers tangled in her hair, dragging her neck back so he could nip at her flesh. The music swirled around them, the keys pounding in time with Niall's strokes. He let go of her hair and gripped her nipple between his fingers. She cried out as the sensation flooded through her.

Niall's pace grew frantic. His fingers dug into her thighs. Aisling's body surged with heat as the magic inside her swelled in tune with the ache forcing itself up from inside her. She cried out as the two forces collided. Ecstasy coiled around her, sinking deep into her veins.

Niall shuddered, hardening inside her. With a final gasp, he collapsed against her back, his body tensing, then slackening. His warmth pressed against her, and her magic wrapped around them both, cocooning them in a state of frozen bliss.

The piano struck one final, haunting note, then fell silent.

"Do you think Lady Greymouth would approve of what we did in here?" Niall asked, stroking her hair. He rolled off her and leaned against the leg of the bench, one heavy arm draped across her back.

"I bet she did it on piano benches every night," Aisling grinned back.

NIALL LAID a small bouquet of June's fabric flowers against the door, arranging the blooms so they fanned out in a beautiful design. Aisling stood behind him, watching the concentration on his face as he tended the display.

"Rest well, my friend, my brother," Niall said, stepping back. He placed his hand over his heart, his eyes gazing up at the ceiling. He muttered a few words under his breath in a language she'd never heard before.

Aisling laid her hand on his shoulder, the hard muscles shuddering under her touch. Niall – her cruel, beautiful fae – was crying. The sobs tore at his body, raw and harsh.

And then, as quickly as they came, the tears stopped. Niall straightened his shoulders. He drew his sword from its scabbard, running his fingers over his brother's eye (still fucking gross). He lifted the weapon over his head, and with a roar stabbed it into the wooden door, splitting open the fabric petals.

That's my fae.

Aisling still felt raw around Niall, like she couldn't predict what he'd do next. That usually excited her, but with the fae outside the fence it made her uneasy. She didn't know if she fully trusted him again, or if she ever could. But she accepted her unease grew out of her love. If she didn't care for Niall, he wouldn't have been able to hurt her. He may have doomed them both with his stupid note, but in the few short months since he came to Hollythorn House, she'd lived more than she had in the last four years; probably in her entire life.

All things considered, the balance sheet was in his favor.

And now, *now* she would get to see him as he was born to be – Niall the cruel, Niall the blood-thirsty, Niall the scourge. This time, he was on her side.

"When will they attack?" she asked.

Niall dragged his sword from the wall and sheathed it. He hoisted his belt higher around his tooth-mail coat. "With the accelerated time, I imagine we have a day, maybe two, to prepare."

"Do you want some tea?"

He gave her a weak smile. "Do you have anything stronger?"

"I do. Something I've been saving for the end of the world."

Niall followed Aisling into the library. She drew a small key from the pocket of her sweatshirt and unlocked the bottom drawer of the desk. From the compartment, she withdrew the dusty absinthe bottle her grandmother kept there, along with two crystal glasses and two delicate silver spoons covered in filigree designs. In the dim light, the liquid shone a clear green color.

The absinthe belonged to Lady Greymouth. It was the last bottle in a case she brought back from France on one of her world trips. The bottle was half-empty. Aisling rarely touched the stuff, which June had saved for special occasions. Bethany drank her way through most of the remaining bottles, then she'd stalk the halls in a violent rage, calling curses down on the fae and the family before vomiting down the steps and passing out in the bathtub.

Cleaning your sister's dried puke out of the Persian carpet is a fine way to turn one off the temptation of the green fairy.

Now, the drink seemed profoundly apt. Aisling poured a measure of absinthe into each glass, balanced the spoons over the rims, placed a sugar cube from her tea tray on top, and then poured iced water slowly over the cube, melting the sugar and transforming the green alcohol into a beautiful cloudy drink.

She handed the glass to Niall, toasting him wordlessly. He tipped his head back and downed the absinthe in a single gulp. Aisling followed his example, her throat burning from the strong drink, the top of her tongue numb from the wormwood.

"Another," Niall said, his voice hoarse. He pushed his glass toward her. Aisling poured them both another measure.

"To the sweetest poison of them all," she said, and tossed hers back. Her head spun. "To our grief."

"To love," Niall said, reaching for the bottle.

They are one and the same.

Aisling started to prepare another measure of absinthe, but then she caught shadows moving along the fence just beyond the window.

"Niall, there are more people outside, in the yard." Aisling got up and walked over to the window, peering out at the figures as they used large pliers to bend holes in the fence. They leaped inside and trampled across her frozen yard. They moved at superhuman speed, their bodies only a blur against the gathering storm.

"Not people. Fairies." Niall came to stand beside her, his hand falling on her shoulder. He watched as fae poured through the breaches and fanned out across the lawns, steadfastly avoiding the corner where the ground bubbled with radiation. Every one of the fae wore tooth-mail and green breeches of the Slaugh, and each carried a curved bone sword or a bow and quiver of arrows strapped across his or her back. "We're seeing them sped up because time's passing out there faster than it is in here."

"There goes the neighborhood," Aisling said. "What do we do?"

Niall didn't answer, but his gaze hardened. "There's Laneth."

Aisling followed his gaze to a tall, thickset fae standing off to the side, surrounded by warriors. He remained bone-still while the other fae bustled around him, his grey eyes darting over the house's facade with a look of intense hunger. His stillness made his features visible – his wide girth and regal face. The fae's eyes fell on the window where they stood. He raised a hand and waved at them, his face breaking into a smile that had nothing to do with happiness.

"You said you couldn't see inside the house," Aisling said.

"I guess they can now." Niall touched the hilt of his sword. "Come closer, Laneth. I'd like to tear off your head with my bare hands."

"Sounds fun. I want to watch." Aisling glanced up at the portrait of Lady Greymouth hanging over the fireplace, her haughty chin held high, that yellow-eyed cat staring out with such derision. She wouldn't sit idle while the fae tore apart the house, either. Aisling thought of Grandmother June binding her power into Hollythorn's walls, giving her life that the house – and their family legacy – may continue. And then trying to stop Aisling from meeting the same fate.

"This is my house. I'm not letting them take it." Aisling's hands closed into fists. "Not without a fight."

Niall looked at her, his eyes wild with admiration. "Look at you, burning with bloodlust. It's gorgeous."

"Are we doing this?" she demanded.

Niall claimed her lips in a devilish kiss, a doomed kiss, a kiss that promised bloodshed. "Damn right we are."

"We have to control the entry points," Niall said as they carried splinters of the headboards into the library. Niall had found Bethany's old ax in the greenhouse, and he'd chopped up all the larger pieces of heavy wood furniture into planks they could use for barricades. Widdershins curled around his feet while he worked, attempting to help in the way only cats could – by getting in the way. "The fae will break through eventually, especially if they're drawing power from Laneth. That's unavoidable. What we need to do is funnel them where we want them to go."

"And where would that be?"

"Into the void, if we can manage it." Niall set down his pile and pulled out the hammers he'd found in the greenhouse. "This house has given you the means to get rid of your enemies. All we have to do is get them to fall into the trap."

Aisling held the boards up to the window while Niall nailed them in place, crisscrossing them to create a solid barrier. She watched the fae bustling around through her dwindling view. They were gathered around campfires, unperturbed with what was going on in the house. Laneth sat in the center of the camp atop a throne made from skulls. He smiled up at her and threw up a hand in greeting.

Aisling didn't see the magic he unleashed with that flick of his wrist, but she *felt* it in her bones. The house rumbled in protest as Laneth's magic crashed over it. Niall's chair wobbled, and he had to grab the boards to keep from falling. He stared up at the ceiling, his expression darkening. "Laneth's toying with us," he said. "It won't be long now."

They finished nailing the boards over the library window, and Aisling placed an array of iron objects at the base of the barricade. If the fae broke through, they would land on the pile of iron candlesticks and tools, and if they didn't have Niall's immunity it might slow them down. As they backed out of the room, Aisling cast a protection spell she'd learned from her grandmother's books, placing a line of salt all around the edges of the library. Her voice wavered over the words. She'd never performed magic like this before, but she felt the energy sizzle in her fingers as she poured the salt. She knew the fae would eventually overcome the spell, but it would slow them down.

Next, they tipped over a large cabinet across the entrance to the east wing and pushed a heavy wardrobe in front of the ballroom doors. Aisling scattered these areas with her grandmother's warding crystals, as well as more salt and more incantations.

With any luck, the fae would feel her magic repel them if they tried to enter those areas, and would follow the far easier path she and Niall had laid out for them.

At the threshold of the front door, Aisling placed another pile of iron objects, hoping to hurt the fae as they came through.

While she did this, she heard Niall grunting with effort as he tore away the boards that closed off the dining room. Aisling didn't want to see what lay beyond that door, knowing that she would be staring into the black hole of space itself. But she felt no guilt about their plan. If the fae wanted Hollythorn, they would learn that the house demanded sacrifice.

She stood at the end of the hallway, watching as Niall tipped over the large hall table to create another barricade and stacked the golden dog statues behind it to use as missiles. That done, he moved to the narrow staircase next to the dining room, the one leading down to the wine cellar. Here he stacked the knives he'd taken from the kitchen, each of them sharpened to a razor's edge.

Aisling didn't have much hope that his battle plan would work, but she had long ago resigned herself to dying in the house, and she was damn well going to die fighting alongside Niall.

You want sacrifice? I'll drown *this altar in blood.*

Aisling ran back into the hall and yanked down four heavy swords that hung between the portraits. She placed two on the staircase and handed one to Niall – a spare in case his bone sword was lost. He swung it in the air, a wicked grin spreading across his face. At least he felt perfectly at ease with a weapon in his hands. Aisling eyed her own blades with apprehension, trying to remember everything Niall had taught her about combat.

"What do we do now?" she said.

"Now we wait." Niall's hand fell around her waist, pulling

her close. She took strength from the warmth of his body, from the warrior's blood pulsing in his veins. This might be the last time she felt his skin against hers. She leaned her head against his shoulder, breathing his scent deep, capturing it in her memory before it was drowned in blood.

45

NIALL

*A*isling made them both dinner. They ate in the library, each with one eye focused on the small gap they left in the window so they could observe the fae. The storm had cleared, giving them a clear view of the thousands of fae warriors filing in ranks, their swords clamoring for the battle to begin.

A chill brushed the room, as if even the house itself sensed its doom approaching.

The Slaugh were too numerous to all fit through the fence, so they lined up on the hill behind, their fires stretching over the lip of the hill and down the valley, beyond their sightline. Niall couldn't pick out individual warriors in the sea of fae. He'd never stood on this side before, staring back at his own army with doom in his heart, watching warriors he once fought alongside raise the blood-soaked banners of impending war.

Beyond the army, the fire still raged. It tore through the spires and swept clear the dead trees. *I guess that's one way to melt the ice.*

It was all his fault.

Aisling yawned. "I don't want to think about this anymore. I'm going to bed. You coming?"

"Woman, I'm a fairy, not a stallion," Niall patted his crotch. "Give me some time to recover."

Her cheeks reddened in that way that never failed to drive him wild. "I actually was talking about sleep."

Niall leaned over and kissed her lightly, his tongue playing along her lips. "I think I'll stay here a little longer. I'll call you if they make a move."

"Make sure you do. I don't want to miss the fun. Goodnight, my fairy." Aisling dragged her fingers over his shoulder, her skin still buzzing with the new power surging through her body.

"Goodnight, dream witch."

The door creaked shut behind her, leaving Niall alone in the library, save for Widdershins who jumped up on the windowsill to paw at the glass. "Meeerow?"

Niall waited until he could no longer hear her footsteps creaking, and then he went to the secret compartment in the wall and drew out the wooden box. He popped the lid and set it on his lap. The withered heart stared back at him, silent and accusing. In the dim glow of the candles, it appeared completely black, as he'd seen it before. It was only when he lifted it out and held it up to the moonlight that he caught the faintest line of blue shimmering on the edges.

There's still life in you yet, old girl.

Niall took Aisling's sword – the one he taught her to use, the one she would carry into battle – and stabbed it into June's heart, smearing the organ down the length of the blade. The blue light flickered as it shimmered into the steel.

June's spell was nearly completed. Soon, Aisling would be the new heart of the house. And there would be nothing left within the walls for Laneth to fight for.

46

AISLING

*S*ome hours later, Aisling awoke. She'd been called from sleep by a disturbing dream. She dreamed she walked to the cemetery to pay her last respects and found the door to the mausoleum open, June's coffin disturbed, her chest hacked to pieces, and her heart missing.

Now, as she stared into the darkness of her room, she felt certain the dream was more than a dream. It was a warning, a calling. She threw out her arm, expecting to feel Niall's warm body beside her. But all she grabbed was a cold sheet.

Aisling sat upright, now fully awake. A nagging unease crept through her body. Why was Niall not here, with her, on what was probably their last night on Earth? Why was he always up and around the house in the middle of the night?

She remembered that time she'd seen him in the shadows. She'd been so distracted by her need for him, it hadn't occurred to her to investigate further.

It occurred to her now.

Something's going on with Niall.

Aisling threw off the covers, causing Widdershins to glower at her grumpily from the foot of the bed. She pulled on the clothes she would wear in battle – Niall's tooth-mail gloves slit open and restitched into a tunic, and a heavy work shirt and leggings underneath. She debated taking a lantern, but she didn't want to alert him that she was coming. Moving carefully so she wouldn't bump the furniture, she padded out into the hall.

First, she peered into Niall's old bedroom, but he wasn't there either. She checked the sheets on his makeshift bed-nest. They were cold.

From somewhere in the house, she heard something clatter on the floor. Niall cursed.

As quietly as she could, Aisling tiptoed to the staircase and started up to the ground floor. She steadied herself against the wall, placing her feet as close to the edge as possible, avoiding the steps she knew had creaks. As she rounded the corner and peeked her head into the entrance foyer, she noticed a dark shadow standing at the front door.

Her breath caught in her throat. In a few moments, her eyes adjusted to the gloom, and she could clearly make out Niall's shape. His head was bent down, focusing on his task, whatever it was.

What's he doing?

She took a step toward him, and then another, craning her neck to see his hands. Her foot caught the edge of one of the statues they'd stacked as a projectile, and it toppled over onto the marble with a mighty *CRACK*.

Niall whirled around, and his face told her everything she feared. In his hands, Aisling saw a strange object. It looked like a box Grandmother June used to store her favorite tea, but she doubted very much there was still tea inside.

Aisling held up her hand, and wished for clarity. A beam of light shot from her fingers and lit up the contents of the box.

"Aisling, you need to go back."

It contained blackened, torn pieces of a human heart.

Aisling choked on bile. *My dream.* She knew without knowing what she was looking at – the remains of June's heart, ruined and taken by Niall, who stared at her with an expression of complete and utter guilt on his face.

Aisling stepped forward, her voice trembling. "Niall, what are you doing?"

"Get back," he hissed, his eyes bright, their icy depths ringed with crimson. "You can't follow me."

"Follow you where?" As Aisling backed up, she saw his other hand resting on the door handle. "Follow you outside, back to your people? It's all been a lie. Everything you've said, everything we did, has just been to lead you to my grandmother's heart."

Pain pounded behind Aisling's eyes and throbbed in her chest. Her body felt cold and shattered, as though the void had seeped inside her and tore all the happiness away.

Niall lied to me.

He never took off his tooth-mail. All this time, he's been hunting the heart. He's been hunting me, *searching for my weakness.*

She couldn't reconcile the Niall she'd come to love – the Niall who taught her how to shoot, who made her breakfast in bed, who did those amazing things to her body – with this conniving fae.

He's not supposed to lie. Not to me.

Niall shook his head. "You and me, that wasn't a lie. That's why I have to do this. But I can't do it with you watching. Aisling, please—"

"I don't care!" she screamed. "Do it, you coward."

Why did he do all this if all he wanted was the magic? Why did he teach me to fight and make me breakfast and and and...

Because he's fae.

Because he lives to conquer, and he wanted to conquer me.

Niall turned back to the door, his shoulders shuddering. He planted his hand on the wood and shoved.

The door swung open.

Aisling gasped.

Outside, the fae horde clamored, rattling their swords, calling for her destruction in a thousand musical voices. Arrows loosed at the house, *thwacking* as they chipped away at the stone porch.

Niall looked up at her, his eyes raw with anguish. "The house demands a sacrifice," he said. "It's the only way you'll have the power to destroy them."

The blood rushed to Aisling's head. Instantly she knew that she misjudged him. Her cruel fae, her warrior with the heart drenched in sorrow. He would lay down his life for her without question, without remorse.

"Niall, *no.*"

She lunged for him, crying his name. But he was too far from her now. The house stretched and bent the distance between them to a great chasm, a yearning, gaping hole where her heart used to be. Aisling's fingers grabbed for him, grabbed only air. He was already lost to her.

Niall stepped outside.

47

NIALL

Niall *felt* the moment Aisling understood his true intention. A cord snapped around his heart, freeing him from the last threads of his guilt. He no longer feared death. He felt like a king – a king who would lay down his life for the kingdom of Aisling's heart.

He walked into Hollythorn House as a dead man, into the beautiful unknown with a smile on his face. He made this sacrifice a long time ago, when he first pushed open the gate of the poison house. Hollythorn had granted him a reprieve from his sentence, the gift of Aisling day after glorious day, but it was time to accept his fate.

The altar demands a sacrifice.

Niall clutched June's broken heart in his hands as he stepped onto the porch. The fae in the leading phalanx recognized him, and he them. They were older now, their hair streaked with grey, which was why they were on the front lines – cannon fodder for the house's defences. He remembered recruiting them as children, instructing them, standing alongside them as they waded into bloodshed for the first time. They shuffled and murmured and stepped back, not yet willing to kill the fiercest warrior they'd ever known.

"Friends," he said, holding the heart out like an offering, a gift. "I bring you the heart of the witch, scoured and stripped of her magic by me. I carry her spirit inside me. If you want to take her, you shall have to devour me."

Arrows sang in the air. A sound that had once filled him with the joy of bloodlust, but now signaled his doom.

At first, he didn't feel them beyond a dull thwack as they struck his mail. He thought perhaps that his teeth still held enough protective magic to deflect them. But then he looked down to see several shafts sticking out of him like porcupine quills. Only then did the pain register.

It *burned* inside him, ripe like summer fruits falling from the trees, splattering their juices across the open wounds of his insides. More brutal than the blood gurgling in his lungs, than the bite of stone arrowheads in his ribs and organs, was the knowledge that these arrows came from fae he fought alongside as brothers.

At least I won't be alive to bear the scars of my loyalty.

Niall was dimly aware that beyond the roaring of his blood in his ears, Aisling called his name.

He smiled.

Pain was truth, and he wore his truth with pride because, for the first time in his life, he knew the meaning of loyalty, of sacrifice. This pain was for her, and so he welcomed it. He *cherished* it.

"Aisling." Her name rushed from Niall's lips as he unleashed his final breath and collapsed on the porch.

48

AISLING

"*A*isling."

He sang her name as he fell, like a priest succumbing to reverence, like a hymn that rose to the heavens to anoint some long-dead saint.

Then he fell.

He fell, and her heart fell with him.

It dropped right out of her body into the floor, and the house swallowed it as it swallowed everything else. All that was left of her was sorrow and hellfire.

The fae surged forward, crying their battle cries, raising their swords to run her through. Aisling longed to open her arms and let them come, let her join Niall and everyone else she loved in death. But that wouldn't honor his sacrifice. She had to fight. She had to live. She would do it for him.

They will not touch him.

They will not desecrate his body.

They won't take him from me.

Aisling ran for the door, not even remembering that she might not be able to pass through. Her hands burned. Her fingers were branches of willow stacked on the altar of her family, lit for the purifying fire. She screamed as she passed through the open door and the fire scorched through her veins, as she stepped onto the ruined porch for the first time in four years and threw out her hands.

Her body trembled.

A wall of fire opened up in front of her, throwing the fae back over the iron fence. They screamed as their bodies hurtled through the air and crashed into the ranks behind. Some were impaled on the iron spikes at the top of the fence. They twitched as their bodies slid down the metal, burning their skin to ash.

Fuck. I didn't know I could do that.

She screamed as the heat flared in her fingers. Aisling sent another wave across the lawn, knocking back another phalanx that surged toward her. All around she sprayed flames that crackled and caught. All around, the Slaugh army burned.

But these were fae, and they didn't give up. They, like Niall, were primed for sacrifice. Warriors surged through the holes in the fence, eager to die for their new king. Arrows flew around Aisling's head. She didn't know how much longer her magic would hold them back.

"Niall." Aisling grabbed the thick collar of his tooth-mail and dragged him up the steps. Her hands hummed with energy – not fire this time but another kind of warmth. Arrows flew at her head but they seemed to bend around her, hitting the side of the house and knocking chips of stonework down on her.

He weighed seven million pounds, but she managed to drag him over the threshold. She slammed the door shut with her foot. As she turned the lock, an arrow embedded itself in the wood beside her hand, the point tipped with a vicious stone head.

The house won't hold them back for long.

Aisling dragged Niall through the salt circles. His head lolled to the side, and the arrows in his chest wobbled. She lay him down in the foyer, beneath the portrait of Lady Greymouth, and she held his cheeks, touched his eyelids, stroked the slack skin of his jaw. "Please, please, please. Wake up."

Nothing. Nothing.

He was gone.

He can't be gone.

She looked up at the portrait of Lady Greymouth, and a flash of memory overwhelmed her – Niall striding into the house that very first day, as if he owned the place, as if he had every right to be here. Niall walking across that threshold *knowing* it was supposed to kill him, but doing it without hesitation, without fear, because he loved her.

Niall, you thought you were broken. You thought you were weak, but twice you've sacrificed yourself for those you love. You gave your strength to those who didn't have enough of their own.

You're gone, my brave warrior. You're gone and I love you and I'll still fight for you.

Aisling gripped the quill that pierced his chest, right above his heart. Her fingers tingled around the shaft. She knew something was happening, but she didn't know what. She tugged on the shaft, but it didn't move.

She tugged again and felt something inside her *stir*. Above her head, the house cracked and groaned. Plaster dust filled the air as a piece of molding fell, then another.

Her hand trembled. The arrow shaft pulled free.

Aisling bent to inspect the wound, but there was none. The material of Niall's coat had knitted itself together again, and there was no blood, no bone poking through. Aisling had no heart left to hope, but she hoped anyway.

She grabbed another shaft and pulled it free, and another. They slipped easily from her hands, leaving nothing but dented teeth and the cruelty of her hope.

Niall coughed.

Aisling fell on him, kissing his lips and his cheeks and holding his head in her still-tingling hands and hardly daring to believe that he was still alive. She held him until his body became hers, his breath her own, his heart and hers beating as one.

"What did you do to me, witch?" Niall croaked, touching his hands to the spots where the arrows pierced him.

"I saved your life, you ungrateful fae."

Niall peered up at her with those wicked eyes. "I was supposed to be the sacrifice. What good is a grand and tragic gesture of love if you go and pull me from the brink?"

"Shut up and kiss me."

He obeyed, pressing his lips to hers even though his body trembled from the effort of it. His kiss was everything – it was summer days and wicked hot nights and beautiful, tragic *life*. Around them, the house groaned as arrows pelted the walls. Somewhere above their heads, a window shattered, then another.

"It won't be long now." Niall peered up at the ceiling, where dark cracks latticed along the plaster, sending a snowstorm of dust down on them. The iron chandelier rocked dangerously as the walls groaned and shook. "The house is weak. It won't be able to hold back both the fae and the void for long."

The house groaned again. Sparks fell down from the chandelier in the hall. Something scraped along the porch. And then the front door rattled against its frame.

BANG BANG BANG.

The sound reverberated around the hall like gunshots. The bangs grew louder, pounding against Aisling's skull. Splintered wood flew off in all directions. The door sagged on its hinges. The house groaned in protest. In the skylight above, lightning flashed as the storm of the century raged overhead.

BANG BANG BANG.

With a sickening *CRACK,* several boards flew off the door, scattering across the hall. The blade of an ax thrust inside, slashing at the door to widen the hole. The walls groaned in protest, and more sparks rained down, but the house didn't have the strength to fight back anymore. Niall had given that strength to Aisling.

The fae had breached Hollythorn House.

Niall leaned out from their hiding place behind the corner of the archway and sent an arrow flying at the door. It caught the first fae in the throat as he swung his body through the hole. The fairy staggered back, his hands grabbing at the arrow, his mouth open. Blood dribbled down his chin. He fell across the threshold.

The next fae stepped over his body, not stopping to check if his comrade was alive.

Aisling's hands burned with righteous fury. She squeezed her eyes shut and flung out her fingers, channeling all her energy at the advancing fae. To her surprise, heat surged from her palms. She opened her eyes and saw a ball of fire spin across the room. The fire caught the fae square in the chest, his tunic bursting into flames. He screamed as he went down, his long hair burning a bright halo around his tortured face.

More Slaugh warriors shoved their way through the hole in the door, tearing it wider. They trampled over the bodies of their comrades as they fought to be on the front lines to capture the witch.

Niall's arrows flew in all directions, hitting their marks with unbelievable efficiency despite his injuries. Aisling's hands burned as she forced her rage out through her skin, as she channeled the energy the house had given to her into destroying its enemies with cleansing fire.

Niall flung his last arrow into the column of fae. He flung down his bow and grabbed Aisling's arm. "Retreat!" he yelled, dragging her back. Aisling scrambled after him, sprinting across the marble into the west hall. She leaped over the heavy desk, grabbing up her sword, holding it the way Niall had shown her. Her whole body trembled – a mixture of rage and fear.

Niall's tactics worked perfectly. Here in the hall, the fae had to come at them in almost single file. They were as evenly matched as they could hope to be. The first warriors rounded the corner, drawing their own swords and grinning their self-satisfied fae grins, as though they'd already won.

Aisling's hands on the hilt felt cold as ice. She didn't think she could summon any more fire. *This is it. This is where I die.*

Niall surged forward. His sword clashed with the first fae.

The fight happened so fast, a blur of limbs and gritted teeth and shining steel. Aisling heard Niall cry out, and her whole body surged with new energy.

She plunged her blade into the fae's neck. None of Niall's training prepared her for the ease at which the steel sliced through the fairy's flesh. His eyes bugged out of his head, and blood spurted from his open mouth as his skin turned green, then black, around the wound. He collapsed to the ground, his blade sliding to the floor with a *CLANG*.

Aisling didn't have time to gloat over her kill. Another bone blade swung toward her face. Aisling ducked. The fae who attacked her faltered as he regained his balance. She flung her sword up, aiming for his throat. But she wasn't fast enough. He blocked her blow. A chip of bone flew from his sword as her steel bit, but he was stronger than her. The force of his blade against hers reverberated up her arms. Her hands shook as she fought at the bind to hold him off.

"I'll have you soon, witch," the fae grinned, as he inched his blade closer to her face. "But don't worry, I'm not going to kill you. Our King will let me take my pleasure with you before he eats your heart and strips the magic from your charred bones."

Aisling gritted her teeth. Her shoulders shook from the pressure of holding his blade back. The point of his sword wobbled in front of her eye.

The fae's eyes widened with surprise. The pressure on Aisling's shoulder relaxed as he collapsed against the wall, the entire side of his face caked in blood. Niall withdrew his blade, dragging the tip along the edge of the fae's temple. Her assailant opened his mouth to scream, but the hilt of Niall's sword caught him across the jaw. The fae's face exploded with blood. He doubled over, landing on top of his fallen comrade.

Another fae came at them, and another, each one fresh to the fight, their skin gleaming, their faces aglow with the joy of battle. Aisling's arms screamed. She swung clumsily, her sword flailing. Even Niall looked tired, his face streaked with the blood of those he'd felled. It was only by the awkwardness of their position that they continued to hold ground.

"Fall back!" he hissed at her. Aisling dropped her arm and sprinted for the end of the hall, Niall hot on her heels. Four fae vaulted the table and raced after them, their feet pounding against the marble.

"Argh!" one of them yelled as his boot caught a statue. He crashed to the floor, bringing the fae behind him down as well. The other two didn't even slow as they surged forward, trampling their comrades.

"Quick, into the dining room!" Niall yelled as loud as he could, loud enough for all the fae to hear. Aisling poured on speed, her feet slipping against the marble, slick now with the blood caking the bottom of her shoes. She reached the end of the hall, where the dining room door gaped open, the inky blackness inside snaking its tendrils around the edge of the wooden door.

Fear rose in her chest as they reached out toward it. One

wrong move, one foot out of place, and she'd fall right into the void.

Niall grabbed her hand. At the last possible second, he yanked her hard, enveloping her in his arms as he shadow-shifted. His darkness shrouded them both as he pressed her back to the hallway wall, disguising them as part of the encroaching darkness. The cold of the void grazed her cheek, and then it was gone. Aisling held Niall as tight as she could and tried to keep her breathing quiet and even.

The fae rounded the corner and flung themselves into the dining room. They didn't have time to scream before they were swallowed, just the way her mother and sister had been devoured.

The warriors who followed directly behind them managed to stop themselves just in time. Their eyes grew wide as they stared directly into the void itself. Niall dropped his shift and sprung at them, dagger drawn. He had the element of surprise. Within moments they had cut down the last of this first wave of fae.

"Where now?" Aisling puffed, her stomach retching as she regarded the bodies littering the hall. Niall bent down and picked up the knives they hid there.

"I think—" Niall began, then clutched his shoulder, wincing as a deep cut opened across his skin. An arrow stuck out of the wall just behind him.

"This is pointless, witch." A single fae stood at the end of the hall, his bow stretched between his long fingers, pointed directly at them. "This house, and all of its power, will be ours."

He raised the bow. Aisling's breath froze in her chest. Niall squeezed her hand. She stared down the hallway at death himself.

She grinned.

The door beside the fae flew open. An invisible wind

plucked him from the hallway and dragged him inside. The door slammed shut again. From inside the room, they heard the fae screaming.

Niall turned to her, his eyes wide with surprise. "What did you do?"

"It's the house! It's fighting for us."

"Quick," Niall yanked her back. "That was only the first wave."

As if on cue, the picture frame on the wall shattered, glass shards raining down on them. Niall shoved Aisling to the ground. Her knee hit the marble floor with a painful *CRACK*. Two more arrows sunk into the wall where they'd been standing.

Niall tugged her hand. "Run," he yelled.

Aisling scrambled to her feet. Arrows whizzed around her head, slamming into the walls as she streamed past, their fletching still quivering from their flight. She pitched herself toward the library.

Niall yanked her into the library and slammed the door behind them. "Help me move this." He shoved the large oak desk they'd already moved next to the door. Aisling took the other end. Together they dragged it across the carpet and barricaded the door.

Aisling sprinkled a line of salt around the desk and cast a protection spell around the door. Her hands felt cold again, and she knew the spell was weak. Just the act of performing it made her feel woozy. "I need to sit down. I think... I'm probably supposed to recharge myself under the full moon or something."

While she slumped against the side of the desk, listening to the banging and voices in the hall as the fae ravaged her home, Niall paced across the room, over the bright square on the faded carpet where the desk had sat.

"We're trapped in here," she said, her head throbbing. "It's a dead end."

"Better than being dead out there," Niall said. "We'll wait them out. See if you can get the house to give you more power."

He sounded so arrogant, so sure of himself, but Aisling knew it was false hope. She raised her hand to the ceiling, trying to force all thought from her mind. It was hard, given how the loud banging in the hall distracted her, but she tried to focus on the house, on the memory of her grandmother. *Please, June, I need more. I just need enough to stop them. Please, give me everything you've got. Lay it on me, Grandma. I can take it.*

Nothing happened.

The warm feeling in her hands didn't come back.

Aisling lowered her arm as another chunk of plaster fell from the ceiling. "It's not working. Maybe the house doesn't have any more power to give. Did you ever find anything in those books?"

"Maybe. Yes!" Niall grabbed one of the open volumes off the stack by the window and thrust it under her nose. Aisling stared at the diagram of sigils, trying to focus on the words DRAWING DOWN SPELL. Her fear made the lines wobble. Nothing made sense. A lump rose in her throat. *How am I going to do this?*

I have to do this.

Aisling reached for the book, but as she did so, the whole desk started to shake. The door banged against its hinges.

"Niall, they're trying to move it!"

Aisling flung down the book and leaned against the desk. She planted her feet into the carpet, straining her whole body against the weight.

In a flash, Niall was beside her, grunting as he shoved it back. Together, they managed to push the desk back against the door. The magic book slid across the floor, just out of reach. Niall drew his sword.

BANG.

A huge force shoved against the door. The desk hurtled across the room. Aisling was pitched into the air. Her body slammed into one of the bookshelves. Pain arced across her skull. Books tumbled on top of her, their heavy corners pummeling her skin. White lights grew large and heavy across her eyes, stealing away her vision as she swam in an ocean of agony.

They're inside. We're doomed—

Then everything went black.

49

AISLING

*A*isling woke in darkness. Pain arced across her skull, then subsided. She managed to pry open her eyes. Remnants of the desk lay scattered across the floor. Books littered the carpet like bodies on a battlefield, their spines torn open, ripped pages fluttering on a cold breeze. Niall lay near the fireplace, his body covered in books, his sword still clutched in his hand, the bone blade snapped in two.

I'll never find that spell book now.

Niall raised his head and stared at the door. Aisling followed his gaze, her stomach tight with dread.

In the doorway stood a fae. Tall and majestic, his body shimmered with a pulsing aura so vivid even Aisling could see it. An aura of violent green that made her think of the pictures of forests boiling she'd seen on TV when the first bombs were dropped. Circling his head was a crown of thorns and teeth.

This fae carried no weapon, but if he alone had pushed the door open, he didn't need one.

This must be Laneth.

The fae glared at Niall with cold, calculating eyes. Then his gaze fixed on Aisling. He smiled, and his smile was more terrifying than anything she'd ever seen in her life.

It was the smile of someone who thought sacrifice meant others laid down their lives for you, and not the other way around.

"Good evening, Niall," Laneth said, his tone light, friendly. It made every word he said all the more sinister. "You didn't think you could keep this treasure from me, did you? I've come for what's mine."

"This isn't your house, Laneth," Niall said. "It isn't your power, and it isn't mine, either."

"Tsk, tsk, that's not a Slaugh talking." Laneth's eyes rested on Aisling's face again. He turned his head to the side as he studied her, like the spider studying the fly. "You've been corrupted, I see. Bewitched by *this*. You should have eaten her heart while you had the chance. Then you might've stood against me as an equal."

She dragged her body up, pain clawing at her limbs. Magic burned in her fingers once more. Only a little, but maybe it was enough.

Above their heads, the house groaned.

"I speak of my own free will," Niall spoke slowly, choosing his words carefully. His voice cut the air like a blade. "You're one to talk about corruption. You've stolen from our own people, Laneth. All those years you kept that magic for yourself while fae died for want of sunlight."

"They did nothing with it!" Laneth yelled. "Don't you see? Power shared is power diminished. If the Summer Queen had seen that, she wouldn't have drained herself trying to keep us tethered to a dying city. As King of both Summer and Winter, I can perform spells of untold magnitude. I can heal the scarred earth the humans left behind and give fae dominion over this new world, as it should have been. We'll be the rulers of all, Niall. There's still a chance for you to be part of it. Join me now."

"Oh, of course!" Niall took a step toward Laneth. Aisling noticed his hand shoved behind his back, his fingers clasped around the hilt of his broken sword. "You're the picture of self-lessness, Laneth. You're just doing this for the good of the fae, for the good of the ruined earth. Never mind that hundreds of fae have already *died* because you hoarded magic for yourself. Never mind you killed Odiana and *ate* my brother—"

"I've done what the Summer Queen failed to do," Laneth scoffed. "Rebellion always comes at a cost. Now, will you join me in draining this witch?"

Niall's face twisted into an unreadable expression. He stepped forward, extending his hand to Laneth in friendship.

As Laneth reached out to take his hand, Niall whipped his other arm out from behind his back. He plunged the jagged tip of the sword into Laneth's chest, driving it in right up to the hilt. Laneth's eyes bugged out, and he stared down at the handle protruding from his broad stomach. Eamon's eye stared back at him, and Aisling swore she saw it blink.

Laneth's chin quivered. Aisling leaned forward, ready to watch him fall. Instead, Laneth's face broke into a wide grin.

"It will take more than that to stop me," Laneth said, his voice calm. He grabbed the handle of the sword and dragged it from his chest. It made a sickening plop sound as the tip pulled free. Laneth tossed the blade on the floor. The wound on his stomach closed over, leaving only a tiny smudge of blood.

Shit.

Aisling didn't need to see auras like Niall did to know Laneth must be holding incredible power. He'd healed himself the way she healed Niall, and she was already nearly spent. That wasn't fae magic; it belonged to witches.

Laneth grabbed Niall by the throat. He lifted Niall off the ground, grinning wickedly as Niall struggled against his grip.

"Let him go!" Aisling yelled. She rushed forward, but Laneth held up another hand. Aisling slammed against an invisible wall. She pummeled her fists in the air, but as much as she struggled, she couldn't get any closer. Niall's face was turning white. Laneth's grin grew wider as he raised his own sword.

"I think I'll keep you on the edge of death," he whispered to Niall, loud enough for Aisling to hear. "I want you to see me eat your witch's heart."

Aisling's hands burned. She raised them in front of her face, and for the first time noticed tendrils of blue smoke swirling from the tips of her fingers. It wasn't as strong as the aura shimmering around Laneth, but it gave her a surge of hope.

She thrust her fingers out, pushing out the energy inside her. This time, her hand sailed right through the invisible wall. The heat burned through her skin and surged outward, heading for Laneth. He dropped Niall and grabbed his arm, wincing as the heat seared his skin. There were no flames this time, but a dark burn mark encircled his bicep. Aisling caught the scent of burning flesh.

"Get out of my house," Aisling growled, the power surging through her body, boiling in her veins. She held out her hand, preparing to strike again.

Laneth tossed his head back and laughed, the sound reverberating through the library. He swiped his fist through the air. Books rained from the shelves, scattering across the floor.

With another swipe of his arm, the books rose from the floor, their pages unfurling as they circled the room in a wild dance, slamming against her body. Page after page tore away as Aisling's most precious possessions became her tormentors.

"No." Aisling raised her own arm. She pulled up all the

power within her, dragging every last ounce of love for Niall, for her family, for everything she'd lost and could still lose. She forced up a great cone inside her, the power churning, desperate for release.

She threw all her rage and anger and pain behind it, all the memories of her childhood trapped inside this house, all the stolen moments of her life that she would never get to experience, all the loneliness and longing and regret, and she threw it all at Laneth.

The power fled through her fingers, pouring from her into him. Laneth doubled over, clutching his stomach, his face twisting in agony. Niall managed to pull himself up. He battled through the flapping books to wrap his arms around Aisling.

"You got him!" he cried, slamming his fist into the attacking books as he pulled her toward the door.

The blue aura around Laneth's body pulsed, fading away, then returning stronger than ever. He raised his head, his eyes blazing with triumph.

"You can't touch me," he cried, standing up and throwing his arms wide.

With another wave of his wrist, the pages in the air turned into birds. Huge, white birds, their wings made from words, their talons the barbs of sonnets. They opened their wide sharp beaks and dived for Aisling and Niall.

Niall threw her body over hers, sending them both scrambling across the room as the birds turned about and dived for them again. Aisling leaped left, her body slamming into the bookshelf. Some of the birds couldn't turn fast enough, and they plowed into the barricade, their beaks sticking into the wood.

Laneth surged forward, his hands raised high, a wicked grin on his face. Aisling raised her hand to her face, her other hand seeking Niall's, wanting to die in his arms. Laneth lunged at them, his hands glowing green as he aimed his sword at her chest, at her heart. Aisling steeled herself for the knife sliding between her ribs.

The shelf behind her opened up and swallowed them whole, collapsing the library into inky blackness.

50

NIALL

The birds were gone.

Laneth was gone.

Niall opened his eyes. He lay on a hard, cold surface, a cloud of dust settling around him. A few feet away, he could see the outline of Aisling's body sprawled on her back, her head bent toward him and her body still.

His chest tightened. *Is she alive? Please let her be alive.*

Aisling blinked. Niall's heart surged. She groaned and rolled over, crawling toward him. Niall managed to move his own arm to clasp her fingers in his. His whole body ached.

Aisling's skin felt warm. She was alive. That meant they were both alive. But how? Niall's head pounded. The last thing he remembered was being pummeled by books and Laneth advancing on them. *So what happened? Where's Laneth?*

Where are we?

Niall rubbed his eyes, lifting himself up to a sitting position. They were lying in a dark hallway, similar to other halls on the ground floor – dark wood paneling with a light wash on the walls above the wainscoting, and gilded portraits hanging from every surface. Candles burned from bronze sconces. Here and there were oak side tables covered with gilded dog statuettes. The marble floor beneath them was made in the same checkerboard pattern as the ballroom and entrance hall.

But this wasn't an ordinary hallway. For one thing, it extended in both directions, on and on into a dark infinity. For another, Niall had explored every inch of the Hollythorn that was still accessible, and he'd never seen this corridor before.

"Where are we?" he croaked out. His throat burned from where Laneth had tried to choke him.

"I've never seen this hallway before in my life." Aisling pulled herself to her feet, then helped Niall up.

"Meerrrrw!" Something furry brushed against Niall's leg. Aisling's face lit up as she bent down and picked up Widdershins, cradling him to her chest like he was a baby. His yellow eyes closed and he tipped his head back in ecstasy as his whole body shuddered with purrs.

Niall gave him a scratch under the chin. "I've never been so glad to see a cat in my life," he said. "You're one of a kind, buddy."

"Meerrw!" Widdershins bolted forward, leaping down from Aisling's arms and darting away into the darkness. Aisling called him, but he didn't return. From somewhere in the distance, Niall heard him meow again.

"I wonder if this is where he's been going," she said.

Aisling looked ready to go after him, but Niall held her hand. "Look," Niall pointed to the gilded frame above. It was an image of Lady Greymouth he'd never seen before. She sat in front of the piano in the ballroom, wearing the emerald green dress from his dreams. But instead of her gaze focusing on the keys, she was staring out at him, her eyes seeming to move in the flickering candlelight. Her left arm was extended, her finger pointing down the hallway to their right, the same way Widdershins had gone. "This sounds crazy, but it's almost as if she's trying to help us, tell us where to go."

"Look at the floor." Aisling pointed to the marble beneath their feet. "It's the same pattern as the ballroom."

"Maybe that means we're nearby." Niall squeezed her hand. "Maybe the house is giving us a shortcut."

"What good will that do?" Aisling said. "The entrance hall is swarming with fae. If we end up in the ballroom, there's nowhere else for us to go."

"We were trapped in the library, and now we're not." Niall tugged her hand. "I can't pretend I understand this at all, but I think the house is showing us the way. It's worth a shot."

Aisling squeezed his hand back. "Agreed," she said. "Take me to the ball, fae."

Hand in hand, they made their way down the hallway, glancing at all the portraits. All of them showed Lady Greymouth in different rooms of Hollythorn or out on the grounds. In every picture she stared directly at Niall, her painted eyes unblinking, and pointed the way ahead. The silence swirled around them. Niall could no longer hear the fae crashing through the house or the flap of those vicious birds. He'd assumed the library was just through the wall, but maybe it wasn't. Maybe this hallway wasn't really a place at all.

He rubbed Aisling's arm, where her bare skin had risen in goosebumps.

Doors became visible on either side of the hallway. Niall tried one of the handles but found it locked. The more they walked, the more uneasy Niall felt. He lost his sword to Laneth. He patted the pockets of his breeches, hoping to find something he could use as a weapon. But he had nothing left save a small golden dog statue he'd picked up to use as a missile, and he didn't think a dog statue was going to do much damage to Laneth.

"Niall," Aisling whispered. "The portraits."

Niall's chest tightened as he peered closely at the wall. He realized with a start they no longer showed images of Lady Greymouth.

Instead, they depicted his own face.

His, and Aisling's.

They were painted inside the house, wearing strange historical clothes, but they were doing all the things they'd been up to over the last weeks – twirling together across the ballroom floor, painting murals in the drawing room, walking together through the forest bathroom, reading in the library, shooting arrows at porcelain dogs, practicing their sword technique in the entrance hall, kissing with fire and fury. The artist had perfected Aisling's lips, her tumble of brown curls, and his haughty expression and toned shoulders.

Fear clutched Niall's chest, freezing around his heart. *How did this happen? Who's been painting portraits of Aisling and me?*

Where did this hallway come from?

More importantly, where is it leading us?

For the first time in his life, Niall didn't have an enemy he could fight. True terror swelled in his gut. This, whatever it was, was so much more powerful than anything he could hope to fight.

Still, they walked on.

Aisling didn't seem as disturbed by the hallway or the paintings. She dragged him along in her haste to discover where the hallway led. The light in the hall grew brighter until it started to blind them.

Niall took a step into the light, and he wasn't in the hallway anymore. The light faded, and he stood in the center of the ballroom, at the very edge of the buckling floor. Long vines, like the ones that hung through the hidden forest, snaked down from the ceiling and crisscrossed the floor.

"How did we get here?" Aisling whirled around. But there was no hallway behind them, only a blank wall.

Widdershins wandered across the floor toward them, his nose lifted high in the air as if he was saying, 'took you long enough.'

"Meeerw."

Sound returned. They could hear the muffled shouts and bangs of the fae trampling through the house beyond. The ballroom doors trembled on their hinges.

"Now is not the time for your nonsense, cat." Niall dragged Aisling toward the back of the room. The wall shimmered, beckoning them. They ducked down behind the piano, holding each other tight. Aisling bowed her head, raising her hand to the ceiling, her eyes closed as thin slivers of blue smoke curled through the air and entered her fingers. But it wasn't enough magic to hold back the fae.

Niall realized with a start that the ballroom hardly glowed blue any longer. The aura that used to glow brightly from every surface of the room had faded. If he squinted hard, he could just make out a faint glimmer in the gilded ceiling above their heads, the threads flowing down and entering Aisling's hand.

The house was nearly spent. It had very little magic left. Would it be enough to keep them from the void before they stopped Laneth?

When her palms glowed blue and there was no more magic falling from the ceiling, Aisling lowered her hand. Niall wrapped her in his arms. Widdershins stalked around the perimeter of the room, occasionally letting out a defiant *meerrrw.*

They waited.

In the entrance hall beyond, the shouting grew louder. They heard something scraping across the ground. *They're moving the wardrobe.* The bolt holding the doors closed started to lift from its hinges. Niall squeezed Aisling's hand. *You can do it,* he willed her. *You can stop them from getting in.*

Aisling squeezed her eyes shut. Her whole body tensed. The bar slammed back down.

"Nice one," he said. Aisling grinned.

"Meeerrrw!" Widdershins let out a loud bellow. Aisling whipped her head around. Niall followed her gaze. The cat was standing in front of the wobbling wall, staring at the door, his eyes wide and frightened, his back arched and fur on end.

"Widdershins, no!" Aisling cried, but Niall knew she was too late. The black cat leaped into the wall and disappeared with a sickening *plop.*

Aisling's whole face fell. Tears pooled in her eyes. Niall gripped her with fierce affection, trying to drive out the pain of her heart breaking with the strength of his embrace.

"He might not be dead," he said, stroking her hair. "Remember, he's gone through there before. We thought the wall might be—"

"He's gone, I know it," Aisling whispered, her hand against her heart. "Don't ask me how, but I can feel it. The house is falling into the void. There's nowhere for him to return. Widdershins is gone forever."

The bar slid back up again. Aisling screwed up her face. Niall watched in awe as she drew back the pain that threatened to overwhelm her and channeled her magic back toward the door. She managed to shove the bar back down, but it was harder this time. Her whole body trembled. Sweat poured down her face. The bar started to lift once more.

'It's no use." She shook her head. "I can't hold it down much longer."

Niall watched the faded blue aura of the house flicker around the door, the tendrils wrapped tight around the bar, trying to hold it down. He glanced at the golden dog statue, lying on its side under the piano where it had fallen from his pocket. His gaze fell on the opposite wall as the surface wobbled, like the icing on a cake before it had set.

Something occurred to him. A wild idea, a crazy idea, an idea so ridiculous and imaginative he knew it couldn't possibly have come from his own mind. The house had given him a gift. He couldn't explain it, but he *knew* that he was right.

"Drop the bar," he told Aisling, his face breaking out into a wild grin. "Let them come."

"Are you nuts?"

"You know it." He flashed her a wicked grin. "I think I know how we get out of this. Or rather, how you get us out of this."

"I'm trying my best, but Laneth is more powerful—"

"No, he's not. Because you're controlling the house. It doesn't need its own magic, because it has you."

"That doesn't make sense! I'm not doing anything."

"All this time," Niall said, "I thought the house was trying to prime us for sacrifice, talking to me through the void. But now I see. Nothing is a coincidence. All along, the house has been giving you and I what we needed *exactly* when we needed it."

"What does it matter? Hollythorn is useless against Laneth."

"Then where did the hallway come from? How are we still alive? Why did the house bring us to *this* room – the room from my dreams? Why did we have the dreams in the first place? Think about it, Aisling. It isn't the house doing all this," Niall stroked her cheek. "It's you. It's been you all along."

"It's not me. I didn't do this." Tears spilled as she shook his shoulders. "I wouldn't know how."

"No, but you have your whole life to learn. I don't think you're doing it now. I think you set all this in motion a long, long time ago."

"You're not making any sense!" Aisling's face screwed up.

The bar dropped another inch. The banging on the door grew louder, more urgent.

"I don't have time to explain it all, but I know I'm right. You have to trust me, okay? Do you trust me?"

Aisling looked stricken. For a horrifying moment, Niall thought she would say no. She squeezed his arm. "Yes, I trust you."

"Then drop the bar."

"I repeat, are you *nuts?*"

"This house is part of you, Aisling. It's an extension of your own powers and the powers gifted by your family, by your grandmother's sacrifice. You've lived inside it for most of your life – for two lives, in fact – and your magic has become part of it, and it a part of you. You've been the heart of the house all along. That's how I know you'll survive, because if you don't then none of this could have happened. Drop the bar."

Aisling closed her eyes. Her body shuddered as she let go, as she gave herself over to Niall's crazy idea. For a moment, nothing happened.

Then the bar clattered away. The doors flung inward, the heavy wood crashing against the ballroom walls. Laneth stood in the doorframe, a silhouette of shimmering blue, tiny lightning forks crackling from his fingers and the top of his head. He was flanked by two warriors, their bows pulled right back against their ears.

Aisling whimpered, her whole body trembling. Niall clutched her tighter, pressing her against the marble floor, using his body to shield hers.

I hope I'm right about this.

"There's no point in hiding, Niall." Laneth strode into the room. "I've taken every last drop of power from the house. It can't protect you any longer. This is still going to end in your death."

"If you want us," Niall called from behind the piano, "come and get us."

He craned his neck right around to watch Laneth stride across the dance floor, heading right for the area where the floor had sunk into a dimple. Beneath him, Aisling's body grew warm. He could see her aura growing around her, around them both. The blue shimmered with flecks of pink light. He'd never seen pink light before. But he didn't have time to ponder it.

"Now, my witch," he whispered in Aisling's ear.

"Now *what?*"

"Maybe I won't kill your little witch friend right away." Laneth stepped carefully over one of the large vines. "Perhaps I'll bend her over that piano and show her how a real fae makes a human submit. Maybe I'll fuck the cavity of her chest when I tear out her heart. Would you like to watch that, Niall? I'll make it fun for both of us—Hey!"

Laneth teetered on his feet. At first, Niall thought he'd just tripped over one of the vines on the ground, but there was nothing beneath him except smooth marble.

Then he noticed it. The floor bucked and rolled, like waves crashing against the shores of Aisling's beach. Laneth screamed as his feet were knocked from beneath him, and he fell heavily on his back. Behind him, the two Slaugh struggled to remain upright as the vines whipped and wriggled across the floor, wrapping themselves around their ankles and dragging them down.

Aisling sat up. She nodded to Niall as she rose up to her full height, which now appeared very high indeed. The blue and pink light of her magic danced across her face, and she raised her hands toward the ceiling, like a priestess calling down her gods.

"Get out of my house!" she yelled. Her voice didn't seem to only come from her mouth. It was as though all the walls, the ceiling, and the floor spoke her command into the world. It was Aisling, but not. It had a rasp and an echo that was familiar to him.

Niall realized it was Aisling's voice – echoing a hundred times through the ages – who had called him from the void, as she now called down the power of her altar.

For the first time, Niall saw fear in Laneth's eyes.

It was the sweetest sight.

The floor turned into an ocean, a swirling maelstrom. The marble flowed toward the center of the room, drawing up in a great wave before slamming down into a deep, dark whirlpool. In its center, a cold abyss beckoned.

Laneth tried to stand, but his feet slipped from beneath him. The vines that held his two guards rose high, dragging their terrified prey across the ballroom to dangle them above the abyss. The fairies cried and gibbered for mercy.

"Let us go! We'll do anything, please just let us go!"

The vines obeyed, releasing the fae, dropping them straight into the swirling hole. They screamed for a long time as they fell, until their screams faded away completely, replaced by the roar of the beckoning abyss.

The floor tilted further. Laneth skidded closer and closer to the edge of the hole. "Help me!" he cried out to Niall, scrabbling against the smooth floor for some hold.

Niall shook his head. He relished the shaking.

Laneth's eyes widened with terror.

He slipped away.

His scream as he toppled into the dark abyss was the sweetest sound Niall had ever heard. It went on and on until Niall thought he'd drown in the pleasure of it.

As the scream faded into the pounding of Niall's own heart, he surfaced from the lake of his grief to find the ballroom filled with light. Not the blue light of Aisling's aura, but a warm, life-giving glow that seeped from the darkest corners, casting the enormous room in a field of bright sunlight.

And in the middle of that light was Aisling.

His Aisling.

His brilliant, wicked witch.

"You did it." He embraced Aisling. She fell against him, her body heavy as she let out the tension that gripped her. "You brave, beautiful woman. You—"

His adulation was cut short by a horrible crash from above. Plaster rained down from the ceiling. Aisling screamed as a large piece crashed onto the piano bench. The light grew brighter – achingly, painfully bright.

The vines that trickled around the edges of the room shuddered and drew away, shrinking and blackening as they withered and died.

It was sunlight all right – the light from an irradiated sun, rising from the void to devour them all.

Another great crash. The room shook. The piano slid across the floor toward the gaping hole. Aisling's aura fizzled and sparked. A long crack arced across the ceiling. As the house continued to groan and shake, the crack opened further, revealing an inky blackness as it spawned a hundred tiny fissures radiating out from its edges.

"What's going on?" Aisling cried. She gripped the edge of the piano to steady herself. "I don't understand. I stopped Laneth."

"But the magic is still gone. Hollythorn is destabilizing," Niall said. "The whole thing is collapsing into the void."

Aisling's face hardened. She broke into a run, skidding across the lurching floor as she tried to scramble toward the door.

"Where are you going?" Niall called after her, reaching out to grab her before she pitched over.

"We have to get outside. If we can find Laneth's stash of

magical items, we may be able to put enough magic back into the house to make it stable—"

From the distance, he could hear the phone in the library ringing. He grabbed Aisling's arm and dragged her back, flinging her against his chest just as the floor pitched again, sending one of the vines twisting down into the void.

"It's too late," he whispered. "Hollythorn is gone."

"It can't be too late." Her face was wet with tears. "We won. Why do we have to die?"

"We're not going to die." He stroked her hair.

"We were so close," Aisling sobbed into his shoulder. "We had happiness. Why couldn't it have stayed this way forever? Why did we have to be the sacrifice?"

"We can still have happiness." Niall pointed at the wobbling wall, remembering Widdershins picking his way across the ballroom, his steps deliberate, purposeful. The cat had made the journey before.

A large piece of plaster broke away from the ceiling, crashing in front of them. Aisling flinched.

"You want us to... jump into the wall? We'll die!"

Niall dragged her across the floor. "We don't know that, and we're going to die if we stay here, so what difference does it make? Besides, your cat looked awfully sure of himself, and I've heard that cats have a sense for these things."

"Where does it take us? Outside? Into another mystery hallway? Won't that just fall into the void as well? Will the destruction of Hollythorn House collapse the void in on itself?"

"I don't know!" Niall grabbed one of the vines, steadying himself as the floor tilted further. He used the vine to drag them both to the wall. The surface pitched and wobbled as more plaster and debris rained down on them. "I'm not a bloody astrophysicist. But I don't think it takes us to the Summer City. I think it takes us somewhere else. Some*when* else. I think it takes us where Widdershins picked up those wheat stalks."

Aisling grabbed the vine, staring into the wall. Her lip quivered. "What if we burn up?"

"If you burn, I burn." Niall wrapped his arms around her. "This might be the last time I hold you. So if we are really going to die, right here, right now, then I am going to make sure the last words you hear are your legacy. I love you, Aisling. I am a better person because of you. You made me understand the meaning of sacrifice. You *gave* me life. You forgave me. And it is the greatest honor to die with you today."

"Oh, Niall," Aisling sobbed.

"But I don't think we're going to die, because you are even more amazing and clever than you give yourself credit for. I think we're going to live a long time and be very very happy together." An almighty crash shook the whole room. One of the gilded pillars crashed to the ground, shattering the marble as it toppled into the void. It was so bright Niall could only just make out the outline of Aisling against the brilliance. He squeezed her extra tight. "We have to go now. Are you ready?"

"If you burn, I burn." Aisling gave him a beautiful, sad smile.

Niall kissed her, his lips ablaze. Aisling wrapped him in her warmth, the magic in her veins pulsing through his skin, tearing out every last doubt. All that remained was *her,* his love for her, his complete and total faith that after everything he'd done to mess things up, this woman, this amazing woman, had saved them both.

Their fingers entwined, their lips together, Niall and Aisling toppled into the wall, sinking into the plaster as the burning sun swallowed the ballroom whole.

51

AISLING

*A*isling slammed against something hard. Her bones crunched, her entire body exploding with the force of the impact. She imagined herself scattered like stardust across the cosmos, her essence a streak of light in the endless darkness of space.

Time passed.

She waited, gasping, until the pieces of her body coalesced again. Her shape took form. Her muscles knitted together. Blood once again ran through her veins. With her blood came the pain, rolling over her like a dark cloud, bringing her mind back to the circumstances of her disembodiment.

Wherever and whatever she was now, it had forever changed her.

Time passed.

Aisling had no way of calculating how long she lay face down, her face crawling with strange fibrous wisps, her skin crushing against her bones, her veins alight with molten lava.

So this is dying.

It fucking sucks.

The pain faded to a dull roar in her ears, an ache coursing

through her body. Aisling lifted her head and forced her eyes open. Brilliant light pierced her vision. After a few moments, her eyes adjusted.

She lay in a field. The wisps tickling her face were long stalks of wheat blowing gently in a cool breeze. A few inches in front of her face, a bright blue teacup sat on its side, half-covered in soil. Right next to it, one of Niall's arrows stuck from the soil like a porcupine quill.

Beyond the edge of the field, Aisling could see trees and the pale line of a dirt road extending on through gently sloping farmland. There wasn't another soul in sight. *Where's June? Where's Bethany? Our parents?*

The only consolation of dying was that she'd be reunited with them, but shouldn't they be here?

Is dying being alone forever?

That double *sucks. That sucks with a shit cherry on top.*

Beside her, someone moaned. *Niall.*

She wasn't alone.

Niall's here.

Aisling wriggled her fingers, finding the satisfying warmth of his hand still gripping hers.

One painful inch at a time, Aisling turned her head toward him. Like her, he lay on his stomach, his arms and legs spread wide, crushed wheat jutting out from beneath him at all angles. A long gash ran across his cheek, and dried blood and dirt marred his angular features and splattered down the front of his tooth-mail.

He's here with me.

That was all that mattered. Aisling squeezed his fingers, the effort causing a spasm of pain to rocket up her arm. Why did her body hurt *so* bad?

"Are we dead?" she mumbled, her tongue sticking to her mouth.

"I think if we were dead, we wouldn't hurt so bloody much." The corner of Niall's lip twitched, and he winced with the effort.

Aisling dropped his hand and pressed her palm into the warm dirt. A little at a time, she rolled her broken body onto its side. Niall followed suit, groaning as he shifted the shoulder where the arrow had sliced him.

"We made progress," she huffed.

"Great." Niall's breath rasped. "With any luck, we'll be on our feet by nightfall."

"There's nothing around," Aisling said, staring across the field at another sprawling expanse of wheat stretching on and on into the distance. "No landmarks or anything. I guess we should follow that road—"

"Look," Niall croaked, raising his finger to point beyond Aisling's shoulder.

She whirled around and saw what he was pointing at. A figure ran toward them through the wheat. A man with a greying bread and kind brown eyes, dressed in dirt-stained over-alls. His tall frame jerked like a puppet as he propelled himself forward on long, spindly legs, and he waved his hat so hard his shoulder looked in serious danger of dislocating. He looked vaguely familiar, but Aisling couldn't place him.

"Excuse me," he called out to them, his words dripping with old-fashioned vowels. "Are you all right?"

"We're—" Aisling started to speak, but her voice came out as a dry croak. She coughed, and tried again. "We're fine, thank you."

The man reached them, and without even pausing to catch his breath, he hauled her to her feet. Aisling gasped for air.

"Lucky I found you, miss. Your horse must've thrown you and bolted. Do you need a doctor?"

"Um..." *I need Dr. Emmett Brown from* Back to the Future, *but I don't think he's available.*

The man peered all about. "I ain't seen the creature around, but he can't have gone far now."

"My... horse?"

"Of course, dear." Niall steadied her arm. "How else would we have landed facedown in this field if we hadn't been thrown from our horse?"

Aisling nodded, understanding Niall was trying to cover for their strange appearance in the middle of the field. "Yes. That's right. Of course. We were taking a shortcut across this farm when something spooked the horse."

"I'm not surprised. I was over yonder when I heard this almighty great clap of thunder." The man spread his arms wide. "I was expecting the heavens to open, but there's not a cloud in the sky. I came to investigate and found you lying here."

"It's odd, isn't it?" Niall rubbed his chin and looked meaningfully at Aisling. "I remember a loud noise too. It might've been a gunshot."

"I hope not. 'Twas probably those rotten Barker boys poaching again."

"What's your name?" Aisling asked.

"George, ma'am." He lifted his hat and tipped it to her. "I work on the Wilcox estate, up at the manor yonder. This here is his land you're standing on."

George? The name tugged at Aisling's memory. There was a George connected with Hollythorn House somehow, in one of her grandmother's old stories...

"It's a pleasure, George." She fell into the formal way of speaking he seemed to expect from her. "Can you tell us..." Her voice trailed off as the details of the landscape started to make sense in her head. The road, the tall oak on the horizon, even the gentle slope of the land... it all looked awfully familiar, as though someone had crawled into her childhood memories and pulled out this picture. Everything was the same, except...

She glanced all around. "Where's the house?"

"Lord Wilcox's seat is just over those fields," George pointed.

"No, Hollythorn House." Aisling walked a few feet away, scanning the horizon, her heart pounding. "It's was a huge house built in the Gothic style. It can't be that far from here." She spun in a circle, a knot tightening in her chest. "It should be here. Why isn't it here? Why can't I see it?"

"Ain't no house around here that looks like that." George scratched his head. "Just Lord Wilcox over yonder and the Meadowford estate to the north."

"You mean…" Her stomach churned. Her knees trembled. *I thought I'd saved it, but I can't have, because it should be here. It should be right here, right where I'm standing, I'm sure of it.*

And this is George, who first met Lady Greymouth on the road and introduced her to his master—

Her heart pounded as she recognized George from the paintings.

We really did it. We traveled back in time. But why isn't the house here?

Niall grabbed her arms, his eyes dancing. "Aisling, stop. Don't panic. I have this all worked out."

"Then start explaining."

"You can't see Hollythorn House because it hasn't been built yet."

"But it should be here!" Aisling wrung her hands. She could feel panic rising in her chest. "This is the exact spot. That's George, who Lady Greymouth set free after he saved her from a horse-riding accident. But he doesn't even seem to know her. It's all wrong."

"Of course he doesn't know her." Niall smiled, gripping her shoulders and staring deep into her eyes. "He only just met her."

Aisling stared into George's kind face, and the truth dawned on her. "No," she shook her head, grabbing Niall's shoulders to keep from falling over. "No. It can't be."

"Are you ill, ma'am?" George stood over her, looking worried. "Should I take you to Lord Wilcox?"

Niall laughed, and wrapped his arms around her. "Welcome to the first day of the rest of your life, Lady Greymouth."

"Lady Greymouth?" George looked shocked. "You're dressed awful funny for a lady, if you don't mind my saying, ma'am."

"These... these are my traveling clothes," she said, the words sliding from her throat easier than she could ever have imagined as she stared down at her torn and bloody leggings. "I'm surprised you haven't seen this ensemble before. It is the latest fashion in the city."

"Then I must take your Ladyship up to the house," George gave her a deep bow. "I know he would want to meet you and your companion."

"I don't think—" Aisling started, but Niall stepped forward and shook George's hand.

"We'd be delighted to meet Lord Wilcox," he said. "In fact, I think we might be able to offer him a deal. Lady Greymouth is quite taken with this site. I think she would like to buy it to build her new home."

"Niall," Aisling hissed. "We don't have any money. How can we—"

Niall grinned wider. He whipped his other arm around, and Aisling saw something clenched in his fist. One of the hideous dog statues, painted a garish gold. The dog's eyes were two large diamonds that sparkled in the sunlight.

"It's not gilded, it's solid gold," Niall said. "In this century, it's worth a small fortune. Certainly enough to buy these fields."

Aisling's mind reeled. "How is this possible?" she asked. "How could I be Lady Greymouth, when she's my ancestor? And how come you don't seem surprised about any of this?"

"Because I've been putting this together for a while now," Niall said. "You were the one who led us here, Aisling. I mean, the you who is Lady Greymouth. You laid all the clues for us to find our way back here. You made the secret hallway to the ballroom. You even played the waltz for us. I think you even gave us our dreams."

"But I didn't do any of that. I don't have the power for that kind of enchantment."

"Yes, you did." He looked at her. "At least, you're going to. Don't you see? Lady Greymouth's incredible life – building Hollythorn House, having all those wild adventures, helping the sick and those in need of justice, having all those magical children, hosting all those elaborate parties, even going to the beach – is really *your* life. Hollythorn isn't your grandmother's design, it's *yours*. All those tales your grandmother told you about her, you get to *live* them. And as you do, you build the clues into the house, you use your architecture degree and weave your own magic into the walls, you master the magic of dreams to bring two unlikely people together. *You* create the secret hallway and make your voice travel through the void, so that in hundreds of years from now, Aisling will come along again with her fae lover, and she will defeat the fae once more. Maybe you've done this a few times. And maybe each time, you change things a little. Maybe you learn more. Maybe one day you can even stop the wars that destroyed Earth and the Summer City."

"But... that's a paradox."

"You said to me once that Hollythorn House *is* a paradox." Niall shrugged. "Perhaps paradoxes are allowed."

"We can go to the beach?"

He laughed and kissed the top of her head. "We could go to the beach every single day. We can travel the world together, and have a hundred beautiful children."

"Probably not a hundred." Her heart fluttered. "Oh, we can find the secret sex dungeon."

"You get to *build* the sex dungeon, witch," he growled as he kissed her. "We'll fill it with everything your twisted heart desires."

Something rubbed against her leg. Aisling leaned down and scooped up Widdershins. "You knew all along, didn't you, bud?" She nuzzled his fur.

"Meorrw."

George stepped back, his face creased with concern. "It's bad luck to cross a black cat like that, ma'am."

Aisling smiled. "This little guy?" She held up one of Widdershins' white-socked paws. "He wouldn't hurt a fly. I have a feeling he's actually a bringer of *good* luck."

"If you say so, ma'am." George gestured over the hill. "We should be going if I'm to get you back in time for lunch. You'll want to attend to your toilette before you visit with my master. I'll send some of our lads to fetch your horse and carriage."

"I think they're well gone now." Aisling passed her arm through Niall's. She rested her head on his shoulder, breathing in the deep, beautiful scent of him. She couldn't believe only a few minutes ago she stared into the void, greeting her own death. And now, after years of being trapped in the prison of Hollythorn, the house had given her the most precious gift of all – the gift of a long life, filled with love. "Thank you, George. Take us to Lord Wilcox. I have a feeling we're about to make his whole year."

THE END

———

I should have kept my mouth shut.

I should have let them win.
Now the kings of the school are out for my blood,
... and they're not the only ones.

The fire took everything.
My parents. My best friend. My life.

Now I have a second chance.
I only have to endure one year at this prestigious academy for
rich snobs.
One year of being the charity case no one wanted.
One year of taunts and insults and bullying. Then I'm free.

But I didn't count on Trey, Ayaz, and Quinn.
Arrogant, privileged, dangerous.
Drop-dead gorgeous.
They want me gone.
They want me to suffer.
They're determined to make my nightmares real.

Tough luck, bully boys – I won't hide away.
I'm not afraid.
But maybe... *I should be.*

HP Lovecraft meets *Cruel Intentions* in book 1 of this dark
paranormal reverse harem bully romance. Warning: Not for the
faint of heart – this story of three broken bad boys and the girl
who stood her ground contains dark themes, crazed cultists,
books bound in human skin, high-school drama, swoon-worthy
sex, and potential triggers.

START READING NOW
http://books2read.com/shunned

Turn the page for a sizzling excerpt

Get your free copy of *Cabinet of Curiosities*, a Steffanie Holmes compendium of short stories and bonus scenes. To get this collection, all you need to do is sign up for updates with the Steffanie Holmes newsletter.

http://www.steffanieholmes.com/newsletter

My dad builds houses for a living. When I was a kid, he would do a lot of the drafting work for these houses, back in the days where the industry wasn't regulated and this didn't require a special degree. He had these huge pads of paper in his office filled with line drawings of houses, and they fascinated me. I loved imagining people living in the rooms, seeing where the pipes went, understanding how the gables of the roof stopped water from getting inside the walls.

Sometimes, Dad let me and my sister have a couple of sheets of paper and we'd set about designing our own dream houses. My sister wanted a Malibu-style mansion with a pool. I wanted a log cabin, or a castle.

I loved watching architecture programmes on TV. From a young age I was interested in the spaces we create for ourselves and how we occupy them – I think this fed into my interest in archaeology, for what is most archaeology but uncovering the architecture of the ancients?

When I was a teen, my best friend was super involved in the local church youth group. One of the guys from youth group used to invite us around to his place for bonfires. He lived in this beautiful old homestead with seventy-million bedrooms and a big games room with a huge pool table. It had been in his family for generations, and the remnants of their family history hung proudly on the walls.

I loved going there because of the *hidden* history of that house – the stories that weren't told in photographs and heirlooms, but were built into its very foundations.

A mirror in the downstairs sewing room swung open to reveal a secret staircase that rose up into the closet of the first floor master bedroom before rising into the attic. And the house had a room with no door or window.

If you looked back at the house from where we had our bonfires set up, you could see the window of the bedroom where my best friend and I slept. Beside it, at least three meters remained on the end of the wing – space enough for a whole room – but with no window looking into it, and no door to access it.

You better believe I made my friend stay up half the night banging on our wall looking for a secret spring-loaded door. We never found one, but I did notice a square at the back of the closet where the wallpaper didn't match up.

How can you live in a house with a secret room for your whole life and NEVER cut a hole in the wall to look inside?

I will never understand this, and we'll never have answers because the house sadly burned to the ground in an arson attack in my final year at high school.

Poison Malice Twisted is, in part, my attempt to reveal the hidden history of that house. What did that hidden room reveal about the person who built it? What secrets did it contain? What do the places we inhabit reveal about our true nature?

I hope you enjoyed this strange story of love, sacrifice, and weird architecture. Thank you for going on this journey with me, even though it's led to some dark places.

If you enjoyed *Poison Malice Twisted* and want to read more from me, check out my dark reverse harem bully romance series, *Kings of Miskatonic Prep*. HP Lovecraft meets *Cruel Intentions* in this dark paranormal reverse harem bully romance that's definitely not for the faint of heart. Hazel is the most badass FMC I've ever written after Claudia, and I think you'll love meeting her. *Read Shunned now – http://books2read.com/shunned.*

You should also check out my other gothic reverse harem series, *Manderley Academy*. Book 1 is *Ghosted* and it's a classic gothic tale of ghosts and betrayal, creepy old houses and three beautifully haunted guys with dark secrets. Plus, a kickass curvy heroine. You will LOVE it. http://books2read.com/manderley1

Every week I send out a newsletter to fans – it features a spooky story about a real-life haunting or strange criminal case that has inspired one of my books, as well as news about upcoming releases and a free book of bonus scenes called *Cabinet of Curiosities*. To get on the mailing list all you gotta do is head to my website: http://www.steffanieholmes.com/newsletter

If you want to hang out and talk about all things *Poison Malice Twisted*, my readers are sharing their theories and discussing the book over in my Facebook group, Books That Bite. Come join the fun.

I'm so happy you enjoyed this story! I'd love it if you wanted to leave a review on Amazon or Goodreads. It will help other readers to find their next book boyfriend (not Gabriel, though – he's mine).

Thank you, thank you! I love you heaps! Until next time.
Steff

Who the hell builds a school on top of an inaccessible cliff?

Whoever built Derleth Academy, my new school. I answered my own question as the car's wheel skidded over the rough gravel on the way up the steep peninsula. A scream escaped my lips as the car lurched toward the edge of the cliff, one wheel spinning completely free.

Muttering under his breath, the driver for the school slammed the car into reverse and backed us onto the road before slamming on the gas again. We continued our wary climb along the narrow gravel path.

Surely the Academy can't be completely *cut-off.* The school had to bring up food and supplies. Parents must visit on the weekends. My driver was certainly giving it his all, tearing around the corners like he was on a Formula 1 racetrack and not a goat path hugging the side of a mountain. I gritted my teeth and gripped the back of the seat as rocks rolled from beneath the wheels and clattered over the sheer drop into the raging waters below. One wrong move, and we'd tumble down a two-hundred-foot cliff and be dashed against the cliffs so hard and fast that boats would mistake our remains for rock paintings.

Not the way I ever imagined I'd go.

We passed into thick vegetation, the cliff and ocean on one side giving way to looming trees that blocked out the grey sky. I let out the breath I'd been holding. Branches scraped the sides of the car, and my phone beeped with protest as we moved out of cell range. *No contact with the outside world*, the school brochure read. *At Derleth Academy, we foster a competitive academic program requiring the full attention of our students. Distracting technology or personal items will not be tolerated.*

In other words, I couldn't call for help. It was the opening sequence to every horror film, ever.

Not that I had anyone to call. Not anymore.

"Almost there," the driver said, swinging the car around a hairpin corner and launching my stomach into my throat. It was the most words he'd spoken to me the entire trip. "You can see the school through the trees."

I squinted into the forest, trying to make out some kind of building that might pass as a school. But I couldn't see a thing. We rounded another corner and—

Well, that's terrifying.

We rolled between two towering stone pillars obscured by creeping vines, past an ornate sign that read DERLETH ACADEMY. A wide, pristine concrete drive flanked by an avenue of towering trees and wide, manicured lawns led up to an imposing stone building, stretching in all directions with narrow arched windows, spiky towers, and a row of leering gargoyles along the roof.

What is this place? It looked more like Dracula's castle than a prestigious preparatory school.

I couldn't believe the wealthiest people in the country sent their children up that winding road to get educated. *Who's the headmistress, Morticia Addams?* But according to the brochure, that was exactly what they did. In droves. Derleth Academy had a waiting list a mile long, and you couldn't even pay to get in. You had to be *invited*.

Somehow, I, Hazel Waite – an overachieving orphan from the wrong side of Philly – ended up on their radar.

I flashed back to the day two weeks ago, when a banging on the door of my dingy apartment dragged me from a deep slumber. A woman with coiffed hair and a designer suit that cost more than a car staggered backward in surprise when I glared at her through the chain wearing only my pajamas and what must have been a terrifying scowl. Well, *she* wasn't the one being dragged from a pleasant Jason Momoa sex dream during the four-hour reprieve between night shift at the diner and cleaning rooms at a retirement home.

"Are you Hazel Waite?" she asked, her brown eyes wide and curious.

"No. Piss off." I glowered, slamming the door in her face. She was probably from CPS, trying to force me into foster care. Fuck that. I only had seven more months to survive before I turned eighteen. No way was I going to spend it in the hell that had killed Dante.

The woman didn't go away. She sat out on the road in her sports car and waited me out. I had to leave for work or I'd lose my job, and it wasn't easy to find work when you were underage and using an obviously fake ID. As soon as I left the house, she ambushed me.

"I'm not here to hand you over to the authorities," she said hurriedly, shoving a thick envelope into your hands. "I'm a scholarship administrator from Derleth Academy in Arkham, Massachusetts. Your current school put you forward for one of our four senior scholarship positions – a fully funded year at a first-class prep school, where our students go on to attend the top colleges in the world. I know the first quarter has already started, but it's taken me this long to track you down. You've only missed a week so far."

I stared at the envelope in my hands, at the red, black and gold school crest – a crooked five-pointed star inside a shield with some kind of Latin phrase beneath it. *This has got to be a joke.*

"I know what you're thinking," the woman said. "It's not a joke or a trick. I promise you that it's not. If you come to Derleth, we will assume guardianship duties until you turn eighteen. You'll be housed, clothed, and have all your schoolbooks and other needs met, as well as receiving a first-class education. You're a promising student, Hazel, and I know you've been dealt a cruel lot in life. This could be where you turn everything around. Don't answer me now. Read over the paperwork, and I'll return tomorrow for your decision."

And now, just ten days after I signed my soul over to this school in exchange for paid tuition, room, and board, I stared up at the imposing facade and wondered if I'd made a terrible mistake.

Sure, my life was miserable. I was drowning in grief, and even working two jobs I could barely pull in enough money to survive. College was out of the question, because I couldn't finish high school without going into foster care. But at least all that was familiar territory. That was the world I'd grown up in – the world of pain and struggle and loss. Derleth Academy was the exact opposite. Every element of this building screamed wealth and privilege and *you don't belong here.*

The driver pulled to a stop on the wide circular drive beside a towering stone fountain. A black woman in a drab grey smock darted out of the shadows of the porch and approached the car. I held my hand out to her. "Hello, I'm Hazel Waite—"

The woman ducked her head, avoiding me. She popped

open the trunk, hauled out my heavy suitcase and bookbag, and hurried off to the house with them before I could offer to help.

Weird much? I swiped a dreadlock off my face. My friend Dante's foster sister had done them for me last year, back when things were perfect and the most I had to worry about was whether my mom would ground me for getting dreadlocks.

An awful feeling twisted in my gut. I wished Mom was here, hating my loss, right now. But she was gone, gone, gone, and so was Dante, and it was just me and this terrifying school and no other options.

Three figures descended the grand stone steps toward me: A woman with translucent skin and a flowing black dress, flanked on either side by two students wearing the Derleth uniform. Fallen leaves skittered away from the woman's hem, and she moved with such poise that she appeared to float over the steps. With her severe features and a gauzy black ribbon pinned in her hair, she looked more like she was attending a funeral. Behind her, the two students – a guy and a girl – glared at me, distrust emanating from their every pore.

The woman stopped on the second-to-last step, peering down her nose at me as if I were a bug that wasn't even worth squashing. "You'll have to do something about that hair. We enforce a strict dress code in my school, Ms. Waite. I'll not have you flouting it on your very first day."

This must be the principal, Hermia West. My Morticia Addams guess wasn't far off. This woman looked like she drank the blood of students to sustain her beauty. The way her grey eyes stabbed right through me sent a cold shiver through my body.

There was nothing in the student handbook about dreadlocks. Although, of course, I'd only skim-read the thing on the bus from Philly. The handbook was boring. And *long.* "I'm sorry, Ms. West. I didn't know—"

"Ignorance is no excuse. That's 3 demerit points for you. And you're to refer to me as Headmistress."

Beside her, the boy sniggered. I turned my gaze to look at him, and my heart nearly stopped. *Wow, he's beautiful.* I had no idea boys that hot existed outside of magazines and Hollywood movies. He stood practically the same height as Ms. West, his broad shoulders accentuated by the tailored cut of his red-trimmed blazer. Prefect and merit badges decorated both lapels. Dark brown curls caught the grey light filtering through the clouds, throwing back beautiful shades of russet and silver. His clean-shaven face and high, majestic cheekbones appeared angelic, but his ice-blue eyes were cold and cruel.

The girl moved closer to him, touching his arm and shooting me a possessive glare, like a cat in heat. She had the appearance of a cat, too – slanted green eyes accentuated with heavy makeup, pointed chin, and the lithe body and long legs of a panther. Beautiful but deadly.

"This is Trey Bloomberg and Courtney Haynes," Headmistress West said. "I've appointed them as your student guides. They will show you the dorm, library, and dining hall, go over your schedule and classrooms, and ensure you understand *all* our rules. You will dine with the student body in two hours' time, and tomorrow you begin classes. I've had a copy of your schedule and the school handbook placed in your room. Memorize them, for failure to comply will result in further demerits. Here's your dorm room key."

In my pocket, my phone gave another defiant chirp. *Great.* I'd practically worn down the battery looking for a signal on the death road.

Headmistress West descended the last step to drop an ancient-looking metal key into my hand. Her pointy black boots lined up with my scuffed Docs. She loomed over me, her disapproval seeping into my bones. "You have a phone in your pocket." It wasn't a question.

"Yes."

Behind her, the boy smirked. I felt naked, exposed. My legs itched to make a run for the woods. Headmistress West held out her hand, unfurling long fingers topped with red-painted nails, the tips pointed like talons. "Hand it over. We don't allow outside technology on campus."

Instinctively, my hand flew to my pocket. "I won't use it to call or text. It doesn't work here, anyway, so what's the—"

"Ms. Waite, failure to obey a teacher's command is an automatic loss of 10 points. You seem most anxious to find out what punishments await the students at the bottom of the class list."

A lump rose in my throat. My phone contained photographs – snaps of my mom smiling demurely or brushing her hair in the mirror before she went out to work at the strip club. Of Dante and I hanging out around the neighborhood, smoking on the rusted playground beside his house, tagging the concrete wall behind the boxing gym on the corner. Every other one of my possessions had been destroyed in the fire. Those photographs were practically all I had left of them.

Trey and Courtney covered their mouths with their hands, barely disguising their laughter. Courtney leaned over and whispered something to Trey. They both cracked up. Despite myself, my cheeks flushed. *Better get used to this.*

Headmistress West, of course, ignored them. She wasn't backing down on this phone thing. My fingers closed around it, the comfortable weight of it in my hand reminding me that it was one of the last connections to my old life.

What does it matter? They're gone. Looking at their photos won't bring them back. But this school could be the only chance I have at a real future.

My hand trembling, I dropped my phone into her talons. As

soon as it left my hand, I itched to get it back. Headmistress West slipped the phone into a fold of her dress, where it disappeared from sight.

"Follow me." The headmistress swirled on her heel and floated up the stairs. Numb, I fell in step behind her. Trey came up beside me. His arm brushed mine, and a jolt of warmth rocketed through my body. I dared a look up at his face. As we moved into the shadow of the porch, the colors in his hair changed, becoming a deep brown and blood red. A curl flopped over his eye, and I noticed flecks of silver on the edges of those arresting blue irises. My fingers itched to reach up and swipe that curl off his face, to touch his smooth skin, feel his cheek move beneath my fingers, to cut myself on his cheekbones. A familiar longing pooled in my stomach, an ache that I'd never been able to sate before, and now never would.

I'd never seen a boy that *perfect.*

Trey's fingers brushed me again. My breath froze in my mouth as his hand lingered on my elbow. To anyone looking at us from a distance, it would appear as though he was helping me, steadying me up the steep steps. The touch on my skin was white-hot, lighting up parts of my body that hadn't felt anything since Dante... since before the fire. *How can this boy with such cruel eyes have this effect on me?*

When he caught me looking, Trey's perfect lips curled back into a sneer. His fingers tightened on my arm, squeezing my skin. Tighter, tighter, until he was cutting off circulation. I yelped in protest.

"You don't belong here," he murmured, his perfect lips forming hateful words. "You should leave now."

He said it so casually, like he was chatting about the weather, and that self-satisfied smirk never left his face. My stomach twisted, the air driving from my lungs as though he'd punched me.

"No thanks," I said brightly, pretending that I misunderstood him. "I'm good."

"We don't want you, and we're used to getting what we want. We're going to eat you alive, new meat." Trey flashed me a smile that was all teeth and violence. The venom in his eyes frightened me. *This is not a guy to mess with.*

Too bad he seemed to already have it out for me, and I hadn't even got inside the school yet. My plan to keep my head down and stay invisible fizzled before my eyes. Already I could see how the school year was going to play out. *We don't want you here.* Trey spoke for the entire student body. He was a King in this school. It was written in his smile, dripping from the menace in his words.

I'd pissed him off. Just by existing. Just by setting foot on the hallowed grounds of his kingdom. *Well, fuck you, Trey Bloomberg.* I could handle a year of insults and loneliness if I got my diploma at the end of it. My life was already hell on earth – if Trey Bloomberg thought he could break me, he'd have to try a lot harder.

I wrenched my arm away from us. "Don't touch me." Behind us, Courtney giggled.

"Yeah, Trey. You should know not to handle garbage. She's a gutter-trash whore who's probably fucked so many guys that your dick wouldn't even touch the sides."

The comment stung. I thought of my sweet mother, all candy smiles and sticky skin as she stripped off her sweat-soaked lace g-string and six-inch heels after her shift and pulled on the cloud-pink pajamas I found for her in a thrift store. A hard lump rose in my throat. I shoved the image aside. *Not now.*

Wait until you get to your room, until you're alone, then you can break down.

"I guess we're not going to be braiding each other's hair," I muttered to Courtney.

"I wouldn't touch that rat's nest on your head if someone hid a *Faberge* egg inside," Courtney sneered. "I bet it's got real eggs in it, though. Insect eggs, laid by the gross things crawling around in there."

Instinctively, my hand flew up to my face, to touch the dreadlock that always fell over my eye, to tuck it behind my ear – a gesture that Dante would so often do when he noticed my loss in my eyes, which was all the time because I liked them unruly. Ever since the fire, I'd been touching my own hair more and more, seeking the comfort of the familiar weight of a hand moving the dreadlocks. But it wasn't the same. It would never be the same.

Courtney wrinkled her face in disgust, while Trey continued to smirk at me. The force of his loathing sank my stomach to my knees. He didn't even know me, but it didn't matter.

At the top of the stairs, the headmistress turned and frowned at me. "Don't dawdle," she snapped. "The school doesn't bite."

"She's wrong," Trey whispered. "Are you ready to find out just how bad we bite?"

The lump of hard, bitterness burned at the back of my throat. They were right. I didn't belong here. I was the poor gutter-trash girl from the wrong side of the tracks, and they were *royalty*. They were the monarchs. *They're going to make my life miserable, and there's nothing I can do.*

Read Shunned now
www.books2read.com/shunned

MORE FROM THE AUTHOR

From the author of *Poison Malice Twisted* and *Shunned*, the Amazon top-20 bestselling bully romance readers are calling, "The greatest mindf**k of 2019," comes this new dark contemporary high school reverse harem romance.

Psst. I have a secret.

Are you ready?

I'm Mackenzie Malloy, and everyone thinks they know who
I am.

Five years ago, I disappeared.

No one has seen me or my family outside the walls of Malloy
Manor since.
But now I'm coming to reclaim my throne:
The Ice Queen of Stonehurst Prep is back.

Standing between me and my everything?
Three things can bring me down:
The sweet guy who wants answers from his former friend.
The rock god who wants to f*ck me.
The king who'll crush me before giving up his crown.

They think they can ruin me, wreck it all, but I won't let them.
I'm not the Mackenzie Eli used to know.
Hot boys and rock gods like Gabriel won't win me over.
And just like Noah, I'll kill to keep my crown.

I'm just a poor little rich girl with the stolen life.
I'm here to tear down three princes,
before they destroy me.

Read now:
http://books2read.com/mystolenlife

What do you get when you cross a cursed bookshop, three hot fictional men, and a punk rock heroine nursing a broken heart?

After being fired from her fashion internship in New York City, Mina Wilde decides it's time to reevaluate her life. She returns to the quaint English village where she grew up to take a job at the local bookshop, hoping that being surrounded by great literature will help her heal from a devastating blow.

But Mina soon discovers her life is stranger than fiction – a mysterious curse on the bookshop brings fictional characters to life in lust-worthy bodies. Mina finds herself babysitting Poe's raven, making hot dogs for Heathcliff, and getting IT help from James Moriarty, all while trying not to fall for the three broken men who should only exist within her imagination.

When Mina's ex-best friend shows up dead with a knife in her back, she's the chief suspect. She'll have to solve the murder if she wants to clear her name. Will her fictional boyfriends be able to keep her out of prison?

Agatha Christie meets Black Books in this steamy paranormal romance collection. Join a brooding antihero, a master criminal, a cheeky raven, and a heroine with a big heart (and an even bigger book collection) for three zany supernatural murder mysteries by *USA Today* bestselling author Steffanie Holmes.

This collection includes books 1-3 in the Nevermore Bookshop series, plus Heathcliff's shop rules, and alternative POV scenes from Mina's heroes. Read on only if you believe one book boyfriend isn't enough.

READ NOW
books2read.com/nevermorebox

OTHER BOOKS BY STEFFANIE HOLMES

This list is in recommended reading order, although each couple's story can be enjoyed as a standalone.

Nevermore Bookshop Mysteries

A Dead and Stormy Night

Of Mice and Murder

Pride and Premeditation

How Heathcliff Stole Christmas

Memoirs of a Garroter

Prose and Cons

A Novel Way to Die

Much Ado About Murder

Kings of Miskatonic Prep

Shunned

Initiated

Possessed

Ignited

Stonehurst Prep

My Stolen Life

My Secret Heart

My Broken Crown

My Savage Kingdom

Manderley Academy

Ghosted

Haunted

Spirited

Briarwood Witches

Earth and Embers

Fire and Fable

Water and Woe

Wind and Whispers

Spirit and Sorrow

Crookshollow Gothic Romance

Art of Cunning (Alex & Ryan)

Art of the Hunt (Alex & Ryan)

Art of Temptation (Alex & Ryan)

The Man in Black (Elinor & Eric)

Watcher (Belinda & Cole)

Reaper (Belinda & Cole)

Wolves of Crookshollow

Digging the Wolf (Anna & Luke)

Writing the Wolf (Rosa & Caleb)

Inking the Wolf (Bianca & Robbie)

Wedding the Wolf (Willow & Irvine)

Want to be informed when the next Steffanie Holmes paranormal romance story goes live? Sign up for the newsletter at www.steffanieholmes.com/ newsletter to get the scoop, and score a free collection of bonus scenes and stories to enjoy!

ABOUT THE AUTHOR

Steffanie Holmes is the *USA Today* bestselling author of the paranormal, gothic, dark, and fantastical. Her books feature clever, witty heroines, secret societies, creepy old mansions and alpha males who *always* get what they want.

Legally-blind since birth, Steffanie received the 2017 Attitude Award for Artistic Achievement. She was also a finalist for a 2018 Women of Influence award.

Steff is the creator of *Rage Against the Manuscript* – a resource of free content, books, and courses to help writers tell their story, find their readers, and build a badass writing career.

Steffanie lives in New Zealand with her husband, a horde of cantankerous cats, and their medieval sword collection.

Steffanie Holmes newsletter

Grab a free copy of *Cabinet of Curiosities* – a Steffanie Holmes compendium of short stories and bonus scenes – when you sign up for updates with the Steffanie Holmes newsletter.

http://www.steffanieholmes.com/newsletter

Come hang with Steffanie
www.steffanieholmes.com
hello@steffanieholmes.com